P9-DDL-340

A Gathering Place

A Gathering Place

A Cape Light Novel

THOMAS KINKADE

& KATHERINE SPENCER

BERKLEY BOOKS, NEW YORK

A Parachute Press Book

A Berkley Book
Published by The Berkley Publishing Group
A division of Penguin Group (USA) Inc.
375 Hudson Street
New York, New York 10014

This book is an original publication of The Berkley Publishing Group.

This is a work of fiction. Names, characters, places, and incidents either are the product of the author's imagination or are used fictitiously, and any resemblance to actual persons, living or dead, business establishments, events, or locales is entirely coincidental.

Cover design by Erika Fusari.
Text design by Tiffany Kukec.

All scripture passages have been quoted from the King James Version of the Bible.

ISBN 0-425-19004-8

PRINTED IN THE UNITED STATES OF AMERICA

Dear Friends

I AM SO HAPPY ONCE AGAIN TO WELCOME YOU TO CAPE LIGHT. The town is much as it has always been—a place where the pace is slower and people stop to savor the simple pleasures.

When I first conceived of the idea of the Cape Light books, I wanted to convey with words the same vision that my artwork expresses with paint—the values of faith, hope, family, and community. I never dreamed that so many of you would write to me and say that Cape Light had become so real and precious to you. I knew that Cape Light lived in my heart, but I am so proud that it has found a place in yours as well.

The painting on the cover of *A Gathering Place* is a portrait of a simple village church, the serene image of a lovely building. When I paint a picture of a building—whether it's a warm cottage, a stately house, or a quiet church—I concentrate on the architecture of the building so that I can paint it, but I must also visualize life *inside* the building. This is the only way I can capture its true essence.

I imagine the people who live in these structures. I think about the role the building plays in their lives. The white-steeple church on the cover of this book is not a grand place. It's not a lofty cathedral. It is very simply a gathering place. A place where people come together to thank God, to ask for his help, and also to reach out to each other.

In *A Gathering Place* you will see hard times for Lucy and Charlie Bates . . . moments of suffering and doubt for Reverend Ben . . . hard decisions to be faced by Emily Warwick and Dan Forbes . . . and the entire town will experience a sad and profound loss. Through it all, the people of Cape Light will hold together and help their neighbors to gather strength and push on.

As you open this book and once again greet the people of Cape Light, my prayer for you is that you find a gathering place of your own: a place where you can find love and support and the peace of mind to appreciate all of God's blessings.

—Thomas Kinkade

CHAPTER ONE

EMILY WARWICK PARKED HER JEEP IN FRONT OF DAN FORBES'S house, then opened the tailgate and carefully removed an apple pie. Covered with foil, it sat wedged between various plates and bowls filled with the makings of a Thanksgiving dinner.

High gray clouds blew across the sky, bringing sunlight one minute and shadows the next. The frost-covered ground and icy roof edges along Emerson Street cheered her, the sparkling white trim looking as if it had been applied by an artist's careful touch. Even Dan's squat little cottage looked more appealing today, which was saying something. A frosty glaze coated the pavement under her steps, and carrying the pie up the path proved to be a bit of a balancing act.

A balancing act, too, in the very gesture, she thought. A Thanksgiving offering to a neighbor and friend. And yet her relationship with Dan definitely seemed more than a friendship these last few weeks . . . but less than a romance.

The pie in one hand, she pressed the doorbell with the other. Though she'd never been a whiz in the kitchen, for some reason she'd been inspired last night to bake for the holiday. One pumpkin and two apple, one pie too many for the small gathering at her mother's house. Dan seemed the perfect candidate for the extra. About two weeks ago, he'd taken a bad fall while working on his sailboat and was now confined to a wheelchair, with no one but his son Wyatt to keep him company today.

It's just a neighborly gesture, the friendly thing to do. *And we are friends,* she reminded herself, *if nothing more.*

The door swung open, and a young woman with honey-blond hair and deep blues eyes stared out at her curiously. "Can I help you?" she asked.

"I'm Emily Warwick, a neighbor. . . . I live down the street. . . ." Emily felt awkward and began to gesture, then noticed the tinfoil slipping off the dish. "I just wanted to drop this off."

"Oh, of course." The young woman smiled. "I'm Lindsay, Dan's daughter. Dad's told me about you. You're the mayor, right?"

"Right," Emily replied with a nod, wondering if that was all Dan had said about her. "I didn't realize both you and Wyatt were coming for the holiday," Emily said, mentioning Lindsay's brother. "I hope I'm not interrupting anything."

"Not at all. Actually, Dad didn't know we were coming. My husband and I sort of surprised him." Lindsay laughed, suddenly sounding and looking a lot like her father. "Come in, please. Dad could use a visitor. Actually, he's starting to drive us all a little crazy," she added in a whisper.

Emily smiled, slipped off her coat, and left it on a nearby chair. The house was filled with the delicious scents of a turkey roasting and cranberry sauce simmering. So poor Dan wasn't going to starve today, after all.

She followed Lindsay to the small kitchen, where Lindsay set the pie on the counter. A young man with thick brown hair and a full beard stood at the stove. Wearing a long white apron, he added fresh herbs to a stockpot, his expression one of complete concentration.

Lindsay waited a moment, then touched his shoulder. "Honey, this is Emily, a friend of Dad. She brought us a lovely pie. Emily, this is my husband, Scott."

"Nice to meet you." Scott stretched out a large hand, and Emily shook it. "Thanks for the pie. Now I don't have to worry about dessert."

"Not counting the pumpkin-mousse napoleons, he means," Lindsay noted. "Scott's a chef. He keeps forgetting we're only four people today, not forty."

Scott gave a good-natured shrug. "So we'll have plenty of leftovers."

"I'm going to have to double up on my workouts," Lindsay said with a sigh. "This happens every year over the holidays. You should have seen last year's feast in New Orleans."

"Is that where you live?" Emily asked curiously. Dan often talked about his son, but he rarely mentioned his daughter.

"We lived there for three years," Lindsay explained. "But we knew we would come back north one day. My dad's accident just made us move up faster."

"Oh, so you're up in New England again for good?"

"It looks that way. Scott may open a restaurant in Boston with some friends. I'm looking for a job, too. I'm in marketing and sales," she added.

"Sounds like you'll be living in the city then."

"That's our plan. We're going to camp out here until Scott's business deal is settled. Dad sure found a cozy little place," Lindsay said, glancing around with a smile. "I guess he didn't expect so many visitors."

"I guess not," Emily agreed. The house was small. Too small really for Dan's entire family to have moved back in with him. There was a certain irony to it, as Dan was such a solitary type and now, to make matters worse, housebound.

Dan's house, which was just down the street from her own, had been for sale a long time before he bought it. He explained it as an emergency purchase. He had sold a larger home in the village, and he suddenly found himself needing a place to go. But he didn't intend to live here long. Only long enough to hand over his newspaper to his son, Wyatt, then take off on a long, rambling trip on his sailboat.

But Providence had something other than early retirement in mind for Dan, something else entirely: An accident on his boat about two weeks ago had left him with a concussion, several broken bones, various bruises, and an impressive black eye.

Following Lindsay, Emily made her way to the family room in back, which seemed to be Dan's headquarters since his accident. More like the lion's den on some days, depending on his mood.

The room, once a screened-in porch, had been nicely renovated. A fire flickered in the stone fireplace that took up one corner of the room. Broad windows lined three of the walls; built-in bookcases beneath them held Dan's many books as well as awards for the newspaper. One long wall was decorated with framed photographs.

Dan sat at a rolltop desk, the antique topped with a notebook computer. His wheelchair was slanted sideways to the desk to make room for the long, straight cast on his broken leg. It looked uncomfortable, but Emily could hardly imagine Dan surviving for a day out of reach of a keyboard.

As the two women entered, he turned in his chair. His blue eyes lit up when he saw Emily, and she felt her heart do a small flip. She suddenly knew she'd done the right thing by coming today.

"Well, look who's here. What brings you around, Mayor? Visiting local shut-ins for the holiday?" he teased her.

"I only had time for one. Your name was pulled from a hat," she said, matching his dry tone.

He laughed and she could see him relax a bit. "Happy Thanksgiving. Nice of you to drop in," he said sincerely.

"I just wanted to say hello." Emily stepped closer. "I didn't realize you had such a full house."

"Doesn't take much to fill up this place. But having Lindsay and Scott show up last night was a nice surprise," Dan said, as he smiled over at his daughter.

"Emily brought us a pie," Lindsay told him. "Looks like apple."

"Mmm, my favorite. I didn't know baking was among your many talents, Mayor."

"It's not high on the list, so don't get your hopes up," she warned him.

"When you're in my situation, you have to think positively," Dan said. "At least about dessert." He gazed at her, smiling in a way that made Emily feel self-conscious in front of Lindsay.

Lindsay must have sensed something. She glanced at her father and

Emily, then said, "I guess I'll go see if Scott needs any help. Would you like some coffee or tea, Emily?"

"No, thank you. I can't stay long."

"Nothing for me, honey. I'm fine," Dan said.

"Okay, just call if you need anything," Lindsay said, as she left them alone together.

"Have a seat," Dan offered, gesturing to the couch. "You can stay for a minute, can't you?"

"Sure." Emily took a seat on the couch, and Dan turned his chair to face her.

Even though she had seen him since his accident, the sight was still a shock. Besides his leg being in a cast, his left arm was in a sling. The bruises on his face were healing slowly. The swelling had gone down, but the abrasions had turned a nasty shade somewhere between red and purple.

"How are you feeling?" she asked.

"A little better than I look. But not much." Dan touched the bandage on his forehead. "These stitches should come out soon. Thank goodness I've got such a hard head. I guess I ought to be grateful. It's still frustrating to be stuck in this chair, though. So much for taking retirement before I turn fifty!"

He smiled at her and Emily didn't know how to respond, distracted by the subtle energy between them. She could feel it, like an electric current in the room.

"And it will be about six weeks until the cast comes off?" she managed to ask.

"That's what they tell me. I should get a smaller, removable cast on my leg by Christmas, and I may need some physical therapy after the leg heals. But the doctors won't know that for a while."

A heavy silence fell between them. Emily racked her mind for something positive to say. The only benefit she could see from Dan's accident was the fact that it had kept him in town and gave her an excuse to see more of him.

But is that really a good thing, she wondered, *since sooner or later he will be leaving anyway?*

"How is Wyatt doing at the paper?" she asked.

"All right, I guess. He's been distracted taking care of me. But now Lindsay can take over around here," Dan said. "You know, Wyatt worked at the paper every summer from grade school through college. He should be able to run the place by now."

Yes, that had always been the plan, as anyone who was acquainted with Dan even remotely knew by now. Dan's great-grandfather founded the *Cape Light Messenger*. Dan's father, and his father before him, had handed over the reins in due course to the male heir apparent.

Wyatt was a photojournalist and had been living on the West Coast, doing quite well in his field, Emily understood. She wondered how he felt about moving back to his hometown now, after roaming around the world. But Dan never hinted that Wyatt had second thoughts about returning.

"Well, at least you're still around to help him," Emily pointed out.

"I try. But it's difficult since I'm not down in the office when problems come up. Wyatt doesn't seem comfortable asking for advice."

"Typical male behavior," Emily teased gently.

"Especially in this family."

"Those Forbes hardheads. You mentioned that before."

"So I did." Dan met her gaze and smiled at her. Emily smiled back, finding it hard to look away. Then they were both distracted by the sound of someone entering the room.

She turned to see Wyatt, wearing a loose jacket with a long striped muffler slung around his neck. He could have passed for a younger brown-haired edition of Dan, she thought, with the same tall, rangy build and lean face. He didn't notice her at first, his attention focused on his father.

Lindsay appeared in the doorway, with a tray of hors d'oeuvres that gave off a mouthwatering warm buttery scent.

"The printer just called," Wyatt said. "He's got a problem with a few pages in tomorrow's edition. I have to run over there and figure it out. So I may be a little late for dinner."

"You can E-mail me some text if you need help cutting," Dan offered.

"No big deal. I can handle it," Wyatt answered quickly.

"Can I come?" Lindsay asked her brother. "Maybe together we can get it done faster."

Emily could see Wyatt hesitating, as if he were tempted to accept, then he pulled his car keys from his pocket. "It won't take long. But maybe you can stop by the office sometime and look over the subscriptions and advertising, that kind of thing. It's piling up, and I never seem to have time to get to it."

"What about Gloria? Isn't she back yet?" Dan asked.

"I forgot to tell you. She called yesterday and quit altogether. Said she found a new job at an advertising agency in Newburyport. I guess she didn't really have the flu," Wyatt added dryly.

"I guess not," Dan agreed, looking concerned. "It's hard to find someone to fill that spot. It's not strictly secretarial."

"Don't worry, Wyatt. I'll help you catch up until you hire someone. I don't have much else to do." Lindsay set the platter down on the coffee table and wiped her hands on her apron. "I have an interview Wednesday, but otherwise, I'm free."

"That would be great, Lindsay. Just until he finds someone good, I mean," Dan said. He looked surprised, Emily noticed, but pleased at the solution.

"Thanks, it would help a lot. I've had Jane Harmon coming in full-time for a while now," Wyatt told them. "And Sara Franklin should be starting on Monday."

Emily smiled at the mention of her daughter's name.

"Sara. That's right. Where did she go anyway?" Dan asked.

"Down to Maryland to visit her family for the holiday," Emily explained.

Sometimes Emily still found it hard to believe that the baby she had given up for adoption over twenty years ago had come to Cape Light to find her. Sara had come to town last May, right after graduating college, but it was several months before she revealed her true identity to Emily. After their reunion Emily had worried that Sara would return to her adoptive parents and disappear from her life again. Fortunately, though, Sara decided to take a job on the *Messenger* and stay in town a bit longer.

Finding her daughter had been the happiest, most blessed day of Emily's life, the single event she felt most thankful for on this special day of Thanksgiving.

"I hope she's good," Wyatt said. "It's hard to put out a paper every day with almost no staff."

Emily saw Dan tense at his son's words. And she also saw him pause before answering. "Sorry I left you shorthanded, Wyatt. Crown News keeps picking off my best reporters. I did mean to fill the spots before you came," he apologized.

"No problem. We'll manage all right. I'd rather hire my own staff anyway," Wyatt added in an offhand manner. "Well, got to get going. See you later. And happy Thanksgiving, Emily."

Emily glanced at her watch. "I'd better go, too."

"So soon?" Dan's reluctance to see her go secretly pleased her. "Why don't you stay? Have dinner with us. We have a real live chef-in-residence. And I have it on good authority that truffles are involved in the menu."

She met Dan's warm gaze and nearly gave in to the invitation. "Sounds very tempting. But I really must get over to my mother's. I'm bringing the dinner, turkey and all."

"All right, another time then." Dan leaned over from his wheelchair and picked up a canapé. Emily could see it was melted Brie with slivered almonds. "You ought to try one of these at least. They look delicious." He held the dish out to her, and she took one. "I hope Wyatt doesn't take too long at the paper," he added wistfully. "It's pure torture smelling that turkey all day. I don't know why I get so hungry sitting in this chair. Just bored, I guess. By the time I'm ready to get back on my boat, I'll probably sink it."

"Unlikely," Emily replied. The gourmet tidbit in her hand suddenly didn't seem as appetizing, but she took a taste anyway, trying hard not to think about the day Dan would leave town.

Then he glanced at her and smiled in that way he had that made her feel they shared some private joke, some secret knowledge. And she smiled back, resolved to enjoy whatever time they had together, even if it was going to be far less than she hoped for.

* * *

TEN MINUTES LATER, EMILY ARRIVED AT HER MOTHER'S HOUSE ON PROVidence Street. It took two trips from her Jeep to carry everything inside, and all the while her mother stood in the foyer, clutching her sweater to her chest and giving Emily directions.

"I've turned the oven on to warm it. But I don't think you should put any of the food in yet. The turkey will dry out. Especially the white meat. It ruins the whole holiday."

"Don't worry. The turkey won't dry out," Emily assured her.

Walking carefully with the use of her cane, Lillian followed Emily into the kitchen. "I thought you'd be here hours ago. You told me eleven o'clock. It's nearly one."

"I believe I told you twelve, Mother. But what's the difference? I'm here now. It's only the three of us."

Their only guest today would be Dr. Ezra Elliot. He had been their family doctor forever, and even after his retirement, he remained a good friend and just about the only person in town who could argue with her mother and win.

Lillian sniffed and pulled a bit of lint off her sweater sleeve. "Three is plenty. I prefer a quiet holiday. I hardly need to be caught in some wild mob scene at the Morgans' house, which I imagine is not well suited for entertaining. Most houses on that side of town are quite small, you know."

"Well, it would have been nice to join Jessica and Sam," Emily said, referring to her younger sister, Jessica, who had recently married Sam Morgan—against her mother's wishes. The Morgans were a warm, charming family, and Sam's parents were wonderful cooks. Emily was sure that their gathering was going to be crowded, but also lively and fun.

"We could still go over after dinner for dessert," Emily reminded her.

"You may go if you like. I don't need to rush through my dinner." Lillian sighed and sat down heavily in a kitchen chair. "Bring me those string beans, please. I'll clean them."

Emily brought her mother a cutting board and a bowl of freshly washed beans. Lillian's fingers moved in a stiff, but determined, fashion as she set about cleaning the vegetables.

Even though Lillian had finally relented and attended Jessica's wedding, she was still holding the line against Sam. Lillian had not for one moment considered Jessica's invitation to join the newlyweds at Sam's parents' house for Thanksgiving. Emily had wanted to go, but she couldn't let her mother spend the holiday alone.

Emily picked up a mushroom and sliced it in half. As always, her obstinate mother needed time. And she and her sister needed patience.

The doorbell sounded, and Lillian turned in her seat. "That must be Ezra."

Emily wiped her hands on a towel. "I'll get it."

When she opened the door, she was surprised to see that Dr. Elliot was not alone.

"Hello, Ezra. Hello, Luke. Happy Thanksgiving," she greeted the two men.

"Happy holiday, Emily." Ezra leaned over and kissed her lightly on the cheek. "I persuaded Luke to come along. I knew you wouldn't mind."

Dr. Elliot looked neat and dapper, as usual, in a black topcoat, a dark gray suit, and a red bow tie. He carried a bouquet of flowers and a box of fancy chocolates for her mother. Luke carried a small pot of dark red chrysanthemums. The peace offerings would be needed today, Emily thought.

"Of course not. Go on in. Mother is waiting for you," she told Ezra. She turned to Luke and smiled. "Happy Thanksgiving, Luke. Glad you could join us."

Luke smiled back but seemed uncomfortable. He'd traded his usual leather jacket and T-shirt for a tweed sports coat and a turtleneck sweater, a definite sign of his apprehension in coming here.

"It was Ezra's idea. He wouldn't take no for an answer," Luke explained. "But I don't want to intrude. If it's any bother at all, please just say so."

"Nonsense, of course it's no bother. We have more than enough food," Emily insisted. She wondered why he hadn't gone back to his family in Boston for the holiday, but didn't feel comfortable asking. "If I'd known you were going to be alone today, I would have called you myself."

She touched Luke's arm, leading him into the living room. "Mother, look who's here—Luke McAllister."

Sitting on the high-backed velvet armchair, Lillian peered up at him and made a disgruntled sound.

"Mr. McAllister. How nice of you to join us," she said curtly, "though I don't believe we've ever met."

Luke's expression remained impassive, though Emily noticed color rising up around his collar.

"Now, Lillian, don't make a liar out of me. I promised Luke you wouldn't mind a bit if he came along," Ezra cut in. "Where's your hospitality, for goodness' sake? Today of all days."

"Yes, Mother. Where would we all be if the Pilgrims and Native Americans had taken the same attitude?" Emily added.

"Thank you for the etiquette tips, Ezra. And for the history lesson," Lillian added, glancing at her daughter. She sat back in her chair and pursed her lips. "Do have a seat, Mr. McAllister. Of course, you're welcome to join us for dinner. I never said you were not."

"Thank you, Mrs. Warwick." Luke sat on the camel's hair sofa and nearly smiled. But not quite, Emily noticed. "Please call me Luke."

Emily cast Luke an encouraging glance, then excused herself to retreat to the dining room. She added an extra place setting, then took Ezra's bouquet into the kitchen and put the flowers in a vase. Her mother could be impossible, she reflected, but Luke, who had been a Boston police detective, had undoubtedly handled worse.

He'll have to get used to her anyway if he and Sara get more involved, Emily thought, as she arranged the flowers on the dining-room table. It was hard to tell if Sara and Luke were actually dating, or whatever it was young people did these days. But something definitely seemed to be there.

Sara had told Emily that at one point she was so torn about whether to tell Emily the truth about their relationship that she almost went back home for good. It was Luke who had persuaded Sara to think it through and stay—and finally to tell Emily who she really was. For that alone, Emily would be forever grateful to him.

Back in the kitchen, Emily checked on the food warming in the oven. Just as she closed the oven door, Luke appeared in the doorway. "Need any help?"

"Escaping from the living room already?" Emily teased him.

Luke grinned. "I just thought you might need a hand."

"There are a few pots in the sink. One has burned stuff on the bottom. You might need to let it soak."

"No problem." Luke draped his sports jacket on the back of a chair and rolled up his shirtsleeves. "Burned pots are my specialty."

"Mine, too. Burning them, I mean," Emily offered, making him laugh.

They worked together in silence for a few moments. Then Luke said, "So, have you heard from Sara at all?"

"She called this morning to wish me a happy Thanksgiving. I was surprised," Emily admitted. "I'm sure she's very busy. It was sweet of her to think of me."

"Yes, it was thoughtful." Luke nodded. "How did she sound?"

"Very happy. I guess she's missed her family more than she's let on." Emily paused and checked the simmering gravy. "I only hope she doesn't decide to stay in Maryland."

"Do you think she will?" Luke's tone was even, but Emily noticed a slight edge of worry.

"No, not really," she quickly answered. "She'll definitely come back to start her job at the *Messenger.* You know how she's dying to see her name in print."

"That's right. Sara Franklin, ace reporter." He smiled and set a clean pot on the drain board. "She'll definitely come back for that."

Despite his easy tone, Emily knew it would hurt him if Sara didn't return. But Luke was, what, about ten years older than Sara? Maybe even ready to make a serious commitment. Sara was really so young and getting a late start as it was. *She'd waited to find me and untangle her past before pursuing a real career,* Emily thought.

It was hard to guess how things would wind up between Sara and Luke. *But motherly of me to worry,* she realized, with a secret grin.

Emily pulled open the oven door again. No clues to be found there, only the warming food, another question of timing, one that was far easier to answer.

"Looks like dinner is ready. Time to sit down."

With the help of their two guests, Emily transported the miniature feast from the kitchen. A few minutes later, the small group sat at the upper end of Lillian's long mahogany dining table. The table had been taken from the Warwick family estate, Lilac Hall, about twenty years ago when the family was forced to vacate after Emily's father's financial scandal.

While Lillian's colonial was among the finest houses in town, it was still not large enough to comfortably accommodate such a grand piece. Nor her mother's grand attitude, which, Emily knew, had never quite adapted to her change of fortunes.

Emily had stopped in yesterday afternoon, and under Lillian's watchful eye, she had set the table with fine china, sterling, and crystal. Now Ezra's bouquet served as a centerpiece, a collection of autumn-colored blooms and greenery. To Emily's surprise, she saw a look bordering on approval on her mother's face as she surveyed her table.

"My word. Everything looks delicious, Emily. You've outdone yourself, truly," Ezra said, smoothing his napkin over his lap.

Not nearly the gourmet fare at Dan's, but it was a good job for a domestically challenged person like herself, Emily thought.

"Looks great," Luke agreed. "Are those fresh cranberries?"

"The genuine article," Emily assured him, "homemade cranberry sauce."

"Not much to that," Lillian scoffed. "You simply boil the berries in water and sugar. Anyone can do it."

Emily noticed Ezra biting back a grin—or a wise retort.

"Why don't you say the blessing, Emily?" Lillian suggested. "Before the food gets cold."

Everyone at the table bowed his head. Emily took a breath, thinking the words of the prayer would come automatically. But for some reason she felt a knot of emotion suddenly well up in her throat. There seemed to be so much that she was truly thankful for; the familiar words of grace didn't seem to cover half of it. She didn't know where to begin.

Finding Sara. Or rather Sara finding her was first and foremost. She had thanked the Lord above endlessly for that gift but knew it could never be enough.

She sensed the others waiting and cleared her throat. "Thank you, Lord, for this wonderful meal and the good friends—and new friends—here to share it. Thank you for the well-being of all our friends and family, including those who are not with us today. Please let us carry the spirit of this holiday in our hearts every day, and keep us ever mindful of the love, guidance, and the many blessings you bestow upon us."

"Amen," Ezra said happily, lifting his head. "You put it perfectly."

"Well said," Luke agreed quietly.

"She's quite adept at speaking impromptu," Lillian said. "Comes from being in politics, I suppose."

The comment was her mother's idea of a compliment, Emily knew. Lillian had never been comfortable with either emotions or spontaneity.

Emily let the remark pass and smiled at Luke. "Why don't you start the turkey along?" she said, handing him the platter. "Ezra, you can pass the sweet potatoes whenever you're ready."

The table was quiet for a few moments while everyone filled his plate.

"I don't hear much about your project lately, Mr. McAllister. Have you given up on it?" Lillian asked. Emily gulped down a bite of food. Leave it to her mother to start off with the most provocative topic—and in the most tactless way possible.

"No, not at all." Luke dabbed his mouth with a napkin.

"Really? That's too bad. I heard those children left town, and I hoped it meant you were finally coming to your senses and throwing in the towel."

Luke had moved to the town last spring. Despite the local gossip about him, Luke tried to keep a low profile when he bought some property from Dr. Elliot that included a few run-down summer cottages. He eventually decided to open a center there for disadvantaged city kids, a plan that caused a lot of conflict in the town and had nearly cost Emily her reelection. Her mother had been among the many who opposed the New Horizons program coming to Cape Light.

"We sent the kids from the program back to Boston about two weeks ago," Luke explained to Lillian. "The cold weather slowed down the outdoor work, so there wasn't anything more they could do at the building site or at Potter Orchard. But we're still working inside, turning the cottages into dorms."

"They look good, too. I took a peek the other day," Ezra added.

Lillian glanced at him. "It wouldn't take much to improve those cottages. You let them run down terribly. I'm surprised you found anyone foolish enough to buy that property." She turned back to Luke. "But, of course, you have a great deal of money from the police force."

Luke left the Boston police force two years ago, after a shoot-out in which his partner was killed and he was injured.

"You managed to get yourself shot in the head or something, I heard," Lillian went on in a disapproving tone.

"In the leg," Luke clarified. Emily could see him suppressing a grin.

"Not as profitable as the head, but worth something, I suppose," Lillian replied.

"Mother, can we talk about something else?" Emily cut in.

"Mr. McAllister and I are just getting acquainted," Lillian insisted. "I barely know the man, and he arrives at my doorstep for Thanksgiving dinner. I can ask a few questions." She promptly turned to Luke again. To his credit, he didn't look the least bit flustered.

"So, I heard you shot your partner? Is that true?" she continued.

"Mother!"

"Now, Lillian, you've gone too far," Ezra said.

Luke glanced at both of them with a look that said he could take care of himself. "No, I didn't shoot my partner. The department investigation concluded that I abandoned him in a high-risk situation. I don't believe I did. . . . But I have very little memory of the event."

"Oh, yes. You were under the influence, I heard. Is that true?" Lillian pressed on. Emily sat back in her chair, her mouth nearly falling open. Ezra dropped his fork with a clattering sound, slowly shaking his head in dismay.

"The memory loss was some sort of stress reaction. The drinking problem came later, after I was thrown off the force," Luke said in a matter-of-fact tone. "But I got through that, too. In case you were wondering," he added politely.

"Yes, I did wonder. You don't look like a drunk, though. I will say that for you."

"Why thank you, Mrs. Warwick. How kind of you to notice." To Emily's amazement Luke managed to sound sincere, almost gallant, instead of sarcastic.

"No wonder you came all the way up to Cape Light," Lillian said, cutting a small bite of turkey on her plate. "Trying to run away from your troubles, I suppose."

Ezra cleared his throat, and Emily was about to interrupt again herself when she noticed that Luke was nearly laughing at her mother's inquisition.

"Actually, it was the sea air, Mrs. Warwick," Luke said, his eyes twinkling. "I heard it has great restorative powers."

"Restorative powers, my foot. Sit gazing at the ocean all day, and you'll end up with arthritis. I guarantee it," Lillian countered.

"The cause of arthritis is not yet known, Lillian," Ezra cut in curtly. "Neither is the cause of unrelenting rudeness, I might add."

Luke laughed out loud. Emily nearly did, then caught the daggerlike glance her mother was directing at Ezra. Eventually, her mother looked down at her plate and pushed it aside.

"The white meat is very dry, Emily. I'm afraid you let the turkey warm much too long."

Instead of being taken aback by the comment, Emily sighed with relief. It was her mother's way of signaling they could finally change the subject. "Here, try some gravy," she suggested, passing the china gravy boat in her mother's direction.

Lillian ladled gravy on her meat, then studied Luke once more. "So, tell me, Mr. McAllister, do you find any truth to the notion that our sea air can restore a melancholy disposition?"

"I do believe that for some it definitely does the trick," he replied, with a thoughtful expression. "Of course, others might spend an entire lifetime here, and it wouldn't do a thing."

His expression was serious, yet Emily noticed his gray eyes lit by a mischievous twinkle.

Lillian's eyes widened with surprise. She was silent for a moment, and Emily feared her reply.

"Touché, Mr. McAllister," she said at last, with the slightest hint of a grin.

Chapter Two

"More turkey, honey?" Carolyn Lewis held out the platter to her daughter, Rachel Anderson.

"There's a drumstick left," Reverend Ben pointed out. "Your favorite," he coaxed.

"Thanks, but I couldn't manage another bite." Rachel sat back from the table and patted her large pregnant stomach. "The baby is so big now, I can't eat that much at one time."

"Which is not to say that she isn't making up for it by eating about twenty little meals a day," Rachel's husband, Jack, teased. "Including strange cravings for chili dogs at two in the morning."

"You found one for me, too. That was sweet." She leaned over and kissed him on the cheek.

"You're a good husband, Jack. I don't know if Ben would have gone to all that trouble when I was expecting."

"Why, Carolyn, don't you remember? When you were pregnant with Mark you woke up at three A.M., madly craving fresh tomatoes. Sounded as if you were going to die if you didn't have some. I went out in my bathrobe and raided the neighbor's vegetable garden."

Carolyn laughed and touched Ben's arm. "Oh yes, I remember now.

They had a scruffy old dog who started barking his head off, then he chased you around the yard and tore a piece off your pajamas."

"Really?" Jack said, laughing.

"Daddy! You didn't!" Rachel exclaimed.

"Did indeed, I must confess. The neighbors were generous folks. Told me to come around any time and take whatever we liked from their garden. Though I imagine they didn't think I'd be taking them up on that offer in the middle of the night," he said, smiling at her.

"I don't think I ever heard that story," Rachel said, still looking surprised. "Did you have any cravings with me, Mom?"

Carolyn shook her head. "Not that I remember. Just with Mark." The quiet, sobering tone she used in mentioning her son's name instantly dampened the high spirits. A few years younger than Rachel, Mark had abruptly left college his junior year. For the last two years he had roamed the country, taking odd jobs, searching for something that he couldn't seem to define. For reasons Ben could only guess, Mark had kept his contact with the family to a minimum.

"How is he? Have you heard from him lately?" Jack asked.

"Just that letter we showed you from Montana," Ben replied.

"It would be great if he could come home for Christmas, in time for the baby." Rachel looked down and rested a hand on her belly. "I guess there's little chance of that now, though."

Ben saw the sadness in her eyes. She, too, felt abandoned by her brother, whom she loved and had always been quite close to. It seemed unfair, he thought. The rift was no fault of hers.

"Well, we've asked him, dear. Several times," Ben stated quietly.

"There's still time for him to change his mind. It's nearly a month till Christmas," Carolyn added on a hopeful note.

"Yes, but it's hard to get a flight if you don't plan ahead, especially around the holidays," Rachel said. "And you know Mark. He always leaves everything for the last minute."

Jack patted Rachel's hand but didn't say anything. Nor did Ben, who couldn't think of anything to say that wouldn't spread false hope.

"Can we call him?" Rachel said suddenly. "I'll ask him myself to come. I'd love to talk to him anyway."

Ben felt surprised at the simple solution. "No harm trying, I suppose," he said slowly. "I have his address somewhere . . . but not the phone number. Maybe we can get it from information."

"We should at least try. I'm sure he'd love to hear from us today. He must be at least a little bit homesick by now," Rachel said, her mood instantly brighter.

Ben thought her assumptions were debatable. His son did not seem the least bit homesick. Why hadn't Mark called today? He could guess they would all be here. But Ben didn't contradict his daughter.

"Let me see if I can find that letter. I think it's in my desk," he said, rising from the table.

Carolyn rose, too. "I guess I'll clear up, and we can take a break before dessert."

"I can help," Rachel said. But when she stood up, she suddenly gasped. With a startled look, she grabbed her stomach.

"Oh, dear, are you all right?" Carolyn asked in alarm. Jack turned toward his wife, as well, with a questioning look.

Rachel took a few deep breaths, then smiled at them. "I'm okay," she insisted, straightening up to her full height. "The baby just kicked me or something."

"Wow, don't scare me like that. I thought that was *it,*" Jack said.

"Me, too," Carolyn added, with a shaky smile.

"I'm not due for at least four more weeks. And first babies are sometimes late," Rachel reminded them.

Carolyn started gathering the dirty dishes. "I just hope the baby is healthy and everything goes easily for you, honey."

"My thoughts exactly." Reverend Ben smiled, then left the room, heading for his study.

They were fussing over Rachel like clucking hens lately. It was only natural; this was the first grandchild in the family, and they were all swept up in a mood of happy anticipation.

Thank the good Lord above for all our blessings. Ben sent up a silent prayer of thanks for this wonderful time in their lives. He thought of them as they had been just a few minutes ago, gathered around the table, enjoying Carolyn's wonderful holiday dinner—a perfect family portrait of contentment.

The only thing missing in the picture was Mark.

Ben found the letter in his top desk drawer. The return address on the envelope read, *Double Bar T Ranch, Deep River, Montana.* Staring down at the address, Ben hesitated. Why hadn't he and Carolyn called Mark sooner? He hadn't sent any phone number, so they assumed he didn't want them to call. Other reasons, too. They were scared to intrude on his privacy, to stir up the pot. They treated Mark with kid gloves. Maybe too carefully, Ben reflected, though he knew Carolyn disagreed with him on that point.

He dialed information, and the operator found the number quickly. Ben jotted it on a notepad. Still, he paused before joining the others. *Would this call do more harm than good?* he worried. *Please Lord, let us have a good talk with Mark,* he silently prayed.

He found the rest of the family in the kitchen, helping Carolyn clean up. "Information had a number for the ranch. I'll give it a try." He picked up the kitchen phone and dialed.

Rachel wiped her hands on a towel and drew closer, but Carolyn stayed at the sink, her back turned.

The phone on the other end rang several times. Ben was about to give up when someone suddenly came on the line—a woman who spoke with a western accent right out of the movies.

"I'm trying to reach Mark Lewis. This is his father calling," Ben explained.

"Mark? He's 'round. I'll see if I can find him for you."

Ben waited, feeling his stomach knot around his Thanksgiving dinner. He hated feeling so much anxiety just because he was about to speak with his son. It wasn't right, he thought. It wasn't right.

"Dad?" Mark suddenly came on the line. "Is everything okay?"

"Everything's fine, son. We just wanted to say hello. How are you doing? Enjoying the ranching life?"

"So far it's been great. I'm still not used to the hard work," he admitted. "Montana is awesome, though."

"Yes, I've heard that." Ben suddenly felt a lump in his throat the size of a football. He had tears in his eyes, as well. "Happy Thanksgiving," he said, forcing a bright voice. "We just called to say hello. There's someone here who really wants to talk to you."

He quickly handed the phone to Rachel, then took out his handkerchief and blew his nose.

"Mark? It's me, Rachel. How are you?" she said, hugging the phone to her cheek. "What in the world are you doing in Montana?"

While Rachel chatted happily, Ben glanced at Carolyn. She had turned around to face him but still stood across the room.

He could tell she felt as he did—almost too overwhelmed to speak casually to Mark, to adopt a calm, relaxed tone that wouldn't emotionally crowd him.

Trying to get his son to come home was like coaxing a frightened cat down from a tree, Ben thought. He suddenly felt frustrated and resentful, and he sent up a quick prayer, asking the Lord for patience and the right attitude.

". . . big as a house. I've only got about four weeks left." Rachel paused, listening, then replied, "I wish you could be around when the baby is born. Maybe you could come back for Christmas. It feels like it's been so long since we've seen you."

For some reason, Rachel was able to say directly to her brother what they all felt, and Ben was glad that they had made the call. Maybe this is just what Mark needed to hear. Then he felt suddenly tense as he watched Rachel's warm expression cloud over. He knew Mark's answer had not been positive.

"Really? I didn't know that. . . . Well, keep in touch, okay? Listen, here's Mom." Rachel turned to her mother, who now stood nearby.

Ben saw Carolyn stare at the phone for a moment, then take it from Rachel, her hand trembling slightly.

"Hello, sweetheart. Happy Thanksgiving," she said warmly. "Oh, we're fine. How are you? Any snow there yet? . . . That much, my word! Do you have enough warm clothes?"

She listened for a few moments and laughed, a forced sound, Ben thought. Her eyes were shining, as if she were holding back tears.

"We missed you here today. There are so many leftovers. . . . Oh, you did. That was nice. . . . Well, take good care of yourself," she urged him. "I will, dear. All right. . . . I understand. Bye now," she said suddenly.

She took a deep breath and hung up the phone. Nobody spoke for a long moment. When Carolyn turned again, Ben met her gaze. "Someone needed to use the phone," she said, her voice carefully controlled. "He had to hang up."

"He said he didn't think he could come home in time to see the baby born," Rachel reported sadly. "Since he's the low man in the group, he has to stay. They don't have many men working on the ranch in the winter. He says he was lucky to get the job."

Ben nodded. "I see," he said.

Of course, if Mark really wanted to come home, he could simply pack up and quit. There were no ties holding him to some ranch in Montana.

"He said he might come for the christening," Rachel added. "I hope he will."

"I hope so, too," Ben said. He did hope so, but he didn't honestly believe Mark would return, even then. "I think it was good to call him," he said finally. "We've shown Mark how much we all miss him and care about him."

"Let's say a prayer about it, together," Rachel suggested.

Carolyn glanced at him. He knew she had been praying about this problem for years now. And so had he. But that didn't mean they should stop praying about it—or doubt that the good Lord was listening to them and doing what was best for all of them.

They made a small circle, joined hands, and bowed their heads. Ben spoke. "Dear God, please bless our son, Mark, and keep him safe. Please let him know how much we all love him and miss him. Please help him on his journey and let him soon find his way back home to us. Grant us patience and understanding while we wait. Amen."

God moves in his own time, not our time, Ben reminded himself. Mark would return in God's own time and not a minute sooner.

The phone's shrill ring broke the silence. Was that Mark calling back, saying he'd changed his mind and would be home soon after all? If so, it was the fastest answer to a prayer Ben had ever experienced.

He picked up the receiver. "Hello?"

"Sorry to bother you, Reverend." Ben instantly recognized the voice of Sam Morgan on the other end, and he felt alarmed at Sam's serious tone. "Something's happened."

"What's wrong, Sam?"

"It's Digger. He took Grace's dog out this morning, and he never came back. It's been over eight hours. The police and some volunteers are looking for him."

"My word! How is Grace?" Ben asked, knowing that the elderly fisherman's disappearance would be hardest on his daughter.

"You know Grace. She's not exactly the emotional type. But she's shook up. Harry is here with her," Sam added, referring to Harry Reilly, who owned a boatyard in town where Digger sometimes did odd jobs. "But he really wants to get out to help search. I'm going back myself in a few minutes."

A widower of many years and a loner by nature, Harry was not a particularly friendly man, but in the past months, he had grown close to the eccentric old fisherman and his middle-aged daughter. Tonight, Harry's support would be important, Ben thought anxiously.

"Yes, I understand. Tell Harry I'll be over right away," he said. He hung up the phone, feeling his pulse race.

"What is it Ben? You're as white as a sheet," Carolyn said.

"Digger is missing. He left the house this morning with Grace's dog and hasn't been seen since," he reported, as he ran to his study for his Bible. "I'm going to stay with Grace."

"Oh, no. How awful." Carolyn shook her head.

"Poor Grace," Rachel said. "She must be beside herself."

Everyone knew how Grace watched over her father. Digger was all she had left. Still, the old seaman grew restless and couldn't stand hanging around Grace's antique store all day. He found work around town or rambled about, often evading his daughter's watchful eye.

"Should I come along?" Carolyn asked, as Ben looked around the kitchen for his car keys.

"I'll go now by myself. If this drags on though, maybe you could come later."

They all knew what he meant but wouldn't say. If Digger was found dead, Grace would need all the support they could muster.

"I'm just going to clean up a bit and put the food away. Then I'll come right over," Carolyn said. "Tell Grace we'll be praying for him. And for her."

"Yes, I will, dear," Ben said, as he pulled on his coat at the front door.

While Grace was no longer a member of the church, Ben had the feeling she would welcome any and all prayers tonight. Her faith had faltered and lapsed altogether about seven years ago when she lost her daughter, Julie, and her marriage fell apart. Since then Ben had repeatedly reached out to her, but she'd remained stalwart in her anger at God. Digger, however, rarely missed a service, and whether Grace attended or not, Ben knew he wouldn't feel right if he didn't go to her now.

"I'll go, too," Jack offered suddenly. "Maybe I can join the search party."

"Absolutely. Sounds like they can use as many volunteers as possible tonight."

Jack grabbed an extra sweater and some gloves. Then the two men kissed their wives good-bye and left the house. Night had nearly fallen, and the chilly, damp air warned of snow. Ben walked quickly to his car, afraid to consider the possibilities.

Lord, please let us have good news tonight about Digger.

LUKE FOLLOWED EMILY'S JEEP INTO THE LOT AT DURHAM POINT BEACH and parked beside her vehicle. The beachfront looked like the set from a suspense film. Police cars, an ambulance, and three fire trucks with huge spotlights on top were lined up side by side, the powerful lights mimicking the sweeping beam of the Durham Point Lighthouse, farther down the shoreline.

Luke jumped out of his truck and slammed the door. The flickering searchlights illuminated the sandy dunes like a moonscape. The ocean waves slammed onto the shoreline with a booming sound, like the roar of a cannon.

A chilling image entered Luke's mind: Digger, already lost somewhere under the dark water, returning to the place he loved best in the world, the deep mysterious sea. He took a breath and pushed the thought aside.

Emily stood nearby. The wind tossed her short hair as she surveyed the scene. The call from the police chief, Jim Sanborn, had shocked everyone at her mother's house. Ezra wanted to come, too, at first but decided to stay with Lillian. Which was just as well, Luke thought. The doctor was hardy but no youngster.

Luke had to hand it to Emily. She hadn't hesitated a moment in coming out here, though the police chief had offered to keep her updated by phone. But Emily was not the type to sit idle, waiting for news, Luke knew. He saw her digging through her trunk then pulling out high rubber boots and a big flashlight.

Luke came around his truck and joined her. "I see Jim Sanborn down there," Emily said, pointing across the lot. "Let's see what's going on."

The police chief stood at the back of a flatbed truck, where a map of the area was spread out beneath a floodlight. He turned when he saw them and nodded.

"Any news, Jim?" Emily asked hopefully.

"Nothing," he said, shaking his head. "We've got most of our manpower down here, since Grace thinks he probably came this way. We've been searching Beach Road and other routes. But there's no sign of Digger. Or the dog. The man could be anywhere," he added grimly.

Sanborn was clearly doing the best he could, but the situation seemed beyond him, Luke thought. And maybe beyond the resources of this small town.

"How many people are out looking for him?" Emily asked.

"About forty-some-odd. Harry Reilly's been getting the word out. Volunteers are still coming to help. They're checking in at the police station with Officer Tulley. He's sending them out in pairs to different areas of the village."

"What about search dogs?"

Luke added. "Does Cape Light have a unit?"

Sanborn folded his arms over his chest, seeming to take notice of

Luke for the first time. His eyes narrowed. "We got some dogs from Hamilton first thing this afternoon. They started off at the Hegmans' house, then lost the scent just outside of town. We didn't find them much help, frankly."

Luke seemed undaunted by the reply. "Well, two-men pairs are okay to cover the town. But you need to cover the large open areas inch by inch."

"Inch by inch, huh? If we had an army at our disposal maybe," Sanborn challenged him, his voice rising. "Are you here to help search, McAllister, or take over my job?"

Luke had expected something like this. He knew that the police chief and others in Cape Light still resented him for bringing in the center. He was used to their attitudes. So used to it, in fact, that it didn't faze him. He was too worried about Digger to let any of it get under his skin tonight.

"I'm telling you, you're doing this wrong. With all due respect," he added. "Like the dunes over there with the high grass. You need to get a long line of, say, twenty men with the search vehicles moving behind them. Have them walk straight across to the other end. As for needing an army to do it, what about the National Guard or even the Coast Guard? They might send some help out here, maybe even a helicopter to sweep over the coastline and marshes—though it's too late to see much now," Luke added unhappily.

"That's not a bad idea. Have we called them, Jim?" Emily asked.

"I've been waiting," he admitted. "But I guess it is time."

The chief's expression looked tight and grim, and Luke allowed himself some sympathy for the man. He probably resented having an ex-cop from Boston—a disgraced cop, no less—telling him how to run his show. It was completely understandable. But Luke had run searches like this before, and he knew he couldn't afford to remain silent when Digger's life was on the line.

The police radio buzzed, and the chief picked up the call. "Sanborn." He listened intently. "Give me the coordinates," he said. Luke watched as he turned to the map and marked a spot. "Yeah, I got it. Keep following the trail. Check back in five minutes. I'll be right there."

As he clicked off, he glanced up at Emily. "Digger's pack was found on a trail that leads into the woods off the Beach Road. Had snow on it, so it must have been there awhile," he said disconsolately. "The officers are still following the trail."

He pointed to the map. "The path must be about here, leading into the woods behind the Cranberry Cottages."

"It's marshland back there, isn't it? Behind the woods, I mean," Emily asked.

"There are high reeds and mud. You can't see two feet in front of your face. A lot of water, which I hope is frozen hard enough to walk on. There's some quicksand in there, too."

"Oh, dear. It will be like looking for a needle in a haystack," Emily said.

"It's no place to spend the night at Digger's age," Sanborn responded. He swallowed hard, as he rolled up the map.

"It's a break," Luke insisted. "This could be the lead you've been waiting for. But now you have to use it."

The older man turned to Luke, his eyes flashing with anger. "So what's my next move, McAllister? You want to run this show, go ahead. What do we do now?"

Luke stepped up to the truck bed and looked over the map. "Call all the searchers to that location. You want to cover this section first. Then this next section here."

"And what if he's not in there? What if he's down here in the flats or in the dunes, where we haven't even looked yet? Or somewhere along the road? We won't have anyone left to check those areas."

"If Digger's still in the woods, there should be more evidence. Even if it's just trampled-down brush," Luke argued. "Without enough people looking at once, you might not get to him in time."

The police chief paused a moment. He glanced at Emily. "What do you think, Mayor?"

"I think Luke's got a point. If it were up to me, I'd say, let's try it and see how it goes, but it's your call."

Sanborn nodded, avoiding her gaze. "All right then. I'll send the bulk of them down to that spot." He glanced at his watch. "I'll meet you over there. There should be some flares on the road."

"Don't worry. I'll find the spot." Emily turned toward Luke. "Okay, let's go," she said to him.

Luke fell into step beside her, his hands digging into his jacket pockets. They reached her car, and he turned to her. The wind off the water was chilling as he tugged at his words. "This is the right way to go, Emily."

Emily pulled open the door to her truck. "I hope so. I don't know if I can live with myself if it isn't."

Luke jumped into his 4Runner and gunned the engine. Farther down the lot he saw Chief Sanborn pull out, followed by three cruisers and the ambulance.

For a moment Luke allowed his doubts to surface. What if he was wrong? It had been Sanborn's call finally, but if they didn't find Digger, Luke knew he would be blamed. He was barely accepted here as it was. He would have to leave, no question. All the work he'd done here, the roots he'd put down—it would all go down the drain.

He would have to leave Sara. That would be hardest of all, he realized. Leave her before they'd even gotten started.

CHAPTER THREE

LUKE KNEW THE VACANT LAND ALONG THE BEACH ROAD WELL. Though he had only moved here in the spring, he'd spent summers in Cape Light as a boy, which was the real reason he'd been drawn back to the town. He knew the road was bordered by a tangled wood, where narrow paths wove between overgrown trees, vines, and brush. The woods were not quite as hard to walk through at this time of the year. But nearly, he thought.

At a certain point, the ground became too soggy for trees, and the terrain turned into a wide meadow, covered by tall dense reeds and scrubby bushes. If Digger had wandered that far, it would be hard to find him tonight. And if they didn't find him tonight . . . Luke couldn't allow his mind to consider the possibility.

They would find him. They had to.

As Jim had promised, orange road flares marked the opening to the woods. A good number of searchers had already arrived, and the road's shoulder was lined with cars and trucks. Luke parked his 4Runner and joined Emily. The volunteers huddled in small groups, waiting for directions. Many greeted Emily, Luke noticed, but only Sam Morgan and Harry Reilly greeted him.

The chief's car pulled up, and Jim walked up to Emily and Luke.

"Well, here they are," he said. "I still don't like sending the whole search crew into the same place."

"It's useless on the trail," Luke agreed, "but we've already established that Digger's not on the trail."

"Good detective work, McAllister. He might have walked into the woods this morning and walked right out."

"Or he might have gone into the marsh and is now stuck in there," Luke countered. "Let them all go down to the end of the trail, where the reeds start. Then have them line up side by side, a few yards apart and walk into the reeds."

The chief took a long harsh breath. "I'm giving this scheme an hour. If it doesn't pan out by then, we'll try it my way again."

"All right, Jim. Fair enough," Emily said. She looked at Luke but didn't say anything more.

The police chief spoke to the officers present, and the group was soon organized as Luke had instructed. Luke pulled on a borrowed pair of rubber boots, turned on his flashlight, then joined the single-file line of men and women marching into the woods.

The line of volunteers and police officers soon came to the end of the wooded trail, and they turned toward the edge of the tall reeds. Finally, they began to move forward, spots of light from their flashlights dancing around their feet. Luke walked behind Emily who was not far from the police chief.

Despite the cold snap, much of the wet boggy ground remained soft and muddy, sucking at their feet with each step. Luke pushed through the reeds and bramble, his gaze searching the ground for any clue, any sign that Digger had wandered into the marsh.

"For the life of me, I can't see why anyone would think the man could be in here. There's no path anymore, and you can barely walk two steps. It just doesn't make any sense." Luke overheard the police chief complaining to Emily.

"Let's go on a bit farther," Emily replied. "We've barely come a hundred feet."

"That's just my point. I'm watching the clock," Sanborn added gruffly.

Luke swallowed hard and kept his head down. He was also watching the clock and knew that time was ticking down.

Still, he had a feeling, a gut feeling, that Digger was in here. Since he'd come to Cape Light, Luke had found himself not exactly praying, but talking to God on a more regular basis. As he pushed through the tall weeds, he started a silent conversation. *God, please help us out here. Give us some sort of sign. Another clue. We can't do this without you.*

The minutes ticked by. One of the volunteers turned an ankle on a tree root and had to be taken out on a stretcher by the EMS crew.

Sanborn turned to Emily. "Had enough yet? This is a downright waste of time," he said sharply. "Digger must have come down the trail, dropped the pack by accident, then realized he couldn't walk in any farther and went back out again. You don't need Sherlock Holmes to figure that one out."

Luke could see worry and indecision flashing across Emily's face. She sighed and checked her watch. "We did put an hour's time limit on the effort," she acknowledged.

Luke knew more than an hour had passed by now. Counting the trek in from the road, it was nearly two. She cast Luke a questioning look. "What do you think? Would Digger have come into the marsh this far? I mean, the chief has a point. There aren't even trails anymore."

Luke shrugged. "Not to you and me. But Digger knew every path and shortcut within a ten-mile radius. He might have been taking some hidden path through the marsh that cuts down to the beach. Or he might have gotten lost looking for it."

It wasn't just his ego talking or some need to be right. He still had a nagging feeling that Digger was around here, somewhere. And it was the kind of feeling that detectives are taught not to ignore.

Sanborn huffed impatiently. "I'm calling the searchers in. We agreed on one hour. It's been far longer than that."

Emily glanced at Luke then back at the police chief. She nodded. "All right. If you think we've come far enough. It is hard to see how he could have made it back here," she added quietly.

Luke turned away from them, staring at the wall of reeds swaying in the darkness. The sight made his heart heavy with dread and fear. Digger was back there somewhere; he just knew it.

"I'm going to stay," he said suddenly.

Emily turned and stared at him. "Alone? Do you think that's wise?"

"You can't stay out here alone, McAllister," Sanborn cut in harshly. "We'll be sending out a search team for you next. I won't permit it."

Luke met his gaze. "Guess what? I don't need your permission. We just crossed the line onto my property. I'm going to keep searching out here."

Sanborn gave him a hard look, then turned to Emily. "You heard him, Mayor. I won't be responsible."

The chief clipped his radio back on his belt, then raised his light straight up, swinging it back and forth, a signal to others that the hunt in this area was over. Police officers at other positions in the marsh signaled back in answer. There was a moment of heavy silence. The sound of failure, Luke thought.

The searchers turned and headed back to the road. Emily stayed behind a moment.

"I don't think it's very wise of you to stay out here alone," she said to Luke, when the chief was out of earshot. "But I can see you're determined. At least take this." She took her key chain out of her pocket, then pulled something off it and handed it to Luke.

Luke looked down at the metal whistle in his hand. "Okay, thanks," he said, slipping it into his pocket. "Don't worry. I won't get lost out here, too."

"I certainly hope not," Emily said in a serious tone. "I'm going back with the others now. But I want you to test the whistle in about five minutes or so. It will make me feel better if I know you can be heard if you need help."

Luke felt a little silly complying with the request, but he nodded anyway. "Sure. No problem. I'll try it in a few minutes."

He'd put Emily's reputation on the line tonight. He could at least blow the whistle if it made her feel better.

"All right, then. I'll be listening for it."

Emily turned to join the others. The last of the volunteers were vanishing down the trail back into the woods, and the area looked suddenly very dark without the reassuring glow of the searchers' flashlights.

Luke pushed forward. It was harder going with his single light. He started onto what he thought was a trail, but it soon dwindled and disappeared. He moved slowly, searching the ground for any clues that Digger had passed through. But he was only one pair of eyes now. If Digger was lying in the reeds unconscious, Luke might walk right by him and never know it.

Luke paused and checked his watch. It was time to signal Emily. Standing in the darkness with his single beam of light, he was suddenly grateful for the whistle. He blew on it sharply, took a breath, and blew again.

He sighed and looked around, wondering if he should walk in a new direction.

Then he heard a sound, coming from deep in the marsh. Something moving, pushing through the reeds. He held his breath, listening, praying it wasn't just a deer or one last volunteer who had gotten separated from the group.

Then he heard a dog barking. A few staccato barks, thin and forced, as if the dog had been at it for hours and its voice and energy were just about gone.

Grace's dog, he thought. She must be trapped back there. Was Digger with her? They could have easily been separated back here. . . .

Luke pointed his light in the direction of the barking sound and plunged into the reeds again. He put the whistle to his lips and blew hard.

The dog soon barked in answer, and Luke moved toward the sound. He felt a surge of energy, and despite his feet feeling like blocks of ice in the rubber boots, he moved through the rushes quickly, a goal finally in sight.

Every few yards, Luke blew the whistle, eliciting more excited yelps from the dog. As far as he could tell, the sound continued to come from the same spot, and Luke wondered why the dog didn't run toward him. She must be wounded or stuck in something. He hoped she wasn't badly hurt.

Finally, Luke pushed aside some branches, pointed his light, and spotted the dog in a small clearing. Panting, she stood still, then looked at him and wagged her tail. She didn't look hurt, Luke thought. He wondered why she hadn't run to him, then realized maybe the flashlight had scared her.

He pointed his light down on the ground and moved forward. "Daisy, here girl," he called out softly. He patted the side of his leg. "Come on, girl."

The big yellow Labrador tossed her head back and barked again, even more loudly. She suddenly turned and leaped, disappearing into the nearby brush.

"Daisy! Come on, Daisy," Luke called, running after her. He quickly crossed the clearing, then plunged into the brush, unmindful of the branches and vines cutting his face and hands.

After a few terrible moments in which he was sure he had lost the dog, he spotted her standing near a thicket, whining and pushing at something on the ground with her nose. At the sound of his footsteps she looked up and barked at him.

Luke felt his blood run cold. He stepped forward, flashed his light on the ground and was finally sure of what he saw.

It was Digger, lying facedown on the ground, his arms and legs at strange angles. Luke dropped to the ground. Gently, he turned him over and felt his neck for a pulse. It was weak, but the old man was still alive. Just barely.

"Thank you, God. Thank you for helping us find him," Luke mumbled, as he pulled open the scarf at Digger's neck to check his breathing. He was breathing, but his skin color was bad, pale and bluish. He needed medical attention immediately. Luke hoped it wasn't already too late.

He pulled off his jacket and bundled it around Digger like a blanket. It wasn't much, but it would have to do until the EMS crew got to him, Luke thought.

Suddenly Digger stirred. He opened his eyes and looked at Luke, though Luke wasn't at all sure that the old man recognized him. Then Luke felt Digger grasp his hand, his eyes filled with emotion. Luke leaned toward him. "You're going to be all right, Digger. Don't worry. I'm going to get help. I'll be right back."

Digger stared at him a moment longer, then closed his eyes. The effort of replying was too much for him, Luke realized.

Luke rose and ran back in the direction he had come, pushing through the reeds with all his strength. He remembered the whistle and began to blow on it again, as hard and fast as he could.

He hadn't gone far when he saw several beams of light coming toward him. It was Sanborn, Emily, and a police officer. "Luke, are you all right?" Emily called out to him.

"I found Digger. He's alive!" Luke shouted. "Get the stretcher!"

The lights came closer, and Sanborn reached him first. His expression was a mixture of anger and relief. "Where is he?"

"Through these reeds, not far. Follow me," Luke said, leading the way. Sanborn paused and took out the radio to call for the EMS crew before following Luke.

When Luke reached Digger again, he suddenly remembered Daisy. He glanced around for the dog, hoping she hadn't run away again. With a sense of relief, he saw her resting at Digger's booted feet, still panting, but looking as if she knew her job was done.

Sanborn pushed into the clearing and squatted down at Digger's side. He then checked the pulse in the old man's neck.

"I heard Daisy barking and followed her," Luke explained. "She led me right to him."

"Lucky break," Sanborn said, glancing up at him.

"Yes, it was. Lucky for Digger, I'd say." He stared back at the police chief, who was the first to look away.

Just then Emily appeared, with Officer Tucker Tulley following closely behind her.

Emily came forward and stopped in her tracks, staring down at Digger.

"Thank God," she said quietly.

Luke couldn't agree more.

* * *

LUKE AND EMILY RODE TOGETHER IN HIS 4RUNNER, FOLLOWING THE ambulance to the hospital in Southport. Neither spoke for a long time. Then Emily said, "You were right to keep looking, Luke. I'm sorry I didn't trust your judgment."

Luke shrugged. "I just had a feeling he was there. I can't say why. I could have been wrong."

"But you weren't. Digger and Grace owe you a lot."

"Me? No way," he said. "It was a group effort. You ought to get some credit yourself for giving me that whistle. Besides, if anyone should be singled out as a hero, it's got to be Daisy. Poor dog nearly barked her head off."

"Yes, she did, poor thing." Emily shook her head. "The town should give her a medal. I'm going to look into it."

Then they both smiled. Luke felt exhausted and chilled to the bone. His clothes were caked with mud, and his feet, wet and numb. But the relief of finding Digger had made him almost light-headed.

He was sure everyone in the search party felt that way right now. But Emily's words had made him feel good, too, as if he had distinguished himself tonight. As if people in Cape Light might look at him differently from now on.

In his own eyes, the feeling was something he could only call redemption. As if in some small way, he'd made up for the missteps of his past. Not that searching for Digger could ever compare with the night that had left his partner dead and branded him a coward and a failure. But he felt as if he'd been given another chance tonight, and he had finally done all right. He sent up a silent prayer, thanking the Lord for His help, for Digger's life, for this feeling.

Suddenly, all he could think about was Sara. He yearned to see her and tell her about what had happened and what it all meant to him. She was the only one he really wanted to be with right now. He smiled to himself, staring out at the dark, empty highway. She'd be back in three days. That wasn't long at all. It suddenly seemed like his reward.

* * *

EMILY ENTERED THE HOSPITAL'S EMERGENCY WING WITH LUKE AND SAW a cluster of familiar faces gathered around Grace Hegman. Grace was wiping her red-rimmed eyes with a tissue, as Harry Reilly stood to one side, patting her shoulder. Carolyn Lewis sat beside her. Grace looked upset, as one would expect, but relieved as well.

"How are you doing, Grace?" Emily asked her softly.

"Not too bad, all things considered." Grace shook her head. "At least he wasn't lost out there all night. Doctor said he wouldn't have had much of a chance then at all."

The mere thought of such an outcome brought a fresh wave of tears to Grace's eyes. Emily's heart went out to her. "So you've already spoken to the doctor?"

"Just for a minute. He won't say anything yet. They need to work on him, give him tests. More waiting," she added, forcing a thin smile. "I don't know what I would have done tonight, waiting to hear word, if it wasn't for Harry and the reverend and Mrs. Lewis. I would have lost my mind, I guess. And if he wasn't found . . . or didn't survive . . ."

Carolyn reached out and took Grace's hand. "We got through it, Grace. That's all that matters now," she assured her. "Don't let your mind dwell on what might have been."

While Carolyn comforted Grace, Reverend Ben steered Emily aside for a more private conversation.

"At least Digger is conscious," Emily said.

"Yes, they let Grace speak to him for a moment when they wheeled him in. He even answered questions. He said he was going to the beach to do some clamming and lost his way." Reverend Ben shook his head. "Digger knows every inch of the woods like the back of his hand. How could he have lost his way?"

"He got confused, I guess."

"Yes, disoriented. The doctors don't think he's had a heart attack, but they're checking him thoroughly."

"Of course." Emily paused. "Maybe I shouldn't say this, Reverend, but coming here, seeing Grace so upset and waiting for word about Digger—it reminds me of the fire last summer."

"Yes, me, too. I had the very same thought."

When a fire broke out at the construction site at the Cranberry Cottages, Digger had sounded the alarm and had later been treated for smoke inhalation. Although it was known to very few, an investigation found the primary cause: the old seaman's charred pipe under the rubble. Emily had persuaded the fire chief to report that the fire had been due to accidental causes, which was true, and no charges had been brought against Digger.

But the incident had been a warning of Digger's decline and need to be closely watched. Grace had done her best, Emily was sure. But clearly, her best efforts had not been good enough to protect her father.

"He's survived. That's the most important thing," Reverend Ben told Emily.

"Of course. But I'm worried, Reverend. Something like this could happen again. Then what?"

The reverend removed his glasses, rubbing them clean with his handkerchief. "First we need to hear what the doctors say. Then what Grace says, of course," he added, glancing across the room. "There are a lot of people in this town who care about Digger. I'm hoping that if people who care about him put their heads and hearts together, they can help the Hegmans work this out—find some way for Digger to retain his autonomy."

Emily didn't know what to say. While she agreed with Reverend Ben, she wasn't sure such an ideal outcome was possible. She only hoped that Grace realized how far things had gone and the dire consequences if action were not taken.

She turned to see Luke talking to a few men from the rescue team, her brother-in-law, Sam Morgan, among them. She didn't mean to eavesdrop, but she couldn't help overhearing them. "Come on, Luke," Sam said. "If you hadn't gone up against Sanborn, Digger would still be out there."

Luke started to speak, but Harry Reilly interrupted him, "Sanborn's all right. He can get on his high horse, though. Good thing you listened to your gut. You even brought Daisy home. That was the icing on the cake for Grace."

Luke tried to downplay his part again, but Sam, Harry, and Jack

Anderson wouldn't deny him the role of Digger's main rescuer. Emily turned away. She had heard enough.

Perhaps people just needed someone to be the hero tonight, she thought. Everyone deserved credit for finding Digger. Even Chief Sanborn had used his best judgment at the time. The entire group had worked together in a cooperative spirit typical of this town. But Luke's knowledge and solitary stand had made all the difference. After all the ill will this town had shown him, she was glad to see him being appreciated.

CHAPTER FOUR

ON MONDAY MORNING AT THE CLAM BOX DINER, THE SCENTS OF strong coffee, hotcakes, and bacon filled the air, along with bantering conversation about Digger Hegman's rescue. So many of the diner's customers had taken part in the search, almost everyone seemed to have some interesting tidbit to offer.

Officer Tucker Tulley sat at the counter in his usual seat, just behind the grill, carrying on his usual, fractured conversation with Charlie Bates, as the diner's owner dished up breakfast orders at a fast, and often furious, pace.

"You should have seen the look on Sanborn's face when McAllister shouted out that he had found Digger," Tucker told Charlie. "When we first heard all that whistling, Sanborn thought for sure McAllister had gotten into some kind of trouble and needed help."

"I would have thought the same," Charlie said, as he flipped a row of pancakes. "Him finding Digger, why that was just dumb luck."

"Come on, Charlie. I know you don't like the guy, but you have to give him some credit," Tucker prodded his old friend.

"I do not. No one's going to make me, either." Charlie glanced at Tucker over his shoulder, sending a warning look. Why, he would have won the election and been mayor, if it hadn't been for McAllister and that infernal center for juvenile misfits of his. Charlie knew he'd never forget that, no matter what McAllister did.

"Seems to me, not too long ago, a lot of folks around here were ready to run that guy out of town. Now, all of a sudden, he's a big hero. It's the dog that's the hero if you ask me," Charlie griped.

"That's exactly what the chief says," Tucker replied, appeasing his old friend. Lucy Bates breezed by with the coffeepot and automatically filled his cup again.

"Don't even waste your breath arguing with him. He thinks he's right about everything. You ought to know that by now," Lucy said, though she was talking more to Charlie's back than to Tucker.

Tucker glanced up at her. "I ought to, but then what would we talk about?" he asked innocently.

"See, Tucker knows I don't mean anything by it. Arguing is just my way, Lucy," Charlie told his wife. "You got an order ready here," he added, pointing at a fried-egg sandwich that the assistant cook, Billy, had just set out.

"You'd better call the new girl. I've got to go," Lucy replied, as she briskly untied her apron and stuffed it under the counter.

"Got to go? Are you crazy?" Charlie stared at her, waving the metal spatula as his voice rose anxiously. "It's not even eight. We've still got the morning rush coming in. You can't go anywhere now."

"I told you last night, Charlie. I've got to get over to school this morning by eight-thirty. There's a review session for my art history course, and I can't miss it."

Lucy pulled her purse and a canvas tote filled with books out from under the counter. She stood there, glaring back at him with that hard "I dare you" look that Charlie had seen a lot of recently—and had come to detest. When she got that look in her eyes, there was no stopping her. He'd learned that the hard way these last few months. Still, he couldn't help trying to appeal to some rational part of her—if there was one left.

"Lucy, come on now. Give me a break. It's Monday morning. We've got a million people in here, waiting for their breakfasts and about a million more coming in. Can't you just skip your review meeting and help me out?" he pleaded. "You can get the notes from someone else tomorrow, can't you?"

Lucy's mouth closed in a tight line, and she tucked her book bag firmly under one arm. "No, I can't do that today, Charlie. Sorry. I need to go. Billy can come out and help serve, if you get too jammed up."

She walked toward him, trying to get out from behind the counter, but Charlie blocked her way. He knew some customers were starting to watch, but he didn't care.

"I need you to stay here, Lucy. Stay and do your job," he insisted angrily.

They stood nose to nose. He stared down at her, feeling so infuriated he thought he might explode. Her eyes narrowed, and she pushed at him with her shoulder. "Let me by, Charlie. I have to go. You're making a scene here," she warned him, in a low tone. "Just let me pass."

"No, I won't." Charlie crossed his arms over his chest, his feet planted in place. He watched as Lucy's fair skin flushed red, a sure sign that she was mad as anything at him. Still, he didn't budge, just waiting to see what she would do. Give in, he hoped.

"Okay, have it your way, then," she said finally. She backed away from him, her head sagging. She sighed as if she were giving up. Then suddenly she hoisted herself up on the counter, and clutching her purse and book bag, she swung her legs to the other side.

"Now, just a minute. You—you can't do that!" Charlie sputtered, starting after her.

He tried to grab her arm, but Tucker stood up and touched Charlie's shoulder, the gentle but firm pressure holding him back. "Let her go, Charlie," his old friend said quietly. "I think something on the grill is burning. You'd better take a look."

Charlie watched as Lucy slid down to the floor, ran to the door, and made her escape, coat in hand. He turned to Tucker, about to complain, then just shook his head. "Something's burning all right," he muttered. "It's my marriage. It's turning into burnt toast, right before my eyes, and there's not a thing I can do."

"Come on now, Charlie. It can't be that bad," Tucker said. "You and Lucy are just hitting a little . . . rough patch."

Charlie stalked back to the grill and turned a row of bacon strips. "It's worse than that, Tucker. Much worse. Lucy is just not the woman I married. I hardly know what to expect from her one minute to the next. You saw the way she bolted out of here just now. Did you ever see anything like that? The old Lucy would never have done anything like that," he grumbled.

"Well, people change. That's true," Tucker agreed. "But it can't be easy for her, going back to college and working here. And taking care of the kids, too," he pointed out.

"I never said it was. My row isn't so easy to hoe, either, you know. But it all seemed to be working fine until she decided to go back to school. That's when the old Lucy disappeared and this new, crazy one took her place. She doesn't listen to a word I say. She doesn't do her job around here, our house is upside down and inside out, and half the time I don't know where she is or who's watching our kids. It's just sheer insanity. And for what? So my wife can study art history? What does Lucy need to know about that for?"

"Because . . . she really wants to?" Tucker offered.

"For goodness' sake, what difference does that make? I really want to be an astronaut and fly around in the space shuttle. You think I ought to run down to NASA and volunteer myself?" Charlie retorted.

"Not unless they have a little grill on those birds," Tucker said, laughing.

"I'm serious, Tucker. Our agreement was to see how this college thing worked out, then decide if she ought to continue. Well, it's a plain disaster as far as I can see. I thought Lucy would come to her senses and give it up. But you can see what I'm dealing with here. I try to reason with her, and she just makes a break for it. Jumps right over the counter like a horse jumping the stall."

Tucker thoughtfully chewed the last bite of his doughnut, then swallowed. "You've got a problem here, Charlie, no doubt about that. Seems to me the two of you have come to what I'd call a crossroads. Now you got to figure out which way to go and who's going where and with whom."

Charlie stared at him. Then looked back at the grill and pushed the potatoes around.

"Well, that makes some sense, I guess," he said finally. "Maybe you can do me a favor and stand out there in that crossroads and direct the traffic. That ought to give me some chance of winning."

He heard Tucker chuckle softly, trying to brighten the mood. Charlie forced a tight smile while inside he felt his gut still churning, his heart heavy with doubt. He didn't know what was happening between him and Lucy. And for the first time, he honestly felt afraid.

SARA FRANKLIN ARRIVED AT THE NEWSPAPER OFFICE AT A QUARTER TO nine on Monday morning, thinking she was so early she might need to wait at the door for someone to let her in.

But the door was open, and she could see through the storefront-style windows that the office—a large room with a row of computers on desks—was already stirring. A woman about her age sat at the desk nearest the door, talking on the phone while she scribbled notes on a pad. Her head bobbed as she spoke, her long dark curls bouncing in time to the conversation. She took Sara in with a sweeping glance but didn't pause to greet her.

Sara kept walking and came to a middle-aged man with a bristly gray crew cut who sat at a desk a bit farther back, against the wall. He stared intently at his computer screen, typing with just his two index fingers in staccato bursts, and he didn't look up as she passed. A bumper sticker on the bulletin board next to his desk read, "The difference between the right word and the wrong one is like the difference between 'lightning' and 'lightning bug.' " The quote made her smile, despite the nerves jumping around in her stomach.

"Good, you finally got here."

She turned to see who had greeted her and realized it had to be Wyatt Forbes. He seemed to have materialized out of thin air. Then she noticed a corridor at the back of the newsroom, which seemed to lead to some other, smaller rooms.

They had spoken once by phone but had never met in person. He looked a lot like his father, she thought, the same blue eyes and even features. But unlike Dan's fair hair that had gone mostly gray, Wyatt's was dark brown with a slight wave. The front fell down across his eyes, and Sara noticed him sweep it back with his hand in an impatient gesture. He was tall like his father, too, and when he stood next to her, she had to tip her head back to meet his gaze.

"Sara Franklin, right?" he asked, holding out his hand.

She smiled and shook hands with him. "You must be Wyatt."

"That I am. Though on a morning like this one, I'd love to deny it." He walked over to his desk, the last one at the back of the room, and Sara followed. "Here, have a seat," he said, gesturing to the chair next to his desk. He sat behind his desk and began sifting through the papers and folders piled up there without looking at her.

"I read your clips. They were okay," he said.

"Thanks." Just as sparing with praise as his father, too, she thought.

"I know when my dad hired you, he said you'd be part-time, doing rewrites, public notices, that sort of thing. But we're low on staff. Just lost two reporters to our competition, the *Chronicle.* It's part of Crown News. Ever read it?" he asked abruptly.

"Uh, no, I don't think so," she answered, wondering if she was giving the wrong answer. Already.

"Well, you need to now. Need to keep up with their stories, make sure we're not missing anything. They keep picking off our best reporters," he continued. "And we're down on office help, too. We could use you here full-time, if you're available."

Sara thought of her part-time job at the library—but only briefly. Looked like she would have to wait to borrow those new arrivals, just like everyone else.

"Sure, I'm available," she replied quickly. "Absolutely."

"Great, you're going to have to jump right in."

"I'll be covering stories right away, you mean?"

"That's right." He nodded, his expression questioning. "Any problem with that?"

"No problem at all. I can do it," she promised. She partly wanted to jump for joy—and partly wanted to run from the room in a panic attack.

He stared at her for a minute, an unsmiling look that made her uncomfortable. He had very blue eyes, she noticed.

"Okay, we'll see how it goes." Wyatt glanced at his watch and pushed back his hair with his hand. She never really thought of Dan as attractive, but somehow the same features on his son definitely were.

"Let me introduce you around, then you can pick a desk and get to work."

Wyatt rose, acting as if he were unaware of her, and again Sara followed him, quickening her steps to keep up. Wyatt walked to the man with the crew cut, who continued to type away furiously until Wyatt knocked on his computer terminal.

"Come up for air, Ed. I want you to meet somebody," Wyatt told him. "This is Sara Franklin, a new reporter. Sara, Ed Kazinsky."

"Right, Kazinsky's Korner. I like your column," she added.

Ed immediately smiled, revealing a row of tobacco-stained teeth and a gold crown. "I'm going to like this girl. She's very sharp." He turned and began typing again. "Now please go away so I can work. Nice to meet you, Sara. If you have any questions, ask one of the others," he advised.

"Thanks for your time, Ed. We know how important you are," Wyatt said dryly. He glanced at Sara and raised his eyebrows, then led the way to the young woman at the front of the newsroom. She was also working at her computer, but she stopped and looked up right away as Wyatt and Sara came toward her.

"This is the new reporter I told you about, Sara Franklin. Sara, this is Jane Harmon. She covers day-to-day stuff, town meetings, school board—"

"Any meeting within a ten-mile radius that lasts longer than three hours and can bore even a politician to tears. That's my specialty," Jane joked, holding out her hand to greet Sara.

"Hey, don't scare her. I'm putting her on the same beat," Wyatt warned.

"It's not so bad. The trick is not to doze off before the good stuff happens," Jane said. She squinted at Sara. "You look familiar. Have we met before?"

Sara smiled self-consciously. She heard that a lot around town. "I worked at the Clam Box during the summer."

"Oh . . . sure." Jane's eyes grew brighter. "Well, hope you like it here better. No tips, but it's more fun. Frankly, I'm glad to see another body. Things have been a little frantic since Dan's accident."

Sara noticed an irritated expression cross Wyatt's face, then disappear so quickly, she thought she'd imagined it.

He turned to Jane again. "Can you help Sara settle in? I have to cover a story at the courthouse in Southport. I have you down for the Water Authority meeting in Hamilton at one," he added.

"Should I take Sara with me?" Jane asked.

"Uh . . . no. I have something else for her. That interview with McAllister."

"Luke McAllister?" Sara asked. "Why does the paper want to interview him?" Was there more controversy over the New Horizon's Center? She hoped not.

"Didn't you know? He's the one who found Digger Hegman," Wyatt told her.

"What happened to Digger?" Sara asked.

They both stared at her in disbelief, before Wyatt said, "Oh, you haven't heard, yet, I guess." He was smiling, but she still felt embarrassed.

"Digger was lost for about twelve hours on Thanksgiving Day," Jane explained. "There was a real manhunt, practically everyone in town came out to look for him. They finally found him in the woods off Beach Road, not too far from the Cranberry Cottages. It sounds like if it weren't for McAllister, the old guy would still be out there."

"Really?" Sara could hardly believe the story—or that she hadn't heard about it. But she had only gotten back to town late last night and hadn't spoken to anyone. "What did Luke do?"

"He probably saved Hegman's life. But everyone's got a different version," Wyatt said. "We wanted Luke's story firsthand, but he said that you were the only one he'd talk to, and he'd wait until you came on the staff. Is he a friend of yours or something?"

"Yes . . . a friend," Sara replied, feeling warm color flush her cheeks. *Or something* was probably the more accurate description, though she couldn't really say what. "I'll call him right now. Maybe he's free this morning," she added, trying to sound professional.

"Good, get right on it. It's late, but we'll make it a feature. Get a photo, something with the woods in the background," Wyatt said. "There's an old Nikon in the darkroom you can borrow. You know how to use a 35mm, right?"

Sara nodded. If the camera didn't have an automatic exposure—and it sounded like it did not—she couldn't promise the pictures would come out. But Luke probably knew how to set it, she thought. She would ask him to help her.

"The story doesn't have to be long, about seven hundred fifty words. Copy deadline is three o'clock."

Sara swallowed hard. Read up on the background, do the interview, write a seven-hundred-fifty-word article, and turn in a great photo. All by three o'clock. Whatever made her think she could do this job?

"Sure." She nodded. "I've got it. Three o'clock."

"Okay, see you later." Wyatt grabbed his coat off a rack near the door and left.

Jane's voice broke into her wandering thoughts. "Don't worry, he's always like that. Sort of rushing around like the March Hare, shouting orders. You'll get used to it."

"It's a lot like the diner so far," Sara joked, making Jane laugh.

"Come on and pick out a desk. We have some good vacancies this week."

Sara smiled back at her. "Lead the way."

Sara was soon settled at a desk just behind Jane with a view of the street. She found recent editions of the paper and read the article on Digger's disappearance as well as the official police report.

Finally, she knew it was time to call Luke. She felt a pang of conscience as she punched in his number. She hadn't called him all week from Maryland. Maybe she should have called when she got into town last night, but it had been very late; she hadn't even called Emily.

Suddenly, she hung up the phone. *I ought to just go out and see him.*

He's probably working outside, and I'll just get the machine. If things are awkward between us, it will be easier to deal with face to face.

Sara picked up her jacket and stuck a new reporter-style notepad in her knapsack, along with the camera. Passing Jane's desk, she said, "I'm going out to see Luke McAllister. I'll be back in a little while."

Jane nodded, her eyes glued to her computer terminal. "If you're back by twelve, you can come with me to the Water Authority meeting. They're going to discuss the new water-treatment proposal," she added in a tempting tone.

"That sounds . . . exciting," Sara said politely.

Jane laughed, and Sara swung through the door, feeling suddenly lighthearted, like the real thing already.

She drove up Main Street and then turned off at Beach Road. It was a short distance to the turnoff for Luke's property, which was still marked by an old sign that said Cranberry Cottages that Luke had never bothered to take down. Sara steered her hatchback down the gravel road to the cottages, carefully avoiding familiar dips and ruts.

Pulling into the lot, Sara spotted Luke's 4Runner parked alongside Sam Morgan's pickup truck. She parked and got out, walking toward the sound of hammers, which echoed through the winter woods. She followed the path to the cottages and looked around the property to see where they were working today. Things looked different to her, though it was only a couple of weeks since she last visited.

Luke had made great progress since the summer. Most of the cottages were now renovated into housing for the kids and counselors who would be coming in the spring when New Horizons opened. Toward the back of the property a foundation had been dug and the framing started on a new building that would house classrooms and a large common room.

Sara spotted Luke on a rooftop, his strong silhouette outlined against the blue sky. He was working on the cottage she had lived in last summer. She had spent time with Luke almost every day when she lived here. They had both been going through so much.

She walked up to the cottage, almost afraid to call out, worrying that she might make Luke lose his balance. Sam saw her first, shouted a hello, and kept working.

"Sara!" Luke called. He waved, then hopped across the roof and climbed down the ladder.

"I wasn't sure if you were back yet." He smiled and stepped toward her, and she automatically returned his quick, tight hug. He wore a thick blue sweater and a tan thermal vest. When he held her close she smelled soap and wood smoke. She had missed him, she realized. More than she had thought she would.

"I got in late last night," she said, as she pulled back. "I'm sorry I didn't get a chance to call you."

"That's okay. What are you doing out here? I thought you started at the paper today."

"I did. You're my first assignment. Wyatt Forbes said you wouldn't give the paper a story about finding Digger unless I wrote it. Is that true?"

Luke looked as if he were trying hard not to smile. He crossed his arms over his chest. "Well . . . yeah. Does that bother you?"

"Surprised me, I guess. So, what's the story? Did you really save Digger?"

"Not wasting any time, are you?" he kidded her. "You were born for this job, Ace."

"Thanks. I hope so."

"Come on, let's go inside. I'll make coffee," he offered.

"Sure." Sara fell into step beside him. "But I can't stay long."

"I know. It is good to see you, though." Luke turned and glanced down at her. "Did you have a good visit with your folks?"

"It was great. We had a lot of time to talk. I think they finally understand why I decided to stay here longer."

"That's good. I'm glad you worked it out with them," Luke said sincerely, and she wondered if he had worried that she wouldn't come back after all.

"They want to come up here for a visit, maybe over Christmas week. They want to meet Emily."

Luke glanced at her. "That should be interesting."

"Yeah, it will be," Sara agreed. She had mixed feelings about the idea but knew it had to happen sooner or later.

They arrived at his cottage, and she waited while he reached around her to open the door. "It seems like you were away a long time," he said.

"Only a week."

"I guess it was. It just felt longer."

Then she heard the door close and felt him right behind her as they walked into the silent house. She thought if she turned around, he would put his arms around her. She stood perfectly still for a moment, then stepped forward, entering the small living room.

She dropped her knapsack on a chair, and a pile of books caught her eye. Thick books with long complicated titles, she noticed. Luke had never been much of a reader. She picked one up. It weighed a ton. *"The Adolescent at Risk in Contemporary Society,"* she read out loud.

"I stocked up on some light reading. I hear the winters are bad up here."

"No, really. Are you going back to school or something?"

He shrugged. "Dr. Santori gave me a reading list last time we met. I want to be able to help out with the kids in the spring. I might take some psychology courses or social work. I'm not sure yet."

"That's a good idea." Sara was impressed; Luke didn't do things halfway. She pulled out her pad and pencil and opened to a list of questions she had jotted down in the office. "Okay, let's get started here."

"Sure." He stepped into the small kitchen and pulled open a cabinet. "What do you need to know?"

"I read the newspaper articles and the police report about the search. What I'm looking for is more of a personal angle."

Luke glanced up at her as he measured coffee into the pot. "Not much to tell. I was with Emily, at her mother's house on Thanksgiving night when she got the call—"

"You were at Lillian's? For Thanksgiving?" Sara couldn't hide her surprise.

Luke laughed. "Ezra dragged me over when he found out I was alone. Your grandmother didn't exactly appreciate a crasher. But Ezra and Emily shamed her into it."

Sara laughed, imagining the scene. "I've got the picture. So, you survived dinner with Lillian. Then what?"

"Chief Sanborn called Emily. He told her Digger was lost and the police had started a manhunt. We went out to Durham Point Beach, where the search was going on."

"Some of the people we've interviewed who were there say you took over at that point and told Chief Sanborn what to do."

"Where did you hear that?" She saw Luke's expression darken, and she could tell she had struck a nerve. "That's not true at all."

"All right," she said evenly. But too many people had given the paper this version for her to be put off so easily. "So, you just followed the chief's orders, like everyone else?"

"Well, I guess I said a few things, about how to look in the marsh, how to line up the volunteers, that sort of thing. But it was Sanborn's call all the way. I was only trying to help find Digger, just like everybody else."

Sara checked her notes again. "So, it would be accurate to say that you gave the chief some suggestions—procedures you knew from having worked in law enforcement?"

Luke looked uneasy with her statement, so he concentrated on pouring coffee. "All right, you could say it that way, I guess."

Her gaze moved down to the next question on her list. "Someone we interviewed said that after about an hour, Chief Sanborn told everyone to turn around. But you argued with him about staying and said you were going to continue on your own."

Again, Luke looked uncomfortable. He ran his hand through his short thick hair and shook his head. "I guess I did say that. I just had a feeling that Digger was still in there, and I didn't want to quit."

Sara quickly scribbled down his statement. "Yes, go on. . . ."

"You're not going to write that, are you?"

"Well, yeah. I think that's a great quote."

"Sara, please . . ." Luke shook his head. "Please don't make a big deal out of this. I really don't want all this attention. I don't want to be the big hero, okay?"

Sara pushed her hair behind her ear. "Sounds to me like you took a stand and saved Digger. Everybody says so—"

"I'm sure Sanborn didn't," Luke cut in. His dark brows drew together in a frown. "Look, I have enough trouble getting along around here. You know that. I don't need to embarrass the chief of police. He was doing his job the best he knows how, and I have to respect that. I've been there. You know what I mean?"

Sara bit the edge of her pencil and nodded at him. She was in a tricky spot. She wanted the story to be accurate, and yet, she understood what Luke was saying. It wouldn't help anyone to embarrass Chief Sanborn.

"Don't worry. I just need to know what happened, how you were involved. Just tell me what you know and let me write it," she pressed him.

Luke gave her a long look, as if trying to decide whether he should go through with this after all. Then he let out a breath and began to tell her his version of the rescue.

"But it was only about two seconds later that Daisy started barking. I just happened to be in the right place at the right time. The dog probably would have led someone to Digger, no matter what."

"Do you want me to say that?"

"Absolutely. I want you to say that Luke McAllister gives full credit to Grace Hegman's dog, Daisy."

"All right." Sara smiled, as she noted his words. "But you know that only makes you look more noble and modest."

Luke shook his head in frustration. "Reporters. They have an answer for everything."

"I'm new at this, but I'm trying." Sara sipped her coffee, and their eyes met. The look of longing in his eyes was unmistakable. Sara felt her heart jump, as she pulled her gaze away.

Resolved not to let herself get distracted, she continued with her questions, trying to get more detail about Luke's feelings as he had pushed through the reeds alone.

Luke shifted restlessly in his chair. "Is this going to take much longer? I really have to get back to work now."

"You said you wanted me to do the story. Well, I'm doing it." She caught his eye and held him in place with a look. His usually serious expression broke out in a smile.

"Be careful what you ask for," he said in a wry tone. "I never realized you'd be grilling me like this. What else?"

Sara asked a few more questions about Digger, then decided she had enough for her story. She sat back and flipped her notebook closed. "All I need now is a picture."

"You're kidding, right?"

"Sorry, Wyatt said I had to get one. A good one. He wants the woods in the background." She pulled the camera out of her pack. "Do you know how to set the lens on this? It's really old."

"Let me have a look." Luke took the camera in hand and rolled his eyes. "Okay, let's get this over with."

Sara grabbed her pack and followed him out. They walked to the wooded edge of the property, and Luke showed her how to read the light meter and set the lens opening and shutter speed. Sara stepped back and started snapping.

She stopped, frowning, after the first few shots. "You look like you're on the way to the dentist."

"Maybe that's because the only thing I hate worse than being interviewed is having my picture taken."

"Can you smile, please? You just saved a man's life," she reminded him, focusing again as she moved in for a closer shot.

"Only one more, and you owe me big time for this," he warned.

"I agree. I should buy you dinner," she said.

"How about I buy you dinner?" he said quickly. "I thought we could celebrate your new job, go someplace special."

She was glad to have the camera hiding her expression for a moment. From the look on his face, she got the feeling he'd been thinking about this for a while. She and Luke had eaten lots of meals together and had even spent a few evenings together. But this sounded like more than pizza or sandwiches on the beach. It felt as if something was subtly shifting between them. The idea made her happy—and nervous.

She looked down and put the camera back in its case. "That sounds great. But I should treat you for giving me the story."

"Just don't misquote me or turn me into some superhero, and we'll call it even," Luke said, walking toward her.

She nodded. "It's a deal."

"Okay then. How about tonight? Are you free?"

"Sorry, I promised Emily I'd go see her. But another night this week would be okay."

"Tomorrow?" he asked.

Wow, he really wanted this to happen. "Um . . . sure. Tomorrow night would be fine." His face broke out in a rare smile, and she smiled back, suddenly looking forward to seeing him again.

"We're set then. I'll pick you up around seven." He moved closer, and she thought he was going to kiss her good-bye—a real kiss. Just as suddenly, she realized that she wanted him to. But instead Luke leaned over and quickly kissed the top of her head.

"See you later, Ace," he said quietly.

"Okay, see you. . . . And *please* stop calling me that," she added, as she strolled away.

She heard him laugh and turned to see him standing with his hands deep in the pockets of his vest, looking uncommonly happy.

IT WAS PAST TWELVE WHEN SARA RETURNED TO THE OFFICE. SHE SOON realized she was alone. Everyone was gone, which gave her a funny feeling. She took a deep breath, settled herself at her new desk, and took out her notes from the interview with Luke. It was getting close to one. She had slightly more than two hours to write the article. Could she do it?

She flipped through the pages and had a strange feeling in the pit of her stomach, as if she were in an elevator that had suddenly dropped a few floors. She squinted at the first page. She had scribbled down Luke's answers in a kind of private shorthand and now could barely decipher her own notes. What in the world had she written, and how was she ever going to make an article out of it?

Sara rubbed her forehead with her hand, suddenly feeling as though she were about to cry. A phone rang, echoing in the silence. She wasn't sure if she should answer it or not, but she checked the blinking lights, pressed the button, and picked it up. "Hello? Uh . . . *Cape Light Messenger,*" she added, trying to sound more official.

It was a woman in the village, calling to take an ad in the classified section to sell a deep freeze.

"It's down in the basement. They would have to figure out how to get it out," she explained, as if any of that information could be included in a three-line ad, Sara thought. She took down the woman's name and number and promised someone would call her back. Still, the woman was determined to talk about her freezer, and it was a good five minutes before Sara was able to politely end the conversation. Five precious minutes taken from her deadline.

Sara put down the receiver, feeling as if she might burst into tears. But she couldn't let herself do that. The one-room storefront office was like a fishbowl. *I'll just have to do the best I can with this. I'll try to match up the list of questions to the notes and try to remember what Luke said,* she told herself.

Finally, she started on her article. Whenever the phone rang after that, she ignored it and kept working. She hadn't been hired as a secretary, she reasoned. She was a reporter, and she had a deadline.

When Wyatt returned an hour later, Sara was so engrossed in writing, she didn't even hear him come in. She felt someone standing right beside her and looked up to find her handsome new boss peering over her shoulder, reading her computer screen.

"Oh, it's you." Startled, she stopped typing and sat back.

"Sorry to sneak up on you." She felt his hand touch her shoulder, then just as quickly, it was gone. "Are you done yet?"

"Not quite. You said the deadline was three."

"Oh, you're the kind who turns in copy at two fifty-nine . . . and fifty-nine seconds," he said in a way that made her smile at herself. He left her desk and headed for his own. "Did you get any pictures?"

She nodded and returned to her writing. "I left the film in the darkroom. But I'm not that great with a camera," she warned.

"Now she tells me," Wyatt answered in an absent-minded manner, as he checked through the mail piled on his desk.

"I left a message on your desk," Sara said, not bothering to add that there were quite a few calls she hadn't picked up.

He picked up her message slip and glanced at it. "Oh, blast," he muttered, and smacked himself on the forehead.

"What's the matter? Is something wrong?" Sara asked.

"Nothing. I'm just a little too scattered lately. I totally forgot about a whole pile of ads that have to run in tomorrow's edition."

Sara wasn't quite sure why this was a disaster, but from the look on Wyatt's face, it seemed to be. "Can I help you somehow? I'm almost done with this," she offered, glancing back at her screen.

Wyatt stared at her a minute, then shook his head. "That's okay. I'll figure it out," he said tiredly.

Sara turned back to her computer and her article. She had managed to decipher her notes pretty well and had even checked the quotes with Luke over the phone. All in all, she thought, it was turning out pretty well.

She was conscious of the fact that Jane and Ed were also back at their desks now, and both had turned in their copy soon after Wyatt returned. Sara kept on working.

Just as the hands of the clock over the door neared two forty-five, a blond-haired woman entered the office and headed toward Wyatt. When she passed Sara, she met her gaze and smiled. Sara smiled back.

"Hi. How's it going?" the blonde asked, as she reached Wyatt's desk. The woman, who was about Wyatt's age, was very pretty. Sara wondered if she was his girlfriend; she seemed so familiar and relaxed with him.

"Terrible," Wyatt replied. "I just realized I forgot to set all these new classified ads for tomorrow's edition. I still have two stories to write up, and all the copy to edit. *And* I have to develop some film and lay out the paper."

"Wow, sorry I asked." The woman shook her head in sympathy. "Why don't you let me do the ads?" She flipped open the folder and glanced at the first few sheets piled there. "These aren't so bad. Some look like reruns."

Sara heard Wyatt let out a deep sigh. "Are you sure, Lindsay? It could take a few hours."

So, her name is Lindsay, Sara thought.

"I'm bored sitting around the house with Dad. Fortunately, Scott just got home, and they're playing chess." Lindsay slipped off her coat and hung it on the old-fashioned coat stand near Wyatt's desk. "I'll help you later with the layout, too. Otherwise, you'll be here until midnight again."

"Thanks, you're a pal," Wyatt said, sounding greatly relieved.

"What are older sisters for?" she asked in a teasing tone.

Older sister? Sara was surprised. The two didn't look much alike. But Lindsay did have Dan's fair hair and blue eyes, she realized. For some reason she didn't want to examine too closely, she felt relieved to hear Lindsay was Wyatt's sister—and not his girlfriend.

Lindsay sat at an empty desk near Wyatt's and began working on the ads. At three o'clock precisely Sara brought her article and disk back to Wyatt's desk.

"Thanks," he said, starting to read it. "Oh, and mark yourself off as delivered on the board back there."

She looked behind him and saw a dry-erase board on the back wall, listing the working titles of assigned articles and the reporter's last name. Sara found "McAllister Interview" and marked it off as delivered.

Wyatt was still reading her article, frowning as he made marks on the copy with a thick black pen. A lot of marks. She felt knots in her empty stomach as she tried to sneak past him, but he noticed her anyway and spoke without looking up.

"Wider margins next time. I need some space to edit."

"Oh, sure. I didn't know."

"By the way, this is my sister, Lindsay." Wyatt looked up briefly and nodded over at his sister. "Lindsay, this is Sara Franklin. She just started today."

"Hello, Sara. Nice to meet you." Lindsay smiled. "How do you like it so far?"

Sara shrugged. "I like it a lot," she answered honestly, and glanced over at Wyatt. "Is there something else you want me to do?"

He was reading the last page of her article. "Yes, there is. Rewrite this," he said bluntly. "It's a mess."

Sara was so shocked that, for a moment, she thought she might burst into tears. She had felt so sure it was good.

"Sure," she said, forcing her voice to sound even. "What . . . what's wrong with it?"

"Well, for starters, this is a news article, not a mystery novel. You need to get the important information right up front."

Sara nodded, even though she thought she had done that.

"And try to trim this fat," Wyatt added, handing it back to her. "There's a lot of fluff in here. Check my marks. You'll get the idea."

Fluff? She didn't think she wrote with a lot of fluff. Sara nodded again, her gaze fixed on the pages. "When do you want it back?"

"Right away," he said, as if she should have already known that. He stood up and turned away, heading to the darkroom.

Lindsay cast Sara a sympathetic look as she passed by. "He's just being tough because you're new. You're lucky my father isn't here. He's even worse."

Well, that's some consolation, I guess, Sara thought. She smiled at Lindsay and returned to her desk. She brought the article up on her computer screen again but found herself staring at the words, unable to focus enough to figure out how to change them. Meanwhile, she felt the minutes slipping past.

Lindsay walked over to her. "How's it going?" she asked.

"Not so great. I'm not sure what's wrong, so I don't really know how to fix it," Sara admitted. "I was a literature major in college. I only took one course in journalism."

"Don't worry. You've got some good stuff in here. It just needs some work," Lindsay said, reading over her shoulder. "Let me take a look at the copy. Maybe I can help."

Sara handed her the printed version of her article, covered with Wyatt's black marks. Lindsay read it quickly, then went over it with Sara, showing her how the important information could be moved and what could be cut.

"Does that make sense?" Lindsay asked, handing her back the pages.

"Absolutely. Thanks a million," Sara said, nearly sighing with relief.

"No problem," Lindsay replied, stepping away.

Finally, at a quarter to six, Sara finished the revision and brought it to Wyatt. "Here's the rewrite. I hope it's better."

He was reading some copy and didn't look up at her. She found herself studying the sharp line of his cheek and his thick brown hair. "Just leave it in the box. You can go."

"Okay. See you tomorrow," she said, walking away.

He grunted but didn't look up.

Back at her desk, Sara gathered her coat and knapsack and shut down her computer. She suddenly felt too tired to see Emily. She just wanted a hot bath and her bed. Emily would understand, she thought, though she'd be disappointed.

But outside the cold, damp air blowing in from the harbor revived her. It would be good to visit with Emily, Sara decided. Emily would be an eager audience for the tale of her first day at the paper. In the eyes of her birth mother, Sara knew she was a walking wonder—to a degree so extreme that even Emily had to laugh at herself at times.

Maybe tonight, that's just what I need, Sara thought. *Some of Emily's questionable cooking and her unconditional adoration.*

Chapter Five

"Have you seen this?" Emily snapped open Tuesday's edition of the *Messenger* and turned to page three. "Sara's first article."

"Is that today's edition? I haven't seen it yet," Dan said eagerly.

She held the newspaper out to him and waited while he slipped on his reading glasses, which were almost identical to her own, she noticed with a secret smile. They were alone in Dan's house, sitting in the family room, where she had found him working on his laptop.

Emily had already read the article but couldn't resist reading it again, and their heads were bent close together as they each held one side of the paper.

Dan sat back first. "Not bad for a start. She managed to give McAllister credit without insulting the police department. That was tricky."

"Not bad at all, I thought," Emily countered, trying not to sound *too* proud of her daughter. "I saw Sara last night. She was worried it didn't come out right. Wyatt made her rewrite it."

Dan took off his glasses. "Good for him. The copy has been a little ragged since I left."

"Really? I haven't noticed any difference," Emily teased him, with a smile. "Sara is so excited about this job, she could barely sit still last night. Thanks again for hiring her, Dan."

"I didn't do it as a favor to you, if that's what you're thinking. She got the job on her own merit. Which is what you really wanted to hear, right?" His warm, knowing smile distracted her.

"Well, yes," she admitted. She looked away. He was getting to know her a little too well lately, she thought. She wasn't used to this. Not with a man, anyway.

"How are you doing today?" she asked, changing the subject.

"I'm horrible. Haven't you noticed?" he replied grumpily. "I wake up every morning, still surprised to find this hunk of plaster on my leg—and mad at myself for pulling such a stupid stunt. You'd think after all these years of sailing, I'd know better than to get knocked out by my own boom."

"Oh, don't be so hard on yourself. It was just an accident. Sometimes things happen for a reason."

What she really meant was: Sometimes God is trying to tell us something. In Dan's case, maybe it was "Slow down, pal." But she knew that Dan wasn't a churchgoer. She also knew this was hardly the time to try to win him over in that direction.

"And what could that reason be?" he asked. "So I can watch more of the all-news channel or sit-com reruns? Catch up on my reading?"

"I don't know." She paused. "Maybe to give me someplace for lunch besides the Clam Box?"

She reached down next to the couch and picked up a picnic basket, then set it between them on the coffee table. She had discreetly stashed it there when she'd come in, while Dan was still distracted with his computer.

"You brought me lunch? Why, bless your heart." He caught her eye with a look that gave her a fluttery feeling in her stomach. "You didn't have to do that, Emily. I can get myself into the kitchen and fix a sandwich."

"Yes, I know. But when I called and spoke to Lindsay before, she said no one would be home this afternoon, so I volunteered. I just hope the menu meets your current standards. No truffles involved," she warned.

"No truffles necessary," he assured her, with a laugh.

Emily spread a red-checkered cloth on the table, then took out some cold drinks, sandwiches, and chips. Dan chose the ham on rye, looking quite content.

He chewed for a moment, and his eyes grew wide. "Mmm, spicy mustard."

Emily bit down on her lip to keep from laughing at his expression. "Too much for you?"

"No, not at all," he mumbled, as he took a drink. "Just snuck up on me. I didn't take you for the spicy type."

She smiled and looked away. "You never know."

As Emily started her sandwich, she suddenly noticed the time. "Mind if I put on channel five? Sophie Potter's show is starting today."

Dan looked puzzled. "Sophie's on TV? When did that happen?"

"Dan, I'm surprised at you. That's been in the works for a while." Emily picked up the remote and found the right channel. The show hadn't started yet; it was just a commercial.

"Some people from channel five came to film the Harvest Fair for the local news, and when they saw Sophie, they thought she'd be perfect for a new show they had in the works," Emily explained. "You know, cooking and crafts, that sort of thing."

"Sounds perfect for her. Sure, let's watch." Dan struggled to turn his wheelchair toward the TV, and Emily quickly rose to help.

"Here, I'll do that," she said. "The wheel got twisted, I think." She rested her hand on his broad, hard shoulder a second, and he glanced up and met her eyes. She smiled back at him briefly then felt self-conscious and looked away.

As she stood behind him, she noticed his hair was actually more silver-gray than blond. It was still quite thick, too. He was lucky, she thought. Most men in their late forties would envy that. He needed a haircut, though; maybe that would be a good project for some future visit. She would have to remember to bring scissors sometime soon.

Then she caught herself. Was she letting herself get too involved?

Too attached? She always knew her friendship with Dan could lead to something more. Maybe it was leading there already. But in a few weeks when Dan got his cast removed, where would that leave her? Emily wondered. With a heart full of feelings for a man moving quickly in the opposite direction?

As if sensing her conflicted thoughts, Dan suddenly glanced over his shoulder. "Anything wrong?" he asked.

"No." Emily came around from behind his chair and sat down on the couch again. "It's just that it's getting late. I need to go back to the office soon. I'll just watch for a few minutes."

Avoiding Dan's curious stare, she turned to the TV. Country-style fiddle music sounded, and the words *A Yankee in the Kitchen* flashed on the screen. The background was a sweeping shot of Potter Orchard and their grand old Queen Anne–style house. Then a pair of hands used a stencil and brush to add *New England Cooking and Crafts. With Sophie Potter.*

"Look, it's the orchard," Emily exclaimed. "I didn't realize they were filming it right at the Potter place."

Sophie appeared on the screen, standing on her porch with a basket of apples over one arm. "Hello, everyone, and welcome to our first show," Sophie greeted her audience.

"Sophie! Yeah!" Emily cheered and clapped.

"Quiet down. I can't hear a thing," Dan said, with a laugh.

"I'm Sophie Potter and this is my husband, Gus." Dressed in a flannel shirt, dungarees, and his ever-present red, white, and blue suspenders, Gus Potter put his arm around his wife's shoulder, smiling so broadly, Emily was sure his face hurt.

"Look at Gus," Dan said. "He looks likes he's just about to burst at the seams with pride."

"They're so sweet together."

"Yes, they are," Dan agreed.

Still in love after decades, the Potters had the kind of relationship that seemed ideal—at least from the outside. Emily had once been madly in love with her own husband. But she and Tim had only been married two years when a fatal car accident turned her into a very young widow.

Would she and Tim have gone the distance, like the Potters? She had always thought so.

"This is our orchard in Cape Light, Massachusetts," Sophie continued. The orchard was set on a bluff above the town, and the camera showed the magnificent view. "We pick peaches in summer and apples in fall. Then there's a berry patch and honey from our bees," Sophie added. "But as much as I love working outdoors, I love puttering around my kitchen even *more.*

"Come on in, folks." Sophie beckoned her audience with an engaging grin, as the camera followed her into the kitchen. "Today I'm going to make Yankee Pot Roast, with seasonal vegetables. It's easy," she promised.

"Mmm, pot roast. My mother used to make it once a week when I was a kid," Dan said.

If he's looking for a cook, he's got the wrong girl here, Emily thought with amusement.

Sophie tied apron strings around her ample waist. "Once we've got the roast going, I'll show you how to make this lovely stenciled apron." She held up the apron edge. "I've got little pineapples on mine, but you can choose any pattern you like. It's a nice touch for curtains or a room border. And stenciling is a simple, economical way to decorate." She grinned again and picked up a large bowl and a wooden spoon. "We'll be right back after this commercial message, so don't go away!"

An advertisement for stain-removal spray came on. Emily and Dan sat back and looked at each other. Then they both started laughing.

"She's a natural. Good old Sophie Potter. I can't quite believe it," Dan said, shaking his head.

"She's wonderful," Emily agreed. "What a big day for her and Gus. I'm going to send her some flowers. If this show works out, I guess they'll be able to keep the orchard."

"I knew Gus had some health problems, but I didn't know things had gotten that bad," Dan said, looking concerned. "In that case, I'll tune in every day to help her ratings."

"Somehow I'm having trouble imagining you stenciling little pineapples on the wall, Dan."

"If it comes to that, you'll know I've really gone off the deep end," he said, with a sigh.

She laughed at him then glanced at her watch. "Gee, it's getting late. I have to get back to the office."

"Oh, that's right. You are the mayor. I almost forgot." The warmth in his blue eyes and soft smile kept her rooted to the spot. At that moment she wished she *could* forget and stay longer. "So, how is everything at the Village Hall?" he added. "Any good news stories brewing?"

"You forget, you're not in the business anymore," she reminded him.

"I'm too old to learn any new tricks now. I'll always be curious about politics. What's going on with that federal grant you applied for? Did the money come through for the Emergency Response Program?"

"Looks like we got it, but there's some red tape. It seems that the funds have to go through the county first. If that happens, the village may never see the money."

"And you'll have a lot of irate voters asking why the town isn't better equipped for emergencies. One of your campaign promises, as I recall."

"Exactly," she replied. "It's not just because of the storm last fall. I had people asking me about it all over again after Digger's rescue. The village does need more equipment and manpower for emergencies, and I thought this grant would be the answer. Now it might just end up a big embarrassment for me."

"Those county commissioners can be pretty slippery," Dan acknowledged. "But I'm sure you can handle them. Have you met with them yet?"

"I'm on their agenda for next week's meeting. I'm going to bring Warren Oakes with me. Having a lawyer along might help."

"Good idea." Dan nodded in approval. "I'll be thinking of you. Let me know how it goes."

"Okay, I will," Emily agreed, closing up the picnic basket.

"Thanks again for dropping by—and for the picnic."

"No problem." Emily finally stood up and picked up her coat. "It was fun."

"Absolutely. You made my day," he replied, gazing steadily into her eyes and making her feel self-conscious all over again.

She picked up her purse and the basket. "Take care of yourself, Dan," she called over her shoulder.

"See you soon," he answered. An unmistakable note of longing in his voice followed her through the empty house.

Out in her car, she still wondered about it. Was he just sorry to see a visitor go, being left alone with nothing to do? Or did he really want to spend more time with her?

She wanted to see more of him; she knew that much. It was risky to get more involved. That was also true. But when she was with Dan, her doubts seemed to fade away, and she simply felt happy. Maybe it was good for her to have some romance in her life after all these years, even for a short time, she reasoned. Maybe Dan would change his mind about his trip.

After all, anything could happen. *So I'll keep seeing Dan,* she decided, *and follow these feelings wherever it is they lead me.* She turned onto Main Street, heading for Village Hall, hoping she was making the right decision.

SARA CHECKED OVER THE COPY WYATT HAD ASKED HER TO PROOFread, then carried it back to his desk. He was talking on the phone, so she waited for him to finish. It was two minutes to five.

Though she'd never been a clock-watcher, she was eager to leave, so she could get ready for her date with Luke.

Her second day on the job had gone somewhat more smoothly than the first. Wyatt had given her two press releases from the state government and asked her to work them up into stories. One was about a statewide rise in real estate value and the other about local levels of air pollution. He had made her revise her copy again, but at least this time, she felt more confident about fixing it.

Finally, Wyatt hung up, and she handed him her work. "Here's the copy you gave me. I only found a few typos."

"Thanks." He put the pages aside. "I have a little problem tonight, Sara. That was Jane. She's stuck in Southport. Her car broke down. She won't be back in time to cover the tree lighting tonight, and I have to go to the county seat for a seven o'clock meeting. So can you cover the tree lighting for us?"

"Uh, when does it start?" Not the best answer for her second day on the job when she wasn't exactly wowing her boss. But she was worried about her date with Luke.

"It's starts at seven. I'm sure it will just be the usual: the high-school choir singing carols and a speech by the mayor. The whole business will be over by eight," Wyatt guaranteed.

Eight? Probably more like eight-thirty or nine, she thought. Luke planned to pick her up at seven.

"Well, to tell you the truth, I have plans. I'm supposed to go out. With a friend," Sara added hastily, not knowing why she felt obliged to describe her date in that way.

"Oh, I see. You couldn't meet up with your friend a little later or something?" he asked. "You don't need to come back and write this up for tomorrow's edition. I'll put it in on Thursday."

The look of disappointment on Wyatt's face made her feel guilty and as if it wasn't very savvy to have refused.

"Okay, give me a few minutes. I'll see what I can do," she said finally. Wyatt smiled, looking relieved and grateful. Also very handsome, she realized. He was wearing a black sweater that made his eyes seem an even darker shade of blue.

"You're a pal, Sara. I knew you'd come through for me."

"That's all right," she said, turning to walk back to her desk. Wyatt was quite charming when he needed to be she thought, as she dialed Luke's number.

Luke picked up right away. He sounded surprised but pleased to hear from her. "How are you doing?" he asked.

"I'm okay, but I have a little problem about tonight."

"That doesn't sound good. Are you standing me up?" His joking tone barely disguised his disappointment.

"No, not at all. I mean, I still want to get together. It's just that

Wyatt asked me to cover the tree lighting tonight at the green. It's sort of an emergency. I was wondering if we could have dinner after? It should be over by eight or so."

Luke didn't answer, and his silence made her nervous. She already knew that when he got quiet like this, it wasn't a good sign. Then she felt annoyed. She'd just started at the paper. He knew how important this job was to her. He really ought to understand.

"I'll go with you," he offered, surprising her. "Unless you would rather I didn't," he added quickly. "I don't want to make you nervous while you're working or something."

"You won't. But it's going to be really corny," she warned.

"I can handle corny. Once a year, I mean," he said seriously, making her laugh. "We can grab a bite in town after you're done. It will probably be too late to go up to Newburyport."

"I guess it will. Maybe next time," she added hopefully.

"Right, next time." He didn't sound mad. More like mildly let down. Sara bit the end of her pencil, wondering if she had done the right thing.

"Why don't we meet at the green?" Sara said. "I'll wait up front, about a quarter to seven?"

Luke agreed, and they hung up.

Sara sensed Wyatt watching her, but when she turned he quickly glanced down at the work on his desk again. "I just spoke to my friend and changed our plans," she told him. "I can cover the tree-lighting ceremony."

"Great." He smiled, looking pleased. "Get some pictures—maybe one of the mayor or Santa. Or maybe the mayor *and* Santa together," he added, sounding excited by his inspiration.

Sara had to smile. She had only worked for him for two days, but already she found the way Wyatt got excited about news stories funny, in an almost endearing way.

"The mayor and Santa." She took her coat and scarf off the rack. "I'll try not to miss that one."

"Thanks. And have a good time with your . . . friend," he said carefully.

Sara wondered if he had listened in on her conversation and guessed she had a date. She slung her long, striped muffler around her neck and pulled open the door. Well, what of it? It wasn't like Wyatt was interested in her or anything. . . . Was he?

No, he was only "managing" you, she told herself, *being extra nice so you'd do the story.*

And it worked, she realized, laughing at herself.

SARA ARRIVED AT THE VILLAGE GREEN AT SIX-THIRTY. THE SEATS SET UP in front of the bandstand were already filled, with more people streaming into the park. It was a cold, clear night, and a pale crescent moon hung above the tall trees. The starry points of light that dotted the dark blue sky seemed to be reflected in the scattered lights out in the harbor.

A line of eager children and their parents gathered near the park's entrance, where volunteers were giving out free candy canes and cups of hot chocolate. Sara nearly laughed aloud, seeing how some of the younger kids were bundled up within an inch of their lives, only their small, surprised-looking faces showing through the mounds of winter clothing. They stared around, wide-eyed, searching the crowd for Santa, no doubt.

She picked up her camera, kneeled down, and took a quick shot of some children pointing up at the tree. A spotlight on the stage illuminating their faces gave just the right touch, she thought. She hoped it would come out.

"There you are. Hard at work already." Sara stood up and found Luke smiling at her. "This is some crowd. I didn't realize there would be so many people here."

"The whole town, it looks like," she agreed. "But we have special seats, right up front. Being a part of the press has its privileges, you know."

"Lead the way," he said, grinning at her.

They found their reserved seats at the end of the front row. On sheets of paper taped to the backs of the chairs, "Press" was written in black marker.

Luke smiled at her again, as they sat down. "Gee, I feel important, like a VIP or something," he whispered. "I didn't realize there would be such perks, taking you out on a date."

Sara glanced at him, feeling another twinge of guilt for her change of plans. It was sweet of him to be willing to go along with this.

The program was just as Wyatt predicted. First Emily said a few words to open the event. Sara took notes, feeling a little strange reporting on her birth mother. It was just a tree lighting tonight, she realized. What would she do if she had to cover Emily on a more controversial story?

The high-school chorus sang "God Bless America," and then a woman named Vera Herbert was introduced as the local Volunteer of the Year, a distinction that seemed to qualify her as official tree lighter. Vera spoke for a few minutes about visiting shut-in seniors and how her volunteer work gave her the feeling of Christmas all year round.

Then Vera pulled the switch, and a collective sigh rose from the crowd. The tree really was beautiful, Sara thought. It towered over the gathering, covered with lights and red ribbons, a glittering star at its very top. The audience cheered and clapped. Luke even let out a low whistle—the type he reserved mainly for sporting events, Sara guessed. The high-school chorus began singing "O Christmas Tree," and everyone joined in.

Sara felt a little misty eyed for some strange reason and blinked. Luke glanced at her and laughed, then he put his arm around her shoulders and gave her a hug.

"What's the matter, got a lump in your throat?"

She pressed her head into his shoulder and nodded, not trusting herself to speak.

"Me, too. Silly, right?" he whispered against her hair. She nodded again, and he held her even closer. They swayed back and forth in time with the music as they sang. Sara had never heard Luke sing before. He had a good voice, smooth and low. It felt good being close to him like this. She was suddenly very glad he was here with her tonight.

The next song was "Jingle Bells," which cheered her, and by the time the chorus sang "Santa Claus Is Coming to Town," Sara had fully recovered from her bout of mushiness and had both her notebook and camera up and running again.

She heard a fire-truck siren in the distance, and Emily stepped up to the microphone again. "Oh, my goodness!" The mayor gasped. "Who in the world could that be?"

The crowd shouted back the answer in a deafening roar.

"Santa Claus?" Emily asked in mock amazement. "You mean the *real* Santa Claus? Coming here? To Cape Light? No, it couldn't be!"

"Yes, he is!" the children yelled back, as the fire truck cruised down a lane blocked off with orange traffic cones and then rolled up to the front of the stage.

Santa waved, then hopped onto the stage and took the microphone. "Ho-ho-ho! Merry Christmas!" he greeted the crowd.

"It's the big red guy, all right. I guess Emily didn't note the meeting in her appointment book," Luke commented dryly.

Sara laughed then handed him her knapsack and notebook. "Can you hold these a minute? I need to get some pictures."

She dove into the crowd that now pressed against the bandstand and started clicking away. The next few minutes passed in a blur, as she dodged the treats Santa and his helpers were tossing out to the children.

Sara struggled to get a good photo of the mayor *and* Santa, as Emily told Santa that all of the children in *their* town were very well behaved and *most* deserving of gifts this year. Finally, their surprise visitor jumped back on the fire truck and headed back to the North Pole.

Sara glanced around for Luke and finally spotted him waiting at the side of the stage. She caught up to him, and he took her hand in a strong grip, leading her out of the crowd.

Finally, they were on Main Street. Luke didn't let go of her hand, she noticed, and she didn't really want him to.

"Should we try the Beanery?" he asked, when they came to the corner. "I hear they serve dinner now."

"Sounds good," Sara replied.

The café's style was a bit trendy for Cape Light, more like a place you'd find in the city. Still, the place had caught on. Tonight Sara and Luke had to wait a few minutes for a table.

"Here's your knapsack," Luke said, handing it to her as they sat down. "I put the notebook inside."

"Thanks," Sara said, taking it from him. "And thanks for coming with me tonight. I hope it wasn't too boring."

"It wasn't a problem. I liked watching you work," he said, the corner of his mouth lifting in a half smile.

Sara didn't know what to say. She looked down at the table and spread her napkin over her lap. "Speaking of my work, what did you think of the interview? Was it okay?"

He hadn't said a word about the interview, and she had wondered all day if something in the article upset him.

"It was great. I clipped a copy and sent it to my mom."

"Did you really?" she asked, with a laugh.

He nodded. "You *almost* overdid it on the hero angle," he added, glancing at her with his eyes slightly narrowed. "But it could have been worse."

"Well . . . thanks, I think."

He reached across the table and took her hand. "I'm really proud of you, Sara. You're out there, writing, doing what you love to do. And you're really good at it."

His praise made her feel suddenly shy. "It's just a little job on a small-town paper. It's not exactly the *New York Times.*"

"There aren't too many people around here who could do it, whether you think so or not. I couldn't," he countered.

"Well, to hear my new boss tell it, he's not so sure yet I can do it, either," she replied.

"Really? What do you mean?" Luke looked surprised.

"He hated the first draft of my interview with you. He put so many marks on it, I could hardly see the text. Then today, the same thing. I had to rewrite an article—twice." Her voice dropped as she confessed her worst thoughts. "I think Wyatt's sorry Dan hired me but feels sort of stuck with me now."

"Maybe he's just being tough on you because you're new."

"That's what Lindsay, his sister, said. It feels more like it's because I'm a bad writer, though," she admitted. "Reporting is different from the type of writing I did in college. I only took one journalism course," she added miserably. "I just hope I get the hang of it before Wyatt fires me or something."

"Hey, don't worry," Luke soothed her. "You'll pick it up. If he gives you too much trouble, just let me know. I'll have a little talk with him," he said in a joking "tough guy" tone.

"Don't be silly." Sara felt herself finally smiling again. Luke was the protective type. When she first met him, it had unnerved her. She was used to being completely independent. But gradually, she came to appreciate knowing that if she needed help, Luke was there for her.

Sara looked down at their hands joined together and thought back to the first time they met. Luke had come into the diner last spring, her first night on the job. He was so distant, she'd almost been afraid of him. Yet, something in his hesitant smile and offbeat sense of humor had touched her, even then. Maybe she had sensed that under his defenses, he was really just hurt and trying to heal. Trying to find his way, just like she was. Now she knew that she'd been right about him all along. He was a good person—a wonderful person. She was lucky to have him come into her life when he did.

"What are you thinking about?" he asked.

"Nothing." She pressed her palm flat against his larger one. "You've got some impressive calluses here from all the construction work."

"Sam says we won't be able to work outside much longer. It's getting colder, and soon there will be too much snow."

"What will you do all winter?"

"There's indoor work—wiring, drywall, that kind of stuff. And those courses I told you about. I think I'm going to audit some classes at the community college, just to start."

"Sounds good," Sara said, impressed at his commitment.

Then she thought of Luke on a college campus, meeting so many new people—so many attractive, single women—and felt a prick of worry. What if he met someone else and forgot about her? But that was silly. Luke wouldn't just disappear with the first attractive woman he met. Besides, it wasn't as if there was anything *really* serious between them, yet. He was free to see whomever he liked. And so was she.

An image of Wyatt flashed in her mind, making her feel guilty and then confused. She didn't even like the guy. He either treated her like furniture or insulted her writing—unless he wanted a special favor, and then he poured on the charm. *Why am I even thinking about him?* she wondered.

A waitress took their orders, and Sara sat back, slowly letting go of Luke's hand. The candlelight flickered over his strong features. He was good-looking, she thought, in a rough-around-the-edges way that she found extremely attractive. She didn't need to give Wyatt a second glance. Not that way, anyway.

They enjoyed the rest of their dinner. Sara told Luke more about her visit to Maryland, and Luke described his Thanksgiving meal at Lillian's house.

" 'Now I heard you were shot in the head? Is that true, Mr. McAllister?' " Luke quoted, doing a perfect imitation of Lillian's imperious tone.

"Oh, no! She didn't really say that, did she?" Sara asked, flabbergasted. She laughed and covered her mouth with her hand.

"That wasn't even the worst of it. Ezra finally accused her of 'incurable rudeness' or something like that," he replied. "I wasn't sure if Emily was going to keel over in shock or cheer."

"Cheer, probably," Sara guessed, still laughing.

Finally, it was time to go. Sara hadn't realized how late it was—past midnight. Luke walked her to her car, which was parked near the café. "I'll follow you home," he offered.

"Don't be silly. I'll be fine," she said. Cape Light was so crime-free, some people didn't even lock their doors. She never worried about being out alone, even at this hour.

"I'll follow you home and walk you to your door. Just humor me, okay?" Luke said evenly.

Reluctantly she agreed, thinking his past had made him overly protective. But when she parked on Clover Street and saw Luke's SUV pull up behind her, she did feel watched over and cared for, as if she was important to him.

Sara's apartment was part of a large Victorian that had once been a single-family house. Her entrance was at a side door on the wraparound porch. Luke met her on the porch steps. The night had grown colder, and their breath mingled in frosty clouds that hung in the air.

At her door she turned and looked up at him. "I had a great time. Thanks again for dinner—and for the tree lighting."

"You're very welcome—for all of the above." He smiled at her and reached out to touch her hair. Then with both his hands gently framing her face, his head moved toward her, and their lips met in a tender, lingering kiss.

"Sara . . ." he whispered against her hair. After a moment, he pulled back, his arms looped loosely around her waist. "Can I see you this weekend? We can catch a movie or something."

"That would be great," she said breathlessly.

"I'll call you. You'd better go inside. I don't want to wake up your landlord."

"It is late," she agreed. Still, it was hard to let him go. Finally, she turned and went inside.

Sara locked her front door and stood there a moment in the dark. She felt herself smile, thinking about the way Luke had kissed her. They had kissed before, once or twice. But never like that. This time had been different somehow.

Something mysterious and exciting was brewing between them. Sara turned away from the door and headed to her bedroom.

If her relationship with Luke was a book, she could hardly wait to turn the page and see what happened next.

Chapter Six

When Reverend Ben arrived at the Bramble Antique Shop on Friday morning, the sign in the window read, "Closed. Please come again." He knocked but didn't hear a sound—not even Daisy, announcing his arrival. Still, he waited. After a few minutes Grace peered out from one of the windowpanes on the door.

"Oh, Reverend, it's you," she said, as she opened the door. "There have been so many people coming by, visitors and a girl from the newspaper, I have to be careful about answering the door. My whole day would be taken up," she explained, as he stepped inside.

"Well, I hope I'm not disturbing you. I just dropped by to see your father. He's home from the hospital, I understand."

"Brought him home yesterday, around noon." Grace nodded, unsmiling. "Oh goodness, look at this mail, piling up out here. Will you excuse me a minute?" she asked. Without waiting for his reply, she emptied the large, old-fashioned letter box, then gathered up some parcels that were piled next to the door.

"I haven't been watching the shop much. Things are getting in a muddle," she explained, carrying the mail to a glass counter near the register.

"Understandably," Ben said, watching as she quickly sorted through the pile of letters.

She was her old self again, Ben noticed. She wore her blouse neatly pressed, her cardigan completely buttoned, and her chin-length hair—brown streaked with gray—carefully held back on the sides with bobby pins.

There was no trace of the bereft, nearly hysterical woman he and Carolyn comforted on Thanksgiving night. He remembered how they prayed together, holding hands. Grace was reluctant at first, admitting that she hadn't really prayed since she lost Julie. But with Ben and Carolyn beside her—and facing the horror of losing her father—she had been willing to try.

Ben wondered now if Grace had talked with the heavenly Father since then. He had hoped to see her in service on Sunday, but he realized now that was expecting too much.

"Look at this, more cards for Dad," she said, holding up a handful of envelopes. "And another box, too."

"Is Digger able to have visitors? I can come back another time if it's inconvenient."

Grace's thin lips drew together, considering the question. "He's resting. But I suppose it won't hurt if you stop in a few minutes. Come on up," she said, turning toward the stairway across from the entrance.

Ben had never been upstairs to the two-story apartment above the shop where the Hegmans lived. At the top of the stairs, he glanced around curiously. The apartment consisted of several small, comfortably furnished rooms. He wasn't surprised to see that the decor looked much like the shop below, filled with antiques as well as plain old furnishings. Pieces of china and figurines lined wooden shelves, and lace covered a pair of end tables. The floors were mostly bare polished wood, but in the living room, an area rug with a flowery pattern muffled their steps.

"My, my," he said, glancing around the room. "Looks like a gift shop in here."

"Yes, just about," Grace agreed.

The fireplace mantel and tabletops were covered with greeting cards, bouquets of flowers, and fruit baskets. There were even two "Get Well" helium balloons tethered to a rocking chair. The colorful array brightened up the somber décor, Ben thought.

"I never knew Dad had so many friends," she said. "I mean, I know everybody says hello to him. But I never expected people would care so much or take the time to send all this stuff."

Ben noted Grace's sincere surprise and realized that at least some good had come from Digger's close call. "People do care, Grace, more than you know."

"Yes, well, Dad is enjoying all the candy and tins of cookies, I'll tell you that much."

Ben was suddenly glad he'd chosen a book as a gift. Everyone knew that Grace frowned on sweets of any kind, though Digger seemed to thrive on them.

"Dad is upstairs, resting. I'll tell him you're here."

"Thanks. I do want to speak to you in private for a moment first. I've been wondering about Digger's health. What did the doctors find? Anything new?"

Grace nodded and pulled at the edge of her sweater sleeve. "As a matter of fact, there has been some news. Seems he's been having small strokes all this time. That's why he's gotten so forgetful lately," she said sadly.

"Oh . . . I see. That makes sense." Ben shook his head. "Is there any treatment for it?"

"He needs to take some medication to keep it from getting worse. But it won't get any better," she reported quietly. "He has to be watched, Reverend. He can't leave the house alone anymore. I'm not even sure he should work. He certainly can't go gallivanting about, like he's used to. Next time he falls into another of those forgetful spells, they'll find him frozen like a statue somewhere," she predicted in a nervous tone.

"Ah, that is worrisome. How did he take it?" Ben asked.

"I haven't told him yet. Not all of it, anyway." She sighed and glanced down at the floor. "I know that doesn't look right, but it's been so difficult, Reverend. These have been some hard days for us. I just wanted to get him back home before I gave him the bad news."

"I understand," Ben quietly assured her. After all these years, he knew he should be used to it, but it still made him uneasy when people viewed him as their moral prosecutor—judge and jury, rolled into one. *Only the Lord above can judge any of us,* he always felt like saying. *Myself included.*

"Digger has to know, Grace," he said gently. "You need to be honest with him about this. Keeping it from him . . . that's not fair to him or you."

"I know what you're saying, Reverend, but it will just break his heart." She paused, and he could see her struggling to control her feelings. "You know how he is. Why, he's up and out and walked around this whole town, even down to the shore and back, before most people have had their morning coffee." She swallowed hard and shook her head. "I'm not sure I should tell him all of it. I'm honestly not sure that would be the best thing. I mean, what if he took it so to heart that he lost his will to keep going?"

Ben was silent for a moment, then said, "That is the risk. But what choice do you have?"

"Well, I have told him that he can't just go wander without telling me his whereabouts. He knows that now, surely," she said. "But he's got to be able to leave the house once in a while, maybe even keep doing those odd jobs he picks up with Sam and Harry. He doesn't have to feel so . . . degraded," she added.

"Yes, I see what you mean," Ben said thoughtfully. "Maybe you can get a few people to help you, Grace. They could stay with Digger for a few hours here and there. Or take him out in town. It's a daunting task to manage all on your own."

"You mean like baby-sitters?" Grace stared at him.

"Oh, not exactly. More like helpers," Ben added.

Grace seemed to consider the suggestion, then shook her head. "Dad would catch on. He wouldn't sit still for it," she said. "Besides I just couldn't impose on people like that."

Ben could have predicted that reply. A loner by nature, Grace had cut herself off from the community after her daughter Julie's death. While she knew everyone in town—most people had stopped in at the Bramble at one time or another—Ben wasn't sure Grace had even one real friend aside from Harry Reilly. She was the type who would rather suffer in silence, even sink altogether, than ask for help.

"But people *want* to help your father—and you," Ben reminded her. "Just look at all these cards."

"Oh, cards and flowers is one thing. Asking someone to give up time is quite another," Grace told him. "Harry will help us. And maybe Sam, a little, though he's quite busy these days. Harry is looking into some sort of electronic gadget that Dad can hook on his belt, so if he gets lost again, we can figure out where he is."

Ben shook his head, his heart heavy with doubt. "Grace, I know Harry has the best intentions, but you can't depend on some gadget to solve this problem. It's too big for that."

Grace gave in to a rare moment of looking completely overwhelmed, and Ben continued in a quiet but firm tone. "Your father must be told how serious the situation has become. That's the most important thing. Then you'll be able to figure out a real plan for his safety." He hoped she didn't take offense, but he couldn't avoid saying it. His conscience wouldn't let him. "Digger's not a child. He can handle it. Don't sell him short."

Ben stopped. He could see his advice and Grace's own strong feelings warring in the expression on her face. Her thick dark brows were knit together in a frown, her mouth a thin line. For the first time, Ben realized that he wasn't even sure he had the authority to advise her. After all, she was no longer a member of the church, though her father was.

"I know what you're saying, Reverend, but I—"

They both turned, startled by a sound out in the hall. Digger appeared in the doorway. A smile flashed on his bearded face, as he caught sight of Ben.

"I thought I heard someone chatting down here. This lazy old hound didn't even bark," Digger said, glancing at the dog at his side. Daisy followed him into the room, her tail wagging as she padded over and sniffed Ben's hand.

"Daisy hasn't left Dad's side since he got home. It's like she's babysitting him or something," Grace remarked. When she met the Reverend's gaze, he noticed two spots of color tinge her cheeks.

Ben rose and shook Digger's hand. "Good to see you home, Digger," he said sincerely. "Here, take my chair." While Digger looked much improved since Ben saw him over the weekend in the hospital, the old fisherman still didn't look his usual hale and hearty self.

"You're the guest, Reverend. You get the fancy chair. I'll sit over here," he said, lowering himself into the nearby rocking chair. "This suits me fine."

"Well, you two have a nice chat. I'm going down to the shop to check on a few things," Grace said, excusing herself.

"Yes, Grace. Take your time. We're fine," Digger said. Ben couldn't help noticing Digger looked relieved to see his daughter go. Probably feels he's being watched every minute now, he thought.

Digger reached into the pocket of his long sweater and took out his pipe. He put it in his mouth, unlit.

"Can't smoke this anymore. Except outside on the sly. But I like having it handy. Almost like fooling myself."

"How are you feeling?" Ben asked.

"Fit as a fiddle," Digger assured him. He thumped on his chest with his fist. "I didn't need to be cooped up in the hospital all that time. Doctors poking and prodding me. Why, that place is for sick people, God bless 'em. I'm not sick."

Of course not, Ben was about to say. Then he remembered that Digger was indeed sick; he just didn't know it. He looked away and adroitly changed the subject. "I brought you something." He offered Digger a rectangular-shaped package, wrapped in gift paper and a bow.

"Why, thanks, Reverend. That was kind of you." Digger took the package and shook it, listening. "Not candy, I hope. Grace will have a fit."

"No, not candy," Ben said, with a laugh. "Go on, open it and you'll see."

Digger tore off the wrapping, revealing a large, thick book. *"Over the Bounding Main: A Short History of Shipbuilding in New England,"* he said, reading the title aloud. He began leafing through the pages. "Hey, now, this looks like a great book you found for me. Look at these photographs."

"Check the index. I think there's a lot in there about this area, even our town."

Digger flipped to the index and scanned the page with his fingertip, leaning his head back a bit to see the words clearly. "Yup. They got a lot in here about Cape Light," he said, looking back up at Ben with a pleased expression. "Maybe I'll find a word or two about yours truly," he added, with a twinkle in his eye.

Ben laughed. "I think the era it covers is well before your time, Digger."

"Sure, I knew that." The old seaman laughed. "My head is just getting swelled with all this attention, I guess."

"I'll say," Grace agreed from the doorway. She had entered so quietly that neither of them had heard her coming, Ben realized.

"Look here, Grace. Reverend Ben gave me this fine book about shipbuilding. It's mighty thick, too. Ought to last me the winter," he said thoughtfully.

"That was very considerate of you, Reverend," Grace said.

"Not at all. I hoped to find something he would enjoy. I'm glad you like it, Digger," Ben said, rising from his seat. "And I'm pleased to see you're feeling better."

"Good enough to hear your sermon on Sunday, Reverend. Don't you worry," Digger assured him.

"I wasn't worried a bit," Ben said, with a laugh. He shook hands with Digger again, and there were some more good-byes as Grace retrieved his hat and coat.

When he got to the stairwell, Grace said, "I'll go out with you, Reverend. Daisy needs a walk. Just let me get my coat."

Ben waited while Grace slipped on a long tweed coat and buttoned it up to her neck. The dog's tail beat wildly when she spotted her leash, and she nudged Ben aside so it could be snapped on. He followed Grace and Daisy down the stairs, sensing Grace wanted to speak to him out of her father's earshot.

"Digger looks well," Ben said, as they stepped out onto the porch. "You're taking good care of him, as always."

"He's coming along," she agreed, as they began to walk together down Main Street toward the harbor. "But he'll never be quite the same again, will he?" She shook her head as she glanced at Ben. "He was lucky, people say. But it was more than luck. The Lord was watching over him," she said quietly, staring straight ahead, "and I'm thankful."

Ben glanced at her, as they continued walking down the street. It was true. Digger had been spared purely by the grace of God. Yet it was almost as great a miracle to hear Grace Hegman give Him credit.

"And I don't think I ever thanked you for coming to sit with me, either. You and Carolyn. I can't tell you what that meant to me, having some company while I waited to hear. And your prayers," she added. Her voice broke off, and she pulled a tissue from her coat pocket. "When we got the call that he was still alive . . . well, it felt to me like God had really heard what was in my heart. This time, anyway."

Ben nodded. He knew what she meant—how when she lost her daughter years ago, it seemed as if God were deaf to her suffering and appeals. And so she had turned away from the church.

"He is listening, Grace." Ben paused, not knowing if he should pursue this topic any further or if the better course was to let her come to her own truth, in her own time. "Have you prayed since that night? Or read the Bible?" he asked.

Grace shook her head. "No, I never was much of a Bible reader. But I guess I have prayed. In my way," she added. "Giving thanks for the rescue and for Dad's recovery." She stared down at the ground and shook her head. "Honestly, Reverend, after the way I've acted toward God—the things I've said to Him in my mind—I feel awfully guilty asking for any more help. Or even just talking to Him, for that matter."

Ben already knew Grace felt this way, but it was a great step in the right direction, he thought, for her to see it so clearly. To see the boulder that blocked her spiritual path. The loss of a child is so life shattering, so incomprehensible, he thought. It amazed him that anyone was able to go on after that. Though he had ministered many facing that unthinkable event, he realized that he could never totally imagine the devastation a parent must feel. He could understand how a woman like Grace would enter into a lifelong, angry stalemate with God. But now she felt remorseful for turning her back on God, it seemed, since this time in her hour of need He had not turned his back on her.

Ben reached out and touched her shoulder. "Grace, God forgives you. Whatever you did or said, the anger in your heart—He understands and forgives. Even if you have never truly forgiven Him for taking Julie," he added quietly.

Grace pursed her lips and stared down at the dog walking just ahead of them. "I'll never understand it," she admitted, "not as long as I live." Her voice trailed off, and she took a deep breath of the cold air. "I don't understand why God spared Dad and not Julie. Maybe someday I will."

"Understand . . . or merely accept that God's ways are often beyond our understanding," Ben said. "Prayer does help, you know."

She didn't answer, as she paused and pulled out a pair of brown woolen gloves from her pocket, somehow managing to put them on while still holding on to the leash.

Ben wondered if he should mention coming to service. She had not attended for years, but it would do her good now, he thought. Yet he sensed it wasn't time to push her any further. She seemed to be thinking a great deal about these questions, working on them. He was grateful for that at least.

Daisy whined and tugged on her leash. Ben noticed that they had already reached the green. "She's caught a scent. I guess I'm going this way," Grace said. "Thanks again for the visit, Reverend. It was good of you."

"My pleasure, Grace. I'll be seeing you."

Grace waved good-bye again, then she turned abruptly onto a path leading toward the harbor. Ben watched her for a moment, the big yellow dog tugging her along.

The weather report called for snow tonight, but the sky above him was clear, a startling shade of blue, the water out in the harbor sparkling in the sun's reflection. Would it snow? he wondered. That was yet another mystery.

God's mysterious ways are beyond our understanding, as deep and fathomless as the sky above, he thought. If he could ever help Grace accept that . . . well, then he'd really have helped her on her journey.

* * *

JANE HARMON BREEZED INTO THE NEWSPAPER OFFICE AND DUMPED HER shoulder bag on her desk, then tugged off her woolen cap. Dark curls flew out in all directions, like a small explosion, Sara thought.

Sara was happy to see her. She had been alone in the office the past few hours and was eager to have someone to talk to. Jane had been really nice so far, offering encouraging remarks on Sara's articles or sympathetically rolling her eyes when Wyatt got into one of his states.

"Listen to this," Jane said. "I just covered that meeting of the Public Services Commission this morning. I thought it was going to be a real snore and didn't even get there on time—don't tell Wyatt, of course," she added in a quick aside. "Then the mayor got into this major brawl with the county commissioner. I mean, I thought good old Emily Warwick was going to haul off and sock the guy. You should have seen it."

"Emily?" Sara wasn't sure Jane knew that she and Emily were related. Closely related. "I've never really seen her lose her temper. Not like that, I mean."

"Believe it. I got a really good shot of her, too. Wyatt is going to love this. I can see the caption now: 'Mayor Avoids Assaulting County Commissioner—but Just Barely.' " She grinned. "I was dying to get more pictures but my shutter jammed."

Lucky for Emily, Sara thought. It was hard for her to realize that they'd be printing a photo and story that would make Emily look bad.

Jane's grin faded, and she stared at Sara for a long moment. "Oh man, I'm sorry. Emily Warwick's your mother, right?" Jane slapped her forehead with her hand. "How dumb am I?"

Sara swallowed and nodded. "She's my birth mother."

"I heard that story a few months ago, but when I met you the other day, I didn't put it together. I'm sorry about what I just said. Really," Jane said quickly. "I think she's pretty cool, actually. That's just the way I get sometimes. I talk first, think later—"

"It's okay," Sara said, cutting her off. "We all need to be able to cover stories the way we see them. I completely understand. So how long have you worked on the paper?" she asked, wanting to change the topic.

"It will be two years in February. But I was only part-time at first. Then in September, when Dan lost two of his regulars to Crown News, he asked me to come in full-time. So I did."

"Crown News again," Sara said. "They're starting to sound like some science-fiction monster that sucks up unsuspecting newspaper staffers like a giant sponge."

"Almost." Jane laughed. "They now own a lot of newspapers around here that were once independent. Our local competition, the *Chronicle,* used to be run by a guy like Dan once, too. But Crown bought it a few years ago. Paid a load of money for it, I hear."

"Really? I wonder how Dan's escaped their clutches."

"They'd buy the *Messenger* in a minute. But Dan would never sell out. He's been saving the paper for Wyatt—the family tradition and all that."

"Right, I've heard about that," Sara said. "Did you grow up around here?" she asked, thinking Jane knew a lot of local history.

"In Ipswich, just south of here," Jane said. "I went to college in Vermont. I wanted to work on a big daily, like the *Boston Globe.* But I got the job here as a stringer and thought it would be good experience. At least for a while." Jane paused and pushed at her hair with her hand. "Working for Dan was okay. He never said too much, though you sure knew when he didn't like a story," she added, with a laugh. "Wyatt is a lot different. It's taking me a while to get used to him."

Me, too, Sara thought, *but I thought it was just because I was new.* "How do you mean?" she asked.

"Well, he gets more excited about the stories, so that's sort of fun," Jane mused. "And he's definitely cuter," she added, with a mischievous grin.

"Yes, he's definitely that," Sara agreed.

"But sometimes I feel like . . . well, like he doesn't really know what he's doing. You always knew what Dan wanted you to do and where you stood with him. Sometimes Wyatt seems like he wants *me* to tell him what my assignment should be."

"He does seem disorganized at times. I guess he's still getting used to running the paper."

Jane shrugged. "Maybe that's it. I sure wouldn't want his job." She took a sip of her coffee and glanced at her watch. "I'd better write up that story."

Wyatt suddenly appeared in the doorway. "What's going on here? Sounds like a coffee klatch," he said, with mock severity.

"It could be. Except that we don't have any coffee left. I had to buy this at the diner," Jane said, holding up her take-out cup.

Wyatt tugged off the long scarf he wore slung around his neck. "I'll put it on my list, Harmon. How was the meeting? I hope you have something for me. I have a huge hole on page three."

"Never mind page three, this is page one. Above the fold," Jane said excitedly. She picked up her notebook and followed Wyatt back to his desk, describing the confrontation between Emily and the commissioner.

Sara didn't mean to eavesdrop, but it was hard not to. Wyatt sounded pleased with Jane's report.

"Sounds hot," he said. "Don't go overboard, though. And call Warwick and Commissioner Callahan for comments. Guess I will have to rip up page one. For once, I thought I'd get out of here at a decent hour." He sat back in his chair and sighed. "Did you get any pictures?"

"I think I caught the mayor looking as if she's just about to have a stroke," Jane replied.

Sara secretly cringed. Poor Emily, she thought. But there was really nothing she could do about it. Rather, nothing she should do about it. She couldn't have anyone here thinking she wanted the paper to give Emily special treatment, just because she was related to her. Besides, Emily had been mayor for the past three years. This was her second term. She had to be used to this by now, Sara reasoned.

Sara turned back to her computer and focused on finishing her article. It was really dull stuff, compared to Jane's story, page-five caliber. But maybe Wyatt would use it for the hole on page three now, she thought hopefully.

* * *

BEN PULLED UP IN THE RECTORY'S DRIVE AND SAW CAROLYN STRUGgling to unlock the front door while holding two bags of groceries. She paused and waited for him.

"You're home early," she said, kissing his cheek.

"Or you're a bit late tonight," he replied. He took the bags from her, and she twisted the key in the lock.

"I stopped in to see Rachel. She was so tired, I stayed and cooked them dinner."

"Aren't you sweet. I'm sure she appreciated that," he said, setting the groceries on the kitchen counter.

"Yes, she did appreciate the help. But that means your dinner will be late."

"Let's just call up for a pizza or something. You don't have to cook twice, dear."

Carolyn cast him a look. "You don't really like pizza, Ben. It always gives you heartburn." He could see her dutiful nature warring with her fatigue.

"That's because I ask for too many toppings," he insisted. "We'll just get a plain one tonight. Maybe pepperoni on half," he amended. "I'll be fine, honestly. I'll call them right now." He picked up the phone before she could argue further. While Ben ordered the pizza, Carolyn began to put the groceries away.

"How is Rachel feeling? Besides tired, I mean," Ben asked.

"Oh, you know. Just what you would expect. Tired of waiting. Very excited."

"That goes for all of us, I'd say," Ben replied.

Carolyn took two dishes from a shelf then turned to face him. "She's still talking about calling Mark. She wants to try to persuade him to come back in time for the baby."

Ben shrugged. "Maybe she should call him again if she really wants to. Maybe she can persuade him."

"I think he wants to come back—but he's still angry at me, Ben. He can't forgive me, so he can't face me." Carolyn put the plates down on the table. The rattling sound unnerved him.

"Carolyn, please, we've been through this before. You can't blame yourself for the fact that you suffered from depression. And you can't blame yourself for Mark's reactions."

"Ben, please, you know what I'm saying is true," she insisted. "My depression doesn't excuse anything. Mark felt ignored, unloved. He didn't get enough from me then, and he never really understood why. Well, on an intellectual level he did, maybe, but deep down, it still left scars. Then he always felt as though you didn't really recognize his feelings. You didn't believe how much it hurt him. You wanted him to just buck up and get with the program—and he never quite could."

"That's not true," Ben insisted. "I bent over backward to understand that boy. All the times he got in trouble, the way he embarrassed the family—deliberately humiliated me," he admitted. "The private school. The counseling. Nobody tried harder than we did."

Carolyn sat down at the table but didn't say a word. Her hurt silence seemed to echo through the room.

Ben tried again. "Mark is an adult, a grown man. Whatever shortcomings you may have had as a mother came about because you were sick. He has to face that and accept it." He paused, trying not to sound impatient with his son—and his wife. But he was tired and it was difficult. "If anyone should take the blame for his anger, it's me. Not you. I agree with that much at least."

"Well, we're both to blame then," Carolyn said, sounding even more upset now. She impatiently swept a lock of hair from her eyes.

"Maybe I could have done more for him," Ben said quietly. "But I was stretched pretty thin just trying to keep up with the congregation. I didn't understand what was troubling him, and he hid a lot from us back then."

"Yes, he did," she agreed. "Or we weren't watching closely enough." She sighed, picking up a napkin and folding it carefully in half. Her hands were still so graceful, he thought, like a young girl's.

"Carolyn, the point is nobody is guaranteed perfect parenting, Mark included. Yes, we both have our shortcomings, yours being more forgivable than mine, I think. But we've always shown him our love. What more can we do?"

"I don't know. . . . I just wish that there was something. There *must* be something," she said. She'd been staring down at the table but now lifted her head to look at him. He saw a film of unshed tears in her eyes. "Don't you want to see him? Aren't you just aching to see him? *Our only son.* It's been two years."

He heard the pain in her voice, a mother's anguish. It tore at his heart, but it only made him feel more angry and frustrated with his son for hurting her so callously.

"Of course, I want to see him. I think about him all the time. I miss him as much as you do," he insisted quietly. "But I also feel at my wits' end. How many times can we call and encourage him to come back? I think we have to wait for Mark to decide he's ready."

"Perhaps there's something we can do that will help him feel ready," Carolyn said.

"Maybe it's something that Mark has to do," Ben said, before he could stop himself. "Maybe being ready means he would finally be willing to sit down and talk, tell us why he's stayed away for so long in the first place."

"That's just the problem," Carolyn said, suddenly angry. "Mark knows you're waiting here, ready to pounce on him the minute he gets in the door. Of course, he doesn't want to come back. Who would?"

Ben felt his own anger well up inside and took a deep, long breath. She was angry with her son for the way he'd treated them, but she couldn't let herself be angry with Mark, not when she blamed herself for Mark's unhappiness and confusion. So instead, she got angry at him. Ben knew all this logically and knew he loved his wife with all his heart, yet it was still hard not to answer her with his own anger.

Give me patience, Lord. This is hard, and it's been a long time coming. There are things that must be said now. Help me say them.

"Carolyn, you misunderstand me. I don't want to attack Mark. I pray every day to have him here with us again. You know that," he appealed to her. "But I wouldn't be honest if I didn't say that if he does come home, we must clear the air. We have to sit down and get at the truth with him. Why is he so angry with us, so wounded? How can we ever heal as a family if we just cover over the wound and pretend it isn't there?"

"What happened to forgive and forget? What happened to turning the other cheek, to unconditional love?" she demanded. "I want him to know that if he comes home, we'll welcome him with open arms—no questions asked, no explanations necessary. I know why he left and I know why he stays away. Why do we need to drag ourselves through this all over again?"

Ben held his tongue. Carolyn's expression was bleak, her jaw trembling slightly. He didn't want to push her any further.

In the silence she seemed to steady herself. "Maybe after the holidays and the baby is born, if he still won't come back, we ought to think about going out there to see him," she suggested in a calmer tone.

"Out to Montana?" Ben was surprised by her suggestion. "It's an idea . . . but I'm not sure it would be the best thing, Carolyn. We'd see him physically, of course. But if he's not ready to open up to us, it might be even more frustrating than not seeing him at all."

Her crushed expression told him he had not said the right thing. "Not for me, it wouldn't be," she said bitterly.

Ben shook his head, hardly able to hear any more of this argument. He and his wife so rarely argued. Mark was almost always the reason when they did.

"Carolyn, I miss him with all my heart. But I can't see what we'd accomplish by running out to Montana if he's not ready to talk to us. I know it's hard, but I think we just have to have patience and pray that someday soon, Mark comes to his senses and is ready to make amends."

"Patience, of course. I knew you were going to say that," Carolyn said harshly. She shook her head in frustration. "That might be good counsel for some family you're advising but not for this one, Ben. Not for your own family. I just don't know why you can't see that."

Ben was at a loss for words, feeling the wind knocked out of him by her verbal blow. That was the bitterest part of this entire situation. It made him feel like such a sham, to walk around counseling others every day, when here at home, he was unable to help his own family with this painful problem.

"I'm sorry you feel that way," he said sadly.

"So am I," she answered quietly.

Carolyn stared at him wide-eyed, unmindful, it seemed, of the tears that rolled down her cheeks. Ben was moved by the sight of her sadness. "Carolyn, please," he began.

The doorbell rang.

"The pizza. I'll get it," Carolyn said, half-rising from her chair.

"No, I will." Ben lightly touched her shoulder and turned to leave the room.

"I'm not feeling very hungry," Carolyn called after him. "I think I'll just go up."

He glanced back at her. He didn't feel hungry now either. "You must be tired. Go on to bed if you like. I'll be along in a little while," he said softly.

Carolyn passed him in the hallway as she turned to go up the stairs. She didn't say anything. The doorbell rang again.

Ben opened the door. It had begun to snow—fat, feathery flakes that clung to the delivery boy's ski cap and jacket and already covered the top of the pizza box. Ben paid, then carried the box into the kitchen and set it down on the countertop. He wasn't sure what to do with it now. At last, he wedged it into the refrigerator, wondering if either of them would want it tomorrow.

He walked to the stairway and glanced up. The house was silent, a penetrating kind of silence that settles in when the only two people inside are in an angry standoff, he thought sadly. He didn't see any light coming from the bedroom and guessed that Carolyn had gone straight to bed. He considered following her, then paused at the foot of the staircase.

No, he needed to read or something. Work in his office maybe. No, a walk would do him good. Some exercise to work out the tension. Despite the snow, or maybe lured by it, he put on his down jacket, gloves, and a hat, and pulled out his thermal boots from the bottom of the coat closet.

When he stepped outside, the white filled the air, whirling in the haze of the streetlights. The snow already covered the world around him, cars, tree branches, rooftops. It would stick, too. The first heavy snowfall of the season. Mark had said that there was already a lot snow out in

Montana. But he'd grown up in New England, so he was used to harsh winters, Ben thought.

Ben looked down and saw his boot prints on the sidewalk, the first to touch the pure white blanket. A snowfall like this usually made him feel optimistic, covering everything over with white, promising a fresh beginning. But somehow tonight the snow failed to work its magic. Some things could not be covered over. Should not be, his mind insisted. He knew that if Mark returned, the past had to be sorted out. They had to talk, all three of them. Why didn't Carolyn see that?

More importantly, why hadn't he done a better job of guiding and helping his family with this problem? Many times it seemed they were making progress, as if with patience and time, they were working it out. Yet tonight it seemed that he had been deluding himself all these years. They had made no progress at all. He had failed all of them, even Rachel. They had all looked to him to lead them out of this shadowy, unhappy place, and he had failed them.

He felt like a fraud, deeply flawed as a minister, spiritual leader, and healer. How could he counsel others when, for years, he'd been unable to find the solution, or even guidance from above, for his own family in this situation?

At the end of the street, where three ambling lanes came together, a triangular plot of land had been set aside by chance or design as a small park. Edged by a few small trees and snow-covered bushes, three benches stood on the walkways, and in the middle, a snow-covered fountain, rimmed with icicles.

Ben stood by the fountain, remembering bringing Rachel and Mark here after dinner on summer evenings when it stayed light until late. The ice-cream truck made a nightly stop at this corner. The kids liked to hide behind the bushes and make Ben catch them. Mark chased fireflies with a paper cup, then screamed with terror if he actually caught one. Rachel dropped flowers in the fountain and watched them float and spin in the swirling water. He suddenly felt as if he might cry and squeezed his eyes shut.

Dear heavenly Father, he silently prayed. *What have I done wrong? Please show me how to bring peace to my family and how to bring them together again. Please show me, Lord. Should we do as Carolyn says? Is that the right way? I just don't know anymore. Everyone seems against me in this. How can I ever reconnect with my son if he doesn't make any effort?*

He blinked, sensing the snowflakes on his face, clinging to his eyebrows and lashes. How long had he been standing there? He sighed and turned back toward the rectory. He reached the path to his front door, feeling frozen to the bone. His heart, too, felt heavy and numb. Not prayer, or even the new snow, the simple, stunning beauty of God's artistry, had helped him tonight.

"WOW, DID YOU SEE THE SNOW? I DIDN'T REALIZE THAT MUCH HAD PILED up." Sara walked toward the windows at the front of the office and stared out at the street. It must have been snowing the whole time she and Wyatt had been working in the back on the layout. It looked like it would reach to her boot tops, and it was still falling.

Wyatt walked up behind her. He was quiet for a moment. "Didn't see much of this stuff in California. Almost forgot what it looked like."

"Where were you living? In Los Angeles?"

He nodded. "I had a job on the *L.A. Times.*"

"You left the *L.A. Times* to come *here*?" Sara couldn't believe she had been so blunt. But Wyatt only laughed.

"Seems like a dumb career move to you?"

"I'm sorry. I mean, I didn't know you were on that big a paper. . . ." She stumbled over her words, not knowing what to say.

"That's all right. Sometimes, I think it's a little crazy myself. But running the *Messenger* is just, well, inevitable for me. No matter where I traveled, or who I worked for, I always knew I'd come back here someday and run this paper."

"I see." Sara nodded. "Of course. Your great-great-grandfather started the paper, right?"

"First edition, June 30, 1852. The headline read, 'Jebediah Wilkes Completes Trans-Atlantic Crossing.' Wilkes was a local who sailed to England and back on a thirty-foot sailboat made here in town. When my great-great-grandfather asked why he did it, Wilkes said, 'Because I'm a darn fool, just like everyone says I am.' "

Sara laughed, and Wyatt smiled at her. A smile that didn't quite reach his eyes, she noticed. Something in Wyatt's quiet, resigned tone was unsettling. He said taking over the paper was inevitable, but he didn't sound as if it was something he particularly wanted to do.

Or maybe that was a given. Maybe the plan had always been so much a part of his life that he took it for granted. Like being in a royal family or something.

"Where else have you been?" she asked, her curiosity about him growing.

"Oh, lots of places. Just about everywhere, I guess. Europe, of course, Turkey, the Middle East, Nigeria, India, Afghanistan, Pakistan, Australia, and New Zealand. Tahiti, of course."

"Of course," she said lightly.

"Russia, Japan, China—just Beijing, mainly. Taiwan, Hawaii—"

"Okay, I got the idea. You really took pictures in all those places?"

"That's what I do . . . or used to do," he amended.

"Don't you miss it?" she said.

He met her gaze then looked out at the snow again. "I haven't had time to miss it, yet. I guess I was getting a little tired of all the traveling, the pressure. It's a certain kind of life. A lot of airports and hotel rooms. It can start to feel very unreal at times." He looked at her. "Unlike this place. Feels like hardly a thing has changed since I grew up here."

Sara knew what he meant. But she didn't think it was quite as simple as that.

"Everything changes," Sara replied. "It seems to me a lot has happened just since I came here a few months ago. People change. That's the heart of it, I guess."

He glanced at her, a flash of surprise in his eyes. "Very true. Everything changes."

They stood there without talking a moment, both looking out at the snow. "I'd like to see some of your photographs sometime," Sara said.

"Sure. I have a bunch back at my father's house somewhere. I'll bring them in. By the way, that shot you caught of the kids at the tree lighting was pretty good."

Sara felt embarrassed by his compliment. Especially since he had asked her to revise the article about three times. "I was just lucky."

"I'll let you in on a little trade secret. Getting lucky like that is about ninety-five percent of taking good photographs."

"I doubt it," Sara said, with a laugh. "But thanks. I'm trying."

"Yes, I can see that." He touched her shoulder in a friendly gesture. Sara turned and met his gaze. They stared at each other for a long moment. She watched something in his expression change, and she felt very aware of his closeness. What was happening here?

Then his hand dropped to his side again, and he smiled. "Thanks for helping me tonight. I'm sorry I kept you so late. I didn't think it would take this long."

"That's all right." She glanced at her watch; it was past midnight. She wasn't surprised. Wyatt was a terrible judge of time and seemed to jump from one task to another during the workday. But when he sat down and finally focused on something, the entire roof could cave in and he wouldn't notice.

She went back to her desk and picked up her coat and knapsack. "I'm glad I have the day off tomorrow," she said.

"You'd better take the phone off the hook, so I don't call you in for some emergency."

"Thanks for the warning. I didn't even think of that." She pulled on her jacket, then slung her scarf around her neck.

"So you survived your first week. What do you think? Coming back on Monday?"

"Sure, I'll be back," she said lightly.

"Good. I didn't want to scare you off. I've been tough on you, I guess. My sister said so, anyway," he added.

Good old Lindsay. She'd been in and out throughout the week, a quiet voice of reason and organization. She had helped Sara more than a few times so far. Wyatt seemed to depend on her a lot, too. More than he'd ever admit, Sara thought.

"I'm okay. It's not as easy as I thought," she admitted. "But I'm learning a lot."

"Yes, I can see that. Your copy is getting better. It's coming along."

"Thanks," she said. It was a small compliment, but something. Her long hair had gotten caught under her jacket collar, and as she pulled it free with her hand, she found him staring at her again.

"Where are you parked?" he asked suddenly.

"Right across the street," she said, pointing at her snow-covered hatchback.

"Need any help cleaning off your car?" he asked.

It was nice of him to offer, but she could tell he was only being polite. Besides, she didn't have the heart to take him up on the offer. He still had more work to do before transmitting the paper to the printer, and he already looked exhausted, with his collar undone and his hair rumpled. The look worked for him, she thought, feeling a tug of attraction.

"No, I'm fine. I just brush off the front and back, and let the wind do the rest."

"Well, all right. Drive safely," he added, as she headed for the door.

"I will. Good night," she said finally.

Sara crossed the street, her boots sinking into the snow even though the plow had passed by at least once. She stood at her car for a moment, taking a deep breath of the cold, bracing air. It seemed to clear her head instantly.

She opened her trunk and pulled out her snow brush, then began to work on her car. The snow was light and powdery, easy to clear away. It felt good to be out and move around after sitting all day and night.

Had Wyatt been flirting with her? *No, he was just being friendly,* she decided. *Maybe he felt guilty after being so mean to me all week. He probably acts that way with everyone,* she told herself. She shouldn't think anything of it. Besides, he hadn't exactly gone out of his way to help her.

She slipped behind the wheel and started the engine. Luke would have come out and cleaned the car for her, she realized. Then she gasped out loud. Luke had been expecting her to call him tonight, and she'd forgotten all about it.

It would be okay, she told herself. She would reach him in the morning. After she slept late.

Chapter Seven

SARA WOKE TO SHARP KNOCKS ON HER FRONT DOOR. SHE squinted at the clock on the table beside her bed. Half past eight. Who could be bothering her first thing on a Saturday morning?

Milky rays of sunlight filtered through her bedroom curtains, the early morning light reflecting off fresh snow. She felt as though it were the middle of the night, then she remembered how late she had gotten home from work.

The knocking continued. "I'm coming. Just a minute," she called out in a grumpy tone. She pulled on her bathrobe. She pulled open the door to find Luke standing on the porch in a down jacket and thick insulated gloves. His eyes were bright and his cheeks were red from the cold.

"Did I wake you? Gee, I'm sorry." He laughed, not looking sorry at all. "I thought you'd be up by now."

"Usually." Cold air seeped into the house, and she pulled her robe around her throat. "I got to bed really late last night. I had to work late. I'm sorry I didn't get to call you."

"That's okay." Luke shrugged. "I guess I should have called, but I wanted to surprise you. Look what I found."

He stepped to one side, and she noticed a long wooden toboggan balanced on the porch rail. The long slats of wood were a golden pine color, curled at the end and trimmed in red paint.

"Wow, that's beautiful! Where did you get it?"

"That shed behind my cottage with all the junk. I was looking in there for a snow shovel. Want to try it out?"

"You're not going to believe this, but I've never been sledding."

Luke looked shocked. "Never? Not even once?"

"We never really got enough snow in Maryland. Not like this, I mean."

"There's enough today." Luke's grin grew wider. "No excuses."

Sara shrugged. It wasn't exactly the way she had planned to start her Saturday, but how could she resist?

"Go on in and get dressed. I need to fix the rope on the end of this thing," Luke said, turning back to the sled.

"Okay, I'll be right out." Sara turned and went back into the house.

"Make sure you wear a few layers of clothes. It can get pretty wet," he called after her.

Sara quickly dressed, gulped down a glass of juice, and met Luke on the porch. "So where are we going?"

"I saw some killer hills out near the orchard. This sled is going to break the sound barrier."

"There are a lot of trees out there. Is it hard to steer?" Sara asked, as they reached Luke's 4Runner. Luke tossed the long sled on top and secured it with bungee cord.

Luke glanced over and smiled at her. "Don't worry. It will come back to me."

"It better," Sara warned, climbing up into the truck.

Luke laughed and started the engine. "Relax, you're going to love this," he promised.

THE SLEDDING AREA WAS MORE CROWDED THAN SARA EXPECTED, A lively scene with brightly colored ski jackets against the stark white snow. She could hear children and adults alike screaming and laughing off in the distance as they parked and took the toboggan down off Luke's vehicle. Sara followed as Luke pulled the sled along, wondering what she had gotten herself into.

They arrived at the top of the hill, and Sara glanced down and felt the bottom of her stomach drop.

Luke set the sled down and straightened out the rope.

"Okay, sit right there," he said in a reassuring voice. "You can hold on to these handles on the side."

She did as he said, then looked straight ahead, feeling her mouth grow dry.

"Now I'm going to give us a push and jump on. All you have to do is hang on, okay?"

She nodded, then turned to him. "This is . . . it's sort of steep. Isn't there a smaller hill we could warm up on?"

"This one isn't so bad," he said reassuringly. "You just think it's steep." She felt him start to push on the back of the sled and gripped the rope handles on the side.

Sara turned her head and stared straight ahead. Off in the distance she could see a fringe of bare trees that were part of the Potter Orchard. And even farther below, the harbor and the village, which looked like a toy village under a Christmas tree.

At least the view is lovely, she thought, wondering if it would be her last.

"Did you ever go on a roller coaster?" Luke shouted, as he pushed faster. "This is sort of the same thing. The first hill is scary. Then you have fun."

"I've always hated roller coasters," she shouted back, as the toboggan picked up speed. She stared straight ahead, watching as the curling end of the sled neared the lip of the hill.

Then she felt the front end of the sled tip over, and she felt Luke jump on behind her, his long legs lined up on the edge of the sled, just outside her own. One of his hands held the rope, the other wrapped tight around her waist. She heard her own voice shrieking, as they flew down the hill. Behind her Luke was yelling, too, only he sounded excited instead of terrified.

The sled picked up even more speed, the trees and snow flying by. Every time Sara thought she was almost getting used to the sensation, they would hit a dip or bump. She would hear herself scream, then feel as if she would have flown right off the toboggan if not for Luke's strong hold around her. She felt his warm breath on her cheek, his soft laughter in her ear.

Finally, they reached the bottom of the hill, and the ground leveled off, though the sled was still moving swiftly.

Just as Sara breathed a sigh of relief, another toboggan crossed their path. Luke gave a sharp tug on the rope and narrowly avoided a collision. But a second later, their toboggan tipped on one side, and Sara felt herself flying off into the snow, with Luke right behind her.

When she opened her eyes, she was staring straight up into the branches of a pine tree, fragments of blue sky outlined by the dark branches. Luke had landed beside her, facedown, one arm slung across her middle, his head just inches from her own.

He didn't move, and she felt her heart pound with alarm. "Luke?" She leaned over and shook him. "Luke!" she called, even louder. "Are you okay?"

His head popped up, and when he grinned, she realized he'd been teasing her. "I'm okay," he said lightly.

"That was mean!" she said, trying not to giggle. She pushed at his shoulder, but he didn't budge.

He shook his head, and bits of snow flew in all directions. "So, you loved it, right? I can tell."

"Loved it? Didn't you hear that woman screaming? That was me!"

He pushed himself up on his arm and stared down at her.

"I'm so sorry. I thought you were having fun," he said sympathetically. "I guess that means we just have to find you a bigger hill."

"Come on, Luke . . ." she began. Then she realized he was teasing her again. A small smile turned up one corner of his mouth, she noticed, just before he leaned down and kissed her. His mouth felt icy on her own as she kissed him back.

She didn't notice the snow seeping through her clothes, didn't notice anything but the sweet, searching pressure of his mouth on her own.

A sled suddenly whizzed by, spraying them with icy crystals. Luke sat up and laughed. "We don't want to get run over out here."

He stood up and offered Sara a hand, then pulled her out of the snow. She felt lightheaded, almost dizzy, and wasn't sure if it was the effect of the sleigh ride or Luke's kiss.

Luke retrieved their toboggan, which had glided under some trees. "If you really don't want to do it again, I'll understand. Honestly," he told her.

Sara eyed the sleigh, then looked up the hill. It didn't seem nearly as intimidating now. "Come on, let's get up there."

"You're sure?" he asked, looking surprised.

She nodded. "Absolutely. Look at all the little kids out here. They're doing fine. I'm not going to let these grade-schoolers put me to shame, for goodness' sake."

Luke shook his head and laughed. "That's the spirit."

They rode the toboggan until they were both soaked and numb with cold. "I'm starved," Sara said, as they climbed back into Luke's SUV. "I never really had breakfast. Want to stop someplace in town?"

He glanced at her and then checked his watch. "Sorry, I have to pick up Digger at the Bramble."

"Is Digger going back to work already? I thought he just got home from the hospital."

"Sam Morgan and I are taking him over to the cottages to do some painting. He might just hang around and help a little. It was Sam's idea, actually. Sort of a favor for Grace," he confided. "She says he's getting restless around the shop."

"That's good of you," Sara said sincerely. Luke struck most people as distant, a loner type. But there was a side of him that was keenly aware of people in need and the ways he could help them. He was just quiet about it.

"Better drop me off at home then," Sara told him. "I should run some errands and clean up. I'm not used to working full-time. My place looks like a tornado struck."

"We're still on for tonight, right?" he added, glancing over at her.

"Sure." She suddenly felt shy with him, thinking about how they'd kissed in the snow. She stared down at her gloves and twisted them around in her lap.

"What if we go up to Newburyport for dinner?" he asked, as he pulled up in front of her house. "Say, around seven. Would that be good?"

"Great. I'll be ready at seven." She started out of the 4Runner. "Thanks again for the sled ride. It certainly was a memorable way to start the day."

"See you later, Sara." Luke smiled and waved at her, then drove away.

Inside her apartment, Sara glanced around at the mess, then went straight to her bedroom and pulled open the closet door. Never mind cleaning up, what was she going to wear? *I might have to run over to the mall and find something new.* Then she realized she had never felt inspired to buy new clothes for Luke before. *Is that a good sign—or a bad one?* she wondered. *Well, I'll find out soon enough, I guess.*

"I KNOW IT LOOKS BAD, BUT IT'S NOT EXACTLY THE END OF THE WORLD, Dad," Wyatt argued.

He sat down hard on the couch in the family room, his father's lair. Dan sat nearby in his wheelchair, his expression grim, his tan complexion mottled with anger.

"We'll just run a correction in the next edition. No problem," Wyatt said.

"Oh, no problem? That's the third time this week. Pretty soon all you'll be publishing is a long correction sheet."

"What are you talking about? The big dailies do it every day."

"We're not reporting on the world at large, only this little corner. It's small enough to get it right the first time," Dan snapped. "The *Messenger* has always prided itself on accuracy. If you don't deliver that, you've lost people's confidence. Subscriptions and advertising will drop off, and then where will you be?"

"You've jumped from a one-line misquote to a complete disaster scenario. Very objective, Dad," Wyatt countered.

"How is the advertising doing?" Dan prodded. "It looked a little spotty this week."

"It's the same as usual, I guess." Wyatt ran his hand through his hair, feeling frustrated. "Lindsay has been dealing with that end of things lately. Maybe you should ask her."

Thank goodness for Lindsay, Wyatt thought distractedly. If she hadn't been coming around, picking up the loose ends, he wasn't sure he'd be able to get a paper out every day.

"Lindsay? What does she have to do with it?"

"She's been helping out, filling in for Gloria and just . . . helping out. I thought you knew."

"I knew she went down to the office a few times. I didn't realize she was so involved," Dan admitted. "You're the publisher now. You have to know what's going on with the advertising revenue. It's your lifeblood. It should be up this time of year, way up."

"I'm sure it should be. But I've got a few other things on my plate right now, Dad," Wyatt said tensely.

Dan was silent for a moment. "If you're having trouble and you don't know what to do, you should just call me."

Wyatt stared at his father, struggling to keep a lid on his anger. "I thought I was running the paper now. Not just warming your seat while you're stuck in this house. If that was the deal, you should have told me. Maybe I wouldn't have quit my job in California and come running back here."

"That was never the deal, and you know it. It was time for you to come back and take over."

"Well, here I am. I'm running it." Wyatt threw his arms up in frustration. "And you haven't had anything but criticism from the day I started."

"That's not true." Dan shifted restlessly. "I just can't help looking at it with a critical eye. I've been doing it long enough, you know."

"Yeah, I know all about it, Dad," Wyatt said. "But I'm doing it now. Did you want me to take over or not?"

"Of course, I want you to. You know how much."

"I thought I did," Wyatt said. "Now I'm not so sure. Maybe you aren't quite ready to retire."

"What are you talking about? If I wasn't stuck in this chair, I'd be a thousand miles away from here by now," Dan argued.

And out of my hair, Wyatt silently added. But meeting his father's gaze, he suddenly felt sorry for him. Anyone could see that it was pure torture for Dan to be confined this way. But being housebound like this, with nothing else to think about, was probably part of the problem, Wyatt realized.

Wyatt stood up and rubbed at a knot of tension in his shoulder. "Look, Dad, I don't know what to say. I'm doing the best I can. You ran the paper for over twenty years. I've been there—what, three weeks?" he pointed out. "I'm going to make mistakes. I'm sure if you think back to when you first took over, you did, too."

Dan met his gaze, then looked away. Wyatt noticed his father's jaw shifting, as if he were carefully considering his reply. Then he let out a long sigh. "Of course, I made mistakes. But I'm just trying to help you. Can't you see?"

Wyatt took a breath. "I do see. But I need to do things my way. Or this isn't going to work out."

Wyatt saw a strange expression flash across his father's face just then, a mixture of shock and disappointment. As if the very idea of his son walking away from the *Messenger* was unthinkable. But just as quickly, it passed, lingering only in his father's eyes.

"Of course, it's going to work out. Don't be ridiculous," Dan scoffed. He turned his chair to face the windows. "Look at all that snow. I guess that's all they're talking about in town this morning, anyway."

"Yeah, I guess it is."

Wyatt took a moment to decode his father's change of subject. Was he saying that the whole town was talking about the snowfall and not the error in his precious *Messenger*? That the front-page error wasn't such a big deal, after all? Wyatt wasn't completely sure, but he suspected that this was as close as Dan would get to an apology.

The doorbell rang. "Expecting anyone?" Wyatt asked, as he turned to answer it.

Dan shrugged. "It might be Emily Warwick. She mentioned she might drop by, if she wasn't too busy. We're in the middle of a chess game," he added, glancing at the board.

Wyatt could tell his father was truly hoping it was their attractive neighbor. Well, at least he had one thing to distract him from worrying about the paper.

"I'll go see." Wyatt left the room and headed for the front door. He pulled it open, happy to see Emily standing there. She looked different in her weekend clothes, a bright yellow parka and jeans. The big blue mittens on her hands made her look very young.

"Emily, come on in. Dad's been waiting for you." Wyatt noticed her cheeks looked red but couldn't tell if she was blushing or it was the cold weather.

"He's in the family room," Wyatt said, leading the way. "Emily is here," Wyatt called out to Dan.

Dan looked up from his computer screen and smiled at his visitor. "So, ready to lose?"

Emily shook her head, as she unzipped her jacket. "False bravado will get you nowhere. As I recall, you're in check and I'm just about to capture your queen."

"Oh, I found a way out of that mess," Dan said, wheeling his chair over to the game table. "You're going to have some problems of your own in a minute."

Wyatt stood in the doorway a moment, as they prepared to resume their match. Wyatt could tell his father really liked Emily. He seemed to light up the minute the woman entered the house. He wondered if the feelings were mutual. She seemed just right for him, Wyatt thought.

"I'll see you later then, Dad. So long, Emily."

Dan looked up, as if suddenly remembering his son was in the room. "Going out?"

"Just down to the office for a few hours. I need to finish Monday's edition." *And draft the correction and look into the advertising situation,* he silently added. "I won't be late. Are you set for dinner?"

"Emily and I are going to call out for something." Dan glanced at

Wyatt, as if there was more he wanted to say. Instead he shrugged and said, "See you later, then."

Wyatt guessed that sooner or later, his father would tell Emily all about their argument. But as he closed the front door, the notion didn't bother him. Emily looked like a good listener, the reasonable type, someone who could put things in perspective. Which might be exactly what his father needed right now.

THE LOW CANDLES ON THEIR TABLE CAST LUKE'S FACE IN FLICKERING shadows. He looked handsome as he read through the dessert menu, Sara thought, his gray eyes silvery in the half light.

She silently studied his face. The narrow scar that ran from his temple down to his jaw had once seemed sinister to her. Now she hardly noticed it at all. When she did, it reminded her of the difficult times Luke had been through and how he had fought to turn his life around. He had a lot of inner strength, a lot of character. It was one of the traits that had first attracted her to him—and still did, she realized.

"See anything you like?" he asked, suddenly looking up.

Sara felt herself blush and hoped he wouldn't notice. "It all sounds great, but I think I'm just too full for anything more."

"Me, too," Luke said. "Why don't I get the check, and we'll walk a little?"

Sara agreed, and Luke signaled to their waiter. Their night out had been perfect, Sara thought. The restaurant was elegant and romantic. Located in a federal-style house in the village of Newburyport, it was decorated for the holidays with fresh pine boughs, velvet ribbons, and white candles everywhere. The food was as classic as the setting, and being with Luke felt easy and somehow right. She found herself feeling sorry that their time together was coming to an end.

They were soon outside, standing on the sidewalk. After the cozy restaurant, the cold night air was a bit of a shock. Luke put his arm around her shoulders, as if it were the most natural thing in the world, and they fell into step beside each other. The street was filled with shops and restaurants, all decorated for the holidays. The antique lampposts were wrapped in green boughs and red ribbons, and the small trees along the street were covered in tiny white lights.

"I can't believe it's almost Christmas. I feel like it was just summer last week," Sara mused.

"I can't believe I've been living here for almost six months," Luke replied.

"Me, too. The time went by so quickly." Sara said, turning her head to catch his gaze. His face was close to hers, almost touching. "So much has happened. In some ways, it feels like another lifetime."

"I know what you mean," he admitted. "Think of how you felt when you first came up here. What you were going through."

"You helped me a lot," she told him shyly. "Especially about finally telling Emily who I was. I was so upset and confused, I don't know if I could have done it without you."

He stopped walking for a moment and glanced down at her. "Oh, I just gave you a push now and then. That's all." His expression barely showed it, but she could tell her admission had touched him. "I'd say we're even. You made me stick with the project. Maybe without you around, I would have quit."

"You were pretty angry sometimes, but I don't think you ever would have quit."

"I thought about it," he confessed. "But I didn't want you to think less of me."

"Luke, if you decided to give up on the New Horizons Center because of all the opposition, I would have sympathized, not criticized," she assured him. "I *never* would have thought less of you. But I've got to tell you—I think what you've done is pretty amazing."

He smiled at her and didn't say anything for a while. "I've done okay, I guess. It doesn't seem real yet. It won't until the kids get here and we're officially open in the spring. I guess then it will all hit home with me."

He didn't have to say more. Sara knew what it had meant to Luke to start this project and see it through. After failing as a cop, he'd found a way to redeem himself, in his own eyes and in the eyes of the world.

A chilly breeze blew up from the harbor, and they nestled even closer. Sara stole a quick glance at Luke, his strong profile against the clear night sky. He had come to mean so much to her in such a short time. But she knew that one day she would leave Cape Light. She was here for her job and for a chance to get to know her birth mother better. But she had never thought of Cape Light as her true home, while Luke had made a commitment to stay. Yet, as he stopped walking and turned to face her, it hardly seemed the right moment to remind him.

Then Luke stared down at her, slipped his arms around her waist, and pulled her closer. She knew he was about to kiss her, and she felt a breathless excitement.

"I think we have a lot to look forward to, Sara," he said softly. "A lot to look forward to together, I mean."

His tone sounded serious to her. Almost too serious, she thought. Sara tipped her head back and closed her eyes. His kiss was warm and loving, and she felt herself melting into his embrace, her sudden apprehension melting, too, as she kissed him back with all the emotion that suddenly welled up in her heart.

Was Luke getting too serious too quickly for her? She wasn't sure. She couldn't say what their future would bring. Nobody could. But she felt happy in his arms, and when they were close like this, it didn't seem to matter.

Chapter Eight

As he started the service on Sunday morning, Ben was pleased to find Digger Hegman seated in his usual spot, second pew, pulpit side. Digger sat beside the newlyweds, Jessica and Sam Morgan, who were probably keeping an eye on him. Ben had hoped to see Grace sitting beside her father today, but she was nowhere in sight.

Grace's appearance would have been the silver lining to Digger's crisis, but that was too easy. *The Lord doesn't usually deliver such tidy bundles,* Ben reminded himself. *You ought to know that by now.* Still, he felt her absence keenly, as though it were a lapse on his part.

The time for his sermon arrived, and he stepped up to the pulpit. He heard a restless shifting and muffled coughs, as the congregation waited for him to begin. He glanced at his notes. They were sketchy, not as well organized as usual. Still upset by his argument with Carolyn, he hadn't been able to focus very well last night when he tried to polish it up. Maybe this was one of those days when he would do better to forget the sermon and just speak from the heart.

"I welcome you all here this morning," he began. "I especially extend a welcome to Mr. Dennis Hegman, better known to most of us as Digger." Ben paused, hearing some good-natured chuckles.

He was among the few in town who knew Digger's Christian name, a perfect question if there were ever a Cape Light version of *Jeopardy*, he thought fancifully.

"We're thankful for your safe return, Digger," Ben said, meeting the old fisherman's gaze. "And for the effort of so many in our town who left their families and holiday celebrations when they heard that a friend and neighbor was in trouble.

"It was a night we'll all remember. One of the most frightening in our town's recent history, I think, but also one of our finer hours. When the news went out, the good people of our town didn't say, 'That's too bad, but I guess the police or whoever will handle it.' They didn't procrastinate. They didn't make excuses. They just came."

Ben paused, pushing up his glasses. He saw in the pews so many men and women who had come out to search. Folks like Sam Morgan and Harry Reilly, of course, good friends of the Hegmans. But also people like Warren Oakes, who barely knew Digger; Miriam Foster, a postal worker who also had a seat on the village council; and even Betty Bowman, a real-estate broker.

"This time of year is called the season of giving," he went on. "Giving gifts to our family and friends and remembering those less fortunate. We give donations of money or clothing or even toys and food. We do it wholeheartedly or out of habit or maybe even guilt. Sometimes we simply find ourselves cornered into giving, our path in the mall blocked by a smiling volunteer ringing a bell."

A few in the congregation smiled or nodded or even looked uncomfortable, recognizing themselves. Others stared at him with blank, unfocused expressions that made Ben wonder if they even heard him.

"It seems to me," he continued in a stronger tone, "there are so many ways to express charity, to give of ourselves to our neighbors and friends. And this is the perfect time to 'think out of the box' about it, if you will—out of the alms box," he added, drawing a few smiles.

"The outpouring of energy and concern I witnessed on Thanksgiving night was charity in action—people who selflessly put aside their own concerns, their own physical comfort, and even personal safety to aid someone in need. A dramatic gesture.

"But consider how many far more subtle ways there are for us to do the same thing—to come to the aid of someone in need—with our time, our sympathy, or maybe just a smile and a kind word. A small gesture of courtesy, like letting the other guy have the last parking space or letting someone ahead of you at the supermarket checkout. Giving makes us feel good about ourselves and about the world around us. It makes us feel more optimistic, more hopeful, more spiritual . . . and closer to God.

"In the First Epistle of St. Peter, Chapter 3, we find these words: 'Finally, *be ye* all of one mind, having compassion one of another, love as brethren, *be* pitiful, *be* courteous.'

"Once you try to imagine how you can express charity in a non-material way, the list is endless, isn't it? Yes, let's remember those less fortunate at this time of the year. That goes without saying. But let's open our eyes to the opportunities in our lives every day. Maybe few will be as dramatic as what occurred in this town on Thanksgiving night, but they will be equally or even more rewarding for you, I promise," he concluded.

Ben gazed around at the congregation. Had he reached them? he wondered. Had his ideas and words penetrated in any meaningful way? He couldn't tell. It had seemed a good idea to depart from the sermon he'd prepared. Now as he left the pulpit to continue the service, he wasn't so sure. He didn't have that certain feeling he would sometimes get, a feeling of connection with his listeners. He was doubting what he had prepared and doubting what he had delivered off-the-cuff.

He saw Carolyn sitting a few rows from the front, beside Rachel and Jack. He tried to catch her eye, but she was looking down at her prayer book. Faulty connections despite the best intentions. It seemed an insidious pattern for him these days.

He turned and prepared to continue with the service. For the next forty minutes he forced himself to focus and ignore his wandering, negative thoughts.

Later, as Ben stood at the front doors to the church and greeted his parishioners, he felt as if he were only half-listening, as they spoke to him. But when Digger appeared, he suddenly felt less distracted.

"I enjoyed the service, Reverend," Digger said, in his typical fashion. "It's true what you said. The Lord was good to me and so were the good folks in this town. I won't forget it. But I wish, by now, everyone else would."

Ben winced inwardly, suddenly realizing how insensitive he had been. "I'm sorry if I made you uncomfortable, Digger. I certainly didn't mean to," he said sincerely. "I was trying to praise the volunteers who came out to help, but I didn't stop to consider that talking about it might embarrass you. That was thoughtless of me. I apologize."

"No apology necessary, Reverend. If the story perked up your sermon, you were welcome to it. It's just that I'm the shy type, you know," Digger said, in a joking tone.

"Shy? Give me a break," Sam Morgan protested from his place behind Digger in line. "The sermon was very good, Reverend. And worth thinking about," he added quietly.

"Thank you, Sam." *If ever there was a man who practiced just what I've been preaching, it has to be Sam Morgan,* Ben thought.

"By the way, Digger, I didn't see your name on the volunteer list for the Christmas Fair this year," Ben said, feeling a flash of inspiration. "You know we really could use more helpers who can handle tools and know how to put things together. Think you might have a few hours to spare for us?"

Digger's eyes brightened. "Well, Grace has been keeping me pretty occupied in the shop these days. It's the busy season, you know. But I suppose I could drop by and lend a hand. If you really need me . . ."

"We certainly do," Ben assured him. "The next meeting is Wednesday night in the all-purpose room. Fran Tulley is our chairperson this year. I'll have her call you."

"Okay, I'll be there. Maybe Grace will come along, too."

Ben tried not to show his pleasure at the suggestion. "I'm sure she'd be very welcome," he replied.

SINCE STARTING AT THE PAPER THE WEEK BEFORE, SARA HAD NOT ALlowed herself to take a real lunch break. She noticed how everyone else ate at their desks, still typing with one hand. She didn't want to look like a slacker, so she did the same.

But by Wednesday, she needed to get out of the office for a while. Wyatt had returned from the weekend tense and irritable. Their few hours of camaraderie the night of the snowstorm hadn't carried over to the workweek. For the last few days, in Wyatt's not-so-subtle opinion, Sara hadn't done anything right. At precisely twelve, she left some copy on his desk, grabbed her coat, and headed outside.

As she rounded Main Street, she considered the Beanery on the opposite corner. But the familiar blue sign for the Clam Box up ahead caught her eye, and she kept walking toward it.

She glanced at the signs in the window as she entered: "Box Lunches to Go" and "Try Our Famous Clam Rolls." For some reason, the faded cards made her smile. She left her job here only a month ago, but somehow it felt like years.

The Clam Box was always quite busy at the lunch hour. Sara stood behind a group of local businessmen waiting to be seated. The aromas of coffee, bacon, and home fries were heavy in the air, bringing her back instantly to her days waiting tables. She had liked working here at times. It had been a good way to get to know the people in town and get ideas for the short stories she liked to write. It also helped her to surreptitiously get to know Emily, who often stopped in.

Probably the best part of the job was making friends with Lucy. Sara glanced around but didn't see her. She hoped Lucy was in today. She had already eaten enough Clam Box cuisine to last a lifetime.

A waitress flew past; no one Sara recognized. *She must be my replacement,* she realized. She spotted an empty seat at the counter and sat down. At the far end, she saw Charlie at the grill, his back turned to her. Just as well, Sara thought. She opened her menu and tried to decide what to order.

"Well, hello, stranger!" Sara turned and saw Lucy standing behind her, her pretty face brightened by a huge smile. Lucy leaned forward and gave her a quick hug. "I thought you went to Maryland, not Mars."

"Sorry I didn't come by sooner. I started at the paper last week, and it's been really hectic."

"I'm only teasing. How was your visit with your folks?"

"Great. They're coming up here soon, around Christmastime. I hope you get to meet them."

"I will if you bring them in here," Lucy replied. "The meal will be on the house . . . but don't tell Charlie," she whispered.

"But don't tell Charlie" was a regular footnote to Lucy's conversations. It was clear to anyone who knew the couple that their marriage was tense and difficult, for Lucy especially. Sara knew more than most, especially about Lucy's struggle to go back to college, which Charlie still opposed.

"How are your courses going?" Sara asked. "Getting ready for finals?"

"Finals and papers and class presentations. I don't know how I'm going to get it all done. Right on top of Christmas, too," Lucy said, waving her order book. "I know it's a lot to ask with your new job and everything, but I hope you can help me out with some of my term papers. Just look them over?"

"Sure, no problem," Sara replied lightly. It really wasn't a problem. She liked helping Lucy and tried to encourage her.

"So how is the job going? I've read all your articles. They're great," Lucy said enthusiastically.

"It's going okay. It's harder than I thought, though," Sara admitted. "Wyatt Forbes makes me rewrite everything two or three times before he'll accept it. Then he ends up chopping it to bits or rewriting most of it himself. Makes me wonder why I bother."

"Oh, dear. Well, you're in the real world now, Sara. Sounds just like a boss to me. I'm sure he thinks you're terrific," Lucy consoled her. "It's not the same around here without you, honestly. But when I pick up the newspaper every morning and I see your name in print, I just sit back and say, 'Wow, that's my friend. She's a real reporter now.' "

Sara's smile widened. Lucy's lavish compliments made her almost feel embarrassed. But they did take the sting out of the rotten week she had been having at work.

The frantic ringing of the order bell distracted them both, and they looked down the counter to see Charlie, slamming his hand on the ringer again. "Order up, Lucy. Have you gone deaf on me or something?" he shouted at her.

"Just a minute. I'll be right there," Lucy called back.

Sara saw Charlie squinting down the counter, as if he didn't recognize her. Then he walked toward them.

"Well, look who's here," Charlie remarked. "Nice of you to drop in, Sara. I thought since you found out you were a Warwick, you decided you were too good for this place."

"Nice to see you, too, Charlie," Sara replied dryly.

"So how's it going at the *Messenger*? Convenient for your mother to have you working there, I guess. Now she doesn't have to worry. She's got the whole town in her pocket."

Sara expected as much from Charlie. He was bitter about his defeat in the election and took any opportunity to criticize Emily. But his words still stung. She was sure a lot of people agreed with him, though they might not say as much to her face.

"Charlie, what a thing to say! I think you owe Sara an apology."

Sara was shocked. She had rarely heard Lucy stand up to her husband that way.

Charlie scowled. "Sure, I'll apologize. Next time it snows on the Fourth of July. You remind me, honey," he said, turning his back to them.

"That's okay. You have a right to your opinions, Charlie, even if they're totally fallacious and misinformed." Sara didn't raise her voice, but she could tell from the way he rubbed the back of his neck that he heard her.

"Guess I'd better go." Sara grabbed her coat and scarf off the back of her chair. Her stomach growled with dismay at the sudden change in plans. So much for lunch.

"Sorry, Sara." Lucy reached out and touched her arm. "Can I fix you something quick to take out?"

Sara shook her head, then managed a small smile at her friend. "I really just stopped by to see you." She leaned toward Lucy and gave her a hug. "Let's get together sometime. Call me when you need help with your schoolwork."

"I will," Lucy promised. "So long now."

"Miss, can I have more coffee, please?" a man in a booth nearby called out. Both women turned to him at once, Sara feeling old reflexes kick in.

Then they looked at each other and laughed. "Go on and get out of here, before someone ties an apron on you," Lucy warned her.

Sara picked up a sandwich at a deli in town, then went straight back to the newspaper office. The moment she walked in, Jane and Ed both stopped working and looked up at her. She could tell from the expression on Jane's face that something had happened. Something bad.

"What's going on?" she asked Jane quietly.

Jane glanced over her shoulder at Wyatt. He was at his desk, going over some papers with Lindsay. "Nothing good. Don't panic, but you're in trouble."

"Me?" Sara heard her voice rise an octave at least. "What did I do?"

"It was that meeting this morning, the Zoning Board. You should have stayed until the end. Something happened. We missed the story—uh-oh, he wants you," Jane whispered, turning her back on Wyatt, so he couldn't see what she was saying.

"Sara, I need to talk to you. Back at my desk, please," Wyatt said curtly.

Sara felt her stomach twist into a million knots. She was suddenly glad she hadn't eaten anything. As she turned to face Wyatt, she felt Jane secretly squeeze her arm. "Hang in there," Jane whispered.

Sara turned and slowly walked back toward Wyatt. Lindsay was now working at a different desk, consulting long sheets of numbers and tapping on a calculator. She looked up at Sara as she passed and gave her a gentle smile but didn't say hello.

Sara's mouth suddenly felt so dry, she could barely speak. "You want to see me about something?"

Wyatt nodded. "I sent you to cover the zoning meeting this morning, and all you come back with is this?" He got to his feet, picked up the article she had handed in, and read her headline aloud in a mocking tone, " 'Zoning Board Questions Golf-Course Development Budget.' "

Sara swallowed again and nodded. "You told me to get the story on the golf-course construction, about the delays and how the builder has been running overbudget—"

"That's what I said. No argument there. But didn't you even read the agenda? Right after you left, they discussed a new proposal to open up the old Durham Point Yacht Club again—"

"But I thought you—"

"Wait, let me finish." Wyatt held up his hand, silencing her. "Apparently, during this part of the meeting—that you walked out on—a group from the Green Coalition broke in and tossed trash and bird feathers all over the board members. It was a real scene. The police came in to break it up and arrested a few of the protestors."

And any *part of that would have made a great photo for page one,* Sara silently finished for him.

"Now, we're stuck. The *Chronicle* will have the story tomorrow, and we'll have . . ." He squinted at her article. "Golf-course budget problems."

Sara suddenly felt as if she might cry. Lucy and Luke and even Emily might be impressed with her. But she wasn't a real reporter. Not by a long shot.

"I'm sorry, Wyatt," she managed. "It wasn't on the agenda you gave me this morning. They must have added it at the last minute."

"Of course they added it at the last minute. That's just the point. They were trying to sneak it by the Green guys . . . and by us." His voice rose on every word. Then he seemed to realize he'd been shouting. Sighing heavily, he sat down in his chair. He was silent for a moment, rearranging stacks of papers on his desk. Sara wondered if he was done chewing her out.

"What else are you working on today?" he asked suddenly.

"Um, let's see . . ." Sara was so nervous, her mind went blank. "There's a story about stiffer fines for unleashed dogs. . . ."

She was feeling more idiotic by the second. The leash-law story was even more trivial than the golf-course piece.

"All right. Hold on to that. Finish it tomorrow," he suggested. "In the meantime, why don't you proof this stuff for me?" He handed her a stack of copy.

"Sure." Sara looked down at the copy and back at Wyatt. She felt totally deflated. In five minutes she'd gone from rising new reporter to resident proofreader.

"Isn't there something we can do to get the story about the protest anyway?" she asked. "I could work on it, make some calls—"

"I put Jane on it. She's trying to pull it together. She might get an interview with one of the protestors later, after his bail hearing."

Sara cringed. She would have given anything to do that interview.

"Problem is, we run the risk of sounding sort of secondhand now. And no pictures," he added. "It's just not the way we want to do things."

"Sure, I understand." Sara nodded. "I'll be more careful next time. I just didn't realize."

"Obviously," Wyatt said. He picked up some copy from his in-box without looking at her, and Sara knew she'd been dismissed.

The rest of the afternoon dragged by. Sara did the proofreading and typed up some classified ads and public notices. She tried not to be distracted by the sound of Jane working on the big story she had missed, but it was hard not to listen in. Little by little, Jane pulled the pieces together using the phone and E-mail, interviewing board members, eyewitnesses, and even the officers who arrived at the scene.

A few minutes after three, Wyatt jumped up from his desk and yelled across the room, "Okay, Jane. They just called. Get down to the courthouse. They're releasing one of the protestors. His attorney says he'll talk to you."

Sitting midway between the two of them, Sara suddenly felt invisible—and useless.

Jane jumped up from her chair, grabbed her coat and shoulder bag, and headed for the door.

"Make it quick. I need you to write the story right away. And try to get a picture of somebody," Wyatt called after her.

"Got it. See you later." As Jane flew through the door, she cast Sara a sympathetic glance.

Sara knew her colleague wasn't trying to make her look bad. She was only doing her job. Jane could be trusted to come back with the story. *And I can't,* Sara thought dismally.

* * *

THAT NIGHT WHEN SARA GOT HOME, SHE FOUND A MESSAGE FROM EMILY on her machine. "I'm just calling about tonight. I'm sorry but something came up, and I'm stuck in the office. Can we get together later in the week, maybe Saturday night? Let me know. I hope everything is going well, honey. Give me a call tomorrow if you can. Okay, bye."

With all the distraction, Sara had forgotten that she and Emily were supposed to get together that night. Just as well, Sara thought. Though she knew Emily would have done her best to cheer her up, she didn't feel like seeing anyone tonight.

She fixed dinner, then stretched out on the couch and wrote in her journal for a while, but even that familiar remedy didn't improve her mood. Her writing sounded like one long whining session. She shut the leather-bound book, feeling even more upset with herself.

The windows in the living room rattled softly in the wind. The old house was drafty, and Sara pulled an afghan over herself. Outside, her street was quiet, as usual. The recent snowfall still covered the ground and clung to the telephone wires and trees.

She wasn't used to the snow and cold. She wasn't sure she wanted to get used to it. The winter had just begun. It would snow a lot more, to hear the locals tell it. What was she doing here? Maybe she should go home, back to Winston. Maybe she wasn't cut out to be a reporter, even in a small town like this one. She hadn't majored in journalism. Her major had been literature, and she wanted to write short stories or a novel. Maybe she ought to go back to waitressing or some other mindless job and try writing fiction in her spare time, the way she did when she worked at the diner. . . .

The sound of the phone ringing broke into her thoughts. She didn't want to speak to anyone, and she let the machine pick it up. It was probably her parents. They hadn't really wanted her to come back here. If she spoke to them tonight, they had a good chance of persuading her to come home, she thought.

But instead she heard Luke. "Hi, Sara. It's me. I guess you're not around right now. I just called to say hello—"

Before he could hang up, she jumped up and grabbed the phone. "Hi, I'm here. Sort of."

"Sort of? Is something wrong? You sound funny."

"I'm just tired." She paused, wondering if she should say more. "I had a bad day at work. I really screwed up."

"You did? What happened?" Luke's tone was interested and concerned, yet somehow, distant enough that she felt able to relate the story.

He listened without interrupting, then said, "Wyatt again."

"Well, he's my boss. And he's making me totally miserable."

"I know. He's not my favorite person," Luke said loyally.

"Or mine," Sara said. "Still, I'm lucky he didn't fire me on the spot. But it looks like I'm going to get grunt work from here on in. Unless he's absolutely desperate."

"Look, you made a mistake, but you've only been there a week. It's not like people are born knowing these things. You just have to pay your dues for a while. It's no big deal."

"It *is* a big deal. I was so embarrassed, I wanted to stick my head under the desk for the rest of the day."

She could tell that Luke was trying hard not to laugh at her. "I know it seems bad tonight, but don't get discouraged," he said kindly. "Your boss will get over it. Tomorrow, he'll be all excited about something else."

"Yeah, I guess he will," Sara agreed, realizing that Luke's words had calmed her, partly because he didn't gloss over the truth. She should have known that she wasn't going to be the best reporter in the history of the *Messenger* from day one. There was a lot she had to learn. She only wished now her first lesson hadn't been delivered in such a humiliating way.

She suddenly missed Luke and wished they were together. His advice was solid and his sympathy, warming. But one of his strong hugs would have been nice right now, too.

"So, how is your week going?" she asked. "Better than mine, I hope."

"That wouldn't take much," he said, making her laugh. "We've been working inside since the snow. Digger was here one day. We had him painting, and he did all right—a neat job. And I've been to school a few times, sitting in on classes. Adolescent psychology, fascinating stuff. If only I knew then what I know now."

"I doubt much got past you. Like for instance?"

"Like how to ask a girl out on a date. So when can I see you? How's Saturday night?" he said, with a touch of laughter in his voice.

"Saturday? Sure. Oh, wait. I might be seeing Emily. We were going to have dinner tonight, but she had to cancel. Would Friday be okay?"

"Friday's fine," he said agreeably. "An entire day sooner. Can't complain about that."

She thought of their last date, the closeness she'd felt, the way they'd kissed while walking through Newburyport. *An entire day sooner would be fine with me, too,* she thought.

"Great. I'm looking forward to it," she said.

"Me, too. Good night, Sara. And don't worry. You've got the right stuff. It's all going to work out. Just give it some time."

She smiled. "Thanks for saying that—and for listening to me."

"It's just true," he replied quietly. "And don't worry so much about what Wyatt Forbes thinks."

"Okay, I'll try not to," she said. Then she said good night again and hung up the phone.

She really hadn't wanted to talk to anyone tonight, but Luke had helped her put things in perspective. As she got undressed for bed, she didn't feel nearly as bad about going in to work tomorrow.

What would I do without him? she wondered, as she slid under her covers.

LUCY HEARD CHARLIE UNLOCKING THE FRONT DOOR. SHE GLANCED UP at the kitchen clock. It was half past eleven. She knew he was exhausted from working all day and would be in no mood to hear her out. But there were things that had to be said. She'd been practicing in her head all night, waiting for him.

"You're still up?" he said, as he walked into the kitchen. "You have to help me open up tomorrow. Did you forget?"

"I had some homework to do." She looked up from her textbooks, which were spread out on the kitchen table. "I'll be all right."

"Homework, right." He looked down at her books and shook his head. "I don't know why you knock yourself out like this, Lucy. What are you trying to prove? I just don't get it."

"I'm not trying to prove anything. We've already been through this a hundred times. I want to finish my degree and go to nursing school. Why is that so hard for you to understand?"

He pulled open the refrigerator door and stared inside. "You're fooling yourself. You'll never finish. You're just making life more difficult for everyone in this house until you give up."

Lucy wanted to put her hands over her ears so that she couldn't hear him, but she willed herself to sit back in her seat and not rise to his bait.

"I will finish. It may take me a while, but I'm going to do it," she said quietly. "With or without your support, Charlie."

"Oh, I'm supporting you, all right. Paying the bills around here, aren't I? The mortgage, the cars, the insurance. I just wish I could come home and find the house in some kind of order or have some clean socks when I need them. This place is a wreck lately, in case you haven't noticed."

"The semester is ending. I have a lot of school work—papers due, tests to study for. . . ." She gestured at the pile of books on the table. "In case *you* haven't noticed."

"How could I not? It's all you seem to do lately. School, school, school," he complained. "What about this family? Aren't we important to you?"

She stared at him, too tired to defend herself again. She sighed and shook her head. How could she be a perfect housekeeper when she worked in the diner almost as many hours as he did and took care of the children and went to school?

"Looks like I'm the one who has to do all the work in this marriage," he said in a self-righteous tone.

Lucy fought back a stab of white-hot anger. They'd had this same argument so many times, she just couldn't stand hearing it anymore.

"This is hopeless," she said suddenly. "Absolutely hopeless."

He sniffed and glanced down at the table. "Trying to go to school, you mean?"

"No, not school. Our relationship. Our marriage, Charlie. It's hopeless. I can't do this anymore."

Charlie shook his head and touched his ear, as if he thought something was wrong with his hearing. "What do you mean, you can't do this anymore? What's that supposed to mean?"

Lucy took a breath. She felt tears well up in her eyes but forced herself not to cry.

"We're always fighting, always at each other. I don't want to live like this anymore."

"Oh, well, how do you want to live? You want to split up? Is that what you're saying? If you would just quit school . . ."

His voice sounded half-angry and half-scared, she thought. The scared part gave her a bit of hope and courage.

"We were on this road long before I went back to school. Things have been bad between us for a long time, and you know it," she insisted. "We need to get some help. We need to see a counselor to help us work things out."

"Oh, a counselor." He waved his hand at her. "What's some counselor going to tell you? I don't want to sit and tell some stranger all my personal problems."

"It wouldn't have to be a stranger. Reverend Ben could give us marriage counseling."

"He could, huh? It sounds like you've already spoken to him about it. Have you been talking about me to Reverend Ben?" he demanded.

Lucy met his angry stare, but soon looked away. She could easily lie and avoid more of his anger, she realized. He would never know. But she didn't want to. It was time to have this out.

"Yes, I've spoken to him a few times. Ever since I decided I wanted to go back to college, and you wouldn't let me. He suggested we go to see him together. He thinks it will help."

"I can't believe this." Charlie shook his head, looking even angrier. "I can't believe you've been complaining about me to Reverend Ben for months now, and you never said a word."

"Not complaining, Charlie. Talking things through. I've needed some advice, someone to talk to," she insisted. She took a deep breath and blew her nose. "I'm at the end of my rope. That's all I know. Will you see him with me—or not?"

Charlie stared at her. "What happens if I say no? Then what?"

Lucy shrugged. "I don't know. I haven't thought that far ahead."

"You'd never leave me. Where would you live? Where would you work?"

"I don't know," she said honestly. "I guess, if the time came, I'd just have to figure it out."

"But you couldn't. Not by yourself, that's just the thing. And what about the boys? I know you. You'd pull the moon out of the sky if it would make those kids happy. It would crush them if we split up, and you'd never do that to them," he said, sounding as if he'd suddenly looked down and found the winning card in his hand.

It was true. She couldn't stand the idea of hurting the boys. But they weren't babies anymore. Charlie Junior was ten and Jamie was eight, and Lucy was starting to wonder if it was any better for them to hear their parents arguing every minute. That couldn't be good either, she reasoned.

And what about her own happiness, her own sense of well-being? She had always put that last on the list, if at all. But lately she was beginning to see that it counted. It counted a lot. She deserved to be happy. She deserved better than this, at least.

"Listen, Charlie. I'm just not going to argue with you anymore. You don't even have to answer me right now. Think it over. I'm not packing my bags and running off anywhere. I'm willing to try to make things better. But I want us to see Reverend Ben. That's what I want. You think about it, and let me know what you want to do."

Her tone was quiet but firm. Charlie met her gaze. He seemed unsteady on his feet, like a prizefighter in a late round, she thought. His eyes looked red rimmed and bloodshot.

"I want to go to bed, that's what I want to do," he said flatly. "Are you coming?"

"No. I have more work to do." She picked up her highlighting pen and looked down at her textbook again. *As if I'll be able to concentrate now.*

"Suit yourself. Don't forget to turn the lights off," he said in a tired voice.

Lucy listened as he walked through the dark house and climbed the stairs. She felt scared all of a sudden, as if she had turned a corner and made a choice that was irreversible.

She looked down at her textbook and the words blurred. Then she clasped her hands together and squeezed her eyes shut.

Dear Lord, I don't know what came over me tonight. I just had to be honest with Charlie about the way I feel. Please help us see our way through this mess. It doesn't look that good. I'm not sure I should have pushed him like that. But I can't see how things can get better if we go on this way. Please help me to do the right thing, Lord. Please help me and my family.

Chapter Nine

By the time Sara returned to work on Thursday, she had resigned herself to the possibility that Wyatt would never trust her to cover another important story for the rest of her life. Time to pay your dues, she told herself, recalling Luke's words.

Sipping her morning coffee, she polished up some short articles, including a report on the village's new leash law. When she handed the copy in, Wyatt handed her piles of proofreading and, after that, other grunt work. Meanwhile, Jane and Ed were rushing in and out, talking on the phone, clacking away at their keyboards, as they gathered the day's news.

Sara cringed every time she heard Wyatt talking about Jane's coverage of the zoning meeting. The *Messenger* had scooped the *Chronicle* with Jane's interview of the head protestor and a photo that included the man holding up a fistful of feathers. A bit staged perhaps, but eye-catching. The feathers had been Jane's brainstorm, and she had resorted to pulling them out of her own down jacket. Wyatt was so impressed that he promised the paper would buy her a new one.

Sara had to listen to him all day on the phone, bragging about how his paper had pulled the story out of the fire at the last minute after their first reporter—who thankfully remained nameless—had totally messed up.

Friday passed in much the same way. As far as Sara could tell, Wyatt still hadn't hired anyone to fill the vacant clerical position, and more and more of that work was coming her way. The only plus was working with Lindsay, since Wyatt's sister seemed to be handling the business end of things now.

Lindsay was calmer than her brother and more organized. She didn't condescend to Sara but took time to explain what she needed clearly, not assuming Sara would automatically know what she had to do.

She appeared at Sara's desk midway through the morning. "I need you to organize these invoices for me; what's been paid in this folder, and what's due in this one. Sometimes it's hard to tell. Gloria was a little sloppy, even though my father thought she was a genius," Lindsay noted, with a wry grin. "Check in the computer when they look iffy, and mark the questionable ones with a sticky."

"No problem." Sara nodded, accepting the menial task as best as she could.

"Listen," Lindsay said, "I know this isn't what you signed on for. But in a small shop, we all have to pitch in. Besides, it's good for you to see the different aspects of running a paper. It's not always about chasing after a hot story. Or even a dull one, for that matter. If not for the boring stuff, we wouldn't have any revenue."

"I guess not," Sara said, meeting her gaze.

Lindsay touched her shoulder. "Don't worry. You'll get back to it. For one thing, Wyatt doesn't have enough staff. Ed's so spoiled, he hardly works anymore, except for that glorious column of his," she confided, with a smile.

"So I noticed." Sara smiled, too. "How did you get to know so much about the paper?"

"If you grew up in our house, it was all you really heard about, morning, noon, and night. You couldn't help learning how it was run," she joked. "I worked here summers and weekends, too, just like Wyatt. I even wrote a little bit. But that's not my thing," she added. "The newspaper is really like any small business. Once Wyatt sees that, he'll take the problems in stride. I think he overreacted a little on Wednesday. Give him time, and he'll get over it."

That made Sara feel a little better. Lindsay seemed so calm and steady compared to Wyatt. Wyatt's mercurial temperament and creativity made him interesting, exciting to be around—he definitely had charm—but those same traits made him hard to work for, Sara decided. She wished Lindsay had more say in running the *Messenger.*

Sara got to work on the invoices. Wyatt didn't speak to her all that day, so Sara was surprised when he called her back to his desk a little before five. He looked tired and frazzled, as usual, with uncombed hair and a shadow of a beard on his lean face. Somehow it all looked good on him.

He sat back in his chair and rubbed the back of his neck. "You could help me out with a little problem tonight, Sara," he began. "The Rotary is going to present their Community Leader of the Year Award at a banquet in town. Can you cover it?"

"Sure, no problem," she said quickly, trying not to sound so excited that he could guess her fear of being forever exiled to the unsorted invoice piles.

"Good. It's at the Bailey House Inn, up near the turnpike. Starts at six. You're dressed okay, I guess," he said, taking in her burgundy turtleneck, long black wool skirt, and boots. Wyatt's appraising gaze made her feel self-conscious. She was relieved when he looked back down at the rough sketch of a layout on his desk.

"I have a huge hole in page three, and this Rotary story better fill it. Get what you need, come right back, and write it up. I'll patch it in last thing."

"Sure, I'll come right back. Anything else?" she asked, worried suddenly about missing something he assumed she would know. Like there would be an unscheduled appearance of the president of the United States at the end of the evening, and she might leave early and miss it.

He shrugged. "Don't forget your camera?"

Sara felt warm color start to rise in her cheeks and turned so he couldn't see. "Don't worry. I won't."

Okay, the story was a no-brainer, but she was relieved to be called back into action so quickly. Lindsay had been right. Wyatt really needed her, like it or not.

Sara had her coat on when she remembered her date with Luke. She groaned, realizing she had to cancel on him. She quickly punched in his number, glancing over her shoulder to see if Wyatt was watching. But he wasn't in the main office. He's probably in the darkroom, she thought, grateful for the privacy.

"Hey, how are you doing? I was just going to call you," Luke answered, sounding happy to hear her voice. "Home already?"

"Um . . . no. I'm still at work." She twisted the phone cord around her hand. "Something's come up. Wyatt asked me to cover a story tonight, some Rotary club banquet. And after what happened on Wednesday, I can't say no. He's had me doing mostly clerical work all week. It's been really awful," she added in a hushed tone.

"You know, I'm liking that guy less every day," Luke said slowly. "What about later, after it's over? We can get together for coffee or something," he suggested.

Sara sighed. "I have to come back and write the article. He needs to run it in Monday's edition. I may be here awhile." She waited for Luke to answer, but he didn't say anything. She knew he was disappointed and felt bad about letting him down. But he understood the pressure she was facing, didn't he?

"What about tomorrow night?" she suggested. "I was supposed to see Emily, but I can change that. She won't mind."

"Sorry, I'm going up to Boston to see my family. When you said you were busy, I promised to drive my mother down to Connecticut for a family party. My dad is out of town for some retired police officers' convention."

Sara was surprised by his plan but thought it was a good sign. When he was kicked off the police force, Luke's relationship with his family grew strained. His two older brothers were both cops, as was his father, a retired detective who took Luke's failure personally. Little by little, Luke had been trying to mend those frayed connections.

"Oh, so I guess you'll be gone the whole weekend then," she said.

"Yeah, that's the plan."

A tense silence fell between them. Sara knew that when Luke's feelings were hurt he grew quiet, as quiet as a stone. She wanted to say the right thing, but didn't know what to say.

She heard Wyatt come back into the main office, shuffling things at his desk. *I should be out of here by now, on my way to that Rotary meeting.*

"Listen, I'm sorry," she said, sounding rushed. "But I just have to do this."

"I know. I'll call you when I get back. We'll get together next week. It's no big deal."

Although he had said the right words, Sara didn't find his tone of voice reassuring.

They said good-bye, and Sara hung up. Then she picked up her knapsack and left the office. She had been given another chance but at a cost, she realized. Why was everything so complicated?

"OKAY, NAME YOUR THREE FAVORITE JIMMY STEWART MOVIES." EMILY set a huge bowl of popcorn on the coffee table, and Sara leaned over and took a handful.

"Let's see, that's a tough one." Sara chewed thoughtfully. "*It's a Wonderful Life*, of course."

"Of course," Emily agreed.

"Then I guess I'd have to say *Mr. Smith Goes to Washington.* And, wait . . . I nearly forgot *Vertigo.*"

"Jimmy Stewart was great in the Hitchcock movies, too," Emily agreed, "but *It's a Wonderful Life* is in a class of its own. I have to see it at least once a year. I usually save it for the night I wrap my Christmas gifts, but I was glad you picked it out for tonight."

"Me, too," Sara said sincerely. It had been great fun to watch the old classic with Emily. Between the two of them, they knew just about every line. Being with Emily had taken her mind off her problems at work and with Luke.

Then out of the clear blue, Emily said, "So where's Luke tonight?"

"Visiting his folks for the weekend. Why do you ask?"

"No reason." Emily shrugged. "I just wondered why you were free to see me tonight."

Sara caught her eye. "I don't see him *every* Saturday night. I mean, it's not like we're going out or anything."

"Sorry, I thought you were. I must have misunderstood." Emily picked up a mug of tea and took a sip.

"Well, we do go out sometimes. We get along really well, but it's not really serious or anything. You know how it is," Sara concluded.

"No, I don't know really. But that's okay. I don't mean to pry." She paused, as if considering what to say next. "Luke seems . . . serious."

"Well, he can seem sort of tough and distant, I guess. Until you get to know him."

"Serious about you, I mean," Emily clarified, glancing at her. Sara looked away. She knew what Emily had meant; she was just trying to avoid getting into this conversation. She suddenly felt that Emily *was* prying, and it made her uncomfortable.

"He cares for you a lot," Emily continued in a careful tone.

"Yes, I know." Sara stretched her legs out and crossed her arms over her chest. "I'd really rather not talk about Luke, though. If you don't mind."

"Oh . . . sure. I didn't mean to pry." Emily looked uneasy, even embarrassed, and Sara regretted that her words had sounded so sharp.

Sara shrugged, feeling uneasy now herself. "I just feel . . . well, my relationship with Luke is private. I'm not ready to share it with the world at large."

Emily nodded. "Sure. I understand."

But Sara could tell from Emily's expression that she'd now hurt her even more. Emily didn't consider herself "the world at large." She clearly thought she and Sara had a closer connection by now. And they did. Still, it was one of those moments that made Sara keenly aware of the fact that she and her birth mother really didn't know each other very well yet. They were trying and making progress day by day. But they still had a lot of lost time to make up for.

Sara didn't know what to say—or if she should say anything more.

Emily nursed her mug of tea. "By the way, what are you doing for Christmas? Will you be going back to Maryland again?"

Emily's question sounded casual, but Sara knew that her answer mattered. "I'll be around."

"Oh, good." Emily sounded surprised. She paused. Sara sensed that she wanted to ask something and felt nervous about it. Finally she said, "Jessica is having a Christmas Eve party and asked me to invite you. I guess I'll be at my mother's on Christmas Day. You're welcome to come there as well, if you like," she added hopefully.

Sara hadn't really thought about what she would do over the holidays in Cape Light. She had assumed she would see Emily at some point, but she wasn't sure how or when. The idea of both parties seemed a little overwhelming. Then again, why was she staying here if not to get to know Emily and the Warwicks better? She knew that the party at Jessica and Sam's would probably be a lot of fun. People in town were still talking about the engagement party the couple gave back in September.

"Sure, count me in on both. I'd love to come," Sara said.

"Great." Emily looked so happy, she practically beamed. Sara still wasn't used to the pleasure Emily took just from being around her. It was touching, an ever-present reminder that her birth mother loved her and had never really wanted to give her up.

At times, though, Sara felt pressured by Emily's love. Sometimes she just needed to take a breath and step back—even knowing her withdrawal would hurt Emily's feelings.

"I spoke to my folks today. They're coming up to New England the day after Christmas and will stay until Sunday. They're really looking forward to meeting you," Sara said.

"I'm looking forward to meeting them, too." Emily still smiled, but her blue eyes had clouded over, Sara noticed. Of course she'd be nervous about meeting Sara's parents. Sara could tell her parents felt the same way about meeting Emily. Sara already felt as if she'd been negotiating between the two camps, and part of her dreaded the event.

"I thought we could all have dinner together one night. But I wasn't sure where we should go," Sara said.

"Hmm, let me think. The Pequot Inn is nice. Very New England, if they're looking for atmosphere," Emily said. "And the food is good, too."

Her parents would be so distracted studying Emily, Sara doubted they'd notice the ambiance or the food. But she thought the suggestion was a good one.

"That sounds good. I'll check it out," Sara said. "I've also told them about Lillian," she added, with a smile. "They're dying to meet her, too."

"We'll have to arrange it then," Emily promised. "But you know how your grandmother gets. We'll have to catch her in a good mood."

"They'll only be here for five days. I'm not sure that will be enough time."

Emily laughed and shook her head. "How well you've come to know her already."

BEN DISCREETLY CHECKED HIS WATCH. THE BATESES HAD BEEN IN HIS office for nearly an hour but hadn't made much progress. On Wednesday nights, he usually made hospital visits, but when Lucy had finally asked to come in for counseling, he had willingly rearranged his schedule for them.

Lucy had done most of the talking so far, while Charlie sat scowling, occasionally barking, "That's not true," at her. Now they were both sitting silent and sullen, mired in their own thoughts and anger.

Deciding that this silence was not a productive one, Ben turned to Charlie. "Lucy has said that you are negative about her returning to school, and that makes it even harder for her. Do you want to say anything about that?"

"What can I say?" Charlie shrugged, his gaze fixed straight ahead. "I pay for her tuition and books and the baby-sitting, don't I? She's cut down her hours at work. That's costing me, too. You ask me, I'm making things easy for her."

"I'm not talking about the money, Charlie. I mean your attitude, the things you say," Lucy replied.

"Of course, you're not talking about money, Lucy. You don't give a thought to what this is costing us. Or you wouldn't be doing it."

"I work in that diner day and night and have for years. But I've never once seen a real paycheck," Lucy declared. "Charlie takes some money from the business account every month and puts it in our house account and says it's for the both of us. But when I want to spend it on something, it's *his* money."

"The reverend isn't interested in our financial arrangements. That's private," Charlie said harshly.

"Let's just back up a moment—" Reverend Ben cut in. He took a deep breath. *Lord, help me out here. Their problems are deep. I feel as if I'm walking in quicksand.*

"Money issues are a problem for many couples, and we'll talk about that, too, at some point," Ben said in what he hoped was a calming tone. "But right now, I think it would help to get back to something Lucy said, Charlie. She said it wasn't about the cost of school. She said it was your attitude."

"My attitude, huh? That's a good one." Charlie took a deep breath but didn't say anything more. He didn't have to. His body language said it all, Ben thought. Charlie sat staring straight ahead, with his arms crossed solidly over his chest, his jaw set, the very definition of a stone lion. The body was present, but the spirit was not willing, Ben thought, paraphrasing the biblical verse.

Lucy had twisted around in her armchair, with her back toward her husband. When she needed to talk to him, she had to glance over her shoulder. Mostly, she looked the other way, dabbing her eyes with a tissue.

"A man has a right to his opinions. In his own house, no less," Charlie said. "You know it even says in the Bible that a woman should obey her husband. Doesn't it, Reverend?"

Ben sighed inwardly. Leave it to Charlie to point to the Bible to justify his behavior, when it was Lucy who attended every Sunday and showed far more kindness, compassion, and patience every other day of the week.

"Good point, Charlie. Let's take a look at what the Bible says, shall we?" Reverend Ben picked up the Good Book sitting on the right-hand side of his desk and opened to the New Testament. "Let's see, here's the First Epistle General of St. Peter, Chapter 3. I think this might be the passage you're remembering. 'Likewise, ye wives, *be* in subjection to your own husbands. . . .' " He looked up at Charlie. "Is that what you mean?"

"Exactly." Charlie sat back, looking satisfied. "Hear that, Lucy? *In subjection.* That means you need to obey me."

"Let's see what it says about husbands," Ben continued, ignoring the look of dismay on Lucy's face. "Same chapter, a little bit further down. 'Likewise, ye husbands, dwell with *them* according to knowledge, giving honor unto the wife, as unto the weaker vessel, and as being heirs together of the grace of life. . . .' "

Ben looked up and met Charlie's eye. "It says, 'giving honor to the wife.' What do you think that means?"

Charlie shrugged and looked away. "You got me. What does it mean, Reverend?"

"It means you need to respect my feelings more, Charlie. You need to listen to what I say and take it seriously," Lucy cut in, before Ben could speak.

Charlie shook his head, looking suddenly infuriated. "Your feelings! I'm sick and tired of hearing about your blasted feelings!"

"Charlie, calm down," Lucy said, clearly embarrassed. But instead Charlie stood up.

"Just a moment, Charlie. Lucy—" Ben tried to restore order to the scene, but it was no use.

"I'm out of here," Charlie grumbled, grabbing his jacket and heading for the door. "I told you this wouldn't work."

Lucy got to her feet, too. "Charlie, what are you doing? You can't just get up and go like that!" she called, as the door slammed shut behind her husband.

"Just let him go, Lucy. It's all right," Ben said quietly.

She stared at the door for a moment, then sat down again, looking stunned. "I knew this wasn't going to work, but I guess I just had to try," she said.

"There are some serious problems here, Lucy. But at least you and Charlie made a start tonight. Nothing can be solved in one meeting. You know that," Ben said, reaching for something positive in the encounter.

"You don't understand, Reverend. I just don't think I can stand it anymore. You saw how he acted, the things he said. He doesn't even want to try to fix things between us. He won't even admit that there's anything wrong."

"Yes, I know, Lucy. I know what you mean," Ben consoled her. "But Charlie took a big step just by coming here tonight. He may not openly admit he needs to change, but he's thinking about it."

"Well, I'm not sure about that. More likely, he just came here tonight, because I forced him to. I doubt I'll ever get him back in here, and I know he won't treat me any differently," Lucy said sadly. "And if that's the case, I just can't . . . can't stay married to him," she finished, as she started crying again.

"That's a very strong statement to make, Lucy," Ben said quietly. He patted her shoulder and gave her a moment to compose herself.

"I know it's strong. . . . But it's true. I guess I've felt this way for a while, but I've always been afraid to say it," she admitted.

Ben felt alarmed. He knew what she said was true. He had sensed as much over the months. He only hoped it wasn't too late to help them.

"It's been a difficult night for both of you. You're upset. It's hard to see anything clearly right now," Ben told her. "Promise me that you'll just get a good night's rest and try to put these troubles aside for a while?"

Lucy glanced up at him, her eyes dry again. "I honestly don't know that I can do that," she said. "But I'll try, Reverend . . . and thank you for seeing us tonight," she added, as she rose and picked up her coat and purse.

"No thanks necessary," he replied, as he watched her go.

Alone in his office Ben sat at his desk, wondering if he had done them any good at all. He felt his doubts about his own abilities swell up, like a wave rising out of the ocean.

One reason he had become a minister was because he believed he had a God-given talent for bringing comfort and for helping people sort out their problems. The problems between Lucy and Charlie Bates ran deep, no doubt. No one was going to untangle those threads in one or even two counseling sessions. Yet, somehow, he felt he had failed them.

They had parted even angrier and at a greater emotional distance than when they came in. Wasn't he partly to blame for that? He just didn't know anymore.

He sat back in his chair. A framed photo of his family on his windowsill caught his eye. It was an old one, taken on a camping trip in Maine. Rachel and Mark were just teenagers. Ben picked it up and held it in his hand. That had been a good vacation, he recalled, a trip that had brought the family closer, despite all of Mark's problems in school at that time. Things had begun to smooth out a bit. He and Carolyn had felt hopeful that the bad times were behind them.

But nothing had ever been really resolved. Maybe real resolution was too much to ask for. His mother used to say that life is never perfect; there are only happy moments, beams of sunlight breaking through the clouds.

Now his failure to heal the wounds in his own family seemed to cast a shadow over everything—over the Bateses' marriage and even his eagerness to see his new grandchild. Rachel and Carolyn both felt Mark's absence keenly, and Ben sensed they somehow blamed him for it.

He sighed and began to clear off his desk, preparing to go home for the night. He reached for his Bible but instead of closing it, he flipped through the pages, pausing at a familiar passage in the book of Ecclesiastes. "Whatsoever thy hand findeth to do, do *it* with thy might. . . ."

He had always tried to follow those words in his work as a minister—to go the limit for his congregation. And he always believed he did the same for his family. He thought he had done everything possible to show Mark that they wanted him to come home. But Carolyn didn't seem to agree. Maybe she was right.

Ben knew he had felt himself pull back, put a limit on how far he was willing to reach out to his son. And that was wrong, a stingy, miserly way to love. He was the parent. He had to make the extra effort, even if that meant flying out to Montana.

The important thing, Ben told himself, was that he didn't lose hope that this would somehow work out—that the good Lord would, in his own way, bring them together. There might be some solution to their problem they hadn't tried yet.

He sat up straight as an idea occurred to him. It might not work, but it was worth talking to Carolyn about.

As Ben left his office, he heard voices coming from the all-purpose room at the back of the church. He walked up to the doorway and peered inside. The Christmas Fair volunteers, he realized. He had forgotten they were meeting tonight.

Nobody noticed him standing there. Sophie Potter sat in the middle of one group, showing the others how to make something with pinecones and candles—holiday centerpieces, perhaps.

Carolyn looked up at him and smiled. He smiled back, then glanced at the other table and saw not only Digger Hegman, but Grace as well. Their group was using scraps of wood to make decorative plaques and birdhouses. Digger was carefully painting the roof on his, while Grace helped Fran Tulley with a glue gun.

"Hello, everyone. How's it going?" Ben asked.

They all looked up and greeted him—all except Grace who met his eyes for a second, then looked down again, as if she had not wanted him to see her there.

Seeing her working on the Christmas Fair was hardly the same as seeing her seated in a pew on Sunday morning. But she was getting closer, Ben thought. He wondered if she had told Digger the truth about his health.

"Want to join us, Reverend? We could use a few more men in the ranks," Digger joked, glancing around at the ladies.

"I'm better with setting up the tables—and sampling the bake sale," Ben replied, with a smile. "I was just on my way out, actually. Do you need a lift, honey?" he asked his wife.

Carolyn glanced at her watch. She took part in these efforts enthusiastically, as if there was nothing more she wanted to do on a Wednesday night than sit in the drafty all-purpose room and make pinecone centerpieces. He knew that there had to be times when she wished she wasn't the minister's wife.

"I think I will leave with you, Ben. I have an early day tomorrow," Carolyn said. She rose gracefully and took her coat from a pile on the next table. They didn't speak at all until they got outside.

"Where's your car, dear?" Ben asked his wife.

"I walked over. Needed the exercise," she said, tugging on her gloves. She was walking a lot lately, he thought. It was her way of coping with stress sometimes.

The night was cold and clear. He looked out over the snow-covered green—the tall, brightly lit tree at the far end—and out on the water, at the harbor lights.

"Why don't we walk a little?" he suggested. "I could use the air."

"All right." She glanced at him with a questioning look but fell into step alongside him.

They walked down a path that crossed the green to the harbor side. Carolyn walked with her hands in her pockets, but Ben twined his arm through hers anyway. "I've been thinking about our argument," he said. "We never really talked about it."

"I don't know that there's anything more to say," she replied quietly.

He took a deep breath. "I've given this some thought. You wanted to think of something more we could do to persuade Mark to come home. I think he has to make up his own mind to do it," he admitted. "But I did have an idea. What if we book him a flight and send him the tickets? I don't see how we could make our desire to have him here for Christmas any clearer than that. Then if he still doesn't come, maybe we should think of going out there after the baby is born."

Carolyn stopped walking and turned to face him. "I thought of sending him tickets, too . . . but I didn't want to bring it up. I thought you'd argue with me about it," she said.

Her admission made him sad. He suddenly thought of Charlie and Lucy Bates, how the failure to compromise—or even communicate honestly—had so eroded their relationship. He never wanted that to happen between him and Carolyn.

"Then would you like to send him the tickets?" Ben asked.

"Is that what you really want to do, Ben? Or are you just trying to appease me?"

Giving into her because he was afraid of her depression, he translated. Not treating her as an equal.

"It's a stretch for me, Carolyn. I won't deny that. But I believe it's what we have to do, as parents. I think we'll both feel better knowing we've gone the absolute limit to reach out to him. So, yes, I'm willing to try it."

"What made you change your mind? The other night you seemed to feel so differently," she persisted.

"Honestly? I do miss him. More than you realize. Maybe I've reached the point where I'm willing to say, I just want to see him on any terms, too."

Carolyn was silent for a moment. "Well, you know how I feel then. Thank you, Ben."

"You don't have to thank me. We're in this together," he replied. "We can call the airlines tonight when we get home and call Mark right away."

"Yes, we had better call right away," she agreed, her face lit with a happiness that made him even warier. Once again they were about to supply Mark with yet another means of disappointing them. But he had to risk it, Ben realized. It was important to Carolyn that they at least try.

They had reached the Christmas tree, and Carolyn stopped to look at it. "This big old pine tree is just standing here, all year round. But I don't think anybody really notices it until they turn the lights on."

"Just like God," Ben said, gazing up at it. "He's standing there twenty-four hours a day, every day, patient and stalwart and evergreen. But some people only seem to notice him at Christmas time."

"Oh, Ben." Carolyn smiled and patted his arm. "No wonder you're a minister."

He glanced at her. "You think it was that inevitable?"

"Oh, yes. Don't you?"

He didn't answer for a moment. "I suppose. Sometimes I do wonder, though," he admitted quietly. He took her arm again. "Ready to go home?"

"Yes, let's go home." She nodded and seemed to walk closer to him, he thought.

* * *

AS SOON AS SARA GOT HOME ON WEDNESDAY NIGHT, SHE REALIZED THAT she hadn't gotten back to Luke. He had called her a few times since he returned from Boston. They just kept missing each other. She checked the kitchen clock. It was late, nearly eleven, but better to have him annoyed at her because she woke him up than to hurt his feelings by not calling at all, she decided.

At first, she heard the machine and started to leave a message. Then Luke's sleepy voice came on the line. "Sara?"

"Hi. I hope I didn't wake you up."

"No, I just dozed off on the couch, trying to read one of these textbooks. Did you just get in?"

Sara paused. The question felt a little like he was checking up on her. But she tried not to be defensive.

"I had to work late. One of us usually has to stay with Wyatt to help get the paper out. It was my turn tonight."

"Why does he need help? I thought he was running the place now," Luke said.

"It's not his fault. Things just come up, and the layout gets changed at the last minute. It's hard to explain." Sara didn't know why the comment rubbed her the wrong way; it just did.

Luke was quiet for a moment, then he said, "So, how's it going this week with your boss? Any better?"

"It's been all right. I've gotten more assignments," she said. "How was your visit to Boston?"

"Oh, that was fine. It seems like so long ago now," he added.

The weekend did seem distant. The last time she had seen Luke, even more so.

"So, when can I see you? How about this weekend? Are you free on Saturday night?"

"Sure," she said, then hesitated. "Uh, no, I'm sorry. That won't work out." She paused, not knowing if she should explain the reason to him. "Someone I work with invited me to a party. Jane Harmon. I think I mentioned her."

"Yeah, I think so. Okay." Luke didn't say anything more. His tone made Sara feel self-conscious.

Did he expect her to ask him to come along? But they weren't a real couple, yet. At least, she didn't think so. She could go to a party without him. . . . Couldn't she?

He was quiet on the other end of the phone. Not a good sign. She wondered if she should confront him about it: *Well, how serious are we? Are you bothered by me going to a party without you?* Then she pulled back from that idea. She was tired and suddenly afraid she would end up arguing with him. Even Emily seemed to hint that Luke had serious feelings for her—expectations about their future. *Maybe I do know the answers to these questions,* Sara thought. *And I also know we see things differently.*

"How about Friday night?" she suggested. "I'm free on Friday."

"Uh, no. Friday's no good for me. I have to go into Boston on Friday for a meeting. I won't be back until late." His tone was even, but beneath it, she sensed impatience building. "I guess that leaves Sunday, but I'm almost afraid to ask."

"I could see you Sunday night," Sara assured him. "That would be fine."

"Good. Whew, that wasn't too hard," he joked. "Let's not try to decide what we're going to do or where we're going to go right now, okay? I'm sort of worn out from negotiating."

Sara laughed but still felt uneasy. "It is late. I guess I'd better get to bed."

"Me, too," Luke agreed. "I'll see you Sunday, then."

"Yes, Sunday. Talk to you soon," Sara promised. "Good night, Luke." Luke said good night, and Sara hung up the phone.

She opened the refrigerator, took out a quart of milk, and poured herself a glass. She hadn't eaten much dinner, but she didn't feel hungry anymore. She downed the milk, put the glass in the sink, and headed for her bedroom, her mind turning over her conversation with Luke.

She hadn't deliberately meant to be difficult, but she did feel suddenly closed in on tonight. Emily's words had made Sara think. Maybe Luke had a different idea about their relationship than she did. She did care for him. But lately he seemed to have certain expectations about their relationship and their future that she couldn't meet.

Right now she needed to focus on her job. She didn't even know how long she would be living here. She didn't want to hurt Luke's feelings, but she wasn't really looking for a steady or serious relationship right now. That was the last thing on her mind.

I'm just tired, she told herself. *When I see Luke it will all be fine between us again.* Then she slipped under the covers and pulled the quilt up over her shoulders, feeling too tired to worry about anything.

Chapter Ten

Sara slipped into the Village Hall meeting room and took a seat in the back of the room. She was a few minutes late and hoped she hadn't missed anything important.

The town council sat up front at a long table, with the mayor in the middle. Emily looked straight at Sara, smiled slightly for a moment, then put on her reading glasses and looked down at her notes.

"While I agree with Harriet DeSoto that we need to fight for the grant that is rightfully ours, I don't think we have to file a lawsuit against the county. Not until we've exhausted our other options. The repercussions could be serious."

A good point, Sara thought, jotting down notes.

"Meanwhile, Commissioner Callahan is free to hand out that money to whomever he likes," Frank Hellinger, one of the village trustees, argued. "By the time we figure out what to do, there might not be anything left. If we file a suit, at least that might put the brakes on him."

Emily turned to Warren Oakes, an attorney who did legal work for the village. "If we filed a suit against the county, would that put the funds out of play?"

"It would," Warren agreed. "But if we lose, we'll be liable for the county's legal fees, and the commissioner will probably be even less likely to pass along anything from the grant. Riling the county that way is like waking a bear from hibernation."

Sara looked around the room. The meeting of the town council hadn't attracted much of an audience. Villagers were vitally interested in good emergency services—especially when some problem popped up. But most residents had better things to do on a Friday night than listen to the town council figure out how to actually pay for those services.

Sara had been sent at the last minute, when Jane called in from Southport and said she wouldn't be able to cover it. In a way, Sara was grateful that she hadn't had much time to think about it—to think about covering Emily, that is.

"Could we get the federal agency to send a letter to the county?" Emily asked Warren. "Maybe if they show that they side with us, Commissioner Callahan will give in."

"I don't know. I suppose I could call on Monday and try to persuade somebody," Warren said.

A good idea, Sara thought, as she noted Emily's suggestion.

"The question is, how did we get into this fix in the first place? Can you explain that to me, Mayor?" Art Hecht asked in an irate tone. "Didn't you or someone in your office read this document thoroughly?"

Art Hecht, a local businessman, had supported Charlie Bates for mayor, Sara recalled. It figured that he would try to blame Emily. But maybe Emily *was* responsible in some way.

"When we learned of this federal program, I presented the information at a council meeting," Emily reminded him. "And you voted in favor of applying for it."

"Who knew about the fine print and the red tape? That was up to you to figure out," Art pressed. "Now we've been given the funds, but we might not see a penny of them. Explain that to the taxpayers next time someone's having a heart attack, and we don't have an extra ambulance to get them to the hospital."

"Now just a minute. No one is expiring from heart attacks because our emergency response system is inadequate," Emily replied. "So far our system is keeping up with the demand. We're trying to improve it, so we can respond to unexpected or extraordinary situations, like the big storm last fall. Besides, this grant isn't the only place for us to get aid. There are two other federal programs we haven't even tried yet."

"Great. We can apply for anything we want. We can apply to send a member of the town council up to the North Pole to visit Santa Claus. The issue isn't getting anywhere with all this paperwork," Miriam Foster said, in a frustrated tone.

Good quote, Sara thought, with dismay, as she jotted it down. It was going to make Emily look bad, but she knew all of these rebuttals were valid points that should be part of the article.

Sara sighed, trying to push her concern for Emily aside. *You have to stay objective,* she scolded herself. *Wyatt is going to be all over this story, waiting to see if you can do it.*

The meeting finally ended with a split vote on the lawsuit—Emily had to table the motion—but with an agreement that Warren would contact the federal agency and ask them to contact the county on Cape Light's behalf.

Sara felt a small knot of nerves in her stomach, as she left the Village Hall. This was going to be a tough story to write. And it was going to take time to get it right. It looked like another long night at the office.

SARA RETURNED TO THE *MESSENGER* AND WENT STRAIGHT TO HER DESK. She took out her notes and got to work. But she couldn't figure out how to start the article. She found herself glancing from her computer screen to her notebook then back at the screen again, without writing a word.

Suddenly, she sensed somebody standing behind her. It was Wyatt, of course. Who else would it be?

"How was the meeting? Did you get anything?" he asked.

Sara looked up at him. "It was pretty tough for Em—for the mayor," she corrected herself. "A lot of people want the town to sue the county. But she wants to move slower, put some pressure on the county in other ways."

Sara described some of the high points of the argument, making sure she sounded objective. "So the vote ended in a tie," she finished.

Wyatt's eyebrows went up, and he smiled, revealing deep dimples that Sara had never noticed before.

"Good . . . very good. I can put that on the front page if we do it right. This was an emergency meeting, called by one of the council members, don't forget that."

"I won't," Sara promised, feeling a knot of dread as she made a note on her pad.

"And don't call it a tie vote. Call it a stalemate or at loggerheads. We'll think of something catchy," he promised.

"Okay." She nodded and looked back at her computer screen.

She thought Wyatt would go then, but he didn't. She felt him standing behind her. What was he waiting for? She glanced at him over her shoulder and pushed her hair back off her face.

"Is there something else you want to tell me?"

He looked like he might say something more, then paused and shook his head. "No, nothing. You write the story. I'm going to make some room on page one—but no pressure or anything," he added, with a mischievous grin.

"Right, no pressure," she agreed, almost smiling back.

Great. Her first chance at a page-one story, and it had to be about Emily getting flogged by the town council. Sara sighed. Sometimes it was hard to remember why she wanted this job in the first place.

About an hour later, she brought her copy back to Wyatt's desk. He was going through some photos and held up two shots of some high-school kids putting on a holiday show at a senior home. "This one or this one?" he asked her. "Quick. Your first impression."

"The one on the left. I love the expression on that old woman's face. It says it all."

Wyatt looked down at the photo Sara had chosen. "Good choice." He put the photo aside, then took her copy.

She hated watching someone read her work. It made her stomach churn. "Can I do anything while you read that? Proofread something maybe?"

"Uh, sure. That would be a big help. Maybe we can get out of here at a decent hour tonight," he said, smiling at her.

She smiled back and took the pages he handed her. She didn't feel like staying forever tonight, either. She hoped there wouldn't be too many revisions.

Back at her desk, she suddenly wondered about Wyatt's social life. He didn't appear to have one, staying at the office until all hours, almost every night. Was it possible he had a girlfriend back in California or in some more exotic locale. *So what if he does? It wouldn't make any difference to me.* Yet somehow the idea intrigued her.

She was so busy speculating on Wyatt's private life that she didn't hear him walk up behind her, and she nearly jumped when she felt him touch her shoulder.

"Okay, I have a few changes for you. But this is good. Very good," he said.

"Um . . . thanks," she mumbled, surprised. She took the copy back and looked at his marks. Not nearly as many as usual.

"You've got some good quotes in there, strong stuff." He paused and sat down in a nearby chair. He looked at her for a long moment in a way that made her nervous. "I guess that wasn't so easy for you, was it?"

"I knew when I took this job I was going to have to write about Emily, sooner or later. Something that wasn't flattering, I mean," she said honestly.

"It's unflattering, all right. No question about that." The corner of his mouth turned up in a small smile. A very attractive one, she noticed. "I mean that as a compliment to your reporting," he added.

She guessed from his expression, he hadn't thought she would be able to do it, and she surprised him.

"I know. Thanks." She tried to return his smile, but it was a half-hearted effort. She had worked hard these last three weeks for praise from Wyatt. It seemed ironic that she finally won it with an article that portrayed Emily in a negative light.

"Don't tell me. You're not sure right now that you love this job so much."

Sara wasn't sure how to answer. "Something like that."

Wyatt reached over and patted her shoulder. "That's right on schedule, too. I knew you were coming along," he said in a kind, encouraging tone.

He stood up and gazed down at her, smiling. "Clean up that copy, and I'll put it in the layout. Then why don't we go out and get some coffee or something to eat? Have you eaten anything yet tonight?"

Sara had to think for a minute. "A package of peanut-butter crackers. Stale ones."

"Aren't they always?" he commiserated. "Okay, let's finish up and get out of here."

Sara went back to work, suddenly realizing she had never quite agreed to go out with Wyatt. Not that it really mattered. She felt too wired to go home to bed, and it made her feel good that he had asked her, as if now he finally thought of her as more of an equal.

A short time later, they were sitting together at the Beanery. Wyatt ordered a sandwich, but Sara felt like having an ice-cream sundae for dinner. She felt as if she was partly consoling herself with sweets and partly out celebrating something. Exactly what, it was hard to say.

She felt tired, almost too tired to be good company. But Wyatt did most of the talking. "I'll be glad when the holidays are over. It gets on my nerves after awhile," he confessed.

"Really? Why?"

Wyatt looked at her with surprise. "It's so commercial. So fake. Just an excuse for the stores to sell people more stuff they don't need."

She considered his words. "I know what you mean. I hate the materialism, too. But I try to ignore that part." She paused, wondering if she should say more. "Every year up until now, the holidays made me a little sad, because I thought about my birth mother. Finding her, I mean. But this is the first year when I don't have to think about that, and I'm actually going to spend Christmas with her. So it's different for me. I'm really looking forward to it."

Wyatt cast her a thoughtful expression. "Good for you. But I would say you're in the minority."

Sara thought that was a cynical thing to say, but she didn't feel like arguing with him. Although she wasn't very religious, she knew lots of people in this town who were—like Emily and Sam and Jessica. Christmas seemed to have a different meaning for them, one that transcended the shopping-mall materialism. But she wondered if Wyatt would even understand or accept that if she tried to explain it to him.

"So are you planning to go back to Maryland?" Wyatt asked.

"No, my parents are coming up here right after Christmas. They want to see the town, meet Emily."

"That should be interesting."

"I'm a little nervous about it," Sara admitted. "I mean, what if they don't like each other? Then what will I do?"

"They're all adults," Wyatt said, with a shrug. "I say, stick them in a room together, and let them figure it out for themselves."

Easy for you to say, she wanted to answer. But then she decided not to. She suddenly thought of Luke, knowing he wouldn't have given her such a flip answer. But Luke tended to take things seriously. Too seriously at times, she reminded herself. Wyatt had a more laid-back approach to life. He hadn't meant anything by the comment. Besides, maybe he had the right idea.

"So what are you doing for the holidays? Staying in town?" she asked.

"Absolutely. We'll all be packed into that little house. Which is starting to get on everyone's nerves, by the way. I'm not sure how we're going to fit a Christmas tree in there, too. Maybe stick it up on the roof or something," he noted, making her laugh. "All the presents will slide down and get stuck in the bushes, though."

"I thought Scott and Lindsay were moving to the city," Sara said.

"That was the plan. But Scott's restaurant deal fell apart. He's looking for a job as a chef in a restaurant around here. Lindsay is still looking, too, though I guess I wish she'd keep helping me out."

"Why can't she do that?" Sara asked.

"Oh, I don't know." Wyatt shrugged. "She's just getting the business end of things in order. She won't want to hang out there forever. But I haven't spent the holidays with her and Father for a while, though, so that should be fun," he added, changing the subject. "Last year I went out to visit my mother. She teaches in Nebraska."

"Really? How was that?" Sara asked him.

"Cold. Cold and bleak. It makes winter up here look like the Bahamas," he joked. "Come to think of it, I wouldn't mind seeing some palm trees pretty soon. It would be a nice break. But I can't even think about escaping for a weekend while my father is still around. He'd have a fit."

"No, I guess you can't," Sara agreed, surprised to hear that Wyatt was longing to take a break from the paper so soon. He had only been there about a month.

"I lived in the Caribbean for a while. It was great," he told her in a nostalgic tone. "Every morning I'd get up early and walk on the beach and take a swim. The water was so clear. I did some amazing underwater photography."

"It sounds wonderful," Sara said honestly. "You sound as if you miss it."

"I guess I do sometimes. Especially in a place like this, when the snow starts piling up," he said, with a good-natured laugh. "I'm starting to miss taking pictures, too," he confessed.

"Well, New England has its own charms." Sara liked it here most of the time, despite the cold and snow.

"You forget, I grew up here, so it's not nearly as charming for me. But you sound like you want to stay," he noted.

"For a while, I guess. I'm not sure how long. I wanted to take this job and get to know Emily. That's why I'm here right now."

He gazed at her a moment and smiled. "There are so many wonderful places to visit and explore, Sara. I hope you get out there and see them all. You're the type, I can tell."

"The type? The exploring type you mean?"

He nodded. "When you're ready to leave here, I don't think you'll run back to Maryland. You'll go someplace else. Someplace interesting, like New York or San Francisco . . . or London, maybe."

Sara considered his words. She hadn't really thought that far ahead. But maybe he was right. Maybe she did want to see more of the world before she committed herself to a job—or a relationship.

"I love New York, but I don't know if I could live there. It's sort of overwhelming to me," she admitted.

"You would get used to it, if you wanted to."

Sara wondered if that were true. Wyatt made it sound as if anything was possible for her. And, Sara reflected, she liked thinking he was right.

They sat talking until the waitress came by and asked if they wanted anything more. "No, just the check, please," Wyatt said.

"Let me split it with you," she offered.

"Don't be silly," Wyatt said, taking out some bills.

She felt awkward, as if they were suddenly on a date. "Well, thanks for dinner," she said.

"The sundae, you mean?" He laughed at her. "That's all right. I admire a woman who goes straight for dessert." He met her gaze, and with an absentminded gesture, pushed back his dark hair. Sara felt herself staring into his eyes, but she couldn't help it.

"Hello, Sara. Done with work already?"

Sara turned and looked up to find Luke staring down at her. He stood near their table with his arms folded over his chest, wearing his leather jacket and an unhappy expression.

Sara stared at him, wide-eyed, her mouth hanging open in a way she quickly realized was awfully unattractive. She quickly looked away, her cheeks flushing, as if she'd been caught at something. Which was utterly ridiculous, she told herself. She glanced back at Luke, wishing he would stop staring at her with that "Gotcha!" cop expression on his face. She was sure Wyatt noticed, and she felt horribly embarrassed.

"Luke, hi. I didn't even see you there," Sara said, trying to force her voice to a normal tone. She leaned back in her chair, putting more distance between herself and Wyatt.

"Yes, I noticed. You were talking away there," Luke said, his gray eyes never leaving her.

I'm just talking to my boss. It's not a crime, she wanted to say, but that seemed too defensive.

"Um, this is my boss, Wyatt Forbes. Wyatt, this is Luke McAllister," Sara said, introducing them.

Wyatt stood up and offered his hand. He smiled in his usual relaxed way. "How do you do?" The two men shook hands briefly, and Wyatt sat down again. "Care to join us, Luke?" Wyatt asked in a friendly tone.

"No, thanks. I just stopped in for some coffee." He held up a paper cup.

"Well, we were going anyway," Sara said. She stood up and picked up her coat and knapsack. "Why don't you walk out with us?" she asked Luke. She almost thought for a moment he'd refuse, but finally he nodded.

"Sure," he said.

Sara fumbled to get her coat on, and at the same moment, both men reached out to help her. Then they looked at each other, stepped back at the same time, and her coat nearly fell to the floor.

"It's okay. I've got it," she assured them, tugging it on herself.

Luke looked annoyed, silently fuming, she thought. Wyatt looked as if he wanted to laugh, but kept a straight face as they left the café. Once outside, he turned toward Sara. "Good night, Sara. See you Monday. Have a good weekend."

"Night." Sara met his gaze briefly, all the while aware of Luke watching her.

"Good night, Luke," Wyatt said. "Stop by the paper sometime," he added in a friendly tone.

"Sure thing," Luke replied. "Good night now."

Sara watched Wyatt cross the street and walk toward his car, which was parked down the block. Once Wyatt was gone Luke said, "I did just drop by the paper. But no one was there." When Sara turned to him with a puzzled expression, he added, "You said you had to work late. I came by with some dinner for you."

"Oh . . ." She wasn't sure what to say. "Thanks. We finished early, so we went out."

"I figured out that much." His tone was calm and remote. But Sara still felt accused by a certain look in his eyes.

"My car is down this way," she said.

"Okay, I'll walk you." Before she could answer, Luke fell into step beside her.

They walked down the empty street, side by side, without touching or even talking. Sara felt tense and self-conscious. Luke had sunk into one of his maddeningly distant modes, which made it even harder.

"I was just hanging out with my boss for a few minutes after work, Luke," she said suddenly. "We were just talking, having something to eat."

Sara knew she sounded defensive, but she couldn't help it.

"Yes, you just told me that. I guess you and Wyatt are getting along better these days."

It wasn't his words exactly, but more his tone that pushed some button inside her.

"What's that supposed to mean?" she asked, feeling suddenly angry.

He shrugged. "I don't know. You tell me. A few days ago you sounded like you hated the guy. This sudden change of heart surprised me, that's all."

"I wouldn't call it a change of heart," Sara said, finding his choice of words unnerving. "He's my boss. I've got to try to get along with him."

"Absolutely. And it looks like you're doing a fine job of it," Luke countered.

Luke was jealous of Wyatt. Sara thought it was so ridiculous, she could hardly believe it. No wonder it had taken her this long to realize what was really going on.

"Luke, you don't have to be jealous about Wyatt."

"Who ever said I was?" he asked in a quiet tone edged with anger.

"Well, you seem like you might be. Or you might think that something is going on between us, and it's just not true. I mean, he's just my boss. We were just sitting there talking. I don't even like him very much. I mean, most of the time." She shrugged. She didn't know what else to say.

She thought her words would reassure him. Instead, they seemed to make him angrier. "Yeah, you were just talking. You don't even like the guy." He looked down at the ground and shook his head. "Come on, Sara. I'm not blind. You were sitting so close you were practically in his lap. You like that guy, at least admit it."

"I do not. I mean, not like you mean," she insisted.

He really was jealous, she realized. For a moment, she felt flattered. Then she felt annoyed and strangely smothered. She knew Luke running into her tonight had been a coincidence, but she still felt cornered. And she didn't like that feeling at all.

They had reached her car, and she pulled out her keys and unlocked the door.

"Look, I'm not going to argue with you about this. It's just too . . . silly. I don't have a crush on my boss. Let's just leave it at that, okay?"

"All right, if you say so," he replied, in an infuriatingly reasonable tone.

She didn't entirely like his answer. Or the look on his face, which seemed to suggest that she was protesting too much—not only trying to convince Luke she wasn't attracted to Wyatt, but also trying to convince herself.

But she didn't feel like arguing with him any further about this. Which really would make it seem as if he was, in fact, right, she fumed.

"I'm tired. I'm going home. Good night, Luke," she said curtly.

"Okay, good night." He nodded. Then he said, "What about Sunday? Still want to go out?"

She met his gaze and looked away. She was annoyed—but she wasn't *that* mad at him. She found the worried look on his face suddenly endearing.

"Of course I do—even though you're sort of thick sometimes," she replied, with a grin.

As she got in her car and closed the door, she saw the corner of his mouth lift in a hesitant smile.

Sara drove away, catching a glimpse of Luke in her rearview mirror, still standing on the sidewalk with his hands deep in his coat pockets. She felt as if she had a lot to think about.

Luke's jealousy had surprised her. Mainly because she really felt he had nothing to be jealous about. But now she had to wonder: Was he right? Did she like Wyatt more than she realized?

Well, whether she liked him or not, nothing had happened, so she had nothing to feel bad about. They had just talked over coffee. Wyatt was the talkative type. The opposite of Luke. It didn't mean anything, she told herself. Still, she had to admit, she felt flattered by his interest.

The things he'd said about her. He had made her feel interesting and attractive, Sara thought.

That did seem like something to think about.

"EMILY, THANKS FOR COMING." LINDSAY GREETED HER AT THE DOOR, wearing a red wool coat. She looked both ready and eager to go out, Emily thought. "I hope this wasn't any bother for you. I'm not wrecking your Saturday, am I?"

"No, not at all. I was thinking of Dan when you called. Wondering how he was doing, I mean," Emily said, as she stepped inside.

It was actually a half-truth. She'd also been wondering if she was being a fool by pursuing this relationship. Sometimes it seemed so obvious that she would only end up hurt.

But when Lindsay called asking for her help, she couldn't resist offering to come over. It had almost seemed . . . well, like a sign.

"He's okay, isn't he?" Emily asked, as she dropped her coat and hat on a nearby chair.

"Well, yes—and no." Lindsay's voice dropped to a near whisper. "I think this recovery process is getting to him. He's really been down these last few days. Won't shave. Will hardly change his clothes or move out of that room. Last night he didn't eat his dinner, and this morning, he hardly touched breakfast. Scott made his favorite, too, banana pancakes."

"Is he sick? Maybe he's coming down with something."

"He doesn't have a temperature. No other symptoms, either. Just grouchy. Wow, is he grouchy," Lindsay warned her.

Emily smiled. "Don't worry. I can handle him."

"Are you sure?"

"Absolutely," Emily assured her. "I'm glad you called me," she said honestly.

She was pleased to see that her friendship with Dan's daughter had grown to the point where Lindsay trusted her enough to ask a favor. And she hated the idea of Dan feeling so down and being alone in the house, so she was glad for the chance to cheer him up.

"You go," she told Lindsay. "I'll stay here with him until you get back. It'll be fine, I promise."

"Thanks. I really appreciate this," Lindsay said. "My cell-phone number is on the fridge if you need me," she called over her shoulder. "See you later."

"See you," Emily called back. She waited a moment until the door was closed before heading for the family room. The small living room was almost completely overwhelmed by a medium-size Christmas tree. Emily stepped around it, careful not to knock off any of the ornaments.

The house was perfectly quiet. She didn't even hear the incessant murmur of the TV usually tuned to the all-news or all-sports channel—or all news *and* sports—whenever she came here.

She reached the doorway and saw Dan stretched out on the sofa. He looked as though he were sleeping, with an open newspaper covering his head. She stepped over and watched him for a long moment. The newspaper rose and fell with his deep, slow breaths.

"Dan, are you asleep?" Emily asked softly. She leaned over the couch and lifted the newspaper that covered his face and chest.

He didn't move for a moment, then slowly opened one eye and peered at her. "Oh, it's you. I thought it was Lindsay again."

Emily stood up and tried to look annoyed but couldn't help grinning a little. "Why were you pretending to be asleep?"

He sat up and sighed. "So they would all just leave me alone. I thought that was apparent," he said grumpily.

He ran his hand through his hair, making it even messier. He still needed a haircut, worse than ever, Emily noticed. But somehow he managed to look attractive to her, in a ruffian sort of way. Today she'd brought along her scissors. Maybe he would submit to a trim.

Lindsay had warned her about his beard, but it still came as a shock. She'd seen him only days ago. When had this happened? She studied his face, not sure if she liked it.

"So, why are you here? Did Lindsay call you?"

Emily avoided his gaze. "Actually, I came over for some tea and sympathy. I'll have to make the tea, I guess," she said. "Have you seen today's *Messenger?*"

He stared at her a minute, thinking. "Oh . . . that." Dan struggled and finally sat up, then rubbed the back of his neck. "They really gave it to you, didn't they?"

"Do you mean the town council or your newspaper?" she asked lightly.

"It's not my paper anymore. It's Wyatt's," he said, sounding grouchy again. "I couldn't help but notice the byline." He glanced up at her. "Whatever made Wyatt send Sara to cover that story?"

"Well, he couldn't have known it was going to get so ugly. I certainly didn't." She sat on the end of the couch. "Sooner or later Sara has to cover events that I'm involved in. It's unavoidable."

"Have you talked about it?"

"She called me first thing this morning—I was still half asleep—to apologize. She felt terrible about it."

"What did you say?" Dan asked curiously.

Emily shrugged. "I told her it was a very good story, and I was proud of her. I knew it was difficult for her to write. I could see it on her face at the meeting. It was difficult for her to just sit there and watch. She's been working so hard at the paper these last few weeks. She sounded awful. I'm sure the poor girl is coming down with something."

Dan shook his head. "Emily, you sound just like a mother now—and nothing like a mayor. But it still must have hurt a little."

She met his eye and nodded. "It was . . . a little tough. She didn't leave much out."

"So what are you going to do about this mess?" Dan asked.

"I don't know," she said honestly. "Warren is getting in touch with the federal office that awarded the grant. If they don't help us out, we're back to square one. I suppose the council will vote to file a lawsuit."

"That would be a disaster," Dan said, sounding alarmed. She noticed that old gleam in his eye—the way he looked back when he was running the *Messenger*, working a story. He was really like a fish out of water, away from that newspaper office. He just hadn't figured it out yet. "You can't sue the county," he told her. "It would be an even bigger mess than this one."

"That's what I said—right here on page five, paragraph two," she pointed out, handing the paper to him. She rubbed her forehead. "I'm pretty clear on what we shouldn't do. What I don't know is what will help at this point."

"I don't know, either," Dan admitted. "But this isn't your fault. It's unfair of anyone to say that. Don't worry. We'll think of something."

She wondered if they really could. After his years on the paper, Dan had one of the more politically savvy minds in town. Not that she expected Dan or anyone else to solve this for her. Still, just the way he stood up for her and said, "*We'll* think of something," made her feel instantly better. "Thanks, Dan," she said quietly.

"Don't mention it." He met her gaze and smiled, an intimate kind of smile that warmed her heart. "How about in the meantime we have a game of chess?"

"How about in the meantime, I give you a haircut?" she countered brightly. She picked up her purse and took out the scissors. "These are genuine barber's shears. I'm quite good at this, I promise."

Dan put his hands over his hair, looking horrified. "No way are you getting near me with those things."

"Dan, you're being silly. You really need a trim," she told him.

"I know I need a trim. The question is, who's going to see me? Who is going to care if I grow my hair down to my knees?"

"Wouldn't that be a sight." Emily smiled at the image. "Did you have a ponytail in college?" she asked curiously.

"A little shaggy around the edges maybe, but no ponytail," he replied.

"I didn't think so," she said, laughing at his indignant tone. "So, you're not trying to relive your lost youth or something like that?"

"Just plain old cabin fever. Nothing more, nothing less."

"Oh well, I know the cure for that." Emily put the scissors away and stood up. "We need to get you out of the house. I think it's time." She took his hand. "Come on, get up."

"I can't go out. Are you crazy?"

"I'm not worried about myself. But you're definitely going to be insane if you stay cooped up in here for much longer. Come on," she urged, "you can do it."

He shook his head, but she held his hand and looked into his eyes, and something in her gaze seemed to melt his resistance.

"Where would we go?" he asked, looking suddenly intrigued by the notion.

"Where would you like to go? How about out to the beach? Or into town?"

"The beach—that would be perfect," he agreed, sounding suddenly excited. "But town would be nice, too."

"We'll do both then."

Dan grinned and pushed himself up with his good arm while Emily reached out to steady him. He leaned forward and was suddenly upright but looked as if he were about to tip over. Emily quickly put her arm around his waist and held on to him. She had forgotten how tall he was.

"This isn't so bad. I think I like it a lot better than crutches," he said, smiling down at her. His good arm was curled around her shoulders, and his face was so close to her own that his beard brushed against her cheek.

She met his gaze for a moment, then looked away, feeling her cheeks flush. She could tell he noticed and was trying to pretend he didn't.

Why did she still have to blush like a teenager, for goodness' sake? She was forty-two years old.

"I'll help you to the wheelchair," she said.

Finally, they hobbled over to the wheelchair and eased Dan into it.

"You need to dress warmly. It's cold outside. Where are your things?" she asked him.

Dan told her where to find a sweater, his parka, scarf, and gloves, and Emily helped him put them on. She was soon dressed for the outdoors, too, and boldly took hold of the wheelchair's handles.

"I think we ought to take the crutches, too. We might need them," she decided.

"Oh, all right, if you insist. I liked the other arrangement though, just fine," he teased her. "Wait, I want to leave a note for Lindsay." Emily brought him paper and a pen from his desk and watched as he quickly scrawled in block letters:

Finally escaped. I'm a free man. I'll be in touch. Love, Dad.

"How's that?"

"Perfect. I'll leave it right here, where she won't miss it," she promised, propping the note up on the TV set.

Out at her Jeep, it took some maneuvering to get Dan into the backseat and the folded wheelchair into the cargo area, but Emily managed.

It was a clear, windless day and quite warm in the sun for mid-December. When they reached the beach, she pulled up to the beginning of a wooden walkway that stretched across the sand to the shoreline.

She got the wheelchair out first, then helped Dan out and into the chair with a fair amount of tugging, huffing, and puffing that made them both laugh.

"Fasten your seat belt; it's going to be bumpy ride," Emily warned, pushing with all her might on the back of the chair.

"Emily—whoa!" Dan gripped the arms of the chair, as the wheels thudded over the uneven wooden boards.

"Hey, this thing can really roll," she observed, as the wheelchair picked up speed.

"No kidding. I'm going to end up in the ocean if you don't watch out," he warned, as the end of the walkway quickly drew closer.

Emily tried to slow the chair with her body weight, but Dan weighed more and the walkway slanted downhill, toward the shoreline. Emily found herself hanging on for dear life, fighting the almost overpowering force of gravity and hoping Dan wouldn't end up headfirst in the nearest sand dune.

"Doesn't this thing have brakes?" she called out to him.

"Somewhere around here—" He reached down to the side of the chair and started moving levers. "I never really needed them around the house."

"Well, you need them now!"

Inches from the end of the walkway Dan found the right lever, and the wheelchair jerked to a stop.

Emily sat down next to him on the wooden planks, so out of breath she could hardly speak.

"Well, that was fun," he said dryly. "How do you plan to terrorize me next?"

She looked up and laughed at him. "Oh, stop complaining. You enjoyed it. I can tell. Besides, you need me to push you back up that hill, so you'd better be a little nicer."

He glanced back over his shoulder. "That is a steep hill. No wonder we were heading into warp speed."

He turned again and faced the ocean. He didn't speak and Emily felt no pressure to, either. She stared out at the water, feeling the tensions of last night and her current work crisis drain away.

"It does wonders for you, this place. Just sitting here." Dan said finally. He reached down and put his arm around her shoulders. "Thanks for bringing me. Sorry I've been a little grumpy."

She touched his hand and glanced back at him, smiling. "A little? You've been perfectly horrible, truth be told. . . . But I guess I like you anyway."

"Gee, thanks." He laughed and tousled her hair with his fingers. "You're *too* honest, sometimes, Emily. . . . But I like you anyway, too. Come to think of it, I like you a lot."

Dan's words and tender touch sent a surge of pure happiness through her. She glanced at him, then stared back at the waves. It had been a long time since she'd felt so close to and so comfortable with a man. She knew when his leg healed and he finally carried out his plan to leave Cape Light, she would miss him. Very much.

Would he miss her, too? Did he ever think about it? she wondered. She felt sure he would miss her, even if he didn't realize it now, but not enough to keep him here. It wasn't like that between them. She couldn't harbor expectations. Dan had made that very clear. She would just enjoy their time together, however long it lasted.

Starting with here and now, she reminded herself.

"So, what would you like to do next? Go into town? Get a bite to eat, maybe?" Emily stood up and brushed the sand off her pants.

"Excellent suggestion. I'm starved. This ocean air really perks up your appetite."

Emily slowly turned the chair around. "So does all this pushing," she added, starting to roll the wheelchair back uphill. "I hope you brought your credit cards. I think you're buying me a lobster."

"I think I owe you one," Dan said, as he tried to help by pushing on the wheels.

Their lunch at the Beanery did end up including lobster salad sandwiches, which Emily enjoyed immensely. They were able to get a table near the door, convenient for maneuvering Dan's chair into the café. The table also put them in a prime spot for people watching. Practically everyone who came in stopped to say hello and ask Dan how he was feeling.

While he discreetly complained about the interruptions to their meal, Emily could tell that he was basking in the attention. He'd had some visitors at home, but isolation had been setting in. This was just what he needed, she realized. Dan Forbes might have the air of a loner, but he was really more social than he would ever admit.

"Gee, if I had known I was going to see so many people, I would have cleaned up a little," he admitted, as they left. "I look sort of ragged, don't you think?"

"You look fine. But you should have let me trim your hair," she teased him.

They were out on the sidewalk. Emily glanced up and down Main Street, wondering what they should do next.

"That reminds me . . . How about cruising past the barbershop? I can't risk you coming at me with those scissors again, Emily."

"Well, I really don't give a bad haircut, but I'm sure Bob is a lot better," she admitted, pushing him along.

"The town looks wonderful," Dan said. "This is the first time I've been out since they put up the decorations. I tell you, cooped up in that house, I hardly felt like Christmas was coming, except for the TV commercials. Now, I really do."

It did look pretty, Emily agreed, with tiny white lights on all the trees on Main Street, and lights strung across the avenue at intervals. There was even a Santa's sleigh, complete with the eight reindeer, strung up across the street in front of the Village Hall. Each of the shopkeepers had set up a small tree, decorated in keeping with his business. The hardware store had trimmed its tree with nuts and bolts and plumbing washers. The stationery store had used pens, pencils, and colored index cards. The Bramble tree was covered with tiny teacup ornaments and bits of lace and ribbon.

Finally they reached Bob's Barbershop. Like everyone else in town, Bob Greenfield was delighted to see Dan. However, he seemed particularly struck by Dan's long hair and beard.

"I heard you broke your leg. I didn't know you were a castaway on a desert island."

"Good one, Bob." Dan glanced at Emily, and she bit her lip to keep from laughing. "Okay, I'm all yours. Let's do it." Dan spun his wheelchair to face the mirror, submitting to the barber with a sigh.

"This may take a while," Bob said to Emily.

She nodded. "See you later."

While Dan got his hair cut, she strolled around town, browsing the shop windows. She returned about twenty minutes later to find Dan looking different—and even more attractive. The barber had given him a short, layered cut, and instead of shaving off the beard, he'd trimmed it back and groomed it.

"Better?" Dan asked, once they were out on the street again.

"Much," she agreed. "I thought you were going to shave off your beard."

"Why? Don't you like it?"

"I didn't before," she said honestly. "But now it makes you look sort of . . . distinguished."

"Oh no, getting to the distinguished stage, am I?" he asked, making her feel that she'd said the wrong thing.

"And dashing," she added. "Definitely dashing."

"Okay. I'll settle for dashing," he said, sounding pleased. "Mind you, I'm not going to shave once I get on my boat."

"That makes sense," Emily remarked mildly. Secretly she felt jarred to be reminded again of his imminent departure.

His plans hadn't changed; that was no surprise. Briefly she wondered what would happen if she drummed up the nerve to be honest with Dan about her feelings. What good would it do? None at all, for either of them, she decided.

Dan's determination to sail off into the sunset wasn't something he was doing to hurt her, she reminded herself. It was just a case of bad timing. The only thing to do was to watch out for her own heart. She had to be careful. She couldn't let herself fall for him completely—though at times like this, it felt as if she already had.

She quietly sighed, as she pushed the wheelchair down Main Street. Together, they checked out the shop windows, and Emily found herself grateful for the distraction.

"I don't know what to get anyone for Christmas. My kids and Scott, I mean," Dan said. "They've all been pretty good to put up with me. Especially Lindsay. I've been looking at things on the Internet, but I don't even know their sizes. And I can hardly run to the door when the boxes come to hide them."

"I could shop for you," Emily offered. "Just give me some ideas, and I'll go out and see what I can find."

"Oh, no, I couldn't ask you to do that, Emily. That's too much extra work for you," Dan argued. "All that rushing around, standing in lines—"

"Don't be silly. That's what the holidays are all about," she kidded him. She met his gaze and smiled. "Honestly, it won't be any trouble at all. I'll be in the stores anyway. I can do it. I really want to," she insisted.

He was quiet for a moment and rubbed his beard with his hand, a gesture she hadn't noticed before. "Well . . . if you would do that, I'd be eternally grateful. Really."

"Then consider it done," she replied.

They stopped in front of a fancy clothing store that had an old toy train circling a miniature village beneath the Christmas tree.

"Look at that shawl. It's gorgeous. Maybe Lindsay would like something like that," Emily said.

"What am I looking at?" Dan asked, in a humorous tone.

"That woolen shawl. See it in the back—that gorgeous azure blue?"

"Oh, sure. I see it now. That is pretty. What color did you call it again?"

"Azure blue," Emily said slowly, gazing at him.

"Yes, azure. Of course." He was smiling at her, a secret sort of smile that made her feel warm inside. Admired. As if he wasn't thinking of the woolen stole at all, just about her.

"Do you think Lindsay would like that?" she persisted.

"I think she might. Let's keep it in mind."

They window-shopped all the way down Main Street, finally ending up at Emily's Jeep, which was parked near the green. Dan had even found a scrap of paper and a pencil in his jacket pocket and jotted a gift-idea list on the way.

By the time they reached the car, the sunshine was quickly fading, and the lights on Main Street glowed in the dusk.

Carolers stood on the opposite corner, under an old-fashioned gaslight that was trimmed in honor of the season. The singers' voices blended in sweet harmonies, and despite the cold, people on the streets stopped to listen.

Emily helped Dan up out of his chair. Once again he leaned on her for support, with his arm wrapped around her shoulders and her arm circling his waist. They turned together to look at the lights and listen to the singing.

"How pretty," Emily remarked.

"Yes, very pretty," he agreed. He turned and gazed down at her, and for one wild moment, she thought he was about to kiss her.

Then the sound of a car door slamming nearby reminded her that they were still on Main Street.

She pulled back, the mood broken. "Ready to go home?"

"Not really . . . but I guess I have to. It's been a great day. The best I've had in weeks," he said sincerely. "I don't know how to thank you, Emily."

"Oh, you'll think of something," she said lightly.

Then she pulled open the car door and began to help him into the backseat. It had been the best day she'd had in weeks, too. One Emily knew she would remember for a long time.

Chapter Eleven

LUCY SAT AT THE KITCHEN TABLE AND OPENED ONE OF HER school notebooks to a clean page. She pushed aside some coffee mugs and cereal bowls, then picked up a pen and started to write.

Dear Charlie, I don't think this letter will come as a surprise. I'm sick and tired of fighting and don't see that we can get along anymore. So I think it's better for everyone, even the boys, if we separate for a while.

She stopped writing, noticing fat wet tears staining the edge of the paper. She found a tissue on the counter and dabbed her eyes and then the paper, too.

I am going to stay at my mother's with the children. You can see them anytime you like. I'll call you tonight.

She wondered then if she needed to tell him she wouldn't be working at the diner anymore. But that would be obvious, wouldn't it? Even to Charlie? It was Monday, her day off. He would come in tonight, find the note, and figure it out.

She wondered finally how she should sign it. The word *love* seemed hypocritical now, but it was so much a habit. She sat very still, trying to figure out what she really felt for Charlie. Did she love him anymore at all . . . or not? *I'm too mad at him right now to know one way or the other.*

Finally, she just wrote her name at the bottom of the page.

She sighed and stared around the familiar room. How could she leave her kitchen, her house, all her things? She had to find a new job, a new place to live. She had to explain this all to the boys somehow. And right on top of Christmas. She wasn't a very good mother to do this to them in the middle of the holidays, was she? Wasn't it easier to just stay?

Still, something inside insisted that she had no choice. She had to go. This morning. Right now. It felt like suddenly something was pushing her forward, right out the door.

She and Charlie had gone through one of their usual arguments this morning. He wanted her to put in more hours this week at the diner, and she'd said she was too busy with school. It would only be another week or so until the term ended. Why couldn't he be more patient about it?

Somehow they'd gotten around to the topic of seeing Reverend Ben again. Charlie said he'd had enough of that, so she might as well stop nagging him. He wasn't seeing a marriage counselor ever again—Reverend Ben or anybody. That was that. Then he just stormed out of the house.

The boys had been upstairs, getting dressed for school. They came down, quiet as mice, and ate their oatmeal without their usual arguments. Her heart ached for them. Then she walked them down to the bus stop with Bradley, their dog, just like every other morning. Only inside something had snapped. Some switch had turned over, and Lucy returned to the house, her heart weighing as heavily as a stone. She didn't even bother to put the breakfast dishes in the sink. She just sat down and wrote Charlie's note, her mind made up.

Now she took the note and left it in the middle of the table, leaning against the sugar bowl. The same place she might leave him a note about walking the dog or a reminder to bring home a gallon of milk.

For a moment, she considered calling Reverend Ben. He would be sympathetic, she was sure. But he might try to persuade her to stay, and she didn't want to be swayed. No, she'd go see him after it was all done. After she moved out.

She headed upstairs. First she would pack the boys' bags, remembering to take some favorite toys and books. Jamie still slept with a worn stuffed tiger. It was going to be hard for them. But children sensed what was going on between adults. She remembered the way her parents fought. Her father drank and flew into angry rages. Her mother had loyally stuck by him for the sake of the family. But recently her now-widowed mother had confided that she wasn't sure she had done the right thing.

"So don't go following after me, in case that's what you're thinking, Lucy," her mother had warned.

Lucy knew her mother would help her now. She would welcome her and the boys. The house where Lucy grew up was empty, with plenty of bedrooms, and fortunately it was close to the boys' school and friends. Her mother would even loan her some money, if it came to that. She'd often hinted as much, but Lucy had always acted as if she and Charlie were working things out. It embarrassed her for anyone to know that her marriage was such a dismal failure.

Well, they were going to know now. Lucy folded a sweatshirt with the green emblem of the Boston Celtics and put it into a blue duffle bag.

Charlie had snuffed out any hope of their relationship ever working. And once you lost hope—well, what you did you have? You didn't have any choices left.

"DAD? I'M GOING NOW."

Dan heard Lindsay in the doorway of the kitchen and turned to look at her.

"What are you doing?" she asked.

"Just fixing this old lamp. I picked it up at a tag sale a while ago. It's just been sitting around, with a lot of other fix-it projects I've never had time for."

"It's pretty," Lindsay said, taking a closer look.

"It will be," he promised. "I want to get one of those silk shades with a fringed edge for it. You know, that real antique style. Maybe you can find one for me sometime in your travels. I'll give you the dimensions."

"I can try. That will look good. Where will you put it? In the living room?" his daughter asked.

"Oh, I'm not sure yet," he said vaguely. He turned to cut a piece of wire. He actually thought Emily might like it. They'd seen one just like it in the window of the Bramble Shop last Saturday, and she practically swooned over it. He was fixing it as a surprise for her, but not as her Christmas gift. He really had to get her something special for Christmas; he just didn't know what.

"So, you look nice. Going on an interview?" he said, hoping to change the subject.

Lindsay nodded. She sat at the table. "In Newburyport, at an advertising agency. It's a small firm, but they sounded nice over the phone. With Scott working in Southport, it doesn't make sense to keep looking down in Boston."

"Of course not. You two will have to find a place around here now. Luckily you didn't sign a lease or anything in the city. You'd be stuck," Dan said.

"Well, we *are* going to move out, so don't worry," Lindsay promised. "We really didn't mean to stay half this long."

"Don't be silly. You stay as long as you want. I know I've been impossible, unbearable, and sort of a big pain in the neck," Dan admitted, making her laugh. "You've been great to put up with me, honey. Honestly. And you've been a great help to Wyatt. He says he couldn't survive without you. What's he going to do when you find a real job?" he teased her.

"I don't know. I guess he'll manage somehow." He noticed his daughter's expression change. She looked uneasy. Worried about her interview maybe?

"How do you think Wyatt is doing so far?" Dan prodded her. He threaded the wire through the lamp base and pushed it up the brass pole.

"You're down there with him every day. I know he's hit a few bumps here and there, but he's doing all right, wouldn't you say?"

"Sure . . . he's doing fine." She looked down at the leather gloves in her hand and smoothed one out.

Dan watched, wondering what had suddenly changed her mood. "Is there something you think I ought to know?"

"You ought to be asking Wyatt that, I think," Lindsay said, with a shrug. "I'm not going to . . . to report on him for you."

"I appreciate that," Dan said. "But you know how Wyatt is. He won't ask for help. He'll barely talk to me about the paper. He says either he's running it or he's not." He looked at his daughter carefully. "You don't have to tell me anything you're not comfortable discussing. It's just that you seem to be down there all the time. You must know what's going on."

"Why do you think I'm down there all the time, Dad?" Lindsay asked bluntly.

"Well, he's been asking you to help with the clerical end of things. I know that much."

Lindsay stared at him a long moment, and Dan felt his heartbeat quicken. There was something going on here he didn't know about. He wasn't at all sure that Lindsay was going to tell him what it was.

"Wyatt is working hard, Dad. He's really trying very hard," Lindsay said. "It's not that he doesn't love the paper. I really think he does. . . ."

"But?" Dan coaxed her.

"I'm not really sure he understands that the paper is more than just what's happening this very day. Wyatt doesn't seem to see the big picture, what the *Messenger* really is, beyond a great headline or a big photo on page one."

Dan was surprised at his daughter's eloquence and passion. He didn't think she thought much about the *Messenger* one way or the other. His wife never had. In fact, toward the end of their marriage, she viewed the paper as her mortal enemy.

"And what do you think it is?" he asked quietly, curious to hear what his daughter would say.

"Oh, well—" Lindsay sighed and pushed her hair back with her hand. "I'm not a writer or even a photographer," she said, meeting his gaze. "So I see it a lot differently, I guess. It's the advertising and the circulation and giving our regular readers information every day to help make their lives a little easier. Even if that only means a bus schedule or a recipe or a coupon for the hardware store. Oh, you know what I mean," she said, looking suddenly self-conscious.

"Yes, I do," he said quietly.

"I don't mean to say anything negative about Wyatt," she said suddenly.

"I know you don't. And I'd never tell him we had this conversation."

"He's doing fine. We just see the paper differently, that's all. And he needs to be more mindful of business matters," she added, with a small smile. "But he can always hire someone to do that for him."

"That goes without saying," Dan agreed, with a sigh. "How is the advertising base lately?"

"It's back up. We're at last year's levels for December or even a bit higher."

"That's good." Lindsay had done that, he was sure. But for some reason, he just couldn't give her the credit that was due. Not right now.

Dan avoided her gaze and scratched his bearded cheek. "I'm still not so sure about this beard. It's scratchy sometimes," he said, purposely changing the subject.

Lindsay came to her feet. "How does Emily like it?"

Dan looked up at her. He was about to ask why she thought he would be concerned about what Emily thought, but he knew his daughter was on to him. Women had a special radar about these things.

"She says it makes me looked distinguished and dashing."

"It does make you look distinguished. I'm not so sure about the other," Lindsay said, with a laugh. "How is Emily's fight with the county commissioner going? Any change on that?"

"Not that I've heard of. She's going to drop by later. I guess I'll hear what's going on with it then."

Emily had done some Christmas shopping for him already and

wanted to show him what she had found. He was hoping she would stay for dinner. He was planning to surprise her with a delivery from her favorite Chinese restaurant.

"Oh, so Emily is coming over. I wondered why you put on that nice shirt and weren't sulking about being left alone all night," his daughter teased him. "You're probably relieved to have the house all to yourself."

"Don't be silly. Emily is just a friend." Dan felt embarrassed, though he knew he shouldn't be.

Ah, Emily . . . He had to figure out what was going on there. The thing was, he had been enjoying their time together too much to start analyzing and tearing it apart. She was a wonderful woman, and he cared for her—more than he wanted to admit. But he had always been honest with her about his plans. It was okay. Emily understood, he told himself.

He fiddled around with the lamp fittings on the table, wondering now if he should give the lamp to her or not.

"Okay, well you have a good time," Lindsay said. "I've got to run. I'll be at the paper later, if you need me."

"Okay, honey. Good luck." He paused. "And thanks for talking with me. About Wyatt, I mean."

She nodded. "All right then. Enough said."

She kissed his cheek and left the house, leaving him thinking she really had grown into a lovely woman. He was very proud of her.

Lindsay's insights about Wyatt disturbed him, though. He knew she was right. He also had never imagined she had such a deep understanding of the paper, what it meant to the readers, how it served the village. Wyatt didn't seem to see any of that. And if he didn't see that big picture, how would the paper thrive and grow? It didn't bode well, Dan thought.

Despite the predictable growing pains, Dan had sensed all along that things weren't going smoothly. This conversation confirmed it, yet what could he do? The one time he had tried to talk to his son about the paper, Wyatt nearly threatened to toss the whole thing back in his lap.

Wyatt will grow into the job somehow, Dan consoled himself. It's just going to take a little longer than a month or two.

Once he got this ridiculous hunk of plaster off his leg, he'd go down to the office and give his son a crash course in running the paper—whether Wyatt liked it or not. Dan knew he could never leave on his trip while wondering if the *Messenger* would still exist when he got back. That would be unthinkable.

"GOOD MORNING, EMILY." REVEREND BEN'S VOICE STARTLED HER, AND she practically jumped.

"Reverend . . . hello," she replied. Seated on a bench on the green, Emily had been staring out at the water, her thoughts wandering. She had walked from her house down to the green without seeing another living soul, feeling as if she were the only one in town awake this early on a Sunday morning.

"Out running in the snow today?" he asked, eyeing her outfit, a jogging suit topped with a down vest, scarf, and gloves. "You joggers are dedicated. I'll say that for you."

"Just a brisk walk. The streets are too snowy. I need to go down to the beach to run. I was up early and felt like some fresh air."

"I see. Good idea," Ben said, indicating in a knowing glance that he saw a lot more than she'd even hinted at. He glanced at his watch, then added, "Mind if I sit for a minute?"

"No, not at all." Emily moved over and made room for him. He settled down at the opposite end of the bench and looked out at the harbor. The water was slate gray, choppy with white caps. The sun, still low in the sky, was a softly glowing ball edging over a fringe of trees.

"So, how's Rachel doing?" Emily asked, with interest.

"Very well, thank you. Won't be long now." He smiled. "It looks like it will be an exciting Christmas for our family. But what about you? This must be an exciting Christmas for you, too. Because of Sara, I mean," he added.

When it had come to her secret about Sara, Reverend Ben had been her only confidant and sole support for many years. Emily realized now that he was the one person who perhaps truly realized what this holiday meant to her.

She suddenly felt too moved to speak and glanced out at the water again. "Sometimes it's still hard to believe she's really here. I wake up and have to remember." She glanced at him briefly and smiled. "What can I say? It's truly been the answer to my prayers, Reverend."

He didn't reply at first, then reached over and patted her hand. "I know, Emily. It's sort of a miracle really. I'm thankful for your happiness this Christmas, too."

Emily didn't answer. Though she knew she could tell Reverend Ben anything, it was hard to confide in him about this latest problem. Her feelings about Dan. Her hopes for a relationship that often seemed so hopeless. She'd been at Dan's house again last night, and this morning she was filled with the same doubts and questions. Why did she let herself get drawn in like this? Why did she open her heart and let herself feel again when there was no future in it?

She had once told the reverend that she hoped to get married again someday. But that was before Sara came back into her life. Now it seemed as if she were ungrateful, greedy, asking for too much.

"Emily, is everything okay?" Ben asked kindly.

"Yes. Of course." She shrugged. "Everything's great. Just a little stressed with Christmas coming. That's all."

She caught herself, wondering if she had just lied to her minister. Then she realized that, in fact, everything *was* great. She couldn't ask for more. *Wouldn't ask.*

Hadn't she once promised the Lord that if she ever found her daughter, she wouldn't ask for another single thing?

She felt Reverend Ben continue to watch her. "Yes, it's a lot of pressure, these holidays," he said. "A lot of rushing around and expectations. For some people, it's the hardest time of the year. They're constantly reminded of things that are missing in their lives. Very painful," he added, in a sympathetic tone.

"Yes, that's true," Emily agreed. She took a deep breath. Maybe that was it. The holidays were just intensifying her feelings about Dan, making everything worse. It was a romantic notion, to be with someone you loved on Christmas. A romantic fantasy, really.

"It is a difficult time of the year in some ways," she said. "I feel so grateful for Sara. You know I do, Reverend. And yet . . . I also feel my life is lacking in some ways—some important ways. But I don't feel able to ask the Lord for more. That doesn't seem right."

Ben gave her a long thoughtful look. "Maybe not to you, Emily. But, for one thing, the Lord knows best of all that we're only human down here."

His light tone made her laugh. "Yes, I suppose so," she said.

"You told me once you hoped to get married again? Is that it?" he asked kindly.

Emily felt quietly stunned. The reverend was remarkably perceptive. It really was a gift—but also sometimes a little unnerving.

"Well . . . yes," she admitted slowly. "I would."

"Are you seeing someone?" he asked. It was a personal question, yet Emily found the hopeful note in his voice oddly touching.

"Sort of." She nodded. "But it's not going to work out. It's not his fault or anything," she said in a rush. "Just bad timing."

She wondered suddenly if Reverend Ben had any idea who she was talking about. She imagined that there was some gossip about her and Dan floating about. Especially since she was the mayor, and they'd strolled around town so conspicuously last Saturday.

"Oh, I see." Ben nodded and stroked his beard with his hand. "But bad timing isn't necessarily the end of the world. Couples encounter that sort of problem fairly often, I think. They work on it a bit and figure out how to . . . how to synchronize their watches, you might say."

Emily smiled and shook her head. "I know, but not this time." Dan had so many chances to say that he was unsure about his trip or that he would delay it further to give their relationship a chance to develop. Yet he never once even hinted at changing his plans.

"You sound pretty sure of that. I'm not sure what to say then," Ben admitted. He paused. "But don't leave the Lord out of it, Emily. Trust in Him. Tell Him your heart's desires. He wants to answer your prayers in the way that He knows is best for you. You never need worry about asking Him for too much. There's no limit to His love, you know."

"Yes, I know that, Reverend. But thank you for reminding me," Emily said sincerely.

"Maybe you will marry again. But maybe Da—this fellow with the bad timing, I mean—is not the one for you," Ben said gently. "But trust that God has something even better in store."

"Yes, I'll try," Emily promised. She forced herself to smile, knowing in her heart how hard it would be to keep that promise.

The reverend glanced at his watch and quickly rose from his seat. "Goodness, sorry to rush off, but I've got to run. I need to take care of about a thousand and one things before the service this morning."

"I'll see you there. Thanks for talking with me, Reverend."

"No thanks necessary, Emily. You know that." He smiled and nodded and headed off across the green.

Emily knew it was time for her to start home and change. Her mother would soon be waiting for her ride to church. Still, she sat a moment longer, staring out at the empty harbor.

The sun had risen higher, and the water now seemed a brighter shade of blue, the waves far less ominous. Talking to the reverend had helped her realize how she had closed the Lord out of this matter. She had to hand things over to Him and trust Him to figure it out for her.

A familiar verse from the Bible came to mind. *And we know that all things work together for good to them that love God. . . .* She repeated the words in her mind, feeling a certain kind of peace and comfort settle all around her.

"SO, WHAT DID YOU THINK?" LUKE ASKED, AS THEY LEFT THE MOVIE theater. "Did you guess the stepbrother was the one?"

"I thought he could be," Sara said. "They kept hinting it was the old woman, but I knew that was just a red herring."

"Really, how did you know?"

She shrugged. "I just had a feeling."

They walked along without saying anything for a few minutes.

"I'm sorry you didn't like the movie," Luke said.

"I didn't say I didn't like it," Sara replied. She heard her voice sounding grouchier than she had intended. It was late and she felt tired. She didn't mean to be cross with him. "It was okay. I guess I expected something different from the review."

"Yeah, me, too. It wasn't as good as they said."

He glanced at her but didn't say anything more. They came to Luke's 4Runner, and he opened her door. They had planned to go down to the Beanery after the movie for a bite to eat. Sara felt so tired, she wished she could just go home and crawl into bed. She had been sick since Sunday with a bad cold and finally returned to work today. At the moment, all she really wanted was a good night's sleep.

But she didn't want to disappoint Luke. He seemed distant somehow tonight. She wasn't sure why. Maybe he was tired, too, she thought.

Luke parked in front of the café, and they went inside.

"Hey, Sara!" someone called out to her. She turned and saw Wyatt sitting with Lindsay at a table in the back. She waved back to him and then noticed Luke watching her.

"That's Wyatt's sister, Lindsay."

Luke glanced over at Wyatt and Lindsay, then touched Sara's shoulder. "I think the waitress is ready to show us to a table," he said, steering her in the opposite direction.

When they were seated, Luke picked up a menu. "I'm starved. How about you?"

"I'm all right. I ate too much popcorn," Sara said.

"Is your cold bothering you? You sound a little tired."

"I guess I am a little," she admitted. "I'm okay."

She didn't want to complain and ruin their date. Luke had been concerned about her on Sunday, when she had to cancel. He even offered to bring over chicken soup and orange juice and anything she needed from the drugstore. But Emily had already dropped by with supplies. Somehow she had guessed Sara was getting sick the day before, though Sara was sure she never mentioned it.

Luke closed the menu and put it down beside his plate. "We don't have to stay, if you don't feel well. I can take you home. It's okay."

Sara was surprised by his offer and tempted to take him up on it. Still there was a subtle tension in his voice that made her nervous.

"I'm fine. Really," she assured him.

"Okay . . . so what else is it then?" he said.

"What do you mean?" She sat back in her chair, not sure of what he was driving at.

"Well, you didn't have to go out with me tonight, if you didn't want to. It's not like I need you to do me favors or anything, Sara."

"What are you talking about?" His accusation shocked her; at the same time it touched on some guilty little truth that she wasn't quite ready to look at. "Of course I wanted to go out with you. We had plans for Sunday, but I had a cold."

"I'm not sure you were dying to see me on Sunday night, either," Luke replied.

"Luke, come on. You know I want to see you." Sara felt uncomfortable and annoyed to be put on the spot. She was so tired, and she didn't feel well at all. "Why are you asking for all these assurances tonight? That's just the trouble sometimes."

She saw a look cross his face; his eyes widened, and she realized what she'd said.

"Okay, now we're getting somewhere. I didn't even know there was any trouble."

"I don't mean trouble. That's not what I mean," she replied, backtracking.

"Well, it's what you said."

She took a deep breath and tried not to look him in the eye. "Listen, you know that I care about you, Luke. I really value our relationship." She paused, unsure if she should say more—and unsure of how to say what she needed to tell him.

"Go on, I'm listening," he said quietly.

"I just feel as if lately, you have some definite ideas about where things are going with us, and I . . . I'm not ready for anything really that definite or serious right now," she managed. "I've got too much going on, with my job and getting to know Emily. I don't even know how long I'll be living here and—"

"Okay, you don't have to say anymore. I get it," he cut in.

Though his face was an impassive mask, she saw hurt flash in his gray eyes. She reached over and covered his hands with her own. "Luke, you know I care about you."

"Well, apparently not the same way I care about you. I didn't realize I was pressuring you. Is this really about being distracted by your job—or by your boss?" he asked bluntly.

Sara felt her face flush. "Luke, let's not get into that again. Please?"

"Why not? You should see the way your eyes lit up when you just said hello to him," Luke told her. He shook his head, looking angry. "Just forget about it. Forget anything I said. I've been a jerk, I guess." He suddenly stood up and grabbed his coat. "Ready to go?"

Sara felt caught off guard for a moment. "I guess so." She came to her feet and stood there awkwardly while Luke helped her on with her coat.

The short ride back to her apartment seemed endless, tense and silent. When they reached her house, she didn't know what to say. Luke shut off the engine and turned to look at her.

"Well, I'll see you around, Sara."

"I'm sorry if I upset you, Luke. I didn't want to hurt your feelings."

"I'm all right. At least you were straight with me," he said.

"But we could still get together. I mean, we've always been friends," she reminded him.

He shook his head, smiling at her. "You don't get it. I don't want to be just your friend, Sara."

"I know that, but—"

"No, Sara," he cut in. "You said what you had to say. Let's just leave it for now. I don't think I can go backward. That wouldn't work for me."

A wave of sadness welled up inside her. Sara blinked back tears. She didn't want him to see her crying. It seemed selfish or unfair somehow, since she was the one who had disappointed him.

"Okay, I understand," she said. "So long, Luke. I'll see you."

She leaned over quickly and kissed his cheek. Just an impulse, and she didn't stop to think if it was wrong or right. Then she slipped out of the truck and ran up the walk without turning around to look back at him.

"I don't think you ought to go for a walk right now, Dad," Grace said, trying to keep her voice calm and even. "I really need you here in the store. You know how it gets on the Friday before Christmas—all those shoppers."

"Most of them are just browsing. They never ask me for any help. They think I'm a mannequin, sitting in this chair near the door. That's what I'm starting to feel like, anyway," Digger complained. "You ought to just prop me up and pin a price tag on me, Grace. See what you can get."

"Now, Dad, don't be like that," Grace said, trying to soothe him. "Did you finish that rocking chair?" she asked, hoping to focus him on a project. "I could sell that in a minute."

"Needs to dry before I can put another coat of varnish on. I don't want to rush it."

"Yes, that's right. Don't rush it. There's a nice plant stand back in the barn I thought you could paint, though. White or light blue," she suggested. "I'll put a bow on it, put it up front this weekend."

"That one with the curly feet?"

"That's the one." She nodded. "Can you do it for me?"

"Sure. I'll need to buy some paint, though. Guess I'll walk down to the hardware store."

"Don't we have any paint? We must have some white paint," Grace said. She didn't want him walking anywhere alone. She couldn't leave the shop right now to go with him, either. She would miss all her business this morning, and she'd missed too much lately already. Her account books were beginning to show the strain.

"Now what's the problem with me walking down to the hardware store for a can of paint?" Digger picked up his wool cap from behind the counter and pulled it on. "The way you fret lately. I know you mean the best for me, Grace. But it's getting on my last nerve."

"I'm sorry, Dad. It's just that I worry—" Grace stopped herself. He didn't even realize how forgetful he'd been lately. And he had no idea of how his periods of disorientation frightened her. Just this morning she had to remind him that it was December and Christmas was coming. She had hoped the medication the doctors gave him would prevent lapses like that. But so far, it hadn't made much difference.

Before she could say anything more, Daisy trotted down the stairs and ran over to Digger, her tail beating the air.

"Oh, you see I got my hat on, do you, Miss?" Digger said to the dog. "Well, where's your leash? I'll take you."

The dog raced to the door and grabbed her leash from the doorknob, then brought it to Digger in her mouth. Digger laughed and snapped it on her collar.

Grace didn't know what to do. She felt a strange foreboding about letting them go. It was just this way on Thanksgiving Day.

She sighed. This was one morning when she really had to be in the shop. She had a delivery coming in, to say nothing of the Christmas shoppers. And how could she stop him? She couldn't keep him a prisoner in his own house.

"Got your gloves?" she said, walking with him to the door.

"I've got 'em," Digger replied, producing a pair from his pocket and waving them at her.

"Now just to the hardware store and right back. No lollygagging," she instructed. "I'll have your lunch ready upstairs when you get back."

"Yes, Grace. I'll be right back," Digger promised. "I'm just going to get some paint. Maybe I'll treat myself to a new paintbrush, too. No need to make a federal case of it."

Grace watched them go from the front door of the shop until they disappeared down Main Street. Finally she had to shut the door from the cold.

She checked her watch. Half past eleven. She'd give him half an hour. She wasn't sure why she had agreed to it this time. Maybe he'd just worn her out finally.

It had been a daily struggle ever since he had come home from the hospital. So far, she hadn't let him go anywhere on his own. For the most part she went with him when he insisted on leaving the house. Luckily, though, a few others had stepped up to help—Sam and Jessica Morgan and Harry Reilly. Even Carolyn Lewis had stopped in the shop last week and ended up taking Digger with her to the library.

Grace was honestly surprised at the kindness people extended toward her and her father. Well, everyone loved her dad. She'd never been the popular one, that was for sure. But despite their help, the day-to-day responsibility came down to her. Everyone had such busy lives. They couldn't be imposed upon all the time, and she couldn't keep him shackled up in here.

She turned back to her morning task, rearranging the contents of a china cabinet—pieces of Depression glass, some bone-china cups and saucers, and unusual dishes. Everything so fine and fragile, it made her nervous just to touch them. It was frightening just to be alive sometimes, walking around in the world. Once you care for something, get attached, well you set yourself up for heartbreak. You could lose someone you loved as easily as dropping a china cup. Just a beautiful, fragile thing slipping through your fingers, and no way to get the pieces back together again. No way on this earth.

That's how life seemed to her, anyway. When her father lost his patience, he would sometimes say, "For pity's sake, Grace. You can find a cloud in every silver lining, can't you?" But she couldn't help it. She just didn't have the kind of happy outlook some people seemed to be born with. And she didn't look to God to soothe her and save her either, as she once did. Maybe it was just as well. The bad times didn't hurt any less, of course, but she wasn't nearly as surprised by them.

By a quarter to one, Grace had finished with the cabinet. She went to the front of the shop and glanced down the street for her father, who was nowhere in sight. Then she went to the phone and called the hardware store. The owner, Tom Gill, answered.

"I'm sorry to bother you, Tom. It's Grace Hegman. Did you see my dad in there today? Oh, about an hour or so ago?"

"Your father? Not that I recall, Grace. Hold on, I'll ask around." Grace held the phone, feeling her breath grow shorter, as she waited for Tom to return. Finally, she heard him come back on the line. "Sorry

Grace, nobody's seen him this morning. Are you sure he was heading here?"

"He said he was walking down to buy some paint. Maybe he went someplace else," she said, thinking aloud. "I have to go now, Tom. If you see him, just make him stay there, okay? And call me?" she said anxiously.

"Of course. We'll call you first thing," he promised.

Grace dropped the phone and grabbed her coat and car keys. She first ran to the barn behind the shop, half of which was a storage area for the Bramble, the other half a workshop rented by Sam Morgan. She felt a bit of encouragement, as she heard the sound of Sam's power tools.

"Sam," she called, rushing into the workshop. "I need your help. He's lost again. It's all my fault, I just let him go out on his own. I should—"

Sam shut off the table saw at once. "Grace, calm down." Gently, he took hold of her shoulders. "Digger's gone?" She nodded, unable to speak at first.

"He was headed to the hardware store for some paint. He really just wanted to get out of the shop a little. It's been so hard for him—"

"What time was this?"

"He left about eleven-thirty. A little over an hour ago, I guess."

"All right. That's not so bad."

"But Tom Gill said that nobody's seen him. He never got there."

Sam paused to think for a second. "I'll call the police and let them know what's happened. Then I'll go out in the truck and look for him. I'll get Harry to do the same."

Grace nodded. "It's all my fault. I should have told him. He didn't understand how sick he is. I want to help look this time. I can't just sit here doing nothing."

Sam stared at her a moment. "Okay. You take the north side of Main Street, I'll go south. I'll meet you back here in, say, an hour?"

"All right. Thank you, Sam," Grace said sadly.

Sam patted her shoulder, as they headed out of the shop. "We're going to find Digger, I promise."

She nodded. She didn't know what to say. She just hoped they found her father in time.

Grace decided not to take her car, but to go first on foot down Main Street. She stopped at each shop she passed on the way to the hardware store, asking about her father, but no one had seen him.

Finally, she came to the village green. She saw the church at the other end. Had he gone into church? she wondered. That was possible. She walked across the green and went inside.

The church was dark and cool, with shafts of golden and rose-tinted light filtering through the arched windows. Her gaze scanned the pews. The place was empty. He wasn't here. But she sat down anyway in the last pew. She bowed her head and folded her hands.

"Oh, God . . . I know I don't deserve for you to listen to me. I'm apologizing in advance for even asking. If my father is hurt or even dead this time, it's all my fault. I should have taken better care of him. I should have taken better care of Julie. Maybe you wouldn't have taken her from me so soon. . . ."

"Grace? Are you all right?" Grace looked up and saw Reverend Ben standing beside her.

"It's my father. He's lost again. . . . You haven't seen him have you, Reverend?" she asked hopefully.

Reverend Ben shook his head. He slipped into the pew and sat beside her. "No, Grace. I'm sorry. I haven't."

"He went off to the hardware store almost two hours ago and didn't come back. Sam called the police for me. He's looking . . . and Harry . . ." Her voice trailed off, and she covered her face with her hands. She felt the reverend's hand on her shoulder.

"I was just trying to pray before," she added quietly.

"Yes, I'm sorry I interrupted you."

"That's all right. It wasn't going that well."

"God knows your heart, Grace. Even if you can't quite find the right words."

"Well, then He knows I'm heartsick. It's all my fault if my father is hurt this time. I should have never let him out on his own. Not after what happened on Thanksgiving. I never told him the truth about his condition," she admitted. "That was wrong. I can see that now. Maybe God is punishing me."

"God wouldn't do that. I don't really believe He works that way. For one thing, it would be too simple," Ben consoled her.

Grace gave him a bitter smile. "It would, wouldn't it?"

Ben's smile was understanding. "Digger hasn't been gone that long. So let's hope for the best," he urged. "Would you like to pray together?"

Grace couldn't meet his eyes. "Reverend, you already went through this once with me. This is really too much to ask. I feel embarrassed to ask you to help me again. I feel ashamed to call on God."

"I want to help you. God wants to help you. No matter how many times we fall, He's there to pick us up again, Grace. He's already forgiven you for whatever you think you may have done wrong. So forgive yourself. You've only acted out of the best intentions. Everyone knows that."

"I've tried to have my father's good at heart. I'll say that." She shook her head. "Doesn't seem to have been enough, though."

"You might be surprised," Reverend Ben said. "Tell you what, I'll send up some prayers for your father—after all, he's dear to me, too—and you feel free to join in or not as you like. Would you be comfortable with that?"

Grace nodded. "I suppose that would be fine. I know he'd appreciate it."

LUKE PARKED AND TOOK HIS BAGS OF GROCERIES FROM THE BACKSEAT of his 4Runner. The grounds around the cottages were still covered with deep snow. He had only shoveled a narrow path from the parking area to his front door. But as he walked toward his cottage, he noticed what looked like footprints in the snow—the imprint of a man's boots and, alongside those, scattered prints from a dog.

He dropped the grocery bags on his doorstep and looked around. "Hello? Anyone here?" he called out.

Having trained as a cop, he couldn't help feeling a certain alert edge, as he followed the path the prints made. The marks curved around one of the cottages, leading to the front door. The door was ajar. Luke paused a moment before opening it all the way. He listened for the sound of someone moving around inside, but didn't hear anything. Slowly, he opened the door and walked in.

The living room and kitchen area were empty, but then he saw the footprints again, all over the newly finished floor. He followed them to the first bedroom, which was dark, its shades drawn.

Still, he could make out a man lying curled in a ball in a heap of canvas drop cloths left in the corner after the place had been painted. His face was turned away, but Luke suddenly noticed the dog that had been lying nearby was now sitting up and staring at Luke, as if on guard.

Daisy . . . and Digger. What were they doing here?

"Easy, Daisy, you know me," Luke said softly. He held out his hand, and Daisy walked over to him and sniffed it.

Luke knelt down beside Digger, his heart pounding, feeling an odd déjà vu sensation as the events of Thanksgiving night replayed in his mind. He moved closer and checked the older man's breathing. Digger seemed to be breathing fine, he thought. He touched his neck and found his pulse; it was beating even and strong.

Digger's eyes flew open with a start.

"Take it easy, Digger. It's okay," Luke soothed him.

He watched as the old man sat up and shook his head. Digger stared around, clearly confused about where he was. Luke waited for him to get his bearings.

"For goodness' sake, I was sound asleep. Sleeping like a baby. I guess I must have fallen asleep on the job. I'm sorry, Luke," Digger said finally.

Digger had helped paint the inside of this cottage about a week ago. Did he think they were working here today? That would make some sense, Luke thought.

"That's okay. You must be tired," Luke told him gently. "Did you walk all the way here from town?"

Digger's thick brows drew together in a frown. "I don't know. You didn't drive me here? You or Sam?"

Luke shook his head. "Sam's not here now, Digger. It's just you and me."

"I'm not sure," Digger said. He looked around again, as if seeing the cottage for the first time, then fixed Luke with a puzzled gaze. "I ought to get home. Grace was going to fix my lunch. She'll be worried."

Luke didn't doubt for a second that Grace was worried. It was almost three o'clock. "Come on, let me help you up," Luke said, offering Digger a hand.

"Thank you, Luke. Grace will be worried. I ought to call her," Digger said again.

Grace and the police, Luke thought. "I have a cell phone in the truck. We can call on the way back to town."

Luke could imagine the scene at the Bramble Shop right now. The police were probably already out looking, the volunteers lining up again. Thank God, Digger hadn't imagined that he was supposed to go out clamming or fishing today, Luke thought, sending up a silent prayer. At least his confusion had brought him indoors.

IT WAS JUST THREE O'CLOCK WHEN BEN FINALLY PERSUADED GRACE TO return to the shop. They'd been out together, slowly cruising the village streets, searching for Digger. Ben drove while Grace stared out the window, twisting her hands in her lap and looking for any sign of her father through teary eyes.

Ben parked in front of the Bramble Shop, bracing himself for another vigil with Grace. All the while she'd been scanning the streets, he'd been silently praying. They got out of his car and headed up the path toward the shop.

"Maybe there's some news for you, Grace," he said.

"I'm afraid to hear what that might be," Grace replied. She paused on the walk and put her hand to her eyes. Ben moved toward her and touched her arm in a comforting gesture.

Hearing a car approach, he turned to see Luke McAllister's dark green SUV pulling into the shop's gravel drive. When he saw Digger's face peering out the passenger window, Ben felt his heart skip a beat. He gripped Grace's arm. "Look, it's Digger, Grace. He's back," Ben said excitedly.

Grace looked up and turned toward the driveway. "Dad, you're back! For heaven's sake! Are you all right?" She ran toward him as he got out of the truck. Ben followed more slowly, watching the reunion across Grace's snow-covered garden.

"Dad . . ." She started crying, then just about collapsed against him, throwing her arms around his shoulders.

"I'm sorry, Gracie. I didn't mean to scare you like that. I'm so sorry to give you a fright again." Digger patted his daughter's back, as she stood crying.

"He's fine, Grace," Luke assured her. "He just fell asleep in one of the cottages. And look who else is here." Luke handed her Daisy's leash.

"I don't know how to thank you. Why don't you come pick something special out from the shop? Anything you like."

"Don't be silly, Grace," Luke insisted. "I think Digger must be tired, though. Seems he walked all the way to the cottages from town."

"That's a pretty long way," Ben said.

Luke nodded. "Sounds like he went there thinking we were going to work."

"I see." Ben glanced back at Digger and Grace. Grace held her father's arm, about to lead him back into the shop, though it was hard to say which of them supplied the support.

"I'll stay and help here," Ben said to Luke. "You can go."

"Okay, Reverend. No problem." Luke said good-bye to Grace and Digger, then turned to go.

"I guess we need to get inside," Grace said, sounding a bit more composed. "I need to call the police and everybody and tell them you've come home," she told her father.

"Oh, golly . . . You called the police again, did you?"

"Well, I'm sorry, Dad, but I really had to," Grace apologized. She glanced over her shoulder at Ben as they entered the shop, then went over to the phone and started making calls.

Digger took off his jacket, then sat on the stairs, shaking his head.

"I lost track of the time, I guess. It wasn't any big deal, Grace. You didn't have to call out the militia."

His tone was more mournful than reproachful, Ben thought. As if he knew in his heart that something was deeply wrong. Something more than forgetting the time.

Her phone calls completed, Grace looked at Ben and bit down on her lower lip. He met her gaze steadily. "Grace needs to talk to you about something, Digger," Ben began for her. "Something important."

Digger lifted his head. He looked first at Ben and then at his daughter. Ben saw him take a breath and sit up straight.

"All right, what is it? Want to read me the riot act for playing hooky from work today, do you?"

Grace came closer. "No, not exactly, Dad," she said quietly. Ben watched her mouth pull into a thin tight line before she spoke again. "The thing is . . . you're sick, Dad. It's worse than I told you. I didn't want to scare you, but I see now, I should have been honest with you."

"I'm sick?" Digger shook his head and scoffed. "I am not. I just lost track of the time is all. You know I've always been that way, Gracie."

"Yes, you always have been." Grace nodded, agreeing with him. Ben almost thought she was losing her nerve, and he cast a supportive look in her direction. She glanced at him nervously, then took a few more steps closer to Digger.

"Dad, please. Listen to me a minute. Remember when you were in the hospital a few weeks ago, and you had all those tests?" she began slowly.

"Yeah, I remember. Poked and prodded me like a bunch of housewives picking out a chicken."

Ben almost laughed out loud at the image but managed to contain himself. He could see Grace smile slightly, too.

"Well, the thing is the doctors did find something wrong with you. Something more than I told you," she confessed. "They said you've been having little spells. Little strokes, they called them. The strokes have affected your memory—and muddled up your thinking, Dad," she added quietly.

"Muddled me up? Why, I know I'm not as sharp as I used to be maybe. But I understand everything perfectly—well, pretty well for someone my age," he argued. He looked over at Ben. "What is she talking about, Reverend? I'm not having muddling up problems like that."

Grace glanced at Ben nervously. He could tell she wanted his help. "Aren't you, Digger?" he asked gently. "Don't you perhaps feel confused sometimes? I think that's what Grace is trying to say," he coaxed the old seaman.

Digger looked away, stubbornly crossing his arms over his chest. When he didn't answer, Ben said, "Now, think about it a moment. Grace tells me this morning you set off for the hardware store to buy paint. You agreed to come right back here to the shop. Then, somehow, you ended up out at Luke's place, asleep in one of the cottages," he pointed out gently.

"I got tired, I guess. From all that walking."

"Yes, but you weren't supposed to walk all the way out to the cottages," Ben reminded him.

"You got confused, Dad. Mixed up," Grace said bluntly. "It's been happening a lot lately. I've never wanted to embarrass you or make a big thing of it." Her voice softened. "But I think you know it, too. You just don't want to admit it."

"I can understand why this is hard for you to talk about, Digger. Honestly, I can," Reverend Ben said. "It would be difficult for anybody."

Digger pulled off his cap and sighed. He bent his head, rolling the woolen cap around in his big hands. "It happens to old people. It's no crime, you know," he said.

"I know, Dad. But it's different with you. It's . . . more than the usual. Because of this problem with your arteries, the blood flowing to the brain or something. Oh, for goodness' sake." Grace shook her head, sounding frustrated. "The doctor can explain it to you much better than I can. The thing is, you can't be going around the way you're used to—just wandering all day alone, without any company. It's just too dangerous. I can't let you. Something could happen next time. Something terrible."

Digger lifted his head. His small blue eyes brimmed with unshed tears. "I see," he said slowly. "I can't leave the house no more. I just have to sit here and molder away. Is that it?"

Grace, too, looked as if she might start crying again. Ben stepped closer and touched her arm, then reached out to pat Digger's shoulder.

"Not at all, my friend. Not at all," he promised. "But you must know the full story here, Digger. Grace has been shielding you from this. She's been worried about how you'd react. But it's a huge burden for her. You need to help her now by taking care of yourself. By being mindful of your own safety," Ben urged him. "She can't do it all on her own."

Digger glanced up at Grace and took a long breath. "Yes, I know that, Reverend. She's a good girl, always looking out for me. Ever since the good Lord took her mother. She's my youngest, you know," he added, as if Grace were still a little girl.

"Yes, I remember." Ben nodded. He glanced at Grace. "I have a suggestion to offer. Why don't you make an appointment with Digger's doctor and have him explain this condition completely. Then he can advise you both on how this will change Digger's routine. I'll come along, if you like," he added.

"I would like to have a long talk with that doctor, now that you bring it up," Digger said. It sounded to Ben as if Digger was planning on talking the doctor out of the diagnosis. But the meeting would be a start at least.

"I was thinking of that myself," Grace said. "I think we can handle it on our own, though. Unless you want the reverend, Dad?"

"Nah, the reverend's a busy man, Grace. He doesn't need to be tagging along at the doctor's office," Digger said, sounding like his old self again. "Besides, my language might get a little colorful for the reverend when I get a hold of that doctor," he added, grinning. "Despite best intentions, of course."

"Oh, Dad, what a thing to say!" Grace scolded, as she helped him up from the stairs.

"I understand," Ben said, with a smile.

"So, did you save my lunch, Grace? I'm awfully hungry," Digger announced, patting his stomach.

"It's upstairs in the fridge."

"Don't worry, I'll find it." He started up the steps, then turned. "So long, Reverend. Thanks for your help here today." His gaze locked with Ben's for a long moment. "I'm going to remember you in my prayers tonight," he promised.

"Thank you, Digger. I appreciate that," Ben said sincerely.

Grace stood by Ben, watching Digger climb to the top of the stairs and enter their apartment. Finally, she turned to Ben, looking somber but relieved.

"Well, it's done now, Reverend. He knows."

"I think he took it pretty well, all things considered."

"Not as bad as I expected," Grace agreed. "I don't think I could have told him without you. I'm grateful for your help—again."

She glanced at him in that way she had of not quite smiling, but almost—her eyes bright and the corners of her mouth twitching nervously.

"Don't mention it, Grace." Ben pulled on his cap. "I'm thankful that he's all right and that he knows the whole story."

"Yes, I am, too. Very thankful," Grace agreed. She quickly glanced away, and Ben sensed she was thinking about the Lord again and her troublesome relationship with Him.

They heard a knock on the shop door. Two women were peering inside with hopeful expressions. "Are you open?" one of them mouthed through the window.

"Goodness, customers." Grace rushed forward to unlock the door. "Yes, I'm open. Come right in," she said, as the women entered.

"Good-bye, Grace," Ben said, at the door.

"Good-bye, Reverend. I'll see you," Grace called after him.

I certainly hope so, he thought, closing the door behind him. He made his way to his car, then glanced back at the Bramble Shop. He could see Grace through the window, carefully taking a piece of china out of a cabinet to show her customers. She fumbled for a moment, almost dropping it. She recovered just in time, her plain features lit by a surprised expression.

Almost doesn't count, Ben thought. Thank you, Lord, for that.

CHAPTER TWELVE

IT WAS SEVEN A.M. ON THE SATURDAY BEFORE CHRISTMAS, AND Ben walked through the church, amazed by the activity around him. The Christmas Fair was going to be remarkable this year, he realized, maybe the best ever.

Droves of volunteers were already at work setting things up. There were displays selling food and crafts in every spare room and lining the corridors, plus a children's amusement center in one of the Sunday-school rooms. The decoration committee had done an inspired job, with paper garlands, glittering stars, and angels with feathery wings, floating just about everywhere.

The first wave of visitors arrived at nine o'clock sharp, most of them heading first to the arts-and-crafts booths in the all-purpose room. Christmas music played over the PA system, though Ben knew that later in the day the church's own choir would be singing carols. Someone had even scheduled a trio of roving minstrels in Renaissance costumes, who played period music and told stories. And at noon the local theater group was providing a puppet show for the children about the little shepherd boy. How had all this work gone on, right under his nose, and he'd hardly been aware of it?

Maybe it was because the preparations at his own house were so elaborate this year, Ben realized. After Mark received the airline tickets, he'd called to say he thought he could make it home. He promised to try his best, anyway, which was enough of a commitment to send Carolyn charging full-steam ahead, buying him more gifts, putting his favorite foods on the menu. She'd even hired a college student to put a fresh coat of paint on Mark's old bedroom and had bought a new bedspread and curtains.

Ben secretly thought she was running herself ragged and would be too tired by the time Mark arrived to enjoy the visit. But it was good to see her in such fine spirits. Very good, he thought. Rachel had been acting only slightly less excited by the news. Of course, she had another imminent event to focus on. It seemed as if his family would be celebrating the happiest holiday they'd had in years, reunited and awaiting their newest arrival. No wonder he hadn't noticed the preparations for the fair, Ben thought, glancing around and feeling almost awestruck. He'd had some distractions.

At the first booth near the door he saw Emily Warwick, selling fresh pine wreaths, poinsettia plants, and garlands. Her sister, Jessica, was there as well.

"You two are hard at work already, I see," the reverend said, as he greeted them.

"I always sign up for this station," Emily said. "I just love the smell."

"There's already a line at the bake table with Sophie Potter in there. Everyone wants to get a look at her, since she's been on TV," Jessica said.

"Yes, I know. As if they'd never seen her before." Reverend Ben smiled. "Well, our new celebrity should boost the cake and cookie sales."

Grace and Digger came in then, and Digger greeted them with a small wave of his hand. Grace glanced their way and nodded her head.

"Gosh, I didn't expect to see Digger and Grace here, after yesterday," Emily said.

"What a scare," Jessica agreed. "But apparently he's all right, thank heaven. I'm glad they came. I think it's good for them to get out and be among their friends right now."

"Yes, I do, too. Especially for Grace," Ben said. "But who's watching her store today? Did she actually close on the last weekend before Christmas?"

"Molly Willoughby is there with her girls," Jessica said, mentioning her sister-in-law and nieces. Grace had come to know them through Sam and had even given Molly's oldest girl, Lauren, an old piano a few months ago, so Lauren could practice at home.

"That's good of Molly. Grace needs more help like that," Emily said. "More help with Digger."

"Absolutely. She can't do it all herself. Maybe now she'll see that." Jessica turned to Reverend Ben. "Sam said we all ought to do something, make a chain to help Grace."

"I think that's a marvelous idea," Ben said sincerely. He hoped Grace had come to a place where she would accept that kind of help. "Could you organize it—get the names of people who would join and when they would be available?"

"We already started," Jessica told him, with a smile. "Sam and I each made some calls. There are a lot of people who said they'd love to take part."

"That's wonderful. But you know how Grace is. I don't think this will work if the burden falls to her to get in touch. She just won't do it."

Jessica nodded, her long reddish-brown curls bouncing around her pretty face. "I understand, Reverend. Don't worry, leave it to me."

Ben smiled. "All right, then. I'll consider it done. It will be a special gift from the congregation to Grace and Digger."

"A perfect one, too," Emily said.

Ben excused himself from his conversation with the sisters. He turned toward the Hegmans, first sending up a silent prayer.

Thank you, Lord, for sparing Digger again. I don't know what you've been trying to tell us, if there's a message in all this. May our efforts to help the Hegmans be pleasing to you. If there is more we can do, please show us. Please help me when I counsel them. At least I have some good news to offer now. I thank you for that.

* * *

SARA DIDN'T USUALLY WORK ON SATURDAYS, UNLIKE JANE WHO WENT IN on the weekend to work on Monday's edition. But when someone had mentioned the church fair yesterday at the office, Sara had said she planned to go. Somehow Wyatt persuaded her to take pictures for him.

"And maybe you could work up a quick paragraph or two to run alongside them when you bring back the film? We'll do a photo spread," he added. "It won't take you long. You've really gotten a lot faster," he added, with an approving smile.

Though she knew very well that he was charming her into working overtime, it worked. His compliments made her want to prove that she had become more professional at her job.

When she came to the large room that held most of the displays, she looked around for familiar faces. Emily and Jessica were the first ones she spotted. She snuck up on them and succeeded in getting a great candid shot with Emily's arms full of poinsettias and Jessica holding a thick, fragrant garland.

"Sara, that's not fair," Jessica protested. "I would have put on some lipstick or something."

"Sorry, we go for the natural look at the paper," Sara apologized, with a grin. Jessica was so pretty, she looked good no matter what. "Seems like you're doing a brisk business here."

"It's a popular stop," Emily said, smiling at her. "We'll probably sell out before the end of the day."

"What are you doing after the fair?" Sara asked. "Want to get together for dinner or something?"

"I'd love to, honey, but I'm going over to see Dan. I've been doing some Christmas shopping for him."

"How helpful," Jessica teased her older sister. "You didn't offer to do mine, I *noticed*."

Sara couldn't help laughing when she noticed how Emily suddenly blushed and fussed with the bow on a wreath she was holding. Jessica caught Sara's eye, and they exchanged a look.

"How about tomorrow?" Emily said. "Jessica and I are going to do some baking for Christmas. Well, I'll mostly be washing the pans," she added honestly.

"Can you, Sara? That would be fun," Jessica said.

"I'm supposed to see Lucy, but maybe I can come by your house after."

"I hope she's doing all right," Emily said. "I heard she was staying at her mother's."

"Yes, she's moved in there temporarily, and she just found a new job at a restaurant in Hamilton," Sara said.

"Well, give her my best," Emily said kindly. "I'm sure it must have been difficult for her to leave Charlie at this time of year. Charlie is taking it pretty hard. I actually feel sorry for him."

"I haven't been in the Clam Box lately, but I guess I can imagine it. I think I feel sorrier for the people left working there with him," Sara said.

More customers came for wreaths, and Sara decided it was time to get pictures of the rest of the fair. "I'll call at Jessica's tomorrow," she said, with a wave.

"See you, honey." Emily leaned over and gave her a quick hug. "And don't work all day. I can tell you're still not over that cold."

Emily's coddling made Sara laugh. She left them, wearing a small smile and feeling very much in the Christmas spirit.

A little further on she saw Carolyn Lewis and her daughter, Rachel, at a table selling Christmas stockings, place mats, and table runners with hand-worked trim. Sara stopped and took a photo of them, then bought a few things for her family and Emily as gifts.

Sara's next stop was the table where Digger Hegman and Sam were selling handmade wooden gifts: plaques, boxes, and children's toys. Digger didn't even seem to notice her as she took a candid shot of him carefully personalizing a small wooden train, painting the name *Alexander* with a steady hand.

At the paper yesterday, they had heard about Digger's second disappearance. Wyatt wanted to run the story, but Sara disagreed and held her ground. It wasn't really news and seemed a needless embarrassment to the family, she argued. Wyatt didn't concede immediately but, about twenty minutes later, announced that he had a better story to run.

After roaming the large room for a while, Sara strolled down the long corridor and found a bake sale, a rummage-sale room, and even a children's show in progress. Reverend Ben stood in the middle of the action, looking astounded as a juggler balanced a spinning plate on the tip of the minister's outstretched finger.

When Sara finally checked the time, she realized she'd stayed at the fair a lot longer than she'd planned. At least she had managed to do most of her Christmas shopping, too, including a special gift for Luke—a framed piece of stained glass with a beautiful design of blue and green that had the motto "Blessings Bright" written in golden letters in the middle.

She knew Luke loved stained glass; he always noticed it. She wasn't sure why she had felt so compelled to buy it for him after their argument. Did she feel guilty for hurting his feelings or disappointing him? Maybe, she thought, as she placed the gift carefully in the backseat of her car. But she also wanted Luke to know how much she cared for him, even though she wasn't ready for the kind of commitment he wanted.

Sara started up the car, unable to stop thinking about Luke. Maybe she wouldn't give him the gift at all. Maybe that would be sending the wrong message or hurting his feelings even more.

There are still a few more days before Christmas. I'll figure it out, she decided.

Twenty minutes later Sara returned to the office and handed in her film. Wyatt immediately took it back to the darkroom to develop, while she started her article. The Christmas Fair might not be earthshaking news, but it was fun to describe. Sara wrote swiftly, feeling as if she was finally enjoying her job. When Wyatt emerged from the darkroom, she felt a familiar tension return.

"Just a sec," she said. "I've almost got the copy to go with the photos. I just have to smooth this one paragraph—"

"Take your time," Wyatt said.

"Really?" she asked, not quite believing he meant it.

"Well, take another minute or two," he corrected himself. "Then take a look at these." He dropped a contact sheet on her desk.

"What's this?" Sara asked, glancing down at the rows of miniature black-and-white images.

"The roll of film you just shot," Wyatt replied. He handed her a magnifying glass. "Take a look and tell me what you think. But finish that copy first."

Sara rolled her eyes, made some final adjustments to the paragraph about the performers, and printed out her story.

While Wyatt read her copy, Sara picked up the magnifying glass and began to examine the pictures. "This one of Digger painting the toy train is pretty decent," she said.

"Agreed. We're definitely going to use that one," Wyatt said, making her feel good.

"Hmmm . . . none of these shots of Sophie Potter came out. Why did I keep clicking the shutter when she was blinking?"

"Yeah, that's one of the great challenges of contemporary photography—snapping the picture when your subject's eyes are open."

Sara ignored his sarcasm, continuing her examination of the contact sheet. "Oh, I got the one of Reverend Ben balancing that spinning plate on his finger!" she exclaimed, with delight. "He dropped it a second after I took the shot. I was sure it was going to be one big blur."

"I want to use that in the center of the spread. And I'm going to use that one of Betty Bowen carrying the stack of wreaths."

Wyatt had pronounced all of his judgments while staring at her article. Now he met her eyes. "You did okay on the photographs, Sara. And you've got a couple of typos here, but the article's pretty good, too. You make it seem like the fair was really fun."

"Thanks," Sara said. "It was." She knew that wasn't a very articulate response, but she was so unused to Wyatt's praise that it was all she could come up with.

Flustered, she busied herself with the contact sheet again. "Oh," she said, as she saw one she hadn't noticed before. It was the first one she'd taken of Jessica and Emily. The two sisters looked like they were having a great time just being together, and Sara thought they both looked beautiful. "This one of Emily and Jessica—" she started to say.

Wyatt frowned and picked up the contact sheet. "Well, it's a good portrait of them, but it doesn't have much editorial content. I want to go with the choices I've made."

"No, I don't mean for the paper," Sara said. She felt shy, as she asked him for a favor. "I was actually wondering if I could have the negative for it, so I could take it into a photo shop and have prints made. If I frame them, they'll make the perfect Christmas presents for Emily and Jessica."

"That's my favorite last-minute gift idea, too," Wyatt said, smiling. "Don't worry. I can make a few prints for you."

"You can?" she asked in surprise. "But you barely have time—"

"All these pictures will fill out Monday's edition. I'll just finish the layout and send it off to the printer. Then I'll do your prints, no problem."

"Okay," Sara said, wondering why he was being so nice to her. "Thank you."

"Give me about an hour," Wyatt said, returning to his desk and leaving her feeling slightly dazed.

Sara used the time to work on a long-term project Lindsay had given her, sending off letters with rate schedules to potential advertisers.

It was nearly an hour and a half later when Wyatt called out to her. "Want to see your photos?"

Sara walked back to his desk, hoping that the image that had looked so good in a thumbnail print would look decent when blown up to a larger size.

Wyatt had the two 8-by-10 prints lying side by side on his desk. For a moment Sara couldn't speak. Wyatt had taken her black-and-white photo and printed it in a soft silvery finish that made Emily and Jessica look absolutely radiant.

"What do you think?" he asked.

"They're gorgeous!" Sara answered.

"Well, you happen to have a very photogenic family," he told her, with a grin. "And you took a good picture."

"But I never imagined it would come out like this."

He laughed. "That's just a darkroom trick. I'll show you sometime. Now go find some nice frames to do justice to our artwork."

The word *our* caught Sara's attention. He'd said it easily, as if taking for granted that they really had something in common. Did they?

He looked at her, his blue eyes alight. "You've inspired me—or at least reminded me of how much I like messing around in the darkroom when I'm not under a deadline. I'm going to develop a couple of my own rolls now, see if I have any Christmas-worthy shots."

"Okay, see you Monday," Sara said, taking the prints from his desk. She suddenly looked up at him. "You made three."

He shrugged. "I thought you might want one for yourself."

"I do," she said, touched by his thoughtfulness. "Thank you, Wyatt."

"You're welcome. See you Monday," he said, as he turned back toward the darkroom.

THE HOUSE WHERE LUCY'S MOTHER LIVED WASN'T FAR FROM SARA'S. SHE found it easily, and as she walked up the path to the front door, she saw Lucy waiting for her.

"Sara, thanks for coming," Lucy said, giving her a hug.

"I'm glad you called me. I was worried when I heard what happened, but I didn't know where to reach you."

"And you couldn't ask Charlie, that's for sure," Lucy replied. "Come on in. Let's sit in the living room."

Sara followed Lucy to the living room, which was comfortably furnished with a big, soft couch and armchairs arranged in front of a small hearth. A Christmas tree, laden with decorations and lights stood in one corner of the room.

Miniature trucks scattered across the hooked rug and the sound of a TV playing cartoons in another room told Sara that Lucy's kids were in the house. She also noticed an older woman cooking in the kitchen.

"So, you've been here since Monday?" Sara said, as Lucy settled herself in an armchair.

"Yes, it will be exactly one week tomorrow." Lucy nodded, and Sara could tell she'd been counting the days. "I brought a bunch of stuff over that morning, then brought the kids after school." Lucy sighed. "I guess it seems a little impulsive or something."

"Not really. I knew you and Charlie were having problems."

"You and everyone else in town. I guess it wasn't a question of 'if' but more like 'when.' " Lucy shook her head, looking a little lost. "I don't know. Some couples seem to fight their whole married lives but stick together somehow. I just couldn't do it anymore."

"Well, maybe you did the right thing," Sara offered, not really knowing how to console her friend. She had thought Lucy would feel relieved or maybe even feel a sense of triumph by having the guts to finally leave Charlie. But she was clearly sad and confused.

"That's just the thing," Lucy said, "I'm still not sure if it's the right move. For the boys, I mean."

"How have they been taking it?"

"At first they just sort of took it in stride, as if they almost expected it. Or were afraid to ask questions. They seemed happy to have some sleepovers at Gram's house. My mother spoils them something silly," she said, rolling her eyes. "But now they're starting to ask, 'When are we going home, Mommy? When are we going home?' I still don't think they really understand what's happening. Even C.J.," Lucy added. Sara knew Lucy meant Charlie Junior. He was older, about ten now. "Maybe they just want to pretend it isn't happening. I don't know. . . ."

"That must be hard." Sara didn't know what to say. When she was working at the diner, she thought she had all the answers about Lucy and Charlie. It seemed crystal clear that Lucy would be much happier if she left her husband and started a new life for herself. But now Sara could see that it was all very complicated. She honestly wished Lucy wasn't married to Charlie—but what did she know? She couldn't give any advice, she realized. And maybe that meant she was becoming a little wiser herself.

"So what are your plans?" she asked her friend. "You said you found a new job in Hamilton?"

"I was lucky. This really nice restaurant had an ad in the paper on Tuesday. Somebody had to leave all of a sudden with back trouble. I went in and got hired on the spot." Lucy's face brightened for the first time since Sara had come in. "I started on Wednesday, and the tips have been great. And it's been easy with my mother here, watching the kids. I don't have to worry."

"That sounds good. What about Charlie? Have you heard from him?"

Lucy's eyes widened, and she laughed. "That goes without saying—though most of it doesn't bear repeating. Then it finally dawned on me, I don't have to listen to him anymore. Every time he started yelling or even raising his voice, I just hung up the phone," she said, with a shrug. "He finally got the message that if he wanted to have a complete conversation, he couldn't do it by yelling at me."

"That's progress," Sara said.

"He's come to see the boys about three times when I've been out working. He can see them as much as he wants. That's fine with me," Lucy insisted. "Maybe he'll even be spending more time with them than when we were together. He's always working or out with his political pals."

"I guess that's true." Sara paused. She wondered if she should ask more—she didn't want to pry, but she was concerned for Lucy's welfare. "Have you talked to a lawyer at all?"

"A lawyer? I haven't even thought of that," Lucy admitted. "I mean, things could change. It might not come to that."

"I didn't mean you had to rush into anything. It's just that you ought to find out what your rights are—I mean, if you and Charlie get legally separated."

"Yes, I know. There's the house and the business and all. My mother said the same thing," Lucy said, making Sara feel a little easier about bringing it up. "But I'm just not ready for that. I can hardly figure out up from down right now. On Friday I forgot to put sandwiches in the kids' lunch boxes. Can you believe that? They both came home pretty mad at me." She laughed, covering her mouth with her hand. "School's over now. The kids are starting their Christmas vacation, so at least I don't have to worry about that for a while."

"What about you? How did you end the semester?" Sara asked.

"Not good." Lucy glanced at her and winced. "I had to take two incompletes. My professors were real nice about it, when I explained I had a family crisis. But the truth is, writing those papers doesn't seem all that important now compared to my marriage. Still, if I lose those credits, it's like Charlie got his way anyway about me going back to school. So that's what really gets me," she admitted. "He kept telling me to give it up, that it was too much for me. And now I just couldn't stand it if I proved him right."

"Maybe I can help you with those papers," Sara offered.

"Would you, Sara? That would be great. I don't know if I can go back for the spring semester, but I just want to finish this one. I really do."

"I understand," Sara said. "Don't worry. Charlie's not going to take all your hard work away from you—even by default."

"I have seen Reverend Ben," Lucy went on. "I talked with him twice last week."

"What does he think you should do?"

Lucy gazed at the Christmas tree. "He thinks this is a hard time of the year to see anything clearly. The holidays have a way of stirring up everybody's feelings. So he thinks I ought to see how Charlie reacts after he calms down a bit. Reverend Ben isn't the type that really tells you what to do . . . which is maybe why I like him so much," Lucy said, with a small smile. "But he did say to go slow and really think things through. And to pray."

All excellent advice, Sara thought. She didn't pray much herself, but from time to time, she found herself talking to God. Or writing him letters in her journal. Luke was the one who had given her that idea when she had felt so stuck about what to do about Emily. She wished she could tell him about seeing Lucy. He would understand how inept she felt, unable to really help or advise her friend. She wished she could tell Lucy about what had happened with Luke. But this didn't seem like the right time.

After a few more minutes, Lucy brought Sara in to meet her mother. Margaret Dooley was a plump, middle-aged woman who looked like an older version of Lucy.

"I've heard a lot about you, Sara," she said, with a broad smile. "And now you write for the newspaper, too."

"Yes, I do," Sara said evenly, realizing that good-hearted Lucy had probably exaggerated her talents to no end.

"Would you like to stay and have supper with us?" Margaret asked. "There's plenty."

"It smells wonderful," Sara said honestly. "But I have to get going. I have to be at a family thing."

"The Warwicks, she means," Lucy said quietly to her mother.

"I know that." Margaret smiled at Sara again. "Well, you come back and see us another time then."

"I will," Sara promised. She wondered how long Lucy would be living here. Maybe a long time, she thought. Then again, maybe she and Charlie would be back together by the New Year. It was really impossible to say.

"AM I DOING THIS RIGHT? I THINK MY FINGER IS STUCK TO THE SPOON." Emily wanted to laugh at herself, but Jessica was so serious about cookie baking, she didn't think her sister would appreciate the humor.

"What's happened now?" Jessica came over and looked over Emily's cookie sheet, which was covered with oddly shaped scattered dollops of dough, a sharp contrast to Jessica's tray, which had perfectly formed dough balls in three neat rows.

"Interesting. Did it take long to get them to look like that?"

"Don't say I didn't warn you," Emily replied innocently, as Jessica carefully removed the spoon stuck to her finger.

"That was close. I nearly thought we had to call Dr. Elliot," Jessica remarked. "That's what the glass of water is for, by the way."

"I was wondering about that. I thought you might have left it there in case I got thirsty. From eating too much cookie dough, I mean."

"Oh, Emily." Jessica shook her head. She took Emily's cookie sheet and started filling it with more bits of dough. The contrast was startling.

"Do all married people get so smug?"

"Only the extra-happy ones," Jessica teased back.

"That's what I thought." Emily tugged a ringlet of her sister's long shiny hair. "It wasn't so long ago that you were domestically challenged as well. You ought to have a little more sympathy, I'd think."

Jessica turned away to put the cookies in the oven. "I think you ought to get married again," she said.

"Married—me? Whatever gave you that idea?"

"Oh, I don't know. Haven't you thought about it?" She turned around and stared straight at Emily.

Emily felt her mouth twist in a smile. "Well . . . from time to time, I guess. Yes, maybe I have—lately."

"Since you started seeing Dan?" Jessica prodded her in a knowing tone.

Emily's eyes widened. The cat was out of the bag now, it seemed. "Partly," she admitted. "But it seems more like finding Sara really gave me the idea. Or made it seem as if now I was really free to get married again. Before that, I felt too sad about losing her—almost as if I didn't really deserve to be so happy again," Emily said honestly.

"And now?"

"Now I do. I know I've been teasing you a lot, but you and Sam do seem so happy. I guess I'm a little jealous or something."

"Emily . . ." Jessica reached out and touched her sister's arm. "Please don't say that. I wouldn't want to make you sad for the world."

"Oh, I know that. And I didn't say sad. I love seeing you two so happy. It's just made me think about my own life. What I had once . . . and what hopefully I can have again. Tim and I were so happy together," she said. "I'd like to feel that way again, to share my life with someone. I know I've certainly taken my time, but I finally think I'm ready."

"Well, what about Dan? I think he's perfect for you," Jessica urged. "I know you've been spending a lot of time with him. Someone even told me . . . Oh, forget it. It was nothing," she said hastily. "I'd better check the cookies—"

"Someone told you what?" Emily prodded, following her to the oven.

"Oh, it was silly, really." Jessica removed a pan of cookies from the oven, put it aside to cool, then glanced over at Emily. "Someone told me they saw the two of you hugging last weekend in the middle of Main Street."

Emily felt her face flush. "Oh. That. I was just helping him get into my car."

Jessica shrugged. "People love to gossip. Especially about their mayor."

"Yes, being gossiped about is part of the job," Emily agreed.

"So, is it serious? I mean between you and Dan?" Jessica asked.

Emily picked up a cookie. It was almost too hot to eat, but she took a bite anyway. "I don't know really. When we're together, it always seems great. Better and better, actually. I know Dan seems sort of—oh, I don't know—stuffy or something. But he's really a lot of fun, and he's so smart. We talk about everything and even when we argue, it just feels right. Really right," Emily said, with a sigh. She blew on the cookie and took another bite. "He's so sweet. Even with his leg still in a cast, he made me this beautiful lamp. Restored one, I mean. A real antique."

"He made you a lamp?" Jessica looked impressed. "Wow, this does sound serious."

"Sam made you a house. *That's* serious," Emily reminded her, gazing around at the beautifully renovated kitchen.

"He already had the house. He just needed the right woman to inspire him to fix it up," Jessica replied, with a laugh. "So what does this lamp look like?"

"It's gorgeous. Wait till you see it. You know that antique reading lamp in Grace's window, with the fringed shade? It looks just like that. Nicer, actually. Well, I think so," she added, feeling suddenly self-conscious.

"I love that lamp. I think he's wild about you," Jessica decided. "A man with a broken leg doesn't just fix up a lamp for a woman if he doesn't really care."

Emily cast her a thoughtful look and took another cookie. "Well, he is cooped up in the house all day. I guess he was looking for some project to keep him busy. Still, it was very thoughtful."

"Absolutely. Want a cup of tea?" Jessica said, turning on the burner under the teakettle.

Emily nodded. "The problem is, we started off being friends, and now it's hard to tell what's really going on. I know what I wish would happen. But I'm not twenty-one anymore—or even thirty-one," she said, with a small smile. "Sometimes I think I'm really falling for him. But as soon as his leg is better, he's going to sail off on his trip. So what's the use of getting more involved?"

"Oh, but you can't be so pessimistic, Emily. Maybe Dan's feeling the same way about you but doesn't know what to do. Remember how it was with Sam and me? I kept telling him not to get his hopes up, because I planned on going back to the city—and when the time came to go, I couldn't live without him."

"I remember," Emily said quietly. "You two are the classic happy ending."

Although Jessica and Sam's story did have a happy ending, Emily knew only too well that not every story did. Besides, it was different for her and Dan. For one thing, they were older. Life just didn't seem that dramatic. They'd both had their hearts broken at least a few times and knew that even if you truly believed you couldn't live without someone, if you had to—somehow—you just did. Not without tears and heartache, not without feeling something whittled away inside. But unbelievably enough, life went on.

She was now in a more cautious stage of life, Emily realized. She didn't want to risk getting her heart broken, if she could avoid it. Deep down she knew she was past the stage of worrying about falling for Dan. She had fallen. Big time. And when she faced it squarely, it terrified her. What was going to happen? What should she do? It all seemed so impossible.

And yet, she still had an irrational glimmer of hope. Dan could change his mind and not go. Things could work out—couldn't they?

She turned to her sister as Jessica returned to the table with two mugs of tea. "I do like Dan—more than like him," she admitted. "It's very hard for me. I haven't felt this way for anyone in such a long time. Oh, I dated a few times, but that was different. I'd forgotten about this—this giddy, swept-off-your-feet feeling. I'm not sure I like it," she confided, with a small smile. "It's sort of scary."

Jessica stared at her. "It's wonderful. I'm so happy for you, Emily." She reached over and squeezed Emily's hand.

"Thanks, but don't get too excited. I don't really know how Dan feels. He hasn't really said or done anything to give me hope. Except for the lamp, I guess."

"Well, that's something. Maybe he's scared, too," Jessica suggested. "After all, he had an unhappy marriage, and though he's had years to find someone new, he hasn't either."

"Yes, that's true," Emily said. "I'm sure Dan has his own fears about relationships. But it's more than that. I just don't want to get my hopes up and end up disappointed. He always mentions that he's leaving town as soon as he's fit and able. He never seems to have any doubts about that, so maybe he's trying to tell me something."

"Maybe." Jessica sipped her tea. "Then why the gorgeous lamp?"

Emily shrugged. "I don't know. He wants me to keep a light in the window for him while he's at sea?"

"Men! They're so dense sometimes, I wouldn't doubt it."

They laughed together for a moment, then Jessica said, "I remember when things looked so bleak between me and Sam, Emily. I'll never forget what you told me."

"Oh, what was that?" Emily was almost afraid to hear her own sage advice tossed back at her. She nibbled on another cookie for distraction.

"You said something like, if I loved Sam, it was worth anything and not to let my pride get in the way and let my chance at happiness pass me by."

"Good advice." Emily nodded. "For you, I mean. I'm not so sure about Dan, though. I'd be willing to put my pride aside and tell him how I feel. I really would," she said sincerely. "I just don't think it would change his plans."

Jessica looked at her for a long moment. "You don't know that, Emily. You don't know what he's thinking. You've more or less just told me that."

"I suppose."

"Emily, I just don't want to see you end up having regrets about this," Jessica said quietly. "If you found someone you care for, you have to just go for it."

Emily stared at her napkin. "Oh, I don't know. Maybe I just don't have the courage. I'll have to see what happens, I guess."

Jessica watched her for a moment. "When will he go, do you think?"

"Sometime after New Year's. He's going to have the big cast replaced by something smaller. Then a few weeks after that, he can leave."

"Well, a lot can happen in a few weeks," Jessica said optimistically.

"You really think so?" Emily tried hard to hide the note in her own voice that showed how eager she was for any bit of hope.

"I know so."

"Well, we'll see," Emily replied after a moment. "At least there's Sara now. Whenever I even start to feel down or lonely, I think about having her in my life, and it makes up for everything."

"I can see that," Jessica said, smiling softly at her.

"I'm just sorry sometimes that I've missed so much." Emily shook her head. "Somehow, getting to know Sara now has made me think about that part even more. She's such a terrific person, such a great young woman. I'm really so proud of her. But I know I didn't have any part in raising her."

"You could have another child, you know," Jessica said softly.

"Oh, I couldn't. It's too late for that."

"Don't be silly; you're only forty-two. Have you ever thought about it?"

"Sometimes," Emily confessed. She'd thought about it more and more since Sara came into her life. She loved being a mother so much, even in the limited way that she tried to be a parent to Sara. She thought it would be wonderful to have another child and be able to raise him or her. But that dream seemed so far out of reach.

"It's hard to think of having a baby when I don't even have a relationship with anyone. Shouldn't you check on the cookies? I think I smell something burning," she said, purposely changing the subject.

Jessica jumped up and ran to the oven, catching the second batch in the nick of time.

There was a knock on the kitchen door. Emily saw Sara's face at the window and rushed over to let her in. "You're just in time to take over," she greeted her. "I don't think I passed the audition."

"What do you mean?" Sara asked, as she shrugged off her coat.

"Emily made these cookies." Jessica held out the tray with Emily's oddly shaped efforts. "Sort of scary, don't you think? More appropriate for, say, Halloween?"

"They taste fine," Emily insisted, biting into another. "Your aunt is very fussy."

"And now she's trying to eat all the incriminating evidence," Jessica continued.

"I can help with that," Sara offered. She swiped a cookie, as Jessica whisked the tray out of reach. "But I'm just warning you guys, I'm really lame in the kitchen."

Emily put her arm around Sara's shoulder. "See, she does take after me in some ways," she said proudly, giving her a hug. "Don't you think?"

Jessica smiled. "Absolutely."

ON THE WAY BACK TO TOWN FROM JESSICA'S HOUSE, SARA COULDN'T avoid passing Luke's property. She slowed to a near stop as she came to the turnoff. She had his gift stashed in the backseat of her car, wrapped and ready, though she wasn't really sure how or when she would give it to him.

She turned and drove down the narrow road to the parking area. The sound of her car wheels on the gravel road seemed terrifically loud to her in the stillness. Luke's SUV stood in the parking area, and she pulled up alongside it and turned off her headlights.

The lights in his cottage glowed behind drawn curtains. He must be home, she reasoned. It wasn't really late, but she didn't want to just knock on his door and hand him the gift. Sara pictured Luke's face the last time she had seen him, the sad expression in his eyes. No, she didn't want to face him right now. She wasn't ready. Why give him the gift at all then? she wondered.

She wasn't sure. Maybe to show him that even though she had disappointed him—and despite what he thought—he meant something to her. It was just something she wanted to do.

Sara grabbed the gift from the backseat and got out of her car. She left it on his truck, on the hood near the windshield, where he would be sure to find it. It was a clear, cold night. The package wouldn't get wet, and there was no one around here to disturb it, she reasoned.

Then she got back in her car and headed home. She felt relieved, as if it had been the right thing to do. No matter how Luke felt about her now.

AFTER HAVING A SUNDAY DINNER WITH CAROLYN, RACHEL, AND JACK, Ben had left to visit two different members of the congregation who were in the hospital in Southport. He didn't return home until nearly ten. He came in to find the house completely dark, except for a shaft of light coming from the kitchen, where Carolyn always left the light on over the stove.

She must be upstairs, gone to bed early, he thought, as he hung up his coat and scarf. He thought of all the work Carolyn had been doing to get ready for Christmas and Mark's visit and the baby coming, not to mention her time helping at the fair. *The preparations will be over soon. Then we can all relax and enjoy ourselves.*

He was about to go upstairs to join Carolyn in bed when he realized he heard someone downstairs in the kitchen. A soft, muffled sound. Almost imperceptible. But there it was again.

The sound of someone crying.

Ben walked toward the kitchen, his pulse quickening as he began to fear the worst. "Carolyn, is that you?" He saw her at the table, her shadowy outline, her head bent in her hands.

"Honey, what is it?" He put a light on and came toward her. He put a hand on her shoulder. "What is it, dear? Why are you crying? Has something happened to Rachel?" he asked fearfully.

Carolyn looked up at him finally, her blue eyes red-rimmed and swollen. "No, it's not Rachel. It's Mark. He's not coming, after all. He just called a little while ago. Left a message on the machine. I didn't even hear the phone. I must have been up in his room, hanging those striped curtains. You know the plaid ones didn't look right. . . ." She paused, starting to cry again.

Ben didn't know what to say. He felt his mouth go dry as chalk. He sat down beside her and pulled her close. She dropped her head on his shoulder as he patted her back. "You can hear the message if you want to," Carolyn said, between sobs. "I saved it for you."

"That's okay. I'll listen to it later," Ben told her, feeling a mounting anger. How could Mark be so thoughtless, so callous toward them? Especially toward Carolyn. Didn't he know what this meant to her? He'd as good as broken her heart—again. Ben was so upset, he could barely see straight. He didn't know if he could ever forgive Mark for this—though he instantly asked the Lord's forgiveness for even thinking such a thing.

He took a deep breath, listening to Carolyn cry and feeling himself sink inside, like a deflated balloon.

"What was Mark's reason for the change in plans? Did he say?" Ben asked cautiously.

Carolyn lifted her head and shrugged. "No, not really. He said he had to work. They needed him to stay, because somebody else had to go, last minute. Or something like that. I don't know." Carolyn shook her head and took a deep breath. Ben could see her struggling to compose herself again. She touched her hand to her forehead and closed her eyes. As if she felt dizzy or even faint.

"Are you all right, dear? Would you like a glass of water or something?"

She didn't answer for a moment, then quickly shook her head, her eyes still shut. "I'm okay, Ben. Please," she said, a bit sharply.

He knew how she hated for him to fuss over her. Especially when something like this happened. He sat back, waiting, watching her, wishing there were something he could do.

Finally, she opened her eyes. "I just have a bad headache. That's all."

"I'll get you something," he offered. He began to get up, but she stopped him with her hand on his shoulder.

"No, that's okay. I'll get it," she said, coming to her feet. She walked over to the kitchen cabinet near the sink and took out a bottle of headache capsules, then shook a few into her hand and turned on the water.

"Have you called Rachel yet?" he asked.

"No, not yet." She sipped a glass of water. "It's late now. I'm sure she's sleeping. I'll call her tomorrow."

"I can do it," he offered.

"No, I will. I have more time." She wanted to commiserate with her daughter, who would be just as disappointed, Ben thought. He felt bad about it, too, but he somehow felt left out from their grief.

Oh, Lord, why did this have to happen? Ben asked silently. *I thought we were going to have such a good holiday. Poor Carolyn. Please help her, Lord. Don't let her get pulled under by this.*

Carolyn placed the glass in the sink, then turned to look at him. "I know you warned me about going too overboard. About getting so excited about Mark coming home. Maybe we shouldn't have even sent the tickets—"

"Carolyn, please. I'm not about to say I told you so. I feel as disappointed as you do. As for the tickets, that was my idea. We both agreed to try it," he reminded her.

"Yes, Ben, I know, but—" She briefly closed her eyes again. "Oh, I don't know. I don't even know what I'm trying to say anymore. Why won't he come home? I don't understand it." Her voice quavered, on the edge of tears again.

Ben placed his hands on each of her shoulders. "I don't know. We did what we could, Carolyn, but it just wasn't the right time. There's nothing more we can do. We have to carry on and try to have a good holiday without him. For Rachel's sake, at least," he reminded her.

Carolyn stared at him. Her eyes looked blank, empty, someplace beyond sadness. The vision scared him.

"I'm sorry, dear," he added, fumbling for the right words. "I really am. I know how bad you must feel. All the work you've been doing around here. I just don't know what to say. I hope someday Mark comes to appreciate you."

She stepped back. "It's all right, Ben. I'm okay," she promised. "Please don't be mad at him."

He looked at her a long moment. "I'm trying not to be. I'm trying to understand," he replied. "It's very hard."

"Yes," she agreed. "It is." She sighed, folding a dish towel and setting it over a chair. "I'm going up now," she said. "Are you coming?"

"In a minute. You go ahead. I'll be right there."

He heard her slow steps climb up the stairs, then head into the hallway leading to their bedroom. He looked over at the answering machine on the far counter. The green message signal blinked in the dim light. Mark's message, he thought. He stood there a long time, watching the light, tempted to hit the replay button, yet unable to do it somehow. He imagined his son's voice, casual yet decided, delivering the bad news. Without a thought to the crushing disappointment he was delivering. An unexpected Christmas gift.

No, he didn't need to hear it tonight. It would rile him up all over again. He needed a good night's sleep—and a long talk with the Lord beforehand—in order to face this cold, unhappy truth tomorrow.

CHAPTER THIRTEEN

SOMEONE HAD TRIMMED THE FRONT DOOR AND THE PLATE-glass windows that read *Cape Light Messenger* with colored lights. Sara noticed them from a half block down the street.

Inside she found two small, brightly wrapped packages in front of her computer, one from each of her fellow reporters. Jane gave her a CD of a blues singer they'd discovered they both loved, and Ed gave her a desk calendar with humorous malapropisms for each day. Sara had gifts for them, too, and she snuck the boxes onto their desks.

She hadn't bought anything for Wyatt, though; she hoped he hadn't gotten her a gift. She had found herself thinking about him a lot since Saturday, especially every time she looked at the print of Emily and Jessica.

He finally came in a few minutes later and breezed by her desk with his usual greeting, which Sara found oddly comforting. Ten minutes later the staff met for the morning briefing, reviewing their assignments. Wyatt brought it to a close, saying, "I think we should all leave on the early side today. It is Christmas Eve, and there's no edition tomorrow."

"Great, I'd love to get on the road early. Kenny's folks are expecting me for dinner," Jane said. Sara knew she was going to Maine to spend the holiday with her boyfriend's family.

"My column is set," Ed told Wyatt. "I can have it on your desk within the hour."

Wyatt glanced at his watch. "It's only half past nine, Ed. I didn't mean quite that early." Jane and Sara shared a glance and tried not to laugh out loud. Ed made a sour face and adjusted his bow tie.

Sara was working at her desk, trying to follow up on the story about Emily's battle with the county, when Lindsay came in, wearing a red felt Santa cap. She gave out presents to everyone—small gold boxes of fancy chocolates.

"I love these," Jane gasped. "I'm going to hide them in my desk and make them last until next year."

"They won't last until next week in my desk," Sara said. "Thanks, Lindsay."

"My pleasure," Lindsay replied. "Have a merry Christmas, everyone."

Soon after lunch Lindsay took off, and Jane and Ed both said their good-byes. Jane gave Sara a hug. "Have a good holiday—and don't let Wyatt keep you here too long," she whispered.

"I won't," Sara promised.

"What are you doing for New Year's Eve?" Jane asked, as she hoisted up her shoulder pack.

"I don't have any plans," Sara admitted. She thought fleetingly of Luke. He must have found her gift by now, but he hadn't even called to wish her a merry Christmas.

"My roommate and I are having another party. Why don't you come?"

"Okay, maybe I will," Sara agreed. She felt relieved. At least she had someplace to go now. "Have a great holiday!"

Sara went back to work, finished her copy, and then brought it back to Wyatt's desk to hand in.

"Ready to go?" he said.

"Just about. I made some calls on that story about the dispute between the mayor's office and the county. No real change. Warren Oakes says the federal agency that awarded the grant finally promised to write a letter to the county, but they haven't done it yet."

"Everything slows down at this time of the year, especially in government offices. Stay with it, okay?"

"No problem," Sara said. "Well, I guess I'll go now." She was about to wish him a happy holiday when he stopped her.

"Wait . . . I have something for you." He opened a drawer in his desk, took out a slender, rectangular package, then came around and handed it to her. "Merry Christmas, Sara."

Sara didn't know whether to be embarrassed or pleased. "Thanks . . . but I didn't get you anything."

"That's okay. It's nothing really. I saw this the other day in a bookstore and thought you might like it."

Sara tore the paper off. It was a book of photographs by different artists—Ansel Adams, Alfred Stieglitz, Alfred Eisenstadt, Annie Liebovitz, and others. She leafed through the pages. "This is wonderful! Thank you." She looked up at him, touched once again by his unexpected generosity.

"I thought you might like it. I'm glad."

"I'm sorry I didn't get anything for you," she apologized.

"Don't be silly. I never expected you to."

Wyatt put his hands on her shoulders and smiled down at her, his eyes filled with a warm, tender light.

Sara met his gaze, not knowing what to say. But she didn't step away from him. She felt her heartbeat quickening. Something was shifting between them. She could almost feel herself being pulled toward something new and exciting.

Wyatt kept looking at her, his hands on her shoulders. He moved closer, and Sara thought he might be about to kiss her. She stood motionless, breathless, staring back at him.

Then the phone on his desk rang, and the shrill sound seemed like a cannon boom to Sara. She jumped back, suddenly embarrassed.

"Oh blast, I'd better get that," he said. He ran his hand through his hair and grabbed at the phone. *"Messenger,"* he said abruptly. "Oh, hi, Dad." He looked at Sara and rolled his eyes. "Can you hold a minute?" He covered the receiver. "It's my father. I'd better talk to him. Have a good holiday."

"Thanks, you, too." She clutched her book against her chest, as she stepped away. "Merry Christmas, Wyatt."

"Merry Christmas, Sara," he said, smiling at her again. He turned back to the phone, and Sara went back to her desk to collect her things.

Now that was interesting, she told herself, as she walked to her car. Wyatt was sending a message, and she rather liked it. She felt flattered that he found her attractive, even though she suspected that part of the attraction was merely her proximity. But maybe that was okay. She liked him a lot and enjoyed hanging out with him. Wyatt might go to Jane's party on New Year's Eve, she realized happily. That could be fun.

Twenty minutes later, back in her apartment, Sara's heart rate picked up a notch, as she noticed the blinking light on her answering machine. She hit the play button and listened.

"Hi, honey. We just wanted to say hello." It was her mother in Maryland. "I guess you're still at work. Don't bother calling back tonight. We're just leaving for Aunt Ellen's. We'll call you tomorrow morning," she promised. "Everything is set for our visit. Can't wait to see you."

Sara was eager to see her folks, too. The holidays made her a little homesick. But she was still apprehensive about bringing her parents together with Emily. She wished she had someone to talk to about it. She didn't really know Jane well enough, yet, though she was becoming a good friend, and Lucy was too busy with her own problems. Wyatt hadn't been very understanding when she'd tried to explain it to him.

She pulled off her boots and took out the outfit she planned to wear to the party—a long, graceful black velvet dress with a round neckline and tight sleeves. She'd worn it last when Luke took her out to dinner in Newburyport.

Luke was the one she could talk to—about anything, really. But he didn't even want to be friends. He'd made that perfectly clear. Sara knew that maybe she didn't have the right, but she felt hurt and rejected by him, too. She just had to get used to the idea. *Luke isn't part of my life anymore,* she thought sadly.

* * *

THE MERE SIGHT OF JESSICA AND SAM'S HOUSE THAT EVENING INSTANTLY brightened Sara's spirits. She'd always loved the quaint Victorian set in the woods off the Beach Road. Sam bought it at an auction years ago but hadn't seriously started restoring it until he met Jessica. Though Sara knew there was still a lot of refinishing to do inside, the outside looked picture-perfect. Painted dark blue and trimmed with cream and hot pink shutters, it was a classic "painted lady," with a peaked roof and a long chimney spouting smoke into the starlit sky.

Tonight it seemed lovelier than ever, decorated with tiny lights outlining the roof, Christmas candles in each window, pine garlands around the porch rails, and a big wreath on the door. Sara felt as though she were walking into a house in a picture-book Christmas story.

Inside, the smells of good food and the sounds of laughter and holiday music greeted her. Sara made her way into the foyer, her arms filled with packages. A band of children, dressed in their Sunday best, ran past, nearly knocking her over.

"Whoa, there! Slow down, kids," Sara heard Sam say. She turned to see her host and smiled, as he took the packages from her arms.

"Hello, Sara. I almost didn't see you back there," he teased her.

"Hi, Sam. Merry Christmas," she said, as he kissed her on the cheek.

"Merry Christmas to you, too, honey. Here, let me take your coat and introduce you around," he offered.

Not all of Sam's eight siblings and their offspring were present, but there were enough to fill the rooms to capacity and set Sara's head whirling, trying to remember faces and names. She also greeted Grace and Digger Hegman and Harry Reilly, whom she knew from town.

"Hello, Sara. When did you get here?" Sara turned to find Molly Willoughby standing behind her. Molly carried a bowl of cold seafood salad and now set it down on one of the long tables in the dining room.

"Just a minute ago. Merry Christmas. Gee, that looks good," Sara commented. "Did you make that?"

"My dad did. I made the breads," Molly said, pointing to another delicious-looking offering. "So, I noticed you've been writing for the newspaper. How do you like it there?"

"I love it, but it hasn't been as easy as I expected," Sara admitted. "What are you up to?"

Molly shrugged. "Just the usual. Running around. Taking care of the girls. You know how it is," she said vaguely.

Sara knew she really didn't. She couldn't imagine how Molly juggled her many jobs and responsibilities: baking for the Beanery and the Clam Box, catering parties, driving a school bus, cleaning houses, as well as taking care of her two daughters. Sara admired her, even though she was a little wary of Molly's sharp tongue.

Molly and Sara had both been bridesmaids in Jessica's wedding party and had gotten to know each other a bit then. Molly could be difficult at times. She didn't have patience for small talk or people she considered snobs. The Warwicks definitely fell into that category, Sara knew, and now she was one, too. But Molly had a fun side once she relaxed and decided you were okay. She was loyal and had a warm heart, even if she tended to keep it carefully hidden.

"Where are your girls?" Sara asked. "I haven't seen them yet."

"Oh, running wild. I'm sure they're both a complete mess by now and will only show up when it's time to eat," Molly replied, with a quick laugh.

"Time to eat already? I've hardly touched the appetizers." Sara turned to see Dr. Elliot.

"Don't worry, Ezra. We'll give you fair warning before the buffet line starts up," Molly said, heading back to the kitchen. "See you later."

"She's always had a sassy tongue, even as a little girl," Ezra remarked to Sara. "Once when I had to give her a shot, she bit my finger," he said, with a laugh.

"I can just picture it," Sara replied. She could, too.

"Where's Emily and Lillian? Aren't they here yet?" Ezra asked her.

"Emily told me they might be late," Sara explained. Emily had actually warned her that it might take some time to get Lillian out of her house, since she still withheld her full approval of Jessica's marriage. Even though Sara had persuaded Lillian to come to the wedding at the very last minute, Lillian had just about ignored the couple ever since.

"Lillian is pulling one of her stunts again tonight, is she?" Ezra said knowingly. "You would think she could put it aside for Christmas." He shook his head. "I hope Emily has the good sense to just leave her home to pout, if she puts up too big a fuss. I know Emily has waited a long time to spend a holiday with you," he went on, meeting Sara's eye. "She's waited half a lifetime. I'd hate to see Lillian go and spoil that on her, too."

"I know," Sara said. "Don't worry. If they don't come soon, I'll go over to Lillian's and see what's going on."

Ezra smiled at her. "You're a good one. I knew that right off. Even before I knew you were Emily's daughter."

"Thanks, Ezra." Sara felt warmed by his compliment. "I think you're a good one, too."

She knew Dr. Elliot had become friends with Luke lately. She wondered if he knew what Luke was doing for Christmas. Had he gone to visit his family in Boston? She hoped that he wasn't home alone, but she didn't feel comfortable asking outright and tried to think of some way to work Luke's name into the conversation.

Just then Jessica appeared, her face flushed from cooking and her long, curly hair springing out from its carefully upswept style.

"Sara, I didn't even know you were here." She greeted Sara with a big hug. "Merry Christmas."

"Merry Christmas. Everything looks beautiful. I love your tree," Sara told her, tilting her head toward the huge pine. It stood in one corner of the living room, to one side of the fireplace. The star that topped it just brushed the ceiling.

"How tall is that tree?" Ezra wanted to know.

Jessica rolled her eyes. "Very. We even had to cut off a little. Luckily, the ceilings in this house are extra high—"

"Or my wife would have had me cutting a hole in that beautiful new plaster," Sam said. He came up behind Jessica and gave her a hug. "She just had to have *that* tree," he teased.

"It's our first tree, and I loved the shape. Look at it. It's perfect," Jessica insisted.

"It is perfect." A fitting first Christmas tree for a perfect couple, Sara thought.

They heard the sound of the front door opening, and Sara glanced over to see that Emily and Lillian had just arrived.

Jessica and Sam exchanged an apprehensive look, Sara noticed. Then Sam's face took on an expression she could only describe as resigned, as he excused himself and went to greet his newly arrived guests.

Jessica lingered a moment with Sara. "Well, they made it," she said softly. "I just hope she behaves herself."

"Everyone knows how Lillian gets by now," Ezra said. "I think she'd have to go pretty far to shock anyone around here."

Jessica didn't looked comforted. "My mother always loved a challenge. Maybe that's why she finally showed up," she joked.

Emily, Jessica, Sam, Sara, and even Ezra were soon gathered around Lillian, making a fuss over her. "I can manage perfectly well, if you would all just give me a little breathing room," she said finally, shooing them back with her cane.

She entered the living room and gazed around with a regal air. It seemed to Sara that everyone in the room grew quiet for a moment. She noticed Joe and Marie Morgan, Sam's parents, had come out of the kitchen and were standing to one side—apparently waiting to greet Lillian, but not looking very happy about it.

"Lillian, you know my parents, Marie and Joe," Sam said, reacquainting them.

"How do you do. Merry Christmas," Lillian said quickly. She looked down at her wrist and adjusted a bracelet.

"Merry Christmas, Mrs. Warwick," Marie Morgan said. "Nice to see you again," she added, though Sara wondered if she could really mean it. Maybe Marie was just relieved that Sam and Jessica hadn't been snubbed once again by Jessica's mother.

"Yes," Lillian replied, not deigning to return the compliment.

"Sara . . . there you are." Emily happily greeted her with a warm hug. "You look beautiful. I love that dress," she said, stepping back to look at her.

"Thanks, you look great, too," Sara said, with a smile. Emily wore a black velvet skirt and a dark green satin blouse, managing to look casual and elegant all at once.

"Why, thank you," Emily replied, looking pleased. "Mother always said I cleaned up nicely," she joked.

"I never said that once in my entire life," Lillian insisted in a huffy tone.

Emily and Sara glanced at each other and laughed.

"Lillian, would you like to sit down over here? There's a comfortable armchair with a nice straight back, right across from the fire," Sam said solicitously, taking his mother-in-law's arm.

"I suppose I could use a seat," she said, after a pause. "It could be a long evening."

"Yes, indeed," Emily agreed under her breath. "But not quite as long as it would have been if we'd gotten here on time."

"I think she'll have a good time," Sara predicted.

"I think she will, too, though she may never admit it," Emily replied, looking, with an indulgent smile, at her mother.

The Christmas Eve party was one of the best that Sara had ever attended, even better than the traditional holiday get-together at her aunt's house. After a wonderful dinner, the entire group gathered in the living room near the tree and sang Christmas songs, while Marie Morgan played the piano and Sam led in his strong bass voice.

Sara sat alongside Emily, sharing one of the music books that Jessica handed out. A few times Sara caught Emily gazing at her fondly, almost glowing with happiness. After the last song, Sara reached over and took Emily's hand. "That was fun. What a nice tradition."

"Yes, we'll have to do it again next year," Emily said, sounding as if it were hard for her to speak.

"Guess it's time to open the gifts," Jessica announced. The children gave a loud cheer, and within minutes, the room was a tornado of wrapping paper and ribbons.

Gifts piled up so quickly at Sara's feet, she couldn't keep up with them. Jessica and Sam gave her a gorgeous sweater set, and Lillian gave her a new novel by an author they both admired.

Emily's box was huge, and Sara opened it to find a beautiful leather briefcase. She had admired the bag once when they were shopping in the mall together, but it was much too expensive for her to afford on a waitress's salary. At the time, she didn't even have a job where it would be useful.

"Wow, this is great," Sara exclaimed, running her hand along the smooth leather. "I can't believe you remembered it."

"I thought it might be useful, now that you're working on the paper," Emily explained. "I thought that was the one you wanted, but I wasn't sure. If it's not right, you can go and exchange it for something you like better. Maybe a knapsack style?"

"Oh, no—it's perfect," Sara told her. "It's exactly the right one. I love it. Really."

"Good," Emily said, sounding satisfied. "I have something else for you, too—but I'll give it to you tomorrow, on Christmas, okay?"

"Sure." Sara leaned over and gave her birth mother a hug. "Thank you, Emily. I know I'll use it forever."

Now it was Emily's turn to open Sara's gifts. Sara had bought her a beautiful hand-painted silk scarf that she found in a shop in Newburyport. It was just Emily's style, and Sara could see she really loved it. Next Emily unwrapped a video.

"Sara . . . what a great present," she said, holding up a copy of *It's a Wonderful Life*.

"I had to get it for you. I couldn't believe you didn't have your own copy," Sara said, with a grin.

"Essential for my old movie collection," Emily replied, tucking it away in her pile. "Now, what's this?" she said, unwrapping the photograph.

"Oh, my goodness, you took this at the fair, didn't you?" Emily asked softly. "And what a beautiful silver frame. Jessica, look at this. Isn't it great?" Emily held up the photo. "I'll have to make you a copy."

"Guess what? I got one, too," Jessica said happily. "Thank you, Sara."

Finally Emily came to the gift that Sara was a bit nervous about. Emily unwrapped it slowly. When she opened the binder with the plain blue cover, Sara could tell she was confused.

"It's some of my writing. The short stories I told you about," Sara explained. "You mentioned you wanted to read them."

"Yes, of course. I'd love to read them," Emily murmured. She looked up at Sara again, her expression a mixture of pleasure and surprise. "What a wonderful gift."

"Don't get too excited; they're not that great," Sara warned, with a self-deprecating laugh. "One or two were published. But some are sort of out there."

"You have a lot of talent. I'm sure they're very good," Emily contradicted her. "Besides, I know I'll love reading them anyway, just because you wrote them."

When it was finally time to go, Sara helped Emily get Lillian to the car.

"Will we see you at my house tomorrow, Sara?" Lillian asked.

"Yes, I'll be there," Sara promised.

"How about church? You ought to go to church on Christmas," Lillian told her. "Everybody does."

Sara did attend services with her family when she was home, but hadn't thought about it up here. Besides, she wasn't all that religious.

"Why don't you come? It will be fun," Emily encouraged. "I'll pick you up on the way to my mother's. The service starts at eleven so say about ten?"

Sara couldn't refuse. She knew it would mean a lot to Emily if she joined them, and there seemed no reason not to.

"All right," she agreed. "I can be ready by ten."

There were some more good nights exchanged, and Sara soon got into her own car. She headed to the village down the Beach Road, and her thoughts turned again to Luke. Ezra had told her that Luke was in Boston with his family, and she'd been relieved to hear that he wasn't spending the holidays alone.

Despite what Luke thought, she did care about him. She cared a lot. And that wasn't going to change so quickly.

CHAPTER FOURTEEN

EMILY HAD JUST FIXED SOME COFFEE, AND SHE STOOD BLEARY eyed, waiting for it to drip through the pot. Despite the late night at Jessica's, she had woken up at her usual time and been unable to get back to sleep. She had enough time to go for a quick jog before getting ready for church, so she'd pulled on her running clothes then set up the coffee.

Her two cats twined themselves around her legs, reminding her that they needed to be fed. Then they bolted in different directions when someone knocked hard on the front door.

Emily ran a hand through her uncombed hair. Who would be stopping by at this hour on Christmas morning?

When she opened the door and found Dan standing there, she had to consciously keep her jaw from dropping open.

"Merry Christmas, Emily," he greeted her, with a huge grin.

"Dan . . ." She looked around her front yard, then back at him. "How did you get here?"

"I walked. I only live a few houses up the road, remember?"

"But what about your leg—your cast, I mean." She looked him over as if to find the trick that enabled him to be standing there. He looked very handsome, she noticed suddenly, wearing a long navy blue overcoat and a cream-colored muffler.

Meanwhile I look a wreck! I haven't even washed my face. She gave a silent, mental shriek.

"Got the big cast off yesterday," Dan was saying happily. "I'm supposed to wear this shorter one. But it's the removable kind. Comes off and on with Velcro," he continued, seeming unaware of her distress. He swung his lower leg back and forth to demonstrate. "Feels a little stiff, but I'm basically good as new."

"That's terrific. What a great Christmas present for you!"

"Speaking of which—" He reached into a shopping bag that stood beside him on the front steps and produced a gift box wrapped in gold paper and thick scarlet ribbon.

"I really came to give you this," he said, holding it out to her.

Emily took the box in two hands, wondering what he'd picked out for her. "This looks almost too pretty to unwrap. I have something for you, too," she said. "Come inside."

In the living room she crouched down at the Christmas tree and found the package marked with his name.

"Wow, this is big and heavy," he said, shaking it. "Oops, not breakable, I hope?"

"No, not at all," she said, with a laugh. She sat on the couch next to him. "Who goes first?"

"You first. Go on," he insisted. He watched her intently, making her nervous. She undid the bow first and found her hands were trembling a bit. She lifted the cover and started to push back piles of tissue paper, still unsure of what it could be.

Then she saw it and couldn't quite believe it. "The blue shawl . . ."

"The *azure* blue shawl," he corrected her, with a grin.

"But how did you—"

"I had Lindsay pick it up for me," he cut in.

"So that's why it was gone when I went to buy it for her!"

"Exactly," he replied, looking a little smug. "Very clever of me, I thought."

"Very," she agreed. "And very thoughtful."

"Do you like it?"

"It's beautiful. I absolutely love it," she said honestly.

"I thought you would." His smile grew even wider. He looked extremely happy to have pleased her, as if it really mattered to him, and that was a kind of gift to her, too.

She ran her hand across the fine wool. It was even softer than she'd imagined. It must have cost a small fortune. She took it out of the box and unfolded it on her lap.

"I love the color," she said, caressing it.

"That's why I got it. It's the same exact shade as your eyes," he said. "Put it on. I want to see how it looks on you."

"Over my sweatshirt?"

"Why not? It's just me," he said, in a way that made her feel special to him. He picked it up and helped her wrap it around her shoulders. She liked his touch, gentle and careful but still somehow strong.

She looked up at him. "What do you think?"

The look on his face said it all. "You look beautiful. Just stunning, I'd say." His quiet, definite tone made her shiver.

She couldn't answer at first. "Thank you," she said softly.

"You're very welcome. Merry Christmas, Emily." With his hands still holding her shoulders, he pulled her near and kissed her. Her hands slipped around his back, and she held him close. It felt so good to hold him like this. This was what life was all about, being with someone you truly cared for.

She was falling in love with him. Maybe she'd loved him for a long time but just hadn't faced it before now. As their kiss deepened, emotions welled up inside, making her feel as if her heart would just take flight. She finally knew there was no getting around it.

The cats jumped up on the couch, suddenly startling her. "I guess I should have fed them," she sighed, lingering in Dan's embrace. "Now they're just trying to get back at me."

Dan laughed quietly and reached out to cup her cheek in his hand. "That's probably true," he said.

They sat back again, and Dan turned to his gift. Emily felt a twinge of apprehension. She had never expected such an extravagant present from Dan. The present she got him was something rather mundane and practical. She hoped his feelings wouldn't be hurt.

While he worked on the wrapping paper, she carefully folded her wool wrap and placed it back in its box.

Once Dan had removed all the paper on his present, he picked up the box and read aloud, "Five-in-one fog light?" He glanced at her then back at the box again. "Gee, this looks great. Just what I needed."

"I got it at the marine store in town. The man said it's a light, an air horn, a flashing distress signal . . . and . . . oh, gee, I forget what else it does exactly," she admitted.

"I get the idea," he said, glancing at the box again. "An electric can opener maybe?"

"No, I don't think so. But something like that." She laughed and then sighed. "You can exchange it. There's lots of things there you might need for your trip," she said, watching his expression carefully. Somehow the scarf had made her wonder if he was having second thoughts about his trip.

"This looks very useful," he assured her. "I don't have anything like it."

"You mentioned that you needed a new lamp for your trip," she reminded him.

"Yes, I did, didn't I? That was thoughtful of you to remember, Emily."

His voice sounded falsely bright, she thought. Was he disappointed that she hadn't bought him something more personal? Or was the fact that she bought him something for his trip somehow hurtful to him—as if she were saying it didn't matter to her if he left. She had to admit, she'd picked out the gift hoping to show she had no hard feelings.

"I really didn't know what to get you, Dan," she confessed. "It's not that I'm eager to see you go, believe me."

He glanced at her and smiled. "I know that. You're sweet to be so positive about it, Emily."

"I do have something else for you," she said, remembering her other gift. "Well, it's for both of us actually," she explained, as she picked up a small white envelope that was propped on the mantel.

She handed it to him and watched as he opened it.

"Tickets?" He paused and tried to read the small print. "Sorry, I didn't bring my glasses."

"They're for a concert at Lilac Hall on New Year's Eve. It's an all-Bach program. Would you like to go with me?" she asked hopefully. It was a risk, asking a man out for New Year's Eve—and it certainly wasn't her style—but Emily had impulsively bought the tickets, hoping for the best.

Dan's expression lit up instantly, and she knew the impulse had been a good one.

"I'd be delighted. I was going to invite you out to dinner that night anyway," he told her. "I'll find a restaurant for after the concert."

"Okay, that sounds good," she said, feeling relieved.

He rose to his feet and stepped over to her. "I've got to go now. Merry Christmas, Emily."

"Merry Christmas," she replied.

He leaned over and kissed her quickly on the cheek, and she closed her eyes, holding on to his arm just a second longer than was absolutely necessary.

When she looked up at him, he was standing back, gazing at her with a thoughtful expression. "You look very pretty first thing in the morning."

She laughed, not quite believing him. "You really do need your glasses. I haven't even combed my hair."

"Really?" He reached out and gently mussed her hair even more. "It doesn't look any different than usual to me." Then he laughed at the expression on her face and leaned over to scoop up his gift box.

"Okay, I'm going now," he said, heading for the door. "See you soon."

"See you," she replied. She stood in the doorway and watched him walk to the street and back toward his house, his five-in-one fog light jammed under one arm.

Dan's Christmas gift had not been a total success, she thought. But maybe she'd given him something to think about. . . .

* * *

EMILY HAD TO RUSH IN ORDER TO GET READY FOR CHURCH. "DID YOU oversleep?" Sara asked, when Emily picked her up late.

"Not exactly," Emily replied, with a secret grin. She didn't know why, but she felt like keeping Dan's visit to herself. Later when she had some time alone, she'd privately sit and ponder its deeper meanings.

"Late as usual," Lillian complained, meeting them at the door with her coat and hat on.

"Merry Christmas to you, too, Mother," Emily answered brightly.

Though Lillian fretted every inch of the way, they reached the church in plenty of time. Gus Potter, one of the ushers, met them at the door and showed them to seats in the front. Emily felt a glow of pride and happiness, following Sara up the aisle.

Finally, they were settled, with Emily sitting between her daughter and her mother. Jessica and Sam sat a few rows back, alongside Sam's family. When Emily turned and caught her sister's eye, Jessica smiled and gave her a cheery wave. Emily also noticed Lucy and her boys, sitting with Lucy's mother, and on the opposite side of the church, she saw Charlie. Christmas was the one day of the year Charlie closed the Clam Box. A few rows behind him, she spotted Lindsay and Scott. Dan and Wyatt were not with them, she realized. Dan was not a churchgoer; she had always known that. It was just another wrinkle in the situation.

Emily forced her mind away from troublesome thoughts. *Not right now,* she told herself.

The church was crowded, filled to capacity. Surrounded by so many friends and familiar faces, Emily felt a deep sense of belonging and contentment—especially because she was seated next to Sara. For the briefest moment, Emily closed her eyes and silently prayed. *Thank you, God,* she said simply.

She opened her eyes again and looked over at Sara, her dark head bent slightly as she looked through the hymnal. It was still hard sometimes to believe that her dream of finding her daughter had finally come true. Did she dare ask for more?

The service started, and Emily turned her full attention to the altar. Finally, Reverend Ben stepped up to the pulpit to give his sermon.

"When I was a boy, back when dinosaurs roamed the countryside around here," he began, drawing a laugh, "I would get a special toy in my stocking every year. Not a toy exactly, more of what you'd call a party favor these days. It was just a long strip of colored paper, rolled into a ball. When you unraveled it, little toys dropped out. A whistle perhaps and maybe a tin soldier or even a coin. You get the idea."

Emily remembered those paper balls, too. They were fun. Funny how she'd forgotten all about them. But where was Reverend Ben going with this pleasant nostalgia? she wondered.

"At the very center," he continued, "there would be a special surprise. Something that seemed so wonderful, it made all that work worth it—usually a big piece of candy. The kind that could last you a week, if you were careful with it," he noted, drawing a few more smiles. "That was wonderful fun, unraveling that ball of surprises.

"That paper ball reminds me of Christmas in a way. But what is at the heart of Christmas? At the very center of all this activity—all the shopping and wrapping and parties? We are bombarded by advertisements, must haves, to-do lists, and money woes. All the new gadgets we get and give. We sit unraveling and unraveling, our attention drawn by the next flashy trinket and distraction that drops from the ball. And then the next . . ."

How true, Emily thought. And you got so exhausted that by the time Christmas arrived and you ended up in church, you were almost too tired to give God any attention at all.

"Slowly we work our way to the center, to the heart of it," the reverend said. "For if you have the patience, my friends, if you don't let yourself get distracted by the jingle bells and penny whistles and worries about your credit-card bills, you will finally find that very, very special surprise at the center.

"For at the heart of it all is something so small, so weak, so fragile, it often gets overlooked—overwhelmed. Blotted out by the rest.

"At the center, there's a baby. Born in a manger. The story of a humble birth so eternally touching, so moving, it has somehow been handed down for the past two thousand years.

"I've heard it said that a baby is a messenger from the angels. Indeed, when you see one up close, it does seem so. You can't help but marvel at his innocence. A pure heart. A new life, another chance."

Emily glanced at Sara, who appeared to be totally focused on the reverend. Looking at her, Emily couldn't help but think about her own hopes for the future, a dream beyond finding Sara—the hope to find love and to marry again. Even to have another baby, if she was perfectly honest with herself. For finding her daughter had made her even more conscious of the precious days she had lost raising her.

Maybe Reverend Ben was right. Perhaps it wasn't wrong to ask God for more. It was at least honest. What was wrong was to give Him instructions on how these matters should be accomplished, she thought, with an inner smile. But it was never wrong to dream, to hope.

"Today, on Christmas Day," she heard Reverend Ben say, "I urge you all to recognize and rededicate yourself to those same spiritual qualities. Today, reach down and take part in a real way, a spiritual way, in the birth of the Lord. God sent his only Son to live among us, so that we would be saved and given a second chance for life everlasting. In honoring and celebrating the birth of our Savior, let us find our Christ-like center, our own spiritual rebirth."

Emily's gaze fell on the Lewis family. They were sitting in a front pew, Carolyn with Rachel and Jack Anderson. Even from across the church, Rachel's pregnancy was obvious. Emily thought about how excited their family must be, waiting for the baby. Maybe that's what had given the reverend his ideas for the sermon. As usual, his words had touched a chord within her, she realized, giving her something to think about.

AS HE ALWAYS DID AFTER THE SERVICE, REVEREND BEN STOOD IN THE church vestibule and spoke to each member of his congregation as they left. Today being Christmas, however, it was special. The organ music sounding the recessional seemed more joyous, more jubilant. His parishioners did as well, with wide smiles and high spirits, as they not only greeted him but greeted each other, spreading the Christmas spirit.

Ben felt a certain anticipation as Grace Hegman drew closer in the line. Finally she and her father stood alongside him. "Merry Christmas, Digger. Merry Christmas, Grace," he said, reaching out to shake each of their hands.

It had done his heart good to find Grace Hegman in the crowded pews today—a small, positive note, despite his disappointment about Mark.

Ben managed to catch Grace's evasive gaze. "It was good to see you here today," he added.

"I came along with Dad. You know how it is now. . . ." Her explanation trailed off, and she glanced at her father, looking uncomfortable. "But I did enjoy your sermon, Reverend." She looked up at him again, twisting her leather gloves in her hand, practically wringing them into a knot. "I'm going to think about what you said—about Christmas being like a clean slate and all. I liked the way you put that."

"Why, thank you, Grace." Ben was profoundly touched. If he had moved one spirit today, he knew his words had been inspired. And if that single spirit had been Grace Hegman . . . well, he considered himself truly blessed, like he had been sent an unexpected Christmas gift from above.

"We've had a lot of people from the church calling," Grace said. "To spend time with Dad, take him places, do things with him. Jessica Morgan has been arranging it. Did you know that?"

The helping chain. Ben had almost forgotten. Jessica had gotten to work quickly, bless her. "Yes, she mentioned it to me. It was her husband's idea, I think."

"Just like Sam," Grace said, shaking her head. "Well, I do appreciate it. I never thought people cared so much about us. I never knew," she admitted. "It's almost like . . . like a family."

"Yes, it is like a family," Ben agreed. "We try to be."

"Well, maybe someday I'll have a chance to repay the favors. I hope so, anyway," she said, sounding more hopeful than Ben could ever recall.

"I guess we ought to be going." Grace hooked her arm through her father's. "Come along, Dad. We don't want to slow up the whole line here."

"You have a happy Christmas, Reverend," Digger said, smiling.

Ben said good-bye to the Hegmans, watching as they descended the steps in front of the church. He might not see her here again until next Christmas, he realized. But he was hopeful. Only the Lord knew her heart.

Then right on the heels of Grace Hegman, Ben spotted yet another Christmas morning mini-miracle. Emily Warwick was next in line, along with her mother, as usual, and Sara Franklin, which was not at all a typical sight.

"That was a wonderful sermon, Reverend," Emily said, as she greeted him. "I don't want to age myself, but I remember those paper balls, too."

Ben smiled at her. "Come now. You couldn't possibly. You must have just heard us old folks talking about them." He turned to Sara and offered his hand. "Merry Christmas, Sara. Good to see you here today."

"Thanks. Merry Christmas," she replied, looking a bit ill at ease.

"We brought Sara Franklin along with us today," Lillian Warwick explained, apparently considering it necessary to supply her own granddaughter's last name. But Lillian had never really acknowledged the girl as such, Ben knew. "Everyone comes to church on Christmas, you know. It doesn't necessarily mean anything," she added, as if concerned he had gotten his hopes up about adding a new member to the congregation.

"Yes, Lillian, I understand. Merry Christmas," he replied, as he and Emily shared a discreet, silent laugh.

"Come along, Mother. We still have a lot to do," Emily reminded her. As Emily walked on, holding her mother's arm, she suddenly turned to Ben again. "Give my best wishes to your family, Reverend. I hope you all have a wonderful day."

"Thank you, Emily. I'll remember to tell them," he promised. He smiled as he watched them go, though in his heart he wondered what the day at home would bring. They would all get through it. He felt fairly certain of that much. But it wouldn't be wonderful. Not by a long shot.

* * *

"DO YOU THINK WE SHOULD OPEN THE GIFTS NOW?" CAROLYN ASKED.

"Sure, why not?" Ben replied. He'd been stoking the fire a bit to get the flame higher. He stood up and brushed his hands off, glancing at Rachel and Jack who were sitting in a cozy huddle on the couch.

"Are you two ready?" he asked.

"As long as I don't have to move from this spot," his daughter said, with a small smile.

Rachel did look just about done in, Ben thought, her head resting on her husband's broad shoulder, her pregnant tummy as round as a watermelon under her pretty Christmas dress. She had tried hard all day to be bright and cheerful. It must have been hard for her, Ben thought, as it was for all of them.

"Okay, here we go. . . ." Carolyn picked up a gift and checked the tag. "Ben, you help and hand them out," she instructed. "This one is for Baby Anderson. And this one is for—"

"Don't tell me," Ben joked. "I think there's someone who isn't even here yet who got most of the loot."

Everyone laughed, but Ben noticed a sad expression on Carolyn's face as she continued to parcel out the gifts.

She was thinking about Mark, of course. Someone who wasn't here, yet on everyone's mind. His absence hung over the gathering like a cloud, casting a chill on their holiday gathering.

Ben was worried about Carolyn. She wasn't quite herself these past few days. The tension of waiting for the baby and feeling disappointed by Mark was wearing on her. Since Mark's call, she had focused on Rachel and the baby's arrival and cooking Christmas dinner. But there was a forced brightness in her smile today, a brittle note in her laugh. He didn't know quite how to help her through this.

Soon all the gifts were open, and Rachel sat overwhelmed by the bounty of gifts for the baby. "Oh Mom, this is really too much. It's like a baby shower all over again."

"Really, you've been too generous, both of you," Jack said, as he helped gather up all the wrapping paper.

"You'll need all those things, you'll see." Carolyn smiled at Rachel and ran her hand down her daughter's long, smooth hair. "You look so tired, honey. I think you ought to go home and get some rest."

"All right. I think we will go. My eyes are just about closing," Rachel admitted.

"Yes, you two run along. We can finish up here," Ben said, when Jack looked concerned about helping to clean up.

Ben found their coats and scarves and then helped Jack bring some shopping bags out to their car. Once they were gone, the house seemed very quiet. Carolyn moved about, seeming lost in her own thoughts, as she cleared dishes from the dining-room table.

Ben carried a platter into the kitchen and then looked around for a place to put it.

"Oh, just leave that anywhere. I'll deal with the leftovers later. You really don't have to help me in here, Ben. Why don't you watch some TV or something?"

"I can help. There's still a big mess out there," he said, watching her.

"No, really. I'd rather do it myself. Besides, you must be tired," she insisted.

He felt dismissed, as if she really didn't want his company for some reason. As if she purposely wanted to put some distance between them.

"Carolyn, what is it? Are you mad at me about something?"

She glanced at him, then pushed a lock of hair from her eyes. "Of course not. Why would I be mad?"

"I don't know, but you seem like you are. The last few days you've been so distant, so short tempered. Are you worried about Rachel?"

She nodded. "It's hard to see her like this. She can hardly move."

"Well, that's to be expected at this point," he said mildly.

Carolyn turned to him quickly. "I know it's to be expected. But she's my daughter and she's terribly uncomfortable and I feel bad for her."

Ben stepped back as if he'd been slapped across the face. "It's not Rachel at all, is it? It's Mark."

"I really don't feel like talking about this right now," Carolyn said. She brushed past him, carrying a bowl to the sink.

"Why not?" Ben persisted. "It's like the elephant that's sitting in the room, yet nobody wants to acknowledge it. You've been thinking about him all day. I know that," he said flatly.

He could see that she was not listening to him, or at least trying hard not to, as she busied herself sorting out the good silverware on the countertop.

"You can't do this to yourself, Carolyn. It's not fair," he said, in a softer tone. "We gave him every chance. You can't say now that we didn't."

He watched her take a deep breath, as if she were trying hard to control the emotions welling up inside. What was she really thinking now? What was she feeling? How could he help her if she wouldn't really talk to him?

"I think you're letting this affect you too much, dear," he said carefully. "You have to think of yourself, of your health. Maybe you'd like to talk to someone about it, instead of me. A counselor or psychologist," he suggested.

"Oh, here we go," Carolyn said, shaking her head angrily. "Can't I feel sad without you thinking I'm going into a depression again?"

"I care about you. I'm trying to take care of you. I know you're sad, but I also think you're mad at Mark and taking it out on me again."

"Oh, my . . ." She looked totally frustrated, as if she were about to stamp her foot or even throw something. "You just don't understand. It's just impossible."

"What don't I understand? Explain it to me, please. I want to know," he said, putting aside his anger at her accusation.

Finally she turned to face him. "Just because you can counsel other families doesn't mean that you're able to be objective about your own," she said. "Sometimes I think you don't understand this whole situation."

Ben stood, stunned. All his doubts and worries about not being able to help his own family and even his congregation suddenly rose up and threatened to overwhelm him.

"I don't have any answer to that," he said shortly. "I try my best. That's all I can do. I've tried my best for all of you."

She looked at him with a sad expression in her eyes. "Yes, I know you have," she said quietly.

Perhaps she meant it in a conciliatory way, but her sad tone made him feel even worse somehow, even more a hypocrite and a failure.

Ben turned and left the room, feeling numb. He went into his study and closed the door, then stretched out on the couch. The small lamp on his desk cast the room in a shadowy light.

He was worried about Carolyn, about her mental state. But maybe focusing too intently on Carolyn was his problem, he reflected. It was easy to focus on "fixing" her and ignore his own shortcomings.

Her angry words had been so painful tonight, because they had rung true, he realized. He wasn't helping his own family, which forced him to question whether he was really capable of helping anyone.

When, exactly, had he lost his confidence that he could be a spiritual leader? Little moments, like seeing Grace Hegman in church today, made him feel he was still on track. Yet, that wasn't enough. The tiny crack in the foundation that once seemed so insignificant was growing wider and wider, fanning out treelike, the branches threatening to undermine the entire structure of his life. He was flailing, emotionally and spiritually, and didn't quite know what to do.

It wasn't that he doubted God or felt he'd lost his faith. He just doubted himself, his worthiness and ability to lead his flock. No matter how hard he tried to put these doubts aside, they lingered, like blackbirds perched on a wire, waiting for the chance to swoop down and get at him again.

You told Carolyn to see a counselor. Why don't you go see one? he asked himself. He thought about another minister who had been his mentor and spiritual support at times, Reverend John Simpson down in Gloucester, Ben's hometown. They had not spoken in a while, except in a superficial way. But now Ben considered giving Reverend John a call.

He sighed and closed his eyes, trying to move his heavy thoughts to visions of Rachel's new baby. That event would cheer everyone, he consoled himself. Yet, as he felt himself drifting off to sleep, all he could see were blackbirds, sitting before a gray sky, waiting on a wire.

CHRISTMAS DAY AT LILLIAN'S WAS QUIET, AS SARA HAD EXPECTED. SHE found it relaxing after the big gathering at Jessica's house, though. After dinner, she sat with Emily, Lillian, and Dr. Elliot in the living room, listening to classical music while Lillian and Dr. Elliot worked on a crossword puzzle.

"I've got it—amaryllis," Lillian said, carefully filling in the blanks with a sharp yellow pencil. "That was too easy. These puzzles are designed for nitwits these days."

"That's a type of Christmas flower, is it?" Dr. Elliot asked, repeating the clue.

"Exactly. I have one right up there on the mantel," she pointed out.

"That's a beauty," he observed. "I didn't know the proper name though."

"You grow it from a bulb. Sara gave me that in the fall," Lillian remarked. She suddenly looked over at Sara. "That reminds me, check under the tree. There's a package there for you," she said.

"For me?" Sara was surprised. Lillian had given her a book last night. She hadn't really expected more.

"That one, with the red wrapping paper," Lillian said, sounding eager for her to open it.

Sara unwrapped the package, revealing a large album with a brown leather cover. Opening it, she found that the pages were filled with old photographs. They were the photographs of the Warwick family that she had brought down from the attic and helped Lillian sort through months ago, before Lillian—or anyone for that matter—knew that she was Emily's daughter.

Sara looked up at Lillian, who had been watching for her reaction. She hardly knew what to say.

"The photographs from the attic."

"Yes, of course. Where else could they have come from? The department store?" Lillian noted sarcastically.

Sara glanced down at the pages again. Her gaze came to rest on one of Lillian with Emily and Jessica when both were just children. Jessica was seated on Lillian's lap and Emily stood beside her, wearing a navy blue dress with a white Peter Pan collar. Emily and Jessica were adorable, and even Lillian's angular features, framed by the wavy hairstyle of the day, had a certain softness then. Before her disappointments had tempered her, Sara thought. Sometimes she still caught a fleeting glimpse of that softness in her eyes.

She looked up at Lillian. "Thank you so much. That was very thoughtful."

"Don't be silly. I had so many extras, I didn't know what to do with them. Seemed a waste to throw them out. And I know you have an interest in . . . that sort of thing."

In your family history, Sara silently amended for her. But she knew that admission was simply too much to ask, even on Christmas. Her grandmother had at first flatly refused to believe that Sara was actually the child Emily had given up so long ago. Even months later, though she was cordial enough in her way, Lillian had never acknowledged Sara as a member of the family. Perhaps this was her way of doing so.

"Well, thank you. I know I'll love looking through this," Sara said, resting the large book on her lap.

"That was thoughtful, Mother. I had no idea," Emily said, coming to stand beside her.

"It's just a few old photographs," Lillian said. "Why is everyone making such a fuss?" She suddenly turned to Dr. Elliot, who was taking his turn with the crossword puzzle. "For goodness' sake, Ezra, haven't you figured out seven down yet? The clue is Yuletide expletive and insect. Six letters, starts with H."

"Why, yes, I think have it." Dr. Elliot looked up with a pleased expression. "Just came to me as I was listening to your conversation. I believe the answer is humbug."

Sara glanced at Emily, who was also trying not to laugh.

* * *

LATER THAT EVENING EMILY DROVE SARA HOME. AFTER SHE PULLED UP in front of Sara's house, she took a very small box out of her pocket and held it out to Sara.

"One last present before you go," Emily said, with a mischievous smile. "Christmas isn't quite over yet."

Sara took the box and glanced at her. The night before Emily had said she had another gift for her. Sara had forgotten all about it.

"Open it," Emily said softly.

It was a velvet jeweler's box, and when Sara opened it she found a gold heart-shaped locket. She held it up to the light to see it better. "It's beautiful," she murmured. "But so extravagant, Emily. You've already given me such a big gift."

"Your father gave me that our first Christmas together," Emily explained. "I wanted you to have it."

"Really?" Sara looked down at the golden heart again. She knew that Emily and her husband hadn't had much time together, and she was sure Emily didn't have much to remember him by. Every little bit was probably precious to her and carefully treasured. "Are you sure?" she asked. "Maybe you'd like to keep it. For yourself, I mean. To remember him."

"I do remember him," Emily told her easily. "He'd want you to have it. Think of it as his Christmas present to you," she said, with a small smile.

Sara blinked, feeling both a genuine warmth and a pang of loss for the father she never knew. It was suddenly easy to imagine that if she had known Tim Sutton, she would have loved him very much. "Thank you." Sara's voice caught a little. "It's beautiful. I'll be very careful with it."

"I'm sure you will. Enjoy it," Emily said.

Sara gave her a quick hug. "Thanks for everything, Emily. I had a great Christmas with you," she said honestly.

"Me, too," Emily replied, squeezing her hand. "The best," she added. She paused for a moment, her expression changing slightly, Sara noticed. "So, when will your parents get here? They're still coming, right?"

"Thursday afternoon. I just spoke to them this morning," Sara said.

"I thought we could all go out on Friday night to the Pequot Inn, if that works out for you."

"Yes, of course. Whatever is convenient for everyone. Just tell me the time. I'll be there," Emily promised.

Though she sounded positive, Sara could tell Emily was nervous. Well, everyone at the table would be, she thought.

They said good night, and Sara went inside. As she got ready for bed, she thought about last Christmas, how she had planned then to look for her birth mother after graduation and wondered if she would ever find her. She had never imagined that this year they'd be spending Christmas together.

The holiday with Emily—and the rest of her new family—had been far more than she'd ever hoped for.

Chapter Fifteen

It was quiet at the paper the day after Christmas. Ed and Jane weren't back yet, and the phone hardly rang at all. There weren't even any dull civic meetings to attend, so Sara hardly left the office. She was at her desk, organizing a huge pile of files for Lindsay, when her extension rang.

"The *Messenger*," she answered automatically.

"Hello, *Messenger*," a familiar voice replied. "What's new?"

"Luke?" Sara sat up and held the phone closer to her ear. "Where are you?"

"I'm in Boston, visiting my family," he replied, sounding casual and relaxed.

"Yes . . . Ezra told me that," Sara said, in a halting tone. It felt so strange to be talking to him like this, after their last talk had ended so badly.

"I need to see the New Horizons people about a few things, so I'm staying here for the rest of the week," he told her.

"Oh, that's nice," Sara said automatically. She knew he had gone to the city, but thought he might be back by now. It sounded as if he would be staying in Boston through New Year's, but she didn't want to ask him outright. "How was your Christmas?" she said instead.

"Not so bad. How was yours? Did you have a good time with Emily?"

"It was great. Even better than I expected."

"How about your parents? How is that going?"

All things considered, she was surprised that he even remembered that her parents were going to visit. "They'll be here tomorrow. It's too bad you're not around. I wanted you to meet them," she admitted.

He didn't reply at first, and she wondered if her comment had surprised him. "Are you going to spend New Year's Eve with them?" he asked at last.

"Uh, no. They'll be gone by then," she said, wondering why he asked. Did he want to get together with her for New Year's Eve, after all? "I really don't have any plans. Well, someone in my office is giving a party. I might go to that."

"Oh, a party. That sounds good."

"I'm not sure I'm going. I won't really know anyone except for the people from the office." She really meant Wyatt, but she didn't want to risk irritating Luke by mentioning him by name. "Will you be back by then?" she asked.

"Oh, I don't know. A lot of old friends are around this week. I've been pretty busy running around, catching up. I might get together with some of them, I guess," he said vaguely.

So he was staying in Boston for New Year's Eve. "Sounds like you're having fun."

"It's been a good break. Good to be back in Boston again. It can get a little too quiet out there in the winter."

"Yes, it can," Sara agreed. She suddenly felt alone, out in the middle of nowhere, while he was having fun in the city with all his old friends. His cheerful tone made her feel as if he hadn't really been thinking of her at all.

"By the way, thanks for that present you left on my car. That was great. Thanks a lot."

"No problem. I thought you might like it." She felt an unexpected flush of embarrassment for giving it to him. As if she'd overdone it. If he'd gotten her a gift, now was the time to mention it, she thought. But he didn't say a word.

"Sorry, but I have to go," she said, forcing an urgent note into her tone. "Thanks for calling. It was good to hear from you."

"Good to talk to you, too, Sara," he said. "See you when I get back, okay?"

"Sure, see you." She hung up the phone, feeling like she might cry. Why had Luke called at all? To thank her for the gift—or just to show that there were no hard feelings? To show her that he'd gotten over her already, she realized with a sinking heart.

She started as she realized Wyatt was standing by her desk. "It's so quiet here, I'm about to fall asleep. Would you like to go out and get some fresh air, get some lunch maybe?" he asked.

Sara glanced up at him. Wyatt's wide smile and dark blue eyes seemed to instantly distract her from her blues. Lunch with Wyatt, the perfect remedy. *That will get my mind off you real fast,* she silently told Luke.

"Sure, I'd love to," Sara said, smiling. She barely noticed Lindsay walking up to them.

"How are you doing with those spreadsheets, Sara? I'm ready to start working on them." Lindsay's tone was pleasant but firm.

"I have a ways to go, actually," she confessed. The task had been so dull and the office so quiet, she'd been working at a snail's pace.

"Can she finish this afternoon?" Wyatt asked. "Or do you really need this stuff?"

"Oh, does she need to cover a story?" Lindsay asked curiously.

"Uh, no . . . just go out to lunch," Wyatt replied honestly. He glanced at Sara, with a small smile. Sara noticed Lindsay looking at her, too, and Sara suddenly felt self-conscious.

"Well, the problem is I have an appointment this afternoon, and I wanted to finish this today. Our accountant is coming in tomorrow, remember? There are lots of calls to make, too," she said, looking meaningfully at her brother. That was one thing Sara knew Wyatt hated and left to Lindsay.

"I can help you with that. There's not much else going on," Wyatt said. He looked back at Sara with a regretful smile. "Guess we're both grounded. I'll call out to the Clam Box if you guys want anything," he offered.

"Thanks, but Scott made me some lunch. Smoked mozzarella and roast chicken with pesto on a baguette, I think," Lindsay said vaguely, as she strolled away.

"Not on the menu at the Clam Box, in case you wanted the same," Wyatt commented dryly to Sara.

She laughed. "Let me think about it. I'll let you know in a minute," she told him, with a smile.

"All right, I know it's a tough decision. And don't forget, you have a rain check on that lunch date."

"Okay. I won't," Sara promised. She turned back to her work, but her mind returned to Luke, and she felt an unexpected wave of guilt. She angrily pushed the thoughts aside.

Wyatt liked her. He was trying to let her know it, too. And she was free to see whomever she liked now, she reminded herself. Wasn't that what Luke's phone call was all about?

"I'M SURE EMILY WILL BE HERE IN A MINUTE," SARA SAID, AS SHE NOTICED her father sneaking another look at his watch. "Maybe she got held up at the office or something. Everyone in town is always calling her."

"Yes, she's a very important person around here. We've heard all about that."

"I'm sure she'll be along in a minute. We got here a little early, I think," Sara's mother told him. "It's fine, Sara. This is a lovely restaurant you picked out."

"Yes, very pretty," her father said. "Very . . . New England."

"I'm glad you like it. I've never actually eaten here. But Emily thought it would be nice."

Sara saw her parents exchange a quick look. They had arrived in Cape Light yesterday, and Sara didn't think she'd talked about Emily *that* much. But apparently, they thought she had.

"Well, everything in this inn seems quite authentic," her mother said, trying to smooth things over again.

"It's been here forever. You should see this place on the Fourth of July. They have this huge reenactment in town. There's a battle on the village green, and they bring the wounded soldiers back here during the retreat. I mean, the guys who are acting like wounded soldiers. Then everyone has a big party."

"That sounds like a lot of fun. But we have some wonderful reenactments down in Maryland, too. We took you down to one when you were about ten or eleven. Don't you remember?" her father asked.

"I think so, Dad," Sara replied evenly. She noticed that her father had emptied the bread basket. He waved to the waiter to bring another.

"Mike, you won't be hungry for dinner if you keep eating bread," her mother said quietly.

"Are you kidding? I'm starving. Where is this woman?"

"Emily," Sara corrected him.

Her father met her gaze and nodded. "Yes, Emily. Emily Warwick. I remember, don't worry."

"Do you think you'll still be in Cape Light this summer, Sara?" her mother asked.

"Yes, what are your plans these days, honey?" her father said, in his familiar, heart-to-heart-chat tone.

Sara had expected that question. If fact, she was surprised it had taken them a full twenty-four hours to get around to asking it.

"Oh, not much different than when I saw you at Thanksgiving. I really like working on the paper. That's been great so far."

Sara had brought her parents over to the *Messenger* office during the day, and they had met Wyatt, Lindsay, and Jane, who had returned from Maine.

"Well, you are getting some good experience and training," her father said. "A few more months and you can look for a spot on a bigger paper. Maybe the *Times-Courier*," he added, mentioning a paper back home. "I have a client there. He can help you."

"Maybe." Sara reached for her water glass and took a long icy sip. "That might be a while, though. I feel as if I just got started here."

Her mother looked distressed by the news but only said, "Pass the bread, will you, dear?"

Sara caught sight of Emily standing at the entrance to the dining room. Sara waved to her, and Emily quickly came over.

"So sorry I'm late," she said in her most charming manner. "I tried to call from the car, but my phone battery went dead. Isn't that always the way? I hope you're not sitting here starving."

"No, not at all. Please, sit down, Ms. Warwick." Her father rose and politely pulled out a chair for Emily, seating her between himself and Sara.

"Please, call me Emily," she said. She smiled at Sara's mother.

"It's very nice to meet you, Emily. I'm Laura, and this is my husband, Mike," Laura Franklin said.

"A beautiful little town you've got," Mike Franklin said. "Sara showed us all around today."

"The beach and the lighthouse are just breathtaking," Laura added. "So unspoiled. It must be wonderful to be the mayor of a place like this."

"It's a great place," Emily said, with a smile. "Sara tells me it reminds her a lot of Winston."

"Why, yes . . . I guess it is something like our town," Sara's father agreed. "Winston is a pretty place, off the beaten track. We like it," he said, glancing at his wife and Sara.

Emily smiled again, her campaign smile, Sara noticed. She was wearing one of her campaign outfits, too, a slate-blue suit with a long jacket that belted at the waist. Even her hair looked a bit more carefully styled than usual. She looked polished and professional, as if she were introducing herself to a group of voters, Sara thought. And she seemed to be trying just as hard to win over the Franklins.

"So," Emily said, "I understand you're a teacher there, Laura?"

Her mother answered Emily's questions, clearly making an equal effort to be gracious. Sara listened to the three of them exchange small talk and predictable pleasantries throughout most of the meal. Even her father remained on his best behavior.

By the time their waiter cleared the dinner dishes, Sara thought it wasn't going badly, despite her apprehensions. Yet, there was a subtle tension between her parents and Emily, and Sara felt as if she were in the middle, being tugged to either side by invisible threads.

". . . naturally, we wondered why it took her so long once she got here. But Sara has to do things her own way. She's her own person. We understand that," Sara's mother said.

"That's the way we raised her. She has her own opinions about things. That's a trait you want to see in a child, and yet, sometimes it makes things hard when you're a parent," her father told Emily.

Emily's smile looked a bit stiff, but she nodded in agreement.

"I remember when Sara was about four years old. I took her and a group of her friends to the beach, and I had them in line to buy lunch. Every child in that line ordered a hot dog and a Coke. A hot dog and a Coke, right down the row," Laura said. "But we got to Sara, and she just looked up at me and said, 'Do they have peanut butter and chocolate milk?' She wanted peanut butter. She didn't care if every other kid in the world was eating a hot dog."

"Oh, Mom, for goodness' sake." Sara cringed. Why did her mother always have to pull out that peanut-butter story as an example of her maverick personality. It was just so . . . silly.

"Well, I think that took courage. You didn't care what the other kids thought."

"I think I just liked peanut butter," Sara said, feeling embarrassed.

"You still do, as far as I can see." Emily laughed and patted Sara's hand. Sara could see that her parents noticed the gesture. "Yes, she's very independent. I think it took a great deal of courage to come all the way up here and find me," Emily said to the Franklins. "I'm grateful to her for that. She's really changed my life."

Suddenly it was so quiet at the table, Sara thought she could hear the ice melting in her water glass.

Mike Franklin looked down at his coffee cup and coughed into his hand. Sara's mother looked at Emily, then looked away.

"It was hard for Sara. We knew she'd never be really happy until she found you—or reached some sense of closure about you. We really wanted her to find you," Laura said. "It's changed her life, too. To come here and get to know you."

"In a *good* way," Sara put in. Her mother sounded so serious and intense all of a sudden.

"It was a mystery for her. A stumbling block in her life, you might say. She just couldn't get past it," Mike explained. "But now she's solved it, and she can go on with her life. I'm sure you can understand that, Emily."

"What do you mean, Dad?" Sara asked, before Emily could reply. "I *am* going on with my life. I'm going on with it every day."

"I just mean that you've spent a lot of time up here, getting to know Emily, and so forth. . . ." Sara knew he only used the expression *and so forth* when he was losing patience and trying not to show his temper. "But sooner or later, you'll be coming home, back to Maryland. I'm sure Emily would love it if you stayed here forever. But I'm sure she can also understand that this is only a temporary arrangement."

"I think Sara has to do what she thinks will make her happy and what she thinks is best for her. I've never tried to persuade her to stay here," Emily said.

"I'm sure my husband didn't mean to imply that you had," Laura said, sounding flustered.

"We want Sara to be happy. That's all we're saying. That's all we've *ever* wanted. Her whole life."

"Well, then we're in total agreement," Emily said evenly. "Just because I gave Sara up, doesn't mean I didn't think about her. I never stopped worrying if she was safe and happy."

Sara could see her answer had somehow made her father more upset.

"Yes, of course, you thought about her. But it's different for us. We're the ones who raised her. We were her parents for twenty-two years. That's a long time, wouldn't you say?"

Sara saw that Emily was about to reply, but she spoke first. "Dad, calm down. I don't see what you're getting so upset about."

"I do," Emily said quietly. "I think your father feels I'm trying to keep you here, when he thinks it would be better for you to move back home." She looked over at Sara's parents. "I'm sure I'd feel the same way if I were in your position. I'm sure I'd miss her very much and wonder about . . . me."

Sara was surprised for a moment by Emily's candor. She could see that her parents were, too.

"We know you're a fine person. There's no question," Laura said quickly. "When Sara started looking for you, though, we didn't know who she'd find. Frankly, we were greatly relieved to hear that you were so accomplished and respectable."

"But Sara is a soft-hearted girl. She worries about other people's feelings. Too much, I think, sometimes," Sara's father added. "And I worry that she stays on here because she doesn't want to hurt your feelings and—"

"I hope that's not the case. Is it, Sara?" Emily cut in.

Sara had heard enough. "No, that's not the reason I'm here. Not at all. I've wanted to get to know you better, but I don't feel sorry for you—"

"I didn't think so," Emily said, looking uncomfortable.

"—and I'm tired of everyone talking about me as if I weren't sitting right here," she announced to all three of them. "I decided to stay to get to know Emily better. That's certainly true. But she's never tried to talk me into it or make me feel guilty," Sara said, looking at her father. "Now I have a job here. I have friends here, too. Emily isn't the only reason. So stop acting as if she's kept me prisoner or something."

Sara's parents exchanged a look. Her father looked a little sheepish, Sara thought. Finally.

"Look, I know you're all concerned about me, but—"

"But you're going to do what you want to do," her mother filled in for her. But not in a defensive tone, Sara noticed. More as if she were stating an irrefutable fact. "I guess that's the way we raised you. We shouldn't be surprised now," she said.

"And you did an absolutely wonderful job," Emily said, gazing fondly at Sara. "I don't think I even got to tell you that yet. Thank you. From the bottom of my heart. Thank you for loving her and caring for her and raising her to be such a wonderful person. I'm not sure if I could have done it half as well."

Emily's voice trailed off, and Sara saw her look down at the table, unable to meet anyone's gaze. Sara wanted to reach out and touch her hand, but something held her back from the gesture.

"I guess when I thought about coming here tonight, that's all I really wanted to say to both of you," Emily finished.

Nobody spoke for a long moment. Sara saw her father make a restless gesture. He coughed into his hand and glanced at Sara's mother.

"That's a lovely compliment, Emily," her mother said finally. "But all the while Sara was growing up, I was grateful to you just for bringing her into the world. So maybe we ought to call it even."

Sara's father didn't say anything but nodded, and watching his gesture, Sara felt a kind of peace settle over her, relief that they had all come to some sort of understanding. It was as if all this time, she and her parents had fit neatly together in a familiar design. Then along came Emily, and that neat pattern had been shaken loose. But now the four of them were rearranged, balanced out again in a new design.

This was not the dinner party she had imagined, Sara realized, but she was finally learning that her imagination rarely matched reality. The truth was often so much stranger . . . and more interesting.

SINCE IT HAD BEEN SUCH A QUIET WEEK, WYATT HAD LET SARA TAKE OFF on Thursday and Friday to spend time with her parents. The Franklins left New England on Sunday morning, and Sara was sad to see them go.

"Well, we'd better get on the road. We have a long drive ahead of us," her mother said, giving Sara yet another hug good-bye. "I'm happy we came up here to see you, sweetheart. We needed to see if you were really happy . . . and it seems that you are. That's what really matters to us."

"I know that, Mom. I'm glad you came, too," Sara said. She thought she might cry as her father kissed her good-bye again, but she tried not to. She watched their station wagon until it disappeared down Clover Street, then she went inside, deciding she'd spend the rest of the day cleaning up her house and getting ready for the week ahead.

* * *

WITH HER PARENTS IN TOWN, SARA HADN'T SEEN MUCH OF WYATT. Everyone in the office was busy on Monday, unexpectedly so since it was New Year's Eve and the week before had been so quiet.

As Sara finished up a story, she sensed someone standing near her desk. She looked up and saw Wyatt waiting to talk to her.

"Do you need this copy?" she asked, glancing at the clock and still managing to type at top speed. "I'm almost done. . . ."

"No, that's okay. I can wait for that one," he said. "You can go when you're done, though. Everyone's leaving early for the holiday."

"Oh, right," Sara said. She stopped typing and turned to him. She kept forgetting it was New Year's Eve. Avoiding it was more like it.

"Are you going to Jane's party?" he asked. His tone was offhand, casual, yet she sensed his interest in her reply.

"Uh, yes, I think so. I haven't really decided, though. Having my parents here sort of wiped me out," she confessed.

"Oh, come on, Sara. It's New Year's Eve. Nobody stays home," Wyatt said, in a coaxing tone. "You have to come. I won't know anybody there except for Jane."

Sara didn't know what to say. Wyatt seemed to be hoping to spend the evening with her. She felt flattered. It could be fun, she realized.

But she'd been thinking too much about Luke, ever since his phone call last week. Brooding about him, actually. Maybe tonight was a good time to get over that. She ought to ring in the new and ring out the old, as they say.

"Okay, I'll try to come," she said. Her vague promise met with an instant smile. "I might be a little late, though, okay?"

"Sure." Wyatt shrugged. "I have to finish up here, so I'm going to get there on the late side myself." He touched her shoulder for a moment, then headed for his desk. "I'll be on the lookout for you," he promised.

Sara didn't know what to say. She smiled back at him, then turned back to the words on her computer screen, which suddenly looked like a foreign language to her. Well, it could be an interesting evening, she considered. If she wanted it to be . . .

At home, Sara had a long shower and a bite to eat, then took a nap, hoping she'd be more in the mood for a party if she didn't feel so tired. When she woke up, it was almost eight. She didn't feel much brighter, but she got up and dressed quickly in a thick brown turtleneck, jeans, and boots.

Main Street looked quiet as she drove through town. The Clam Box was closed, but the Beanery was brightly lit, and Sara could hear live music as she drove by. As she passed the green, the village tree caught her eye, making her think back to her evening with Luke the night of the tree lighting. She pushed the thought aside, but it still brought her spirits down.

Did she really want to go to this party? It was starting to feel more like a chore than something she really wanted to do. Jane had invited a huge crowd of people. *She might not even notice if I don't show up,* Sara thought. Though Wyatt certainly would. Somehow the notion of meeting him there was starting to feel intimidating. He clearly wanted to spend the evening with her. It was almost like a real date.

She glanced at her watch. It was still too early to arrive at Jane's. Wyatt had to stay at the office and close the issue. He wouldn't be there until much later, and she didn't want to look as if she'd been sitting there hours, waiting for him. *Even if a guy liked you, it was always better if you didn't seem too eager,* Sara thought. Then she realized she really was thinking of Wyatt with a dating strategy, and that made her feel nervous again. Nervous but excited in a good way, too, she mused, with a small smile.

At the end of the block, Sara turned her car around and drove through the village to Providence Street. She parked in front of Lillian's house, assured by the lights in the living-room windows that her grandmother was home.

I'll just look in on Lillian and wish her a happy New Year. When she starts to drive me crazy, I'll go to the party, Sara decided.

As usual, her grandmother took a long time to answer—partly because she walked so slowly and partly because she had to check carefully to see who was calling. Some visitors found that, though they knew full well that Lillian was home, she just didn't let them in.

Sara always felt as if she'd passed some secret test when the door finally opened and her grandmother greeted her.

"Oh, it's you," Lillian said curtly. "What is it? Is something wrong?"

"No, nothing's wrong. I just came to wish you a happy New Year."

Her grandmother looked surprised. "Oh . . . well, come in then." She stepped aside so that Sara could enter. "I detest New Year's Eve. It's a ridiculous tradition, so much enforced merrymaking and revelry. Most people aren't happy at all and end up crying in their soup," Lillian remarked, as Sara followed her to the living room. "Just another day on the calendar, if you ask me."

"That's one way of looking at it," Sara said.

"And why some freezing night in the dead of winter? I would think April or even May would make much more sense as the start of a new year—" Lillian continued.

The phone rang, interrupting her diatribe. Sara was grateful. This visit could turn out to be even shorter than she'd expected. Lillian picked up the phone and said hello. Sara could tell that it was Emily calling to wish her mother a happy New Year before she went out.

"You'll never guess who's sitting here with me," Lillian remarked. "Sara Franklin," she continued, as if Emily would need her own daughter's last name. "All right, say hello if you wish."

Lillian handed over the phone, and Sara heard Emily's voice. "Sara, what are you doing there?"

"I just stopped by to wish Lillian a happy New Year. I didn't realize she doesn't recognize the holiday," Sara joked. "Happy New Year, Emily."

"Happy New Year, dear. I wish you all good things. I hope it's a great one for you."

"You, too," Sara said sincerely. She gave the phone back to Lillian, who continued her conversation.

"Well, enjoy yourself. Yes, I'll speak to you tomorrow."

Lillian hung up the phone and gave Sara a meaningful look. "Dan Forbes again tonight. She's been seeing a lot of him lately. Do you think it's getting serious?"

"I don't know," Sara said honestly. "She doesn't say much about him to me."

"Me, either. But there are signs, you know. She's been looking brighter lately. I thought it was a new lipstick. But she hasn't gone out like this on New Year's Eve since . . . well, since I don't know when. I think it's time I ask to meet him," she said, nodding her head.

Sara smiled at the image of Lillian questioning Dan on his intentions. Dan would handle her well, she thought.

"Dan planned to leave on a long sailing trip before he had that accident," Sara said. "As far as I know, he's still going."

"A man's plans can change. History has shown us that. A man will even give up a crown, if he meets the right woman," Lillian stated flatly. "I'd hate to see Emily disappointed at this stage in her life," she added.

Sara felt the same. Privately she also sensed that Emily had fallen hard for Dan. But she'd never heard Lillian openly express that kind of concern for her daughter.

The doorbell rang. Lillian stared at her. "Now who could that be? I hope it's not Ezra, trying to drag me off to one of those senior-center soirees he's so fond of."

So she did have an invitation for the evening, Sara realized. Good old Dr. Elliot. He never liked to see his old friend Lillian left alone, even when Lillian defied most attempts to include her.

"I'll get it. Be right back," Sara said, smiling to herself.

"I thought I'd have a peaceful evening on my own, and I'm bombarded with company," she heard Lillian mutter, as Sara left the room.

The bell sounded again. "Be right there," she called, crossing the foyer. She swung the door open, expecting to find Ezra.

The last person she'd expected to see was Luke McAllister.

CHAPTER SIXTEEN

"LUKE! WHAT ARE YOU DOING HERE?"

"That's a fine greeting. You sound just like your grandmother." When she didn't answer, he said, "I just spoke to Emily, and she told me you were here."

He'd been calling people in town looking for her? That was interesting. Sara felt her heart jump-start with a hopeful spark.

"Can I come in?" he asked.

"Sure. Of course. Come in the living room," she said, leading the way.

"Who is that?" Lillian's voice called out to them before they even reached the doorway.

"It's Luke McAllister, Lillian. You know Luke," Sara said, feeling wary of her grandmother's reaction.

Lillian watched them enter, with a guarded expression. "Of course, the famous party crasher. This is becoming a habit with you, young man. This is the second time you've come to my home on a holiday, uninvited. Don't you think that's odd?"

Sara thought Luke would be angry, but he only laughed.

"*Very* odd, considering the welcome I get. You think I would have learned my lesson the first time, Mrs. Warwick."

Lillian looked surprised at his reply, at first. Then her eyes narrowed, and she sat back in her chair. "Slow learner, I suppose. Well, sit down, the both of you. It's unnerving to have you standing there, gawking at me."

Sara and Luke glanced at each other, then they each sat down at opposite ends of Lillian's old-fashioned sofa.

"So, how is your project coming along? Any new developments?" Lillian asked Luke.

Sara knew that her grandmother had been opposed to Luke's efforts. But Lillian respected anyone who persisted despite obstacles, and Luke certainly met that criteria.

Luke briefly updated her on the plans, and Lillian seemed impressed. "So, you spent the week in Boston. Why didn't you stay for the big holiday tonight? I imagine it was far livelier there than up here in Cape Light."

Luke looked uneasy for a moment. "A little too much noise for me, I guess. . . . I needed to get back anyway."

Lillian stared at him a moment, then glanced at Sara. "Yes, I'm sure." She yawned—very theatrically, Sara thought. "Excuse me. While your company is stimulating, it's getting close to my bedtime. I'm sorry to end the party early, but I'm old and boring and I do need my rest."

Sara was tempted to laugh out loud but decided to let her grandmother get away with this transparent ploy without remarking on it.

"All right, if you say so," Sara said, coming to her feet. Luke stood up, too, looking very relieved, Sara noticed. "I guess we'd better go then," she said, glancing at him.

"I guess so," he agreed.

They said good night to Lillian, and Sara leaned over and kissed her cheek. "Happy Monday night in December, Lillian," she teased her.

"Thank you. The same to you, I'm sure," Lillian replied.

Once they were outside together, alone on the porch, Sara felt awkward with Luke. "Well, what now?" she asked him.

"Why don't we walk into town and see if anything is going on? I think I noticed something at the Beanery."

"Yes, I did, too," she said, falling into step beside him. "When did you get back?"

He glanced at her, then looked ahead again. "Just now."

"Oh."

"I was surprised to catch up with you. What happened to your party?" he asked curiously.

"Oh, that." Sara paused. She'd forgotten all about the party. "It was too early to go there. Besides, I don't really know anybody there except for Jane . . . and Wyatt," she added.

He looked over his shoulder at her, but didn't say anything.

Wyatt. Oh, dear. Well, she'd have to make up some polite excuse on Wednesday, Sara thought. It looked like she wasn't going to be meeting him at Jane's after all. Lillian was right; plans can change.

"How's the job going?" Luke asked evenly.

"It's all right. It was quiet this week."

"No big front-page stories?" he said.

"Not really." She jammed her hands in her pockets, sensing a certain note of derision in his voice. He was still mad at her, she guessed. She wished he wasn't.

"Luke, listen . . . I'm sorry," she said haltingly. "I know I've been sort of . . . awful lately. As if this job is the biggest thing in the world. I've been terribly self-centered about it, and I'm sorry if I hurt your feelings. I didn't mean to."

He stopped walking and turned to her. "Okay. Your apology is accepted," he said simply.

She felt puzzled. He didn't sound as if he really forgave her or even understood what she was trying to say.

"What does that mean? You still sound mad at me."

"I'm not mad," he said slowly. "I've just had some time to think about things since we had that argument."

His quiet words made her apprehensive. There was something sad—almost final—in his tone.

"I'm happy you like your job and that things are working out for you, Sara," he went on. "But I can see now that things aren't going to work out between you and me. It was sort of foolish of me to even hope for that."

Sara felt breathless, as if the wind had just been knocked out of her. "That's not true. We had an argument. It doesn't have to be the end of everything," she insisted.

"Isn't it? Think about it. I thought that once you had settled things with Emily and started at the paper, things could go forward with us. I guess I was waiting until I thought you had some room in your life for a real relationship," he confessed. "But to hear you tell it, you have even less room and time now. Or maybe you just want to keep your options open—in case someone more interesting comes along."

Sara knew he meant Wyatt, and she also knew that there was some truth to his accusations, however painful that was for her to admit.

Sara took a deep breath. She looked down the sloping street, edged with mounds of snow that took on a bluish shadow beneath the streetlights.

"I know what you're saying is partly true. I know I've acted sort of fickle or something. I think I just got scared," she admitted.

"Well, at least that's honest," he said. "That's just what I was trying to say. You're not ready for a real commitment and I am. It's nobody's fault," he added, in a kinder tone, which somehow hurt just as much as if he'd been yelling at her.

"Why did you come back here then and look all over town for me, if that's the way you feel? Now who's acting fickle? I don't get it, Luke."

"I have a lot of feelings for you, Sara. Even after the way you've acted, I still wanted to be with you tonight. I guess I missed you."

She felt a little better, hearing this admission. "I missed you, too," she said sincerely. "I felt so awful after we had that fight. I care about you. A lot. I know that now. Doesn't that count for something?"

"Of course, it counts for something. It counts for a lot," he said softly. He looked down at her briefly, then looked away. He seemed uneasy, and Sara had a bad feeling that she was not going to like what he had to tell her.

"But there's something else going on now. I'm leaving here. I decided to go back to Boston. I really just came back tonight to say good-bye."

Sara felt breathless and stunned. "You're leaving? You mean . . . forever?" She felt as if she might burst into tears and struggled to hold them back. "I don't understand. How could you leave? The center isn't even open yet—"

"I know it seems abrupt, but I think it's the right thing to do. New Horizons offered me a job last week. Dr. Santori said they could send their staff here to run the center in the spring, but I don't have to stay. They'll train me, so I can help set up new centers in other cities. It sounds like interesting work, with lots of travel. Besides, I've been wondering what I'm going to do with the rest of my life."

Sara couldn't believe it. She'd never imagined that Luke would want to leave Cape Light. Not after he'd worked so hard to establish himself here.

"I didn't know you were thinking of leaving here," she said. Her voice sounded flat and distant to her, as if someone else were caught in this awful conversation. "I thought you were set on opening the center and working there as a counselor."

"Well, I was. But this just came up, out of the blue. It made me start thinking that I might be ready to go back to the city."

Ready to go back. He said the phrase as if he thought of his time here as some long convalescence. Maybe it had been, she reflected. Maybe he needed to go back to Boston just to prove to himself that he could, that he wasn't hiding out here in the country. Lillian had definitely been right. Plans change.

"Listen, I'm sorry you're so upset. I honestly didn't think you would be. I mean, you always tell me you don't plan on staying here forever."

True enough, Sara thought, glancing up at him through a watery gaze. Was he trying to get back at her in some way? Leaving first so she couldn't leave him later? She bowed her head and rubbed her eyes. No, that wasn't it. He was really eager to go. He just didn't see a future for them any longer.

Finally she looked up at him. "So you just came back to say goodbye? What was the point of that?"

She knew she sounded bitter and hurt, but she couldn't help it. She had been so happy and hopeful when he showed up at Lillian's door. She'd never imagined this.

"Sara . . ." He reached out and touched her shoulder. "Not everything works out the way we want it to. You're young, yet. When you've had more relationships, you'll understand."

"Oh no, not the age thing again," she said wearily. It seemed whenever Luke got backed into a corner, he resorted to reminding her that he was older and, presumably, wiser.

"Well, I can't help it. It's true. I just wanted to set things straight with you and tell you what was going on with me now. . . . I don't see things working out for us anymore. Maybe you were right to put me off."

Was he hoping she would argue with him? Sara felt too hurt to fight with him about it anymore. She had put her heart on the line, and she was too late. His feelings for her had changed.

"You didn't seem to think so at the time," she reminded him sadly. "But what's the difference? You sound as if your mind is made up."

"It is," he said quietly.

Sara stared up at him, willing herself not to cry. "Okay, then. Happy New Year, Luke. Good luck with your new job," she added bitterly.

"Sara . . ." He stepped toward her, but she moved away. She turned and started walking quickly to the corner, her head bowed as she tried not to cry.

"Sara, wait a minute. Let me walk with you," he called after her.

"No!" She turned and nearly screamed the word at him. "I don't want you to. Just leave me alone."

She could tell from his expression that she'd convinced him not to follow. Then she turned and started running back toward her car.

"SO HOW DID IT GO WITH SARA'S PARENTS? YOU NEVER TOLD ME," DAN asked, leaning back in his chair. The lighting in the restaurant was low, and a small candle on the table between them cast his face in a warm golden light. Emily secretly studied his handsome features. It was hard to keep her mind on the conversation.

"Well, it was sort of a disaster. But maybe that was good in a way," she replied. "We all needed to clear the air. Sara was stuck in the middle. I felt bad for her." Emily sighed. "I think I'm having too good a time now to get into it."

"That's all right. I just wondered."

So far they had spent a wonderful evening together. The chamber music had been beautifully performed, and the restaurant Dan had chosen was perfect. They'd talked and laughed for hours and now lingered over dessert, as they waited for midnight to ring in the New Year. Emily didn't want to spoil the mood by fretting over something she couldn't really do anything about.

Dan smiled at her. "Would you like to dance?"

"I'd love to, but does your leg feel all right?"

"I'm all right," he said, coming to his feet. He held out his hand to her, and she took it. "You'll just have to hold me up if I stumble."

"I'll do my best," she agreed, as they stepped onto the dance floor.

The music was slow and dreamy, and Emily felt herself relax in Dan's strong embrace. He was a good dancer. Even with a bad leg, he moved deftly for such a tall man.

"You're very quiet," he said, his voice close to her ear. "Anything wrong?"

She shook her head. "Nothing at all. Everything's perfect. . . . That's just the thing. Why talk?"

He glanced down and smiled at her, but didn't say anything. She felt him pull her slightly closer as they took a turn.

They stayed on the floor for two dances, both slow, familiar songs. Emily couldn't remember when she'd felt so comfortable with someone and so happy. Except for Tim, of course. But that was so long ago. When she thought back, her memories of those days had a hazy, dreamlike quality, almost as if she'd imagined it all. It was sad, but with time, everything had faded, like an old photograph, even the pain of her loss.

"I must confess," Dan said, as they returned to their table, "New Year's Eve was never my favorite holiday. Most of the time I go to bed early and just pull the covers over my head."

"And why would you want to do that?" she asked, laughing at him.

"I don't know. Because everyone else seemed so infernally happy—and I wasn't."

"Oh. Are you happy now?"

"I am tonight. With you," he said, smiling. He reached out and took her hand. "You've never told me much about your marriage. Were you happy together?"

"Yes, truly. It seems like that now, anyway." She met his gaze. "What about you and Claire? You must have been happy at first."

"We were. At least I thought so. But there was always tension, I guess, about the newspaper, mostly. How much time I spent there. I think I did spend too much time there," he admitted. "I missed a lot with Lindsay and Wyatt. I know I'd do it differently now. But when they're little, you just think they're going to stay like that forever. You think there's always going to be some other baseball game or piano recital you can go to if you miss one." He paused. "You must think I was a bad father."

"No, not at all. I've met your kids, and I think you're a pretty good father."

"I'm okay. Nobody's perfect. I had the same problem with Claire. She wanted more from me—more time, more attention. By the time I started paying attention, it was too late. We were too distant, too angry at each other. And she was already involved with someone else."

"That's sad," Emily said. She noticed that he didn't blame his wife for what had happened, even though she had left him for someone else.

"We were supposed to go on this trip together. We talked about it all the time."

"And now you're going on your own."

"Yes, I am. One of these fine days. Next week I'm going back to the office to give Wyatt some pointers on being a publisher, whether he likes it or not," Dan said in a definite tone. "After he's settled in, I'm off."

"Sounds good," Emily said lightly.

Dan looked confused for a moment, as if there were something he wanted to say but wasn't sure he should.

"It's hard to believe I'm actually, finally, going. It's something I've talked about, dreamed about, even mapped out, for years. And lately I've been wondering, well . . . if maybe I'm just going to prove something to myself."

"Such as?"

"That I'll do it anyway, with or without her."

"Oh. I see." Emily frowned. She hadn't known about this part of the story. It changed things in a way. "Do you think that's it?"

Dan shrugged. "I'm not sure. It started out as something I planned with her, but now it seems to have become my own thing."

"I think once you're out there, it *will* be your own thing, and you'll have a wonderful trip," she told him.

"I hope you're right. Maybe I've just been stuck in that house thinking too much. Thinking has always been my downfall. I try to avoid it whenever possible." Dan smiled at her. "You're great, you know that?"

"Thanks. Why?" she asked, with a breathless laugh.

"A lot of other women would be trying to talk me out of this, not encouraging me to go."

"Not buying you a five-in-one fog horn and flood light, you mean?"

"Exactly."

"It's okay. I understand." Emily took a breath as she decided to venture into delicate terrain. "I know things are . . . happening between us. But that's sort of a fluke. I mean, you're not even really supposed to be here. So I can't get mad or try to make you feel guilty for going, when I know how much it means to you," she said sincerely. "I wouldn't even want you to stay if that was your reason. If you really care about someone, you want them to be happy, don't you?"

"Theoretically. It's amazing to me how often the real world doesn't seem to follow that theory."

"Well, that's how I feel. Really."

"That's why I think you're so great. You're probably the greatest woman I've ever met in my life," he said. "I do care about you. I care very much."

"I know that," Emily said. The tender expression in his eyes told her it was true beyond any doubt. She felt her pulse quickening, as she wondered if her own feelings and Dan's might actually be closer than she had dared hope.

"What do you see in your future, Emily? What is it you think will make you really happy?"

Emily looked up at him, unsure of whether she should answer him honestly. But he had asked the question. If ever there was a time to let him know where she stood, this was it. Hadn't Jessica told her to just go for it?

Here goes nothing, she thought, feeling as if she were about to dive headlong off a cliff. "Well . . . I guess all these weeks, getting to know you, has helped me finally figure that out," she began slowly. "I'd like to get married again."

Dan stared at her, his mouth hanging open a bit. He realized it and snapped it shut. "Well, that was honest."

Emily swallowed hard, feeling crushed inside but struggling not to show it. Obviously, Dan wasn't about to leap across the table and propose to her. Oh, how could she ever have expected anything like that? She'd been such a fool.

She fought back the tears that she felt welling up. *You cannot cry,* she told herself sternly. *That would make it even worse. You cannot even look remotely distressed.*

She forced herself to smile. "You did ask me."

"So I did." He took a breath. "So, while I'm off sailing around, you'll be looking for a husband?"

Was he perhaps a little jealous? It almost sounded that way under his joking tone. *No, stop right there!* she told herself. *He's not jealous. Get the message: He doesn't care. At least, not enough to change his plans. Better I know now.*

"Something like that," she finally answered, managing a lighter tone. "But you make it sound a little calculating."

"Sorry, didn't mean to. You'll let this future husband find you?"

"Maybe. Then again, I don't have all that much time, I guess."

"Is there some time limit you've set for yourself on this project?" he asked curiously.

"Not me, personally. But the other part is, I'd like to have a baby."

Now his eyes widened, as if he were caught in headlights. Emily would have laughed at his shocked expression, if it didn't hurt so much.

"A baby, huh? Well, that's a surprise. You've never mentioned that."

"I know. It almost sounds silly saying it aloud," she admitted. "But I've been thinking about it a lot, ever since I started getting to know Sara. I always thought if I ever found her, I wouldn't care so much about that part. But it's been just the opposite. The more I get to know her, the more I feel I've missed out on raising her."

"I understand," he said slowly.

"The odds are against me, I guess." She shook her head and laughed at herself. "You know, they say you can't get what you want until you know what you want. Well, at least I finally know, right?"

He took both of her hands in his. "I hope you get what you want, Emily. I know you deserve it."

"Thank you, Dan," she said, unable to meet his intent blue gaze.

I was right. He's not the one. It just won't work out, she told herself, overwhelmed by an aching sadness. She struggled to keep a reasonable perspective—or to at least not burst out crying right in front of him. *For goodness' sake, I didn't even realize how much I was hoping he'd have some change of heart. How could I have let myself fall so deeply in love? Please Lord,* she prayed quickly, *please let me soon see that this is all for the best.*

Meanwhile, she sat there holding his hand, feeling something deep inside crushed and ruined, like a flower trampled underfoot.

The band struck a loud chord, and they both turned at the sound. "—nine, eight, seven, six, five, four, three, two, one . . ." The band leader led the crowd in the traditional countdown. "Happy New Year!" he announced.

Noisemakers and horns sounded. Confetti flew overhead. The familiar strains of "Auld Lang Syne" filtered through the chaos.

Dan moved closer and put his arms around her. He smiled and stared into her eyes. "Happy New Year, Emily," he whispered.

She wound her arms around his broad shoulders and kissed him for the New Year without even answering. She'd already said what she had come to say.

CHAPTER SEVENTEEN

ALONE IN HER APARTMENT, SARA STARTED THE NEW YEAR by first brooding and then cleaning in a frenzy. She only wished she could clear her heart of unwanted feelings as easily—just stuff them all in a big black trash bag and leave them on the curb to be carted away. But it wasn't nearly that easy. She'd tried hard not to think about Luke, but she kept glancing at the clock, wondering if he'd left town yet or if he would call her today.

By nightfall, she realized she wouldn't hear from him again. *Well, that's that,* she told herself. *It will hurt for a while, but I'll get over it. He was right in a way. I'm probably not ready for a real commitment. It's really just as well,* she decided. This reasoning gave her a sense of resolution, even if deep inside she was still raw and aching.

On Wednesday she was eager to get to the office. Wyatt sent her out on a story right away, a boring meeting about parking meters, but Sara didn't mind. He also asked her if she could find some candid shots around town of villagers enjoying the winter. There wasn't much news this week, and he wanted some photos on hand for filler.

Sara returned that afternoon, surprised to see Dan in the office, working with Wyatt. She sensed a definite tension in the air that eased about twenty minutes later when Dan left. What was going on? she wondered. It didn't seem like a good time to ask, though, so she focused on her work.

Jane and Ed had already gone for the day when Lindsay stopped by her desk to say good night. "I have to run. I'm meeting Scott to look at apartments. Wyatt's back in the darkroom. I didn't want to bother him. Could you let him know I had to go?"

Lindsay left, and Sara returned to her writing. She was just finishing her piece, when she heard Wyatt return to his desk.

"Here's the copy to go with the photos," Sara said, handing it to him, "Oh and Lindsay had to go. She has to look at some apartments with Scott."

Wyatt sighed and ran his hand through his hair. "Uh-oh. I really needed her tonight. Oh well, I'll manage. And you're still here," he said, casting her a bright grin.

Sara felt put on the spot. But she quickly returned his smile. Hanging out with Wyatt tonight wasn't the worst idea. It sure beat going home and sulking about Luke.

"I want to show you something," Wyatt said. "You got some great shots of those ice skaters. Come in the darkroom, and take a look."

Sara had never been inside the darkroom before and was curious to see it. The narrow room was dimly lit by a red bulb, which she knew wouldn't affect the developing process. One counter held an enlarger. Another, next to the sink, held a row of trays with chemicals for the various solutions used to develop and fix the prints. There was also a clothesline strung near the sink, with wet photos hanging from clips.

"Look at this one." Wyatt turned on the enlarger, and an image of a woman in a fur-trimmed cap twirling on the ice was projected on the wall. "You really got her."

"Thanks," Sara said. She appreciated the compliment, especially coming from Wyatt.

"Let's go through the negatives together and decide what to use," he suggested.

"Sure." Sara felt a little awkward stuck in the tiny room with Wyatt, but so far he hadn't let her have this much say about which photos of hers they would use. She felt it was a silent acknowledgment that her work was improving.

They reviewed the negatives and chose six photos. Wyatt's praise of her pictures had Sara glowing; she was glad that the darkness hid her expression. They were almost done when Wyatt reached around her to adjust the enlarger. She felt him very close for a moment, his arm coming around her shoulder, his cheek brushing her hair.

She froze in place, not daring to turn her head or meet his eye. But just as quickly, he stepped away and turned to place the negatives on a light box on the counter behind them.

"Have you ever considered studying photography?" he asked.

"Uh, no, not really. I've always liked taking pictures, though."

"You're really good," he said. "I thought at first it was a fluke. You know, those shots you took at the tree lighting," he confessed, making her laugh. "But now I can see it's more than just lucky breaks. You're good with a camera."

"Thanks." Sara felt a little overwhelmed. "I'm not sure photography is something I'd really pursue, though. I really think of myself as a writer."

"You're good at that, too, no question," he said, turning to her. Even in the dim light, she could sense a certain intensity when he looked at her. She felt uneasy and looked away.

"Well, I have a lot to learn about reporting. I know that now," she admitted.

He smiled at her and reached out to touch her shoulder. "I've been hard on you. Maybe too critical. I've been stressed a lot, I guess. You're doing a good job," he said. "And you've been a great help to me around here. Really."

He gazed at her a moment, and Sara felt a wave of sympathy for him. He didn't have it that easy, either, she thought. Though he'd never said as much, she knew he was trying hard to live up to his father's expectations.

"Thanks." Sara met his gaze a moment, then looked away. "So what do you do next in here?"

"Make some prints, fix them. Want to see how it's done?"

"Sure, I'd love to."

Wyatt explained the printing process, using the negatives they had chosen. Sara helped, intrigued to learn the different steps. The odd thing was that, as they worked together, she finally started to feel comfortable with him.

While the prints dried, they went back out into the office, where Wyatt looked over her copy and made a few small changes. "You could move these lines up and then cut down here," he explained, as he marked the text.

"Right, that is better," she agreed, appreciating his explanation.

"Well . . . I guess that's it," Wyatt said finally. He sat back in his chair and folded his hands behind his head. "Unless, of course, you want to hang out and help me finish the layout?" He flashed a charming grin, making it almost impossible for her to refuse. "I'll throw in a pizza."

"A pizza, huh? Okay, I can stay," Sara replied. She did feel like hanging out with him. It was definitely better than going back to her empty apartment to think about Luke.

"Great." Wyatt looked pleased. "In that case . . ."—he glanced at his watch—"let's order now. We might be here awhile. Are you hungry?"

"Actually, I am. I don't think I ate lunch," she commented.

"Me, either. I'm starved. Let's get a lot of stuff on it," he said eagerly. "Where's that menu? I just had it—" he said, searching around his messy desk.

Sara had to smile. Sometimes she was amazed that he got a newspaper out every night without any pages missing.

"I'll call. What do you want?"

They were hard at work by the time the food arrived. They managed to eat at the drafting table where the paper was being set up, hardly missing a beat. There weren't any last-minute articles to fit, so the work went smoothly.

At last Wyatt transmitted the text and photos to the printer by E-mail.

"Excellent. It's a wrap. You've made my day, Ms. Franklin." He glanced up, his dark hair falling over his eyes, and he reached out to shake her hand. Sara took his hand, feeling his strong, warm grip in her own. His hands were wide and his skin smooth, much smoother than Luke's, which was covered with calluses from construction work.

She felt odd thinking of Luke all of a sudden and turned away. "I guess I'll get going. See you, Wyatt."

"Wait, I'll walk out with you," he said, grabbing his jacket from the coatrack behind his desk. Sara put on her jacket and scarf and waited for him by the front door while he made sure all the computers were off and then turned off the lights.

"I can't believe we finished already. This is a record for me," he said, as he locked the door.

"I guess you're getting the hang of it now," Sara remarked. It was true, too. He hadn't really needed her help at all. Sara had a feeling he'd just wanted the company.

"So, what do you think of the paper lately—I mean, since I took over?" he asked. "It's okay, you can be honest."

She felt nervous about answering. After all, he was her boss, and she didn't want to insult him. But it was a fair question, and she knew he'd pick up on it if she tried to hedge.

"It's not the same as when your father ran it, not quite as consistent. But I think it's been good. Some issues have been really good," she added. "More provocative."

He glanced down at her, his hands in his jacket pockets. "Thanks. I guess I think so, too. Seems like I don't have to worry anymore *if* I can do it. It's more whether I *want* to do it."

Sara was surprised by his candor, though she'd often sensed Wyatt had mixed feelings about the paper, acting as if it was more a duty than a pleasure—or the prize he'd been waiting to get his hands on since childhood.

"What about your father? Does he know that?" she asked him.

"We don't communicate that well when it comes to the *Messenger,*" Wyatt said, pronouncing the name of the paper in a mock-solemn tone. "Not that it's all his fault, either. I don't even know how to bring it up. Something like, 'By the way, I know you've waited for years for me to come back, but I'm really having second thoughts about doing this. I sort of miss taking pictures, traveling around, having a real life. . . .' "

"I don't know your father all that well," Sara said, after a moment, "but I think you should be honest with him. It doesn't do either of you any good if you're not."

She had learned that lesson the hard way, taking so long to reveal her identity to Emily, when honesty was the only thing that had helped either one of them.

Wyatt was quiet for a moment. He looked out at the harbor across the street, and she wondered if what she said had made him angry.

"Sara, that's good advice, really. But I don't think my father will understand. You were right the first time. You don't know him. Once he has a plan—well, it's nearly impossible to change his mind."

Sara had a sinking feeling she'd said too much, given advice when he hadn't really asked her for it.

Wyatt must have guessed what she was feeling because he said, "Listen, it's okay. I know you're just trying to help." He smiled, then reached out and briefly touched her cheek.

Sara stared up at him. She suddenly realized she liked him. She liked him a lot. Luke's words came back to haunt her. Had she had a crush on Wyatt all this time and not even realized it? She suddenly knew that yes, she really did like him.

She felt his hand drop away, as his voice broke through her trance. "Where's your car? I'll walk you over."

"I didn't drive today. I just walked to town."

"Let me give you a lift then. My car's right here."

"Okay. Thanks." She nodded, trying to keep her voice normal. It seemed hard in the wake of her sudden revelation.

They crossed the street to his car, and Wyatt opened the door for her. He drove a small black sports car, a two-seater with patches on the convertible top. It looked a little shabby, but also, somehow, classy and hip, Sara thought. It definitely suited him.

He started the engine and a few moments later, they were cruising through the village and then turning down her street. Sara pointed out her house, and he parked in front.

"Thanks for staying tonight. I appreciated your help—and it was fun."

Almost like a date, Sara wanted to say. But she caught herself. "I had fun, too. For work, I mean," she added in a serious tone that made him smile again.

"Yes, for work," he agreed, his smile deepening. "But you still owe me for that lunch date," he reminded her. "I didn't forget."

"The lunch date—oh, right," she said, glancing at him.

"What are you doing Saturday night? Would you like to go out?" He stretched his arm along the back of her seat. Not around her shoulder exactly, but the car was small enough that the gesture was definitely distracting.

"Yes. I would," she said, hoping she didn't sound too eager.

"Good." He smiled at her. "We'll figure out the details later in the week. There's a movie house in Newburyport that shows foreign films. Maybe something interesting will be playing there."

"Sounds good to me."

She found herself staring at him again, wondering how dumb she to had been not to realize she was attracted to him. Had he noticed all this time, she wondered uncomfortably. *Gosh, I hope not,* she thought.

She suddenly panicked and turned away, her hand fumbling for the latch on the door.

"Well, see you. Thanks for the lift," she said abruptly. She jumped out of the car and nearly slid on the snow, catching herself just in time.

"See you, Sara," he called out from his window.

He sounded as if he was trying not to laugh at her hasty escape, but she felt too embarrassed to turn around and look at him again.

Sara still felt a little rattled as she opened her apartment door and let herself in. No calls on her answering machine, she noticed. But who was she expecting? Luke wouldn't be calling again. He was gone, she reminded herself. Gone from this town—and her life.

She felt sad all over again, then almost guilty that she'd had so much fun tonight with Wyatt.

But she didn't have anything to feel guilty over. She was free to see whomever she liked. Now more than ever, she told herself.

She'd felt closer to Wyatt tonight, as if they'd gotten to know each other much better, and she'd grown to like him even more. He was fun, clever, even irreverent at times. The opposite of Luke, who was usually so serious.

Maybe she didn't need deep, serious feelings right now. Wasn't that the real problem between her and Luke? A relationship with Wyatt might be just right.

"LOOK, DAD, I KNOW YOU HAVE YOUR SYSTEMS AND ALL YOUR LITTLE timesaving tricks. But these things don't work for me. I'm trying to work out my own way of doing things. In case you haven't noticed," Wyatt said in a tight voice.

"I know that," Dan replied. "But if you'd just try it my way once, I think you'll see that you're not only saving time but some money, too. That goes directly to the bottom line, Wyatt. Which you don't seem to think about too much, I've noticed."

"What are you talking about? Overhead hasn't gone up at all since you left. Did Lindsay tell you that?"

"Your sister has nothing but positive words about what you've been doing here," Dan replied, which was basically true, he thought.

He stared at his son, feeling weary. It was nearly eleven, and they still hadn't transmitted the issue to the printer. Dan had never realized that his son could be so stubborn and inflexible. The more Dan tried to help him—show him a few shortcuts or problem areas to watch out for—the more Wyatt closed down, shutting him out.

They'd been at each other like this for days now, ever since he started coming into the office last Wednesday. Somehow they'd managed to make it through the week, but Dan could see they weren't getting anywhere.

"Listen, I haven't come down here the last few days to check up on you or make your life miserable. This is your paper now. I know that. I just want to feel sure that you really have control over things before I go. That's all I'm trying to accomplish," he said tiredly.

Wyatt looked up at him and leaned far back in his chair. "Right, your big trip," he said. "I'd trade places with you in a heartbeat."

Dan almost thought he hadn't heard him right. But he knew that he had.

"Getting restless already?" He tried to keep his tone light. "You just got here."

"Oh, I think I've been here long enough to figure some things out," Wyatt said slowly. He looked up at his father in a way that made Dan distinctly uneasy. "Dad, I've been thinking about this a lot, so don't think I'm saying it just because we were arguing," he began.

Dan felt his mouth going dry. He didn't like the sound of this. "Okay, you've been thinking. I'm listening."

"I don't think I'm really cut out to run the paper," Wyatt said flatly. "I know it's been our plan. I know it's the family tradition and all of that. But I have to be honest with you: it's not for me."

Dan didn't know what to say. He felt a tightness in his chest that made it hard to breathe. *He just didn't get off to a good start,* Dan told himself. *If only I'd been here with him from the beginning. He got a bad taste in his mouth and now he wants out.*

"Look, I hear what you're saying, Son. I understand. But I know where this is coming from. You're too hard on yourself. You've always been that way. You want to pick something up and master it immediately—no learning curve." When Wyatt didn't answer, he kept going. "Remember when we bought you that guitar? You stayed up in your room for a week and then came down one day, totally frustrated that you weren't playing like some rock star," he said, trying to lighten the mood between them.

"Dad, I'm not seventeen anymore. This isn't because I'm not running the paper in my sleep—like you've been doing for most of your life," he said in a cutting tone. "It's because I don't ever want to turn into that guy, who's sitting here . . . running this paper in his sleep."

Now Dan felt hurt and angry, but he tried his best to hold on to his temper. He had to go slowly—and carefully.

"Okay, you don't want to be running this paper in your sleep. You don't want to turn into me," Dan said in an even tone. "Fair enough. I know how you feel. I felt the same way when my father handed me the keys to this place. What was I doing with my life, I asked myself, coming back to this nothing little town, throwing my life away on this nothing little paper."

"I didn't say that," Wyatt argued, shaking his head. "I didn't say it was without value. I know it has value."

"You didn't say it, but you didn't have to," Dan told him. "It's easy to say the paper has value. But you don't feel that inside, where it counts."

Wyatt met his eyes, then slowly nodded. "Maybe I don't. It's not for me," he repeated again. "I need to travel, see things. I can't sit here every day, staring out at that harbor, feeling like I'm missing out."

"You will feel that way at first. I felt the same way when I took over," Dan confessed. "But after a while you get used to it. You get involved with the paper, lost in it. It becomes part of you. Then you get to the point where you wouldn't give it up, even if you had the chance. Believe me, it happens. I had this same exact conversation with my father."

"You don't understand. I didn't think you would," Wyatt said sadly. "In time, though, I hope you'll see that I'm doing the right thing."

"Doing the right thing? What do you mean?" Dan asked, feeling panicked.

"I'm going back to L.A. I spoke to my old boss. There's an opening there for me. I can go back to the *Times.*"

"You can't go back to the *Times.* You're staying here. You're running the *Messenger,*" Dan insisted. He was shouting now, but he couldn't help it.

Wyatt didn't answer. He looked down at his desk, then rubbed his forehead with the palm of his hand. "Look, it's late. We haven't even sent the paper to the printer, yet. Let's talk about this more tomorrow," he suggested.

"As if I could sleep for five minutes tonight, after you've dumped this news on me?" Dan took a deep breath and tried to pull himself together. His leg was hurting him something fierce. He knew he'd been up on his feet too long today.

Still, he couldn't sit down. Restlessly, he paced in front of Wyatt's desk.

"Look, maybe I made a wrong move coming here this week. I butted in, and I shouldn't have done that. It's your show now. You run this place however you want to. I'm going to start packing tomorrow and get out. That's it. No more advice," he promised. "Just an occasional postcard."

"Dad, I told you before. It wasn't the advice—though there has been way too much of it," Wyatt agreed. "I'm trying to be honest with you. Even if you leave tomorrow, I'm not taking over. You'll have to make other arrangements. Maybe Lindsay would do it for a while."

"Lindsay? What are you talking about? I'm not going to give the paper to Lindsay. She's not even in the business!"

"Maybe not, but she's a quick study from what I've seen," Wyatt remarked. "The point is, I've accepted this job offer and I'm going back to California. I can stay a few more days if you need me," he offered.

Suddenly, Dan felt as if the fog had lifted, and he could finally see Wyatt clearly. Nothing he could say to his son was going to change his mind.

He let out a long, painful breath, unable to even look at his son. "All right. I got the message. Why don't you just leave now then?" he said in a low, angry voice. "I can get the paper out, no problem. I can do it in my sleep, remember?"

"Dad, come on. I didn't mean it that way—" Wyatt came to his feet and looked at his father. "I'm sorry I said that."

"I know what you meant," Dan said. "You want out. There's the door. You don't have to bother coming back here anymore. I don't see the point."

Wyatt's face filled with emotion as he met Dan's gaze. For a moment he looked as if he were going to say something more. Instead, he grabbed his coat from the stand behind the desk, nearly knocking it over in the process, and stalked out.

Dan didn't watch him go, but he heard the door to the street slam shut with a thud, making everything in the still, silent office tremble for a second—including his heart.

"WHEN IS HE LEAVING?" EMILY ASKED.

"Tonight. That ridiculous little car of his needs a tune-up before he tries to drive it cross-country. I just hope he makes it in that thing. I told him he didn't have to rush off like this, but maybe it's better not to drag it out." Dan sighed and stared out at the water.

Emily had been surprised that morning when he called and asked if she wanted to meet at the beach for a walk. They had both more or less retreated to their separate corners after New Year's Eve. But they were, above all, friends, and she could tell from his voice that something was bothering him. She'd never expected this. She could see that Dan still couldn't quite believe it.

"I know it seems awful right now," she said. "But if Wyatt is really unhappy, then maybe it's for the best. You wouldn't want him to stay here feeling miserable, just because he felt he had to."

"No, I suppose it's better for me to feel miserable. I'm the parent, after all."

"Oh, I didn't mean that," Emily said.

"I know. I'm just a mess today. I'm sorry," he apologized. He took her hand, and they started walking again.

Dan seemed lost in thought, and Emily wondered if she should say anything more. So far, nothing she'd said seemed to have much effect. Dan could be so narrow-minded sometimes. Once he'd fixed his mind on something, he couldn't seem to admit to any other possibility.

The beach was beautiful today, and though the air was cold, there was very little wind, so it wasn't hard walking. The sky was a startling deep shade of blue, and the blue-green waves rolled in long and flat along the shoreline. Far up on the sand, clumps of icy snow clung to a fringe of seaweed and driftwood.

"I know it's hard for you to see it this way," Emily said slowly, "but I'm sure it wasn't easy for Wyatt to confront you. I'm sure he was pretty terrified."

"Yes, it took some spunk. I'll grant him that much," Dan said wearily. He shot her an annoyed glance. "Why are you so keen to see things from Wyatt's point of view?"

"Maybe because I've felt pressured my entire life to live up to my mother's ideals. At least Wyatt was honest in a way I could never be," she admitted.

"That's just my point. You turned out pretty good," Dan said. "Maybe your mother knew what she was talking about."

"Dan, you know what I mean," she said, pushing at his arm.

They walked silently for a while, Emily matching Dan's stride and watching the foamy edge of the water slide up the sand and nearly touch their shoes.

Dan bent down, picked up a piece of driftwood, and tossed it into the waves. "I don't know. Rejecting the paper is rejecting me in a way. It feels like that, anyway."

"Yes, I guess it must," Emily agreed sympathetically. "But Wyatt seems to love newspaper work. He's followed in your footsteps that far. Maybe he's just not ready right now to take over. Right now he needs more time on his own, but in a few years, his life could be very different. He might wake up one day and decide that running the *Messenger* is a pretty good deal."

"I suppose you're right. Wyatt might come around sometime. But where does that leave me? I didn't plan on hanging around a few more years," Dan said gruffly. "I didn't even plan on a few more weeks!"

Emily felt quietly stung by his words, though she knew he hadn't meant to offend her. But she was part of his life now—the life Dan sounded so eager to leave.

She suddenly felt so angry and frustrated, she just wanted to shake him. Oh, it was so hopeless. He had the perfect chance once again to cancel that infernal trip of his, but the thought never even crossed his mind.

"I guess you're stuck," she said flatly.

"Yeah, I am," he agreed, oblivious to her dismay.

"Isn't there anyone you can hire to take over while you're on your trip?"

"No, that wouldn't work. I don't want to bring someone in from the outside. Who would come out here anyway for a temporary job like that?"

"What about Lindsay? You said she's been down there helping Wyatt out almost every day. Sara's told me the same thing. Couldn't she do it?"

"She's good with the business end of things, but . . . I just don't think it would work out."

"Is it because she's a woman?" Emily asked bluntly. Dan generally wasn't like that, but maybe that was the problem here.

"No, of course not. Lindsay's intelligent, capable—I couldn't respect her more," he insisted. "But I can't see her taking the paper. It just wouldn't seem . . . right to me." He glanced at Emily, as if she just didn't get it. She wasn't sure she did. "It's hard to explain," he said finally. "I saved the paper all those years for Wyatt. Not Lindsay."

"So now that you've ruled out the one possible candidate, what are you going to do?"

"I really don't know," he said, after a moment. He turned and looked out at the waves, then crossed his arms over his chest. "I'm thinking of selling to Crown News."

"Crown News?" Emily felt her heart jump in her chest. "What are you talking about?"

"They've been trying to buy me out for years. You know that. I never considered it before . . . but things are different now. I guess I'm going to sit down and finally hear what they have to say."

Emily was stunned. "I know you're upset right now about Wyatt," she said carefully, "but you can't be serious."

"Really? Why not? I've given enough years to the *Messenger.* If Wyatt doesn't want it, what's the difference? At least I can cash in and get something for all my trouble."

"Dan, you despise Crown News," she reminded him. "You can't sell the *Messenger* to them. The town won't have a conscience left—or a heart, for that matter."

"Oh, you'll all survive," he said darkly. "The paper will still be there, bigger and better than ever. I'm sure they'll expand it, maybe even add a little color printing."

"No, it won't be there," Emily argued. "It will turn into some banal, interchangeable clone of all their other chain papers—with no identity, no soul. If you sell the *Messenger,* you'll be making a huge mistake. Surely, you know that."

Dan's eyes were dark with anger. "I don't need any more advice right now, Emily. I didn't ask you out here to make me feel worse than I already do."

She didn't know what to say, so she turned to look at the ocean, her arms hugged around her chest.

Maybe she hadn't been very sympathetic, but sometimes he was really impossible to talk to. This was one of those moments when she wished Dan had more faith. She wished he could believe, as she did, that even though things looked bleak, God was watching over him, ready to help if Dan called on Him. If only Dan could just let go a little and try to let God show him what to do, Emily thought in frustration. But though Dan respected her faith, he didn't share it, and this was yet another place where they weren't entirely compatible.

He let out a long breath, then turned to look at her, his expression suddenly composed. "I'm sorry. I'll figure it out. I just don't see a lot of choices here."

"Sure . . . I understand. You don't need a lot of advice right now; you need to think." Emily gestured toward the shoreline. "I thought I'd take a short run out here. Do you mind?"

"No, not at all. Perfect day for it." She heard regret in his voice. Normally, Dan would have joined her, but his leg wasn't strong enough for that, yet. "I'll wait right here for you," he offered.

"Okay. I'll be right back." She turned and started jogging.

Dan seemed relieved to be left alone, she thought. Maybe it was a good idea to put some distance between them, before she said anything more she might regret.

The shoreline stretched out ahead, seemingly endless and empty. Emily decided to pray silently as she ran. *Please God, help Dan get through this. He's feeling so hurt and angry. He's just not seeing clearly right now. Please help him forgive Wyatt and figure out the right thing to do.*

ON SATURDAY AFTERNOON SARA WALKED INTO TOWN TO DROP OFF SOME books at the library and stop at the post office. She passed by the *Messenger* office and thought about stopping in to say hello to Wyatt. She'd see him soon enough, she decided.

She felt nervous about their upcoming date—not for the usual reasons but because she'd done some thinking about him and her feelings for Luke.

They hadn't spent any time alone together at work the past few days, which was just as well, she thought. Dan had been in the office, trying to carry on some sort of crash-course, editor-in-chief indoctrination, as far as Sara could see. She could also see that it wasn't going very well for Wyatt. She expected that he'd want to talk about it tonight.

She had something to talk about with him, too. She didn't think she could start seeing him. Maybe someday in the future, but not right now. Ever since he asked her out, she'd tried hard to forget about Luke. But in her heart she knew it still hurt far too much for her to get involved with anyone new—even Wyatt, who was about as smart, funny, attractive, and charming as they get, Sara thought, with a sigh. That had to tell her something. Something like she really loved Luke and would probably love him for a long time. You just didn't get over feelings like that so easily.

A lot of her friends said the best way to get over a breakup was to start dating again. That didn't feel right to Sara. It wasn't fair to Wyatt, for one thing. She didn't know exactly how she would tell him, but she knew she'd have to be honest.

Returning home, she turned up Clover Street and headed for her apartment. As she drew closer, she noticed a man on the porch, standing by her door. His back was turned to the street; she couldn't tell who it was. Her first thought was that it might be Luke.

Then he turned, and she could see it was Wyatt. "There you are. . . . I thought I might miss you," he called out, as she stepped onto the porch to meet him.

"Hi, what's going on? I didn't expect you until seven. Need some help at the paper?" she asked.

"No, nothing like that," he said. "I just came to say I can't make our date tonight. . . . I'm going back to California." He smiled and shook his head, as if he were laughing at himself. "How's that for a creative reason to stand someone up? Sounds a little nuts, right?"

"It's a real good one," Sara replied, still feeling confused. "You mean, you're going back for a visit or something?"

"No, more like a permanent change of address. Well, as permanent as it gets with me," he amended. He leaned on the porch railing and crossed his arms over his chest.

"I don't understand," she said, staring up at him. "You mean, you're leaving here? Giving up the paper?"

"I'm leaving tonight. That's why I came—to say good-bye." He nodded, not looking entirely happy, she thought, but greatly relieved. Even his eyes had taken on a brightness she'd never noticed before. "It was a tough call," he said, "but I think I've done the right thing."

"Sometimes you sounded as if you weren't happy," Sara said. "I thought it was just taking you time to get used to the place and coming back here."

"So did I at first. And so did my father," he added.

"Oh, gee . . . How did Dan take it?"

"Not good. Not good at all." Wyatt looked down and shook his head, letting out a breath. "I hope eventually he'll understand I did the right thing. It's a good paper. A great little paper, really. But running the *Messenger* is not for me. At least, not for now," he said, looking back up at her.

He sounded clear on his decision, and Sara sensed it was the right one for him.

"Who's going to take over?" she asked.

Wyatt shrugged. "Don't know. I don't think my father's figured out what to do yet. But I'm going back to the *Times.* They've offered me a great job."

"That's good, then," Sara said, slowly smiling at him. "I think your father will see you've done the right thing someday."

"Someday. He can be sort of slow with these things," Wyatt said. He stood up again and looked down at her. "I just wanted to say good-bye. It feels like we were just getting to know each other. I enjoyed working with you, Sara . . . and knowing you."

"Thanks. Me, too. I mean, when you weren't tearing my writing to shreds," she reminded him, with a smile.

"Oh, I wasn't so bad, was I?"

"Yes, you were awful," she cheerfully agreed. "But I learned a lot."

"You did," he agreed. "Maybe you could come work for me at the *L.A. Times* someday. What do you think?"

"Maybe someday," she replied wistfully. "I need to sharpen my style a little first, though. Trim out the fluff."

"Right." He nodded, laughing at her. She felt sad all of a sudden to see him go. Wistful over something that had never really gotten off the ground, she realized. Well, no matter what, it had been fun to know him, even for a short time.

She put out her hand. "Good luck, Wyatt. I'm going to miss you," she said honestly.

He smiled and shook her hand, then pulled her close for a quick hug. "Good luck to you, Sara Franklin. I'm going to be watching for your byline."

She leaned back and smiled at him as he walked away. He was a great guy, she thought, but what her old college roommate would call "a definite almost." Although she would miss him at the paper, Sara realized she didn't regret that a real romance had never quite sprung up between them.

DAN RETURNED TO THE PAPER ON MONDAY IN A BLACK MOOD. HE curtly greeted the staff as he passed by their desks. He could tell from their faces that they already knew Wyatt had bailed out. Still, when they gathered at his desk for the regular Monday morning meeting, he felt obliged to make an announcement. "As all of you know by now, Wyatt isn't coming back. He's taken another job in California."

They weren't surprised at all, as he'd expected. Jane had been the first in today, and when he mentioned it to her, she said that Wyatt had called her yesterday to say good-bye. Maybe he'd called all of them. Still, it hurt him to say it out loud again.

"Does that mean you're back now for good, Dan?" Ed Kazinsky asked, sounding hopeful.

"No, I'm not coming back permanently," Dan said, more sharply than he intended. "I . . . I'm not sure what's going to happen, Ed. I haven't figured it out, yet. But I still intend to retire from the newspaper business."

Dan looked down at his notes and then over at the story board. "So, let's see, you've got the Zoning Board today and the town council tomorrow night, Jane—"

"The town council is still figuring out that fight with the county over the grant money," Lindsay cut in. "Sara's working on that story now," she reminded him.

"Oh, right . . ." He glanced at Sara. "I guess you ought to take it then."

Sara nodded and made a note for herself.

"So you take the School Board meeting, Jane. Has anyone seen the police report from the weekend? There's an item in there about some kids skating on thin ice near the mill bridge. They fell in, but a guy working on phone lines fished them out."

"I just put a call in to Officer Tulley about that. He's going to get right back to me," Ed said.

"Good. Let's see, what else do we have?" Dan continued. He was back again. Almost as if he'd never left. He felt as if he were in a dream he couldn't wake up from.

"YOU HAD A CALL WHILE YOU WERE OUT, DAD. I TOOK A MESSAGE FOR you," Lindsay said. "It's on your desk."

Dan walked over to his desk and put down the bag that held a sandwich and coffee. It was Thursday afternoon. The staff was out covering stories and only Lindsay was left in the office. He sat down at his desk, then noticed Lindsay still standing nearby, staring at him.

"What is it? Something the matter?" he asked.

"Why are you having a meeting with Ted Kendall?"

He felt frozen. Caught. He glanced at the message slip and saw that the business manager at Crown News had called to confirm their appointment.

"I'm going to talk to him about possibly selling the paper."

Lindsay drew closer, nearly dropping the folders in her hand. "Dad, I know you feel bad about Wyatt, but you can't do that," she insisted.

"That's funny. Emily said the same thing. Why can't I sell the paper if I want to? It's mine, isn't it? Nobody else wants to take it over," he argued.

He knew he sounded hurt, even petulant at this point, but he couldn't help that. He'd been blindsided by his own son, and he still felt stunned.

"Oh, really?" she said harshly. She slammed down the files on her desk and turned to glare at him. "I can't believe you sometimes."

Dan sat up in surprise. "What did I say?" he asked quietly. "It wasn't my plan to sell the paper. But I can if I want to."

"What about me? What about giving me the paper? Didn't that possibility ever cross your mind?"

Now she'd caught his full attention, her distress finally shaking him loose from his torpor.

"I did think of you, Lindsay, but—"

"But what? Too far afield of the family tradition?" she chided him. "I've been here for weeks, pulling the slack for Wyatt, keeping things afloat. I thought when we talked about the paper before Christmas that you realized that."

"I do realize that," he insisted. "You've been a great help here. You've done a great job—"

"But what?" she repeated, cutting him off again. "You never really considered giving me the paper, Dad. If you had, you wouldn't be sneaking off to see Ted Kendall."

"I wasn't sneaking anywhere," he said. "I was going to tell you."

"When? After you signed the contract?" Lindsay looked infuriated, her fair complexion mottled and pink. "I can't believe you shut me out like this. I can't believe you didn't even talk this over with me. Even if you thought maybe I didn't really want the paper, or I wasn't ready to run it . . ."

Her voice trailed off, and he thought she might cry. He felt heartsick. How had this happened? He'd never meant to hurt her. Not Lindsay, of all people.

"Lindsay, honey, let's just calm down a minute and talk."

"No. I'm too mad at you now. I'm not going to try to talk you into it, if my taking over the paper was so unthinkable in the first place," she said flatly. She took a deep breath, and he could see her calming down a little.

"Scott and I have some money to invest now that he's not going to open that restaurant," she said. "Maybe I'll buy the paper from you. Would you let me run it if I paid you for it? I can't see why not. You'd let Crown," she added.

Her offer sent him reeling. Lindsay buying him out? He had no idea she had such strong feelings about the paper.

"You don't have to buy it from me. Don't be ridiculous. This paper is a family asset. I was going to give you and Wyatt some of the proceeds," he told her.

"I'm going home now. You don't need me here," she said quickly, as she gathered her things.

"Lindsay . . . wait . . ." He stood up and reached out to touch her arm.

"No, Dad. I mean it. It's okay," she insisted. "I guess I hoped that once you got over losing Wyatt, you'd think about me. Sometimes it's like you're walking around with blinders on. You're so rigid and stubborn, you can't see past your own nose."

"That's not true. I thought about this a lot. I considered all the possibilities," he sputtered.

"Then I just can't believe that selling to Crown seems the preferable choice," she said in a cutting tone. "I guess that makes it hurt even more."

Before he could say another word, she pulled away from him and rushed out. Dan stood at the back of the empty office, watching her pass in front of the windows. Though it was just past noon, the sky was so dark it looked like dusk.

Snow had begun to fall, he noticed. The weather report predicted it would get messy later, but right now it was benign enough, feathery flakes coating everything in a soft layer of white. He hated the first weeks of January, the holidays over and a long, dull winter stretching out ahead.

I can't wait to get away, Dan thought glumly. *Away from the paper—and everyone around here. Why is everyone so mad at me? Why is everybody yelling at me, then running away? Wyatt, Lindsay, even Emily out on the beach Saturday.*

He thought of Lindsay's accusations and rejected them at once. He didn't walk around with blinders on. She made him sound like . . . like an old broken-down plow horse. No, not a horse. A mule. A plodding, stubborn old mule.

Dan sat down hard and put his head in his hands. He felt so alone in this now. Everyone seemed to have lined up against him. It just didn't seem fair.

CAROLYN HAD BEEN TEACHING LAUREN WILLOUGHBY A SIMPLE PIECE BY Brahms these past few lessons. Lauren was coming along well, but Carolyn suspected she hadn't practiced very much in the last week or so, with the holidays and school recess. Carolyn watched her stumble over the last two bars on the page, then she finally interrupted her playing.

"Wait, dear. Let's stop just a minute right there. Those are eighth notes, remember? You want to hit the keys like this, quick and crisp." Carolyn put her hands to the keys and demonstrated on the lower end of the piano. "And don't forget your fingering. You'll get yourself all muddled up—"

Just then, she heard the phone ring. She listened intently as the machine in the kitchen picked up the message.

"Carolyn? Are you there? It's Jack," the voice said.

"My son-in-law, Jack. I need to get this," Carolyn said to Lauren, as she rose and headed for the phone.

"—Rachel's ready. We're about to go to the hospital," he continued.

Carolyn finally reached the phone and picked it up, feeling breathless. "Jack, are you still there?"

"Oh, there you are," he said, sounding relieved. "We just spoke to the doctor. He thinks she's ready to go in. Here, I'll put her on," he said.

"Hi, Mom. We're going now," Rachel said, sounding bright, but a bit nervous. "I don't feel that bad, yet, honestly."

"Good, that's good then," Carolyn said in an encouraging tone. You will, though, she wanted to add. But she stopped herself. Every woman has a different experience, and nobody really remembers the worst of it afterward.

"It won't be long now, honey. I'll call your father and let him know what's going on. Are you sure you don't want us to wait at the hospital? We'd be happy to," she reminded her.

"Yes, I know, Mom. But Jack will be with me, and the doctor said it might take a few hours or more. You know, first birth. I guess I'd feel better if you just waited at home. Jack will call you as soon as the baby is born."

"All right, dear. We'll come right away. I understand," Carolyn told her. She really wished she could wait at the hospital, but it was Rachel's decision. "I love you, honey. I know everything is going to go perfectly."

"I love you, too, Mom," Rachel said. "Jack will call you later and let you know what's going on."

"I'll be waiting," Carolyn promised. And praying for an easy time of it, she silently added. They said good-bye and Carolyn hung up, feeling a chill sweep through her body. Her hands were ice cold, she realized, rubbing them together. She was so excited now that the news had come, she actually felt light-headed.

She dialed Ben's office but only reached the church secretary, Irene Mills, who told her that Ben had gone to visit an elderly parishioner at a nursing home in Tewksbury.

"Oh dear. Well, if you hear from him, let him know I called, would you? Rachel's just left for the hospital," she told Irene.

Tewksbury? That had to be at least sixty miles away, Carolyn realized with distress.

Irene promised to relay the message and wished Rachel luck. Carolyn hung up, only to see Lauren watching her from the hallway, a questioning look on her face.

"I'm sorry, Lauren. I didn't mean to forget you in there."

"That's okay. Did Rachel have her baby?"

"No, not yet. She's just on her way to the hospital. But it won't be long now." Carolyn checked her watch. Ten more minutes at least before Lauren's mother came to pick her up.

"Let's go inside and see if we can make any more headway today with Mr. Brahms," she said, touching Lauren's shoulder, though Carolyn sincerely doubted she could focus on Lauren's efforts for three notes in a row.

Chapter Eighteen

Carolyn felt as if she had been sitting by the phone forever. It had been almost two hours since Rachel and Jack had called. She hadn't heard from Jack, yet, or even Ben. She'd been after him to get a cell phone, but he couldn't stand them. He would joke that if there was ever anything really important he needed to know, God would get a message to him.

Carolyn wondered if the heavenly switchboard was in operation this afternoon. It was hard to just sit and wait. She'd been outside twice, cleaning the snow off her car and shoveling the driveway, so she could get the car out easily when Jack called. She'd felt a bit light-headed and breathless after both trips but hadn't really minded the exercise. At least it gave her something to do.

She sat with her boots and hat on, her coat and bag by her side. She didn't know if she could stand it much longer.

With her cold hands wrapped around a mug of tea, she stared out the window. The snow was falling heavily now. She hoped Jack and Rachel had reached the hospital without any problem. Again, she told herself not to worry. Jack knew how to drive in snow. He'd lived here his whole life.

The phone rang, and Carolyn snatched it up.

"Hello, Carolyn? It's me," Jack said. "I thought I should call you—"

She could tell from his voice it wasn't good news. "What is it, Jack? What's happened?"

"Well, there are some complications. The baby must have turned since Rachel's last sonogram. He's not facing the right way, so he's sort of stuck."

"Oh, dear. That doesn't sound good. . . ." Carolyn felt dizzy and sick to her stomach, as if she might black out. She forced herself to focus and took a deep breath. "How is Rachel?"

"Rachel's holding up okay. She's a trooper. But she thinks you ought to come now. She wants you to."

"Yes, right away. I'll be there in no time. What are they going to do, a C-section?"

"The doctor said it's too late for that. The baby is too far down the birth canal. They have to do something quickly, though. The baby is under stress. His heartbeat is erratic—"

Carolyn didn't want to hear another word. "I'm coming right away. Tell Rachel I'm on my way."

Jack thanked her and hung up. Carolyn stared around the silent kitchen a moment, wondering what to do first. She pulled on her coat and grabbed her car keys. Then she remembered Ben hadn't called yet. He might not even know. She grabbed a pad from the counter and started writing him a note.

Just then the phone rang. She grabbed at it and said hello, praying it wasn't Jack with more bad news.

"Carolyn? I just called Rachel's house," Ben said. "There's no one home. . . . Is it happening?"

"Oh, Ben, thank goodness it's you." Carolyn sagged with relief. "Yes, she's at the hospital, but it's not going well, Ben. There are complications. The baby is stuck in the birth canal."

She tried to deliver the message calmly, but she knew her voice sounded on the edge of panic.

"Oh, no! That is bad news. How is she doing?"

"Jack said she's doing well, under the circumstances. But she wants us to be there with them now. I was just on my way out the door. Where are you? Can you meet me?"

"I'm not far, up in Tewksbury," he said, and Carolyn's heart sank. He was still there. He'd have a slow trip back with the snow. "The roads are bad. I don't want you out driving alone in this, Carolyn, especially under the circumstances. Wait for me to get home. We'll go together."

"I'm sorry, Ben. I just can't wait. Rachel needs me. I have a bad feeling about this," she confided, feeling ready to weep.

"Dear, please. It's going to be okay. Doctors can do the most amazing things now delivering babies—"

"I know, but it doesn't sound good, Ben. I promised Rachel I'd be there as fast as possible. She's counting on me. I can't wait. You'll have to meet me there."

He didn't answer, and she almost thought they'd been disconnected. Then finally he said, "I can tell you'll probably leave anyway, even if you try to wait. I'll meet you. I'm on my way. And Carolyn, drive safely, please."

"Yes, I will, Ben. I promise. You, too," she said. Then, before hanging up the phone, she added, "I think we should call Mark. I think he needs to know what's happening."

Again, she waited for his reply. "Yes, he needs to know. But don't worry about that now. You get on the road. I'll call him when I get to the hospital," he promised.

They said good-bye, and Carolyn rushed out the door. She jumped in her car and started the engine. While it warmed up a moment and the wipers went to work, she closed her eyes and said a short prayer out loud. "Please God, let everything work out all right with the baby, and let Rachel and the child come through this unharmed."

She clipped on her seat belt and slowly backed out of the driveway. Her tires crunched in the deep layer of fresh snow, and the car fishtailed a little as she turned it to head down the street. But once outside of the village and on the main road, the driving was easier, and she relaxed a bit.

Carolyn had been on the road for about fifteen minutes, feeling frustrated that she had to drive so much slower than usual, when she felt a strange tingling in her arm. She took her hand off the steering wheel and shook her arm, flexing her fingers. *I must have strained a muscle shoveling the snow,* she thought. *I'm so out of shape.* She knew she hadn't felt anything odd at the time, but these things could creep up on you afterward.

Then, suddenly, she felt as if she couldn't get a deep breath. She opened her jacket and even opened the window, mindless of the snow and cold air rushing in at her. The air didn't help. She felt a hot wave of dizziness and then a piercing pain in her head, like something popping inside. The sight in one eye went black. She blinked but couldn't bring it back.

"Dear God! What's happening to me?" she cried out loud. She hit the emergency warning flashers and struggled to slow the car down and steer it over to the shoulder of the road.

As the car coasted, Carolyn blacked out, her head dropping to the steering wheel. The horn blared under her body weight, a deafening sound, but she didn't stir.

The car bumped along unguided for a few yards, then, as if in slow motion, it plowed into a chain-link fence.

WHEN BEN REACHED THE HOSPITAL IN SOUTHPORT, HE WENT STRAIGHT to the maternity ward. He knew every wing of the hospital from the many times he had gone there to visit members of his congregation.

He walked up to the nursing station just outside the labor area. "I'm Reverend Ben Lewis. My daughter, Rachel, came in this afternoon," he said. "I think my wife must be here by now," he added.

"Oh, Reverend Lewis . . ." The nurse looked down at some papers on her desk. Her grim expression set off instant alarm bells. Something awful had happened to Rachel and the baby, he just knew it.

But before he could ask, the nurse said, "You need to go down to the emergency room. I'm sorry, sir. Your wife was just brought in."

"My wife? No, you don't understand. I'm here for my daughter, Rachel Anderson. She's having a baby. There were complications—"

Just then Jack came through a door that read, "Labor Area—No Admittance."

He walked toward Ben with a grave expression on his face. "Ben." Ben felt his son-in-law grip his shoulders. "I have some bad news. It's Carolyn. It looks like she's had a stroke. She's downstairs in the surgical unit. We've all been waiting for you. They need to operate."

"Carolyn? No!" he shouted, as if his adamant refusal could change this bleak reality.

Ben felt as if the room were spinning in circles. He couldn't think, he couldn't see straight. He realized he must have sat down—or collapsed—in a chair because suddenly Jack was crouched down next to him.

"Are you all right? Do you need a doctor?" he asked quietly.

"No, I'm fine," Ben insisted, though he was anything but. He came to his feet, trying to orient himself. "Where do I go?" he asked Jack abruptly.

"To the third floor. I'll go with you," Jack said, taking his arm.

"But what about Rachel? How is Rachel? And the baby?" he asked, suddenly remembering his daughter.

"She's fine. She's resting now," Jack reported, as he led Ben to the elevators. "The baby was born about fifteen minutes ago. I haven't told her about Carolyn. I'll tell her as soon as she wakes up again," Jack added. "They had to take him out with instruments. It was frightening for a while," he admitted. "But he's all right."

"Thank God for that," Ben said, breathing heavily.

"Yes, thank God," Jack repeated. The elevator doors slid open, and the two men entered. They were the only ones inside, and Ben prayed silently, passionately, for his wife's well-being. *Please don't take her from me, Lord. Please let her live. Please have mercy on us.* A silent cry to heaven rose up from his heart.

Down on the third floor, Ben was brought together with the attending physician and surgeon on call. They quickly explained Carolyn's condition, which they diagnosed as a cerebral hemorrhage. They took him into a darkened room and showed him some X rays of Carolyn's skull.

"This is the clot right here," Dr. Whittaker, the surgeon, pointed out. "Not stupendous in size, but it's doing some damage. We've got to get it out before it does any more." He turned to Ben. "She was lucky, actually. She must have felt the stroke coming on and was able to pull her car over in time."

"The car rolled into a fence," the other physician, Dr. Lin, said. "There were no injuries from the collision. We've run all the tests. We know what we need to know. She needs surgery, Reverend. Immediately."

"Yes, yes, of course. Whatever you think has to be done, do it," Ben said, feeling overwhelmed. "What . . . what are her chances? Will she live?" he forced himself to ask.

"The chances of her surviving the surgery are good," Dr. Whittaker answered. "But we have no idea what state she'll be in if she makes it through. She may never come out of the coma. And if she does, there may be complications. Her speech, vision, mobility, and even mental faculties may be impaired. At this point, we have no way of guessing the extent of the damage—or if it's reversible."

"Yes . . . I understand." Ben nodded, feeling numb. He felt Jack's hand, heavy on his shoulder, but he didn't even glance at his son-in-law. "Can I see her?"

"Yes, of course. We're prepping her for surgery. But you can go in for a moment."

Ben followed the two doctors and soon found himself behind a curtained area. Carolyn was lying in a hospital bed, attached to an array of frightening-looking tubes and machines. Her head had been shaved and her scalp painted with some reddish-brown disinfectant.

Ben walked toward her, feeling as if he were in a dream. Her face looked strangely peaceful, he thought, as if she were in the midst of a dream. A very pleasant one, from the looks of it, the opposite of his.

He sighed and took her hand, then leaned over and kissed her on the forehead. "My darling," he whispered. "I love you so very much. I don't know what I'd do without you. . . . Please don't leave us," he begged.

He heard someone behind him and turned to see two nurses in blue scrubs. "I'm sorry, Reverend. You have to go now," one of them said in a soft tone. "There's a special waiting room for surgery. The nurse outside will show you," she said kindly.

"Thank you." He nodded and took one more lingering look at Carolyn before he left. "God bless you, my love," he whispered to her.

Ben turned to Jack as they reached the special waiting room for family members of surgery patients.

"Rachel," Ben said sadly. "She might be awake again by now. You'll need to tell her what's happening." In his heart he wished there were some way to spare his daughter this news.

Jack agreed and left him, promising he'd be back soon. Ben took a seat in the waiting room. It was practically empty. There were clusters of empty blue chairs, a table of magazines and newspapers. A coffeemaker with Styrofoam cups piled next to it stood nearby. Ben looked up at the TV that hung from the upper corner of one wall. He recognized the face of a famous newscaster, but he turned away, unable to watch.

He got up and went out into the hall, glancing around to get his bearings. Then he took the elevator to the first floor, and when he got out, he walked down the nearest hallway and found the hospital's small chapel.

It was dark and shadowy inside, except for a few small lights behind the stark, modern-looking altar. There were three rows of pews, and he sat in the last one at the back. There he knelt down and closed his eyes to pray.

Dear God, please hear my prayers. Please help me through this ordeal. This has to be the worst night of my life. Please let me feel your presence in my heart. . . . The voice inside his head trailed off. He bit down on his lip, feeling empty, frustrated, and scared. He didn't feel in touch with God tonight. He felt himself reaching out, grasping, into emptiness.

God, why is this happening? Why have you let this happen to Carolyn? Dear, sweet Carolyn. She doesn't deserve this.

Immediately he knew it wasn't for him to ask the Lord such questions. Hadn't he counseled families in distress on this very matter, time and time again? But tonight it was his own family, his own wife, caught between life and death. He knew all the soothing, supportive words about accepting God's will and how it was hardest for those left behind, not for the loved one that God has chosen to take home.

He knew those words. Yet they sounded dull and empty to him tonight. Meaningless. Is that how he sounded trying to console the men and women in this very same spot? Like a rattling tin can. He bowed his head.

Don't let me doubt like this, God. Not tonight. I need to be strong. Strong in my faith and trust in You. I'm scared, God. I don't know if I can face it if You have to take her. I just don't know, he repeated dully in his mind.

Ben wasn't sure if he sat there for minutes or hours. When he picked his head up, his neck felt stiff. He opened his eyes slowly and sat back. He had to call Mark. He'd promised Carolyn, and he'd forgotten all about it.

This was going to be hard, but he couldn't put it off. Carolyn would want Mark to know what was happening; Ben was sure of that much.

He went to the phone booths in the lobby and got Mark's phone number again from information, feeling relieved that he remembered the name of the town and the ranch so easily.

After a moment or two, Mark came on the line. The crew had been at dinner in the main house, and Ben could hear a lot of voices in the background.

"Dad, what's going on?" Mark asked curiously. "Did Rachel have her baby?"

"Yes, she did. About an hour or so ago. Everything is fine," he added, feeling surprised by the question because he was so focused on Carolyn. "But there's something else going on. Something serious. It's your mother. . . . She had a stroke on the way to the hospital tonight. She's in surgery right now, so we don't know what's going to happen. . . ."

"Mom had a stroke?" Mark sounded devastated. "How . . . how is she? Will she make it?" he asked in a rush.

Ben could tell he was in shock and not really able to take it all in. He felt sorry for Mark, out there all alone and having to deal with this news. But that was Mark's choice, he reminded himself. He sighed and tried to gather his patience again.

"That's just it, Son. We don't know. The doctor doesn't even know if she'll wake up out of the coma after the surgery." If she survives the surgery, he added silently.

Mark didn't say anything. Ben wondered if he was crying.

"I . . . you have to come back now, Mark," Ben said in a quiet but emphatic tone. Back to see your mother if she lives . . . or for a funeral, he meant. But, of course, he didn't put it quite that bluntly. "Do you still have the ticket we sent?"

"Yes, of course, I do," Mark said.

"Well, use it then. How soon do you think you can get here?"

"I don't know. . . . I need to get to Billings first. Then catch a flight out of there, I guess, to New York. I don't think I can fly directly to Boston," he replied, thinking aloud.

"All right. You work on it," Ben said. It sounded as if it was going to take him some time to get back. Not too long, he hoped. He gave Mark the phone number at the hospital. "I'll be here all night and tomorrow. Stay in touch. Let us know your plans."

"I will, Dad," Mark said in a thick voice. "And if Mom wakes up, tell her I'm coming, okay? Tell her that I love her."

Ben felt immensely sad. And angry. Had it come to this? Had such dire circumstance been necessary for his son to send this message?

"You can tell her yourself when you get here," he said. He hadn't meant for the words to come out harshly, but they had. "I've got to go now," he said a little more gently. "There might be some news."

"Okay, Dad." Mark said good-bye and hung up. Ben sat listening to the dial tone a moment longer than normal, as if mesmerized by the sound. Then he finally hung up and stepped out of the phone booth and into the lobby.

He blinked as he recognized a group from the church, obviously waiting for him; Sam and Jessica Morgan, Sophie and Gus Potter, and Emily Warwick. They walked toward him and, more or less, made a circle around him. He might have felt surrounded or even trapped, he thought, except for the deep concern and affection written on all of their faces. He felt nothing but their warm wishes and caring, radiating out to him like warmth from the sun. Finally, tonight, he felt God's presence in his life through the love and caring of these good people.

"Reverend Ben . . . we came as soon as we heard," Sam said. "How are you holding up?"

"All right, I guess. Carolyn's still in surgery. I was just going to check on her progress."

"Is Rachel all right?" Jessica asked.

"Yes, she's fine. The baby is fine, too, I understand. I haven't gotten to see him, yet, though—oh, there's Jack now," Ben said, noticing his son-in-law walking toward them.

"Ben, the surgery is almost completed. The doctor sent word that it went well. They need you upstairs now."

Ben stared at Jack a moment and gave silent thanks to God for sparing Carolyn's life.

"I have to go," Ben said, gazing around at his friends.

"Yes, of course, you'd better get up there," Emily urged him. "I'm going to wait for a while. Just until Carolyn is in the clear."

"We will, too," Jessica said, nodding at Sam.

"Oh, so will we," Sophie Potter said, touching her husband's arm. "We can't leave before we know Carolyn's all right. We're all going to just sit right here and pray," she stated flatly.

Ben gazed around and felt lifted by their support. "So be it. I'll try to let you know what's going on," he promised. "And thank you," he added, as he walked away, following Jack to the elevators.

"No thanks necessary, Reverend," Gus Potter called back. "No thanks at all . . ."

As Jack had told him, Carolyn was soon out of surgery and moved to a post-op recovery area where she was closely monitored. Dr. Whittaker came out to talk with him.

"The surgery was largely a success," the surgeon reported in measured tones. "Your wife remains in a coma, however, and in critical condition. She's fighting for her survival right now. That's the best way I can describe her condition to you, Reverend. If she lasts the next twenty-four hours, she might make it," he said somberly.

Ben nodded. "I understand," he said. "May I see her now?"

"Yes, that would be all right. But only for a minute," the doctor instructed him.

Ben was led into the post-operative area, and he found Carolyn behind another curtained partition. Her entire head was now covered with white bandages. Her skin was as pale as paper. He had once heard that people in a coma could still hear. He'd heard amazing stories of coma patients waking up when they heard their favorite music or some meaningful words that penetrated their death-like sleep.

"You're alive, Carolyn," Ben whispered. "You lived through the surgery. You have to fight now, the doctor says. This is the fight of your life. We're all waiting for you to wake up and see your new grandson. He's just fine. Rachel is fine, too. And I called Mark, like you asked me to. He's coming to see you, Carolyn. He's on his way."

He paused there, wondering if those were the words that would rouse her. But she lay motionless, barely breathing it seemed to him. Looking as if she had only a little life left. He was afraid to even touch her. Her hand lay palm up outside the blanket, as if frozen there, reaching toward him. He lightly touched his fingertips to hers. Her wedding ring had been removed for the surgery, he noticed, but he saw the slight dent at the bottom of her ring finger clearly.

She had such fine hands, graceful and fluid, a musician's hands. That was one of the things he'd first noticed about her. Her hands had always been such a distinct expression of her entire personality. Would he ever feel her conscious touch again?

How could he ever live without her?

BEN SAT OUTSIDE THE POST-OP AREA, PERMITTED TO TAKE A LOOK AT Carolyn for a few minutes every hour. There was no change at all that he could see. He kept telling Jack to go home, but his son-in-law insisted on staying.

During a break, they went upstairs and managed to sneak a peek at Ben's new grandson through the nursery window.

"There he is. That's the little guy. Isn't he something?" Jack crooned, pointing out the baby right up front.

Red faced with a patch of dark hair covered by a tiny baby cap, the newest member of the family lay curled on his side, his tiny fist pressed to his mouth, eyes shut.

"My word . . . he's beautiful, Jack." Ben felt his eyes fill with tears, and he was finally unable to hold them back. "Look at him, an absolute miracle. Have you picked out a name yet?"

"We're going to call him William, after my dad," Jack answered.

"William. That's a fine name," Ben said. "Very fine . . ."

His voice trailed off, his mind flooded with a thousand thoughts and feelings—the sight of his own two children as newborns, looking so fresh and frail, not nearly strong enough to be out in the world yet. He felt Carolyn's absence keenly. She should be here with me now, sharing this moment. *Dear God, let her wake and see this child,* he silently pleaded.

On the way out of the maternity ward, they looked into Rachel's room. She had the bed near the door, and Jack looked in first. "She's not quite asleep," he said. "I think you can go in for a moment and say hello."

Ben walked in softly. Rachel lay with her head on the pillow, her long hair fanning out around her. He felt for a moment as if she were a child again, and he was looking in on her late at night, before he went to bed. Sensing him near, she opened her eyes and held out her hand to him.

"Hi, sweetheart," he murmured. "I just saw the baby. He's beautiful. Looks just like you."

"Oh, Daddy . . . he looks like a scrunched-up little elf. But he is gorgeous." She pushed herself up on one arm, clearly an effort. "How's Mom? Jack said she's still in a coma."

"Her vital signs are strong," Ben replied, trying to find some positive thought for Rachel to hang on to. "The doctor said the next twenty-four hours are crucial. The blood pressure is the real problem. They can't seem to get it under control. We just have to hang in and ask for God's mercy. We just have to have faith," he added, wishing the words didn't feel so hollow.

Rachel nodded, blinking back tears. "I've been praying for her.

That's all I've been doing up here. I think I'll be able to come down tomorrow. The nurse said I could."

"All right, dear. You get some rest now. You have a baby to take care of," he reminded her. He leaned over and kissed her on the forehead, smoothing his hand over her brow.

"Have you heard from Mark?" Rachel asked suddenly. "Jack said he's coming back."

"All I know is he said he's on his way. I haven't heard anything yet. Maybe soon," he said hopefully.

They said good night, and Ben left her. Thank heaven for Rachel. She was such a comfort to him, always had been. And to her mother, he thought. He met Jack in the hallway, and they began walking down the hall again.

"I'm worried about Rachel. She'll take it hard if anything happens to her mother," Ben said aloud.

"Yes, she will. She's very close to Carolyn," Jack said somberly. "We'll all take it hard, don't you think, Reverend?"

Ben glanced at him and nodded, his throat tight. There wasn't more he could say.

When they got back downstairs, there was a message from Mark. He'd left a phone number, and Ben called it right away.

"Mark? Where are you?" Ben said, as soon as he heard his son's voice on the line.

"I made it to Billings," he replied. "But looks like I'm stuck here a while. There's a major storm. How's Mom doing? The nurse told me she's in recovery but wouldn't say more."

"The surgery was successful. But her condition is very unstable. We really don't know what's going to happen," Ben said honestly. "How soon do you think you'll get here?"

"I don't know. It's bad. The airport is shut down," Mark replied, with a tired sigh. "There's snow all over the country—between here and the east coast, anyway. All the flights in that direction are canceled. I'm trying to get anything now, even if I have to fly south first, say to Ohio or Texas, and then connect going north again."

That would take him forever, Ben thought. He won't be here until tomorrow—or maybe even Saturday.

"I see. That's too bad." He knew it wasn't Mark's fault. How could it be? All the same, he felt an irrational wave of anger and frustration flooding up inside him. Why had Mark waited so long to come back was the question. Why had he waited for a crisis like this, when any minute might be his mother's last?

"Dad . . . are you still there?"

"Yes, I'm here. How are you set for money?" he asked, sounding a bit harsher than he intended.

"I'm okay. I have plenty and a credit card." Mark sounded confused at the question. "How are Rachel and the baby?"

"Rachel is fine. Exhausted, but she'll be okay. The baby is beautiful—dark hair but you can't tell anything by that. They often lose that first patch of hair and then something completely different grows in. . . ."

The same thing had happened to Mark, Ben recalled. Then he caught himself; he was rambling. He felt as if he hadn't slept for a week.

"I have to go," Mark said. "Someone wants the phone. I'll call when I find a flight out of here, okay?"

"Okay, do your best. I know you will," Ben amended.

They said good-bye, and Ben hung up, still feeling discordant chords of anger at his son, who he felt had somehow brought this drama upon himself. Like he did the whole time he was growing up. It was no different now, only this time the consequence might be that Mark never saw his mother again, Ben thought darkly. He caught himself. *She's not gone yet, thank God. Where there's life, there's hope,* he reminded himself.

Finally, at nearly two A.M., the doctor on call reported that Carolyn's condition had stabilized. Though she was still in danger, he encouraged Ben to go home and get some rest.

Ben went home with Jack. The snow was too deep to get the car in the driveway, so they parked on the street, which had been partially plowed. They tramped across the lawn up to the house, so tired they were practically unaware of the knee-high drifts. Although the two men were too exhausted to speak, Ben appreciated having his son-in-law's company. Ben slept in the guest room. The next morning they rose early.

Ben borrowed some fresh, ill-fitting clothes from Jack, and the two men returned to the hospital.

Jack went up to see Rachel, and Ben went straight to Carolyn. In the surgical recovery area he learned Carolyn had just been moved to a room. The nurse wrote the number down on a slip of paper for him, so he wouldn't forget, and he realized he must look as exhausted and overwhelmed as he felt.

"Has my son called?" he asked. "Mark Lewis. He's traveling. He may have left a message for me."

"There are no messages for you, Reverend," the nurse said, checking an in-box. "If he calls, we'll give him your wife's new room number."

Ben thanked her and headed for the elevator. The doors opened, and Jack stood there, supporting Rachel with his arm. She barely looked able to stand, much less walk around the hospital, but he knew how she felt about seeing Carolyn.

"They've moved her to a room upstairs. The fifth floor," Ben said, stepping into the elevator with them. "Apparently, she's still in the coma. We'll just have to wait."

"Then we'll just wait," Rachel said, sounding far stronger than she looked. "Any word from Mark?"

"No, not today." Ben glanced at her. "We spoke last night after I saw you. There's bad weather all over the Midwest. It may take him a while to get here."

He heard his voice taking on an irritated edge, and he was glad to see the elevator had come to a stop and the doors were sliding open on the fifth floor. He didn't quite trust himself to say anything more.

CHAPTER NINETEEN

SARA STEPPED OUT OF HER FRONT DOOR ON FRIDAY MORNING and stopped, astounded by the amount of snow that had fallen overnight. It made her think of the morning Luke had come to her door with the toboggan. He wouldn't be back again with another sledding invitation this time, she realized sadly.

She glanced at her car—or what she thought was her car—completely buried by the snow. She didn't feel like digging it out. *I can walk into town,* Sara thought. It was early and it seemed as if hardly anyone was up yet; the snow-covered lawns on Clover Street still looked fresh and untouched. Maybe she'd stop at the diner and have some breakfast. She had plenty of time.

As she passed the turn for Providence Street, Sara decided to take a side trip and check on her grandmother. The huge, old house looked quiet and still, the curtains tightly drawn. Suspecting that Lillian was still asleep, she decided it was best not to bother her.

She was about to head for the diner when she noticed a snow shovel on the porch. Sara tramped up the walk to retrieve it. She shoveled off the steps and made a path on the walk to the street. The snow was light and dry, and the work went quickly. She glanced at the long driveway, knowing she didn't have time to tackle it. But Lillian didn't have a car.

It was Emily who mostly came to visit, and she could park in the street, Sara thought.

Sara heard a car approach, the wheels crunching on the snowy street, and she turned to see the very object of her thoughts, as Emily, in her dark blue Jeep Cherokee, pulled up and parked along the sidewalk.

Emily quickly got out and walked over to her. "Hey, that's what I'm here for. Looks like you beat me to it." Emily smiled at her, looking pleased at the favor.

"I was just passing, and I had some extra time," Sara explained.

"Does Lillian know you're here?"

"No. I don't think she's up yet."

Emily glanced at her watch. "Probably not. Let's not wake her. I'll tell her you came, though. Where's your car? I didn't see it when I drove up," she said, glancing around.

"I couldn't deal with cleaning it off and warming it up," Sara admitted, feeling as if she'd revealed herself as a total foreigner to this climate. "I'm just going to walk to work today. I can go back later and get it if I need to go cover a story outside of town."

"Want a lift?" Emily offered. "It's getting late."

"Sure." Sara's early burst of energy had burned off with the snow shoveling, and she was glad for the ride into town.

"Did you hear about Carolyn Lewis?" Emily asked, as she started driving.

"Um, no. What happened to Carolyn?"

"Rachel went into the hospital yesterday afternoon to have her baby, and Carolyn had a stroke on the way to be with her."

"Oh no, how awful!" Sara exclaimed. "How is she?"

"She had surgery last night. I went over there with Jessica and Sam and some others from the church. She's out of the critical care unit but still in a coma."

Sara felt instantly disheartened at the news. She didn't know Carolyn very well, but she had always seemed like such a warm-hearted person.

"I wish there was something I could do," Sara said. "Are you going to the hospital again?"

"Yes, maybe tomorrow. Would you like to come with me?"

"I would," Sara said.

Emily smiled at her. "Good, I'd love the company. It's hard to see the reverend's family like this. They're always there for everyone else. You just don't know what to do for them."

They reached the newspaper office, and Emily pulled up across the street to let her off.

"How's Dan doing?" Emily asked, glancing over at the office. She didn't need to add, "Since Wyatt left."

"Not too good. I never knew him that well to begin with, but he couldn't have always been such a pain. I don't think you would have put up with it," Sara said, with a laugh.

Emily grinned. "That bad, huh?"

"Yes, that bad. Now Lindsay is gone, too," Sara told her. "I think they had an argument. Jane says she heard Dan is going to sell the paper to Crown News. She's already looking for another job."

"Dan mentioned that to me last week, right after Wyatt left. I didn't want to tell you, though," Emily said honestly. "I was hoping he would change his mind."

"I still hope he will," Sara admitted. She wasn't sure if she wanted to work for the *Messenger* if Crown News took over. That meant she might consider returning to Maryland. But she decided not to go into that with Emily now. She was sure Emily was putting those pieces together for herself.

"Didn't you know about Lindsay? I thought you and Dan were sort of seeing each other," Sara said.

"Well, we've both been really busy this week. I'm sure we'll catch up at some point," Emily said vaguely.

Sara stared at her. "Aren't you going out anymore?"

She could see that Emily felt put on the spot; she pressed her hands to the steering wheel and stared straight ahead.

"I'm sorry. Maybe it's none of my business," Sara said.

"No. I can tell you." Emily turned and touched Sara's arm. "I want to, really." She took a breath. "I do care about Dan, and I know he feels the same," she started off, sounding as if she needed to defend him, Sara thought. "The thing is, Dan is just dead set on leaving on this trip. He's been thinking about this for years. He has to do it.

"So I think we've both figured out that there's no real future here. Now we're more in the phase-out period, if you know what I mean."

Emily sounded calm and resigned about the situation, but Sara could sense the sadness beneath her words.

"I'm sorry. I guess it's hard for you," Sara said sympathetically.

"Oh, I'll be okay. He was always honest about it. It's not a surprise."

"Well, I think he's missing out, passing up on you in favor of a sailing trip," Sara consoled her.

"I do, too," Emily agreed, smiling again. "Men can be so dense. Even the good ones."

"Absolutely," Sara agreed. She pulled her new leather bag from the floor and turned to go.

"By the way, give Warren a call today. I think he has some news for you about that story you've been covering."

"The emergency services grant? What happened?" Sara asked excitedly.

"I'm not at liberty to say. But you can call me for a comment after you talk to Warren. And don't let him know where you got the tip," Emily added, giving Sara a wink.

Sara leaned into the car before closing the door. "Thanks, Emily."

"No problem. I owed you for all that shoveling this morning. Have a good day, honey."

Emily waved good-bye and pulled away. Sara stood on the sidewalk a moment, steeling herself before she faced Dan again this morning. At least she had a good lead to work on today.

As soon as she got settled at her desk, she called Warren Oakes. It took some wheedling, but she managed to get him to admit that the federal agency that had awarded the grant was now putting pressure on Commissioner Callahan to pass the money through to Cape Light.

"Does this mean the village won't sue the county now?" Sara asked.

"It's too early to say, but if the county does as the feds say, then we'll have no reason to sue."

"So if the county bows to the pressure from the feds, will there be repercussions for Cape Light later?"

"You'll have to ask the commissioner that one," Warren said, with a laugh. "I'd say it's highly likely, but don't quote me on that," he hastily added. "In fact, I wish you'd keep this entire story under wraps until the county has made some public response. You know putting it in the newspaper too soon might weaken our position."

"That's up to my editor," Sara said curtly. "I guess he'll decide if enough has happened here to justify a story."

After talking to Warren, she called the commissioner, but he wouldn't speak to her. She thought of calling Emily, then decided it was too soon. She would take it to Dan first.

"Interesting," Dan said. "Did you just try Oakes on a hunch?"

"I've been after him for a while—and I did get a little tip from someone in Village Hall," Sara admitted.

He met her gaze, then looked away. If he had guessed her secret informant, he didn't comment.

"This latest wrinkle must be making Em—er, the mayor happy," he said. "Have you called her yet?"

"I was just about to. Then thought I'd check with you first. Should I bother to get her statement yet? Maybe there isn't enough here to run a story."

He frowned and considered the paper's options. Or was he just thinking about Emily, Sara wondered.

Dan turned in his chair and glanced at the board, then made a notation by the story. "Let's watch this. It's Friday. I don't think anything more is going to happen until next week. You can call the mayor's office, if you want, but I don't think she'll have much to say until the commissioner responds to the feds. Keep on Callahan. Let him know you really want to keep this story evenhanded, and you're interested in his side of it."

"Okay, thanks. I'll try him again." Sara stood up and started to go.

"Oh, and Sara, good work," Dan remarked, nodding at her.

She thanked him and walked back to her desk. High praise coming from Dan Forbes. She'd have to remember to write this down in her journal tonight.

FRIDAY WAS A LONG DAY OF WAITING. IN SOME WAYS, EVEN HARDER THAN last night, Ben reflected, as he stared at Carolyn's motionless body.

Last night there had been so much drama, so much going on, he had run on sheer adrenaline. But today the minutes crawled, and every hour felt like a lifetime. Jack and Rachel looked in from time to time. Nurses checked in on their appointed rounds, and eventually, Dr. Whittaker stopped by, too.

"Her blood pressure is still unstable, and that's not a good sign," the doctor explained. "We're giving her medication to control it, but it could bring on another stroke. One that would be more severe."

Ben nodded, saying nothing. When the doctor left, he closed his eyes and prayed by Carolyn's bedside, yet he felt somehow his prayers were not heard.

Mostly, Ben sat alone in the room with her. Without anything else to do, he read aloud some of her favorite passages from the Bible, eventually coming to Psalms. If she was really slipping from this world, if she could really hear his voice in her deep sleep, then perhaps these familiar words would give her some comfort, he thought.

He found the Twenty-third Psalm and began to read slowly, "The Lord *is* my shepherd; I shall not want. He maketh me to lie down in green pastures: he leadeth me beside the still waters. He restoreth my soul: he leadeth me in the paths of righteousness for his name's sake. Yea, though I walk through the valley of the shadow of death, I will fear no evil: for thou *art* with me. . . ."

Ben stopped, his throat so thick with tears that he couldn't continue. He put the Bible aside and simply held Carolyn's cool, unresponsive hand, an awful realization dawning on him—if she had to have last rites, he didn't think he could do it.

Night fell. Jack persuaded Ben to have a bite to eat downstairs in the hospital cafeteria. "Rachel had a call from Mark," Jack told him, when they sat down. "He's gotten as far as Fort Worth. He was trying to book a flight to New York or Boston. He thinks he might get here late tonight."

Ben nodded, feeling too drained to react. "I hope he's in time," he said simply. He pushed the bits of food around on his plate; he had no appetite.

He wondered why Mark hadn't called Carolyn's room to speak directly with him. *Probably afraid I would be angry at the delay. Or maybe he just wanted to speak to his sister.* Then he was annoyed at worrying at all about Mark's feelings. Too much attention had already been focused in that direction today by Rachel and Jack and even himself. He resented it. The real focus should be on Carolyn. Only Carolyn.

Later that night, just past eleven, Sophie and Gus Potter arrived. Ben could hardly believe his eyes when he saw them standing in the darkened doorway. For a moment he wondered if his sleep deprivation had finally gotten to him.

"We heard you were still here and thought you needed some rest, Reverend. Let us stay the night with her," Sophie said. "We'll call you if anything happens."

"Yes, Reverend, let us stay. We have a big thermos of coffee and a few good books here. We were hoping you'd let us help you out tonight," Gus added.

Although his first impulse was to refuse their generosity, Ben did feel exhausted. The doctor on call had looked in earlier and said he didn't expect any dramatic changes that night. He, too, had urged Ben to go home and get some sleep.

"All right, I guess I can leave for a few hours. You're sure you'll be all right?"

"We'll be just fine. We'll take good care of her," Sophie promised. Gus hugged him before he left, and then Sophie did, too, her eyes shining with sympathy. He hugged her back, feeling a moment of relief, comforted by his old friends.

* * *

BEN RETURNED TO THE HOSPITAL AT FIVE O'CLOCK THE NEXT MORNING, feeling guilty that he had stolen even a few hours of sleep. As he approached Carolyn's room, he heard someone crying inside. His first thought was that it must be Rachel or Jack and the worst had come in his absence.

He rushed into the room, his heart in his throat, and saw Mark seated at his mother's bedside. His hands covered his face as he cried, his body shaking with each wrenching sob.

Ben started toward him, instinctively wanting to comfort his son. Then as Mark lifted his head and looked at him, Ben stopped, feeling only anger at his son's selfish, unfeeling neglect, his rejection of their love and concern—especially Carolyn's. As if his mother was going to live forever. As if he had eternity to work out his grievances—real or imagined—against them. Well, he didn't. He didn't have all the time in the world. Nobody did. And this scene sadly proved it.

"Hello, Mark," Ben said quietly, still standing in the doorway.

"Dad . . ." Mark began to speak, then he squeezed his eyes shut and rubbed his forehead. He looked as if he had been up for the past three days. Well, he probably had, Ben thought.

"I can't believe this. I can't believe it," Mark repeated, as if in shock.

Ben felt his jaw grow rigid with anger and knew he shouldn't speak. But he couldn't help himself. The anger that had been building for years came spewing out.

"You love her so much? You realize that now?" he began in a low, ragged tone. "Where have you been all these months? *All these years?* Her very last words to me were about you." He nearly choked on the admission, remembering. "Concern for you, Mark. Love for you. You have no idea how much you've hurt her all these years. Hurt both of us," he added harshly.

Mark stared at him, his red-rimmed eyes wide with disbelief. "Dad, how can you say this to me? I just got here. I've been traveling for days. You know why I couldn't get here any sooner—"

"You could have come back any time in the last two years," Ben told him in a low, furious voice. "We all but begged you to come home. And now you're sorry. You want to tell her how much you love her? Well, go ahead. She's right there."

Mark rose and stared at him, shaking his head. "I knew you would be like this. I knew it. Even now," he added, glancing at his mother. "You couldn't wait five minutes to start in on me."

Ben started to answer him then stopped. He took a small step back, appalled at his own loss of control. What had he done? Exactly what he'd promised Carolyn he wouldn't do: greet their son with a tirade of accusations.

He looked past Mark to Carolyn's bed, feeling deeply ashamed of himself. Not so much for his son's sake. He had been honest with Mark for once and didn't totally regret it. But looking at Carolyn, he felt as if he'd failed her. Let her down, now, when what he wanted most was to honor his promises to her.

Rachel walked in and glanced first at him, then at Mark. From the expression on her face, Ben could tell that she knew she'd walked in on something. Wordlessly, she went straight to her brother and opened her arms to him. Ben watched his children embrace, feeling completely outside their circle of love. Then they stood together, side by side, and Mark put his arm around Rachel's shoulders, as they stared down at their mother.

Ben's heart ached for them both. They were adults, and yet in many ways, they needed Carolyn even more than when they were younger. The loss would be deep and devastating for both of them, he realized. For Rachel, because her mother was almost her best friend; for Mark, because he'd had so little time with Carolyn since he was a teenager. He had never worked out the adult connection Rachel had with her mother. His bond to Carolyn was still fraught with so many unresolved issues. If she died now, Mark might never forgive himself, Ben thought sadly.

He felt an urge to speak to them, to offer some loving words that could bring them together as a family. But he stood there silently, feeling the odd man out and feeling, too, as if he deserved to be. He still felt so angry with Mark for having waited so long to come back. Every time he looked at him, he could only think of one question: Why had he waited so long? Too long, maybe. Too long for all of them.

Feeling shaken, he slipped out of the room and walked down the hallway, trying to compose himself. He took the elevator to the first floor and walked to the chapel. He was relieved to see that he would be alone there. He took a seat in a pew, knelt, and folded his hands, trying to pray.

Help me handle this anger, Lord. Give me the right words to say to Mark. The right attitude. I can't come around on my own. I'm stuck. I'm blinded. I can't find my way through this without Carolyn to help me. I want to keep my promise to her, but I don't have the strength. Or the mercy in my heart for my son, he confessed. *Why can't I forgive him? Please help me.*

He sat back and lowered his head, his eyes closed. He felt weary and drained, right down to his spirit. This was the moment when his faith should be lifting him up, giving him the strength to support his family, to bring them together with words of comfort, consolation, and hope.

What kind of man of God was he? In this dreadful hour, he was cowering, fading, exploding like a powder keg, and berating his son. *This is my test, and I'm failing. I'm failing everyone, especially Carolyn.*

"FORTUNATELY WE GOT HERE EARLY, FOR ONCE," LILLIAN SAID TO EMILY, in a hushed voice. "I haven't seen this many people in church since . . . since Christmas."

Christmas had only been three weeks ago, but Emily knew what she meant. The church was filled to capacity, with some members of the congregation even standing in the aisles.

"I guess everyone wants to show support for the reverend and his family," Emily said.

"Yes, of course. How is she doing? What do you hear?" her mother asked in her usual way, with more curiosity than concern.

"I visited last night with Sara. We only stayed a minute or two. There's been no change in Carolyn's condition. Reverend Ben looked exhausted. I think he's been there night and day. I wouldn't be surprised if we had a guest minister here today."

"I see the family," Lillian said, surveying the pews up front. "There's Rachel and her husband . . . oh, and Mark. I barely recognized him with that long beard. He looks like a lumberjack. Hasn't he been away in the mountains, logging or something?"

"He's been traveling, Mother, out seeing the world. I think he just got back from Montana." Emily hated to gossip about anyone but especially about the Lewis family at this time.

"I heard he became a Buddhist monk. Do they have many Buddhists in Montana these days?"

"Mother, please. Look, it's Reverend Ben. I never thought he would be able to give a service today," Emily said sympathetically.

Ben started the service, amazed to see how many had attended today. There would be the same showing at Carolyn's funeral, he thought sadly.

That morning he had woken at dawn with a start, as if shaken by some unseen hand. It was still dark outside, and he thought about the service, sure he wasn't going to be able to do it. He'd nearly called his old friend Reverend Simpson, who was standing by to take his place.

He had dressed quickly, then went over to the hospital and looked in on Carolyn. There was still no change. She was clinging to life, and he knelt by her bed and prayed for a while. He knew she would want him to give the service today, so he'd turned around and come back to town, with just enough time to ready himself and get to the church on time.

The words and the music, which he knew by heart, carried him along for a while, the ritual acting as both a bulwark and support to his flagging spirit and energy.

Ben sat listening as the celebrant read today's Gospel. He barely heard the words, his attention on the sermon he was about to give. He looked down at his hastily written notes and then out over the rows of sympathetic faces. His gaze fell on those of his own family, Rachel, Jack, their new baby, and Mark.

How long had it been since Mark had sat in this church? he wondered. Several years at least. Everyone must be talking about it, the prodigal son who has finally returned home. But this version was not much like the biblical tale. Here, the past problems that plagued the family had never been resolved—and everyone in Cape Light knew it. Ben looked at Mark and felt his own deep inadequacy. He wasn't fit to be a minister, to preach to these trusting people when he couldn't even solve the problems in his own home. He felt it keenly, like a sharp blade pressed against his heart.

But it was time to give the sermon. He took a deep breath and walked to the pulpit, looking far more assured than he felt.

"Stop and smell the roses," he began. "How often have you heard that one? It's so corny and trite. The simple words have lost all meaning for us. Who has time to stop and smell anything these days? Even the food that we eat to fuel our bodies is tossed to us through a car window and hastily consumed before we reach the next traffic light. . . .

"What about lying out in a field and watching clouds roll past? Or purposely taking a walk in the snow or in the rain? Do you ever have time for those things? What about watching the sunrise? Who here has made time and room in his life for any one of these useless, unproductive pursuits?

"Life is too short, people often say. Is it too short to be wasted waiting with a child for the first star to appear? What would be a better use of that time—watching more TV? Balancing a checkbook? Keeping your house neat enough to be in a magazine, or even working overtime? Do you think your children will remember that the house was clean or that you made cookies with them? Will they remember that the family had a new car or that you were home early enough to read them stories every night?"

He paused, not sure if he had the energy to go on. "Life must be more than earning and spending and worrying. We can get so focused on being responsible, on working and keeping up with our to-do lists that we forget to just stop and enjoy the harvest that our efforts have produced. More importantly, we forget to enjoy and appreciate those nearest and dearest to us.

"Each day is a precious, sacred gift, my friends. We walk this earth for a blink of an eye. As we face our final moments, does anyone say, 'Gee, I didn't work enough. I didn't worry enough. I wasted too much time, enjoying beauty, God's wondrous creation. Oh, and I told my family that I loved them way too many times. . . .' "

A few nervous laughs erupted. Ben paused, quickly wondering when he had last told Carolyn he loved her. He couldn't remember. Distracted, he lost his place in his notes.

His gaze fell on the empty space where Carolyn should have been, the sight hitting him full force in the center of his being. For a moment he could barely breathe, but he held on to the edges of the pulpit and steadied himself. He saw concern on Rachel's face and then on Mark's.

He rallied and continued. "We take so many little things for granted. It's only human but not one of our finer qualities." His gaze fell on Mark again. His son stared up at him, his arms crossed tightly over his chest. Ben could see that he was growing uncomfortable; the sermon was upsetting him, but Ben couldn't help that.

"Some people think that they have forever on this earth to hold a grudge or a grievance, to avoid facing a problem squarely and making amends. We put it off. It's hard work and unpleasant. And painful," he added, looking at Mark again. "We make excuses and let ourselves off the hook self-indulgently—not realizing how we might be hurting others and ourselves. Not realizing that the golden tomorrow when we planned to say, 'I love you' or 'I'm sorry' or 'Please forgive me,' may never come. . . ."

Mark jumped up from his seat and pushed his way out of the pew, as if someone had just yelled fire. He ran quickly down the center aisle and out of the church.

The building was so silent, Ben heard his heart pounding in his chest. The familiar creak and groan of the church's heavy front door sounded seconds later, followed by a loud slam.

Ben suddenly realized that everyone was staring up at him. He could barely believe what had just happened. Rachel looked horrified. Jack put his arm around her shoulder and whispered something to her.

Ben pulled a hanky from his pocket and pressed it to his forehead. Then he turned abruptly, left the pulpit, and walked across to the altar. He forced himself to focus on the liturgy and continued the service, all the while feeling as if he, too, wanted only to run out of the church and hide his head in shame.

CHAPTER TWENTY

"WELL, IT'S SWOLLEN," DAN EXPLAINED TO HIS DOCTOR, ON Monday morning. "Swollen and . . ."—he put down the phone briefly to check his leg—"a little bluish around the ankle. I've been putting ice on it, but that hasn't helped much."

"Did you fall or turn your ankle?" the doctor asked.

"I don't think so. I was shoveling snow on Friday—"

"Shoveling snow? With the cast I gave you?"

"It didn't fit under my snow boots," Dan hedged. The truth was, he'd barely worn it at all.

"Hold on for a minute, Dan. I need to pull out your file," the doctor said wearily.

While Dan waited, Lindsay drifted into the room, dressed and ready to go out. He wondered if she had an interview, but hesitated to ask her.

"Good morning. There's coffee," he said. He looked up at her, and she smiled slightly.

"Aren't you going to work today?" she asked curiously.

"Not yet. I needed to talk to the doctor."

"Oh," she replied, not even glancing at his leg. She picked up a section of the newspaper and started reading.

They were on speaking terms but just barely. He'd tried to talk to her about their argument, but she refused to discuss it. Now she and Scott were about to sign a lease on an apartment in Ipswich, and they planned to move out by the end of the month. Dan had told Lindsay that wasn't at all necessary and offered them the house while he was away on his sailing trip. She'd flatly refused him. He only hoped by the time he left, they would have a chance to set things right. Of course, when the sale of the paper went through, she would be angry all over again. That might take her years to forgive, he thought. He still had not struck a deal with Crown but expected to any day.

"Okay, I have it. You need to come in for an examination and an X ray. We may need to give you another hard cast. And I want you in here today," the doctor said curtly. "No excuses. You don't want to end up walking with a permanent limp, do you?"

"No, of course not."

"Here's the receptionist. I'll see you later."

Dan let out a long slow breath. Another hard cast. How long would he have to wear that? he wondered. He knew he couldn't sail alone with a hard cast on his leg. *With my luck lately, I'd be washed overboard and sink like a stone.*

The receptionist came on and offered him an appointment in the middle of the day. He had no choice but to take it, even though it meant he wouldn't get anything done at the paper, what with getting to the doctor's office and back.

He slammed down the phone so hard, the ice pack slipped off his leg. When he bent to pick it up, he slammed the back of his head into the edge of the kitchen table.

"For crying out loud!" he groaned, grabbing the back of his head.

"Dad? What in the world is going on?" Lindsay finally put the newspaper down long enough to look him in the eye.

He shook his head. "I'm a complete idiot. But that should be no news to some people around here."

"What's with your leg? Does it hurt again?"

"I've done something to it." He sighed. "I need to go to the doctor today . . . and I can't drive like this. I know it's an imposition, but do you think you or Scott could take me? You could just drop me there. It may take a while."

"I'll take you," Lindsay said. "What time is your appointment?"

"At eleven. But they make you wait for at least an hour to see the doctor and then wait for the X ray and then wait to talk to the doctor again. And he sounds pretty sure he'll have to put another cast on, so there goes another hour."

"That does sound miserable," Lindsay said. "What about the paper? Who's going to cover for you?"

"I don't know." He shrugged and tried to get the ice pack to balance again. "I'm going to call in and go over their assignments, but there's nobody there who can put the paper together. I guess I'll just have to miss an issue."

"Dad, did you hear what you just said?" Lindsay asked.

"I know what I just said." Of course, it sounded strange to his daughter. But she had no idea how he'd been feeling lately about the paper—about everything. Hopeless.

He couldn't talk to her about it, though, and he no longer had Emily to confide in. He really missed her. Since she'd stopped visiting, the days had taken on a flat, empty quality. His life seemed a mess lately, collapsing around him in all directions, and sometimes it seemed all he could think about was Emily.

"You can't miss an issue," Lindsay said. "You haven't missed an issue since . . . before I was born."

"No, not even when your grandfather died," he said, thinking back. "I don't think he ever missed one either. But I can't be in two places at once. The doctor said if I don't take care of this right away, I could end up with a permanent limp."

She was quiet for a moment, then said, "Scott will take you to the doctor. I'll put the paper out."

He hesitated, surprised by her generosity. "You don't have to do that, Lindsay. It's good of you to offer. And I'm grateful, honestly. But you really don't have to go to all that trouble. Especially after . . . after our argument. I'll—"

"I'm not doing it for you," she cut him off. "I'm doing it for the paper. The *Messenger* isn't going to miss an issue. Maybe it doesn't mean anything to you anymore, but it does to me," she stated flatly.

Dan sat dumbfounded. Even after all she'd said to him about the paper when they had argued, even after all she'd done for the paper while Wyatt was still here, he had still been blind to the depth of her attachment, her commitment, and her passion for the *Messenger.*

Wyatt would never have gone to such lengths, Dan thought, wondering what to say to her. But Scott lumbered into the room. Yawning, he walked over and kissed his wife. He'd worked the dinner shift last night and looked like a bleary-eyed bear.

"Morning," Scott said, sitting down next to Dan at the small, round table. "Hurt your leg again?" he asked kindly.

"Scott, you need to take my father to the doctor today. He can't drive, and it's sort of an emergency."

"Oh, okay. Sure thing," Scott said agreeably. "Do you have an interview or something today?"

"I did, but I'm going to cancel it. I have to go down to the paper."

Dan looked up and caught her eye. She stood before him, her travel mug filled with coffee in one hand.

"I hope it goes all right at the doctor," she said. "Call me at the office when you get back."

"Okay, honey. I will," Dan promised. He felt his mouth form a small, apologetic smile. "Thank you."

"Don't mention it," she said. She kissed Scott good-bye and left the two men together.

Scott was shaking cereal into a bowl while reading the sports section. Dan thought it odd that his son-in-law was such a gourmet, yet he still had a surprising penchant for Cap'n Crunch every morning.

LUCY HEARD THE DOORBELL RING FROM UPSTAIRS. SHE WAITED FOR HER mother to answer it. She knew it was Charlie, bringing the boys back. She just hoped he wouldn't ask to speak to her.

"Lucy?" her mother called up, from the foot of the stairs. "Charlie is here. He'd like to speak with you."

No such luck, Lucy realized. She put down the book she'd been reading for school and checked herself quickly in the mirror. She picked up a hairbrush, then put it down again. She didn't care anymore what Charlie thought about her looks.

He was in the living room with the boys, who were fooling around with their jackets still on. "Come on, boys. Put your things away and get ready for bed. It's almost nine," Lucy said.

"Have they done all their homework?" she asked Charlie.

"Jamie had to do a report on the solar system. I had to take him to the library," Charlie said, as if he had taken their son all the way to the moon.

"The library. Wow. I guess it's been a while for you, Charlie," she said dryly. Now he had a taste of what she'd been going through with homework assignments ever since the boys had started school.

Charlie glanced at her but didn't rise to the bait, she noticed. "Okay, boys, come on and kiss me good night and get upstairs," he said to his sons.

She noticed he'd become more affectionate with the kids since the separation. He never used to kiss and hug them half as much, so that was one benefit.

When the boys were upstairs, he said, "I wanted to talk to you. Can we talk?"

"Sure, go ahead." She sat down, steeling herself for what might be coming next. Since they separated nearly a month ago, Charlie had only asked to talk to her twice—the first time about making a set schedule for visiting the boys, the second, about getting their broken family together for at least some part of Christmas. Lucy had compromised with him on both matters. In general, though, she tried to avoid speaking to him, not saying more than hello or good-bye when he had the children.

Now she wondered if he had met with a lawyer and wanted to finally work out a legal separation. Maybe it was time, she mused sadly as she watched him sit down.

"I've been doing some thinking, Lucy," he began slowly. "The house is empty. I'm just rattling around in there by myself. There's no one around to distract me from my thoughts," he tried to joke.

She forced herself to smile a little, wondering where this was going. "Do you want to sell the house or something?"

"No! No, that's not what I meant," he said, shaking his head. "I meant I'm all alone. I'm lonely. With a lot of time on my hands," he stated bluntly, staring at her.

"Oh . . ." She felt nervous and looked away.

"I miss the kids. Even their fighting and the way it got on my nerves. I haven't tripped on a toy truck or a building block in weeks now. I miss Bradley," he added, mentioning their dog. Lucy hadn't thought twice about taking him along to her mother's. The boys loved him, and Charlie just complained about walking him and how the dog's fur stuck to his clothes.

"You miss Bradley? I don't believe that," she said doubtfully.

"Sure I do," he insisted. He paused, looking nervous. "I miss you. I miss you a lot."

"Well, I'm runner-up to the dog, but at least I made the short list," she said, with a nervous laugh.

"Now, Lucy . . ." His voice began to go up a notch, but he stopped and took a breath. She wondered for a moment if he was counting to ten.

"What I want to say is, I want us to get back together again. I'm tired of this . . . this separation. I've learned my lesson," he announced, looking her straight in the eye, his face a picture of regret and repentance.

"And what was that, Charlie? What was your lesson?" she asked, trying not to sound as cynical as she suddenly felt.

"I have to learn to keep my temper, for one thing."

"That's one," she agreed.

"I have to . . . hear you out. Not just act like I know what's best all the time for everybody."

What had he been reading in the library tonight? she wondered. Some self-help book? This did not sound like the man she was married to.

"All right. That *is* something that you do that I won't put up with anymore," she agreed.

"I know there's more. I would go to see a counselor again, if that's what you want," he offered. "I'd go back to see Reverend Ben and try to talk things out."

"And not start yelling at me and run out of the room?"

"I lost my temper," he admitted. "Talking like that isn't my style. You know that."

"Yeah, I know."

"But I would do it," he hastily added. "I think I'm ready now to try again."

He stared at her hopefully. She could hardly believe it. He was still the same old Charlie. She knew that. But he seemed more reasonable somehow. A little more self-aware, maybe?

Still, Lucy didn't feel tempted to rush back into their marriage, their old patterns, their familiar pain.

"So, what do you say? I thought I could take off from work tomorrow afternoon and move you and the kids back," he offered.

"No, I don't think so," she said slowly. She braced herself, wondering how he'd take it.

"What are you saying? Never? You'll never come back?" he asked nervously.

"I didn't say never. I'm not sure," she explained. "I'm just not ready yet to get back together. Though I think if we ever did, more counseling would be a must."

He sat staring at her, his mouth set in a tight line. He seemed to be on the verge of anger but struggling to control himself. For once, she thought.

Lucy saw him swallow hard, as if holding back the harsh words that could ruin everything again.

"Well, I don't understand why," he said in a reasonable tone. "You can't be comfortable living here, without any of your own things. And having to handle the kids by yourself all the time—that can't be easy," he pointed out.

"It isn't," she agreed. "But there are benefits for me."

He didn't seem to like hearing that, and he twisted his mouth in a sour expression. He didn't ask her what she meant. He didn't want to know, she realized.

She liked the freedom she had to come and go as she pleased. And not having to tiptoe around Charlie's temper and ego every minute, like a dysfunctional ballet dancer. She'd never had a life as a single person. She'd gone from living with her folks to being a wife and mother. But in the past few weeks she'd felt more her own person than ever. She wasn't ready to just give that feeling up.

"Are you starting school again?" he asked.

"I registered for the spring semester. Classes don't start until next week," she said.

"I see." He rubbed his hands together. "Well, will you think about what I've said? It would be worlds better for the children, Lucy. You know that. Now, if you set out to teach me a lesson, I've learned it. I have. But we don't need to give the boys a rough time for any longer than necessary, do we?"

"The boys are fine," she stated flatly.

She wasn't really sure that they were, though. Both were having nightmares and acting out in school. But she wouldn't admit that to him now.

She stood up, indicating that the talk was over and that he had to go. "I'll give it some thought," she told him.

"All right. That's good enough for now, I guess." He stared at her a moment, his brown eyes full of sadness and something else, a look of strange longing, she thought. Like pining after some possession that's been taken for granted, one that is really missed once it's broken or lost.

She felt unexpectedly emotional all of a sudden and quickly walked to the door. She pulled it open, barely glancing at him again. "Good night, Charlie. Thanks for stopping in," she said politely.

"Good night, Lucy. I'll see you," he said, walking slowly into the cold, dark night.

"MARK'S BEEN STAYING AT MY HOUSE," RACHEL SAID TO BEN, WHEN SHE met him at the hospital on Tuesday morning.

"I appreciate you telling me," Ben said.

Mark had managed to avoid him ever since the Sunday sermon. When Ben came into Carolyn's room and Mark was there, Mark got up and left. Though Rachel hadn't said anything, Ben knew the rift upset her. This was the opposite of how a family should be acting in a crisis, he thought tiredly.

"Are you okay in the house on your own?" Rachel asked.

"I'm fine," Ben assured her. "Except for missing your—" He broke off his statement of the obvious as Doctor Whittaker came into the room.

"Carolyn's blood pressure has finally stabilized," he told them. "It's a good sign. She's in far less danger of having a second stroke. But the symptoms of her coma remain unchanged. There's no telling if she'll wake up soon or remain in this state indefinitely."

"At least there was some good news," Ben said to Rachel, after the doctor left. He gazed down at Carolyn again. Her skin looked smooth as porcelain. He'd do anything to see her blue eyes open again, to hear her voice.

"I think Mark should know what the doctor said," Rachel told him. "He's downstairs getting something to eat. I'll go talk to him."

"No, I'll go," Ben said, getting up from his chair. It was time he spoke to Mark. Long past time, he thought.

Ben left the room and started down the corridor. He met Mark face-to-face just as his son stepped out of the elevator.

"No, don't run away from me," Ben said quietly, when it seemed Mark was about to duck his head and turn away. "I want to talk to you. I have some news about your mother's condition," he said, hoping to lure him. "And you know we need to talk anyway."

"Fine." Mark nodded, his expression showing little emotion.

They went into the family conference room Ben had noticed near the nurses' station. Once inside he closed the door. There was a table and some chairs. The large windows framed a view of a snowy courtyard.

Mark sat at the table, his hands neatly folded in front of him. "What is it about Mom? Did you talk to the doctor again?"

"Yes, he just came by. He had some good news. Her blood pressure is finally stable. She's mainly out of danger of having another stroke."

"That is good news," Mark agreed, looking visibly relieved.

"There are no signs of the coma lifting, though. No signs at all," Ben repeated.

Mark looked up at him. "That could happen suddenly though, right?"

"Sometimes."

Mark stared straight ahead again. Ben waited, unsure of whether he should speak first.

"Why did you humiliate me at church on Sunday?" Mark said abruptly. "Was that really necessary?"

"I didn't mean to. I wasn't talking about you specifically. I was talking about people in general. Maybe my words just struck a chord. Maybe you felt guilty," he added.

"Maybe you just think I should," Mark shot back at him. "That's your job, right, parceling out guilt and forgiveness?"

Ben felt put down and goaded. But his volcanic anger at his son seemed spent. Maybe during the long days of watching over Carolyn or in church on Sunday his angry energy had burned off, leaving only a bitter taste on his tongue.

"Your mother couldn't control her depression. She did everything she could to make it up to you—whatever it was you thought she'd neglected to give you. But you just could never let her off the hook. Let both of us off," Ben said tightly. "Why is that, Mark? Why do you feel such a need to . . . to punish us?"

"I haven't punished you," Mark said. "What have I done? Left school when I knew I wasn't getting a thing out of it for all the money you were spending. Yes, I traveled around, trying to make some sense of things. *My own* sense of things," he emphasized. "How was that punishing you? How did that have anything to do with you or Mom, for that matter? I didn't take the mindless way, the easy way—sleepwalk through college, get the expected job, marry the expected girl. I tried something different. Is that how I punished you?"

"No, not at all. That's not what I mean," Ben cut in.

"Okay, I've made my life harder than it has to be," Mark admitted. "But I'm the only one who's suffered from it."

"That's where you're wrong," Ben told him. "There are people who care about you. All this time we've felt as if you've rejected our caring, our love, our concern. You've even rejected our faith."

Ben paused, taking a long breath. He couldn't tell if his words had any impact at all. Mark sat so still, his face a blank, staring out the window at the frozen scene below.

"Can't you see how that's hurt us? Especially your mother. You've withheld your love from her, no matter what she's said or done. It's been terribly painful for her. Didn't you have any idea of that?"

Mark didn't move. He barely seemed to be breathing, as if he'd put himself in some sort of trance.

Finally, he spoke in a quiet, almost gentle voice. "You have no idea what it was like to be your son. To grow up in this town with everyone watching my every move. Just like Sunday, back in church. Hearing them whisper behind my back. 'The minister's son, always acting out. Poor Reverend doesn't know what to do with him.' " He turned to face Ben. "How could I ever live up to those expectations? Or breathe within those rules? I couldn't, Dad. I had to get out just to get some sense of who I really am and what I want from my life. I had to go where nobody knew me—or our family," he added.

Ben didn't know what to say. He'd always recognized that those pressures existed for both of his children. Rachel had just taken them in stride. Mark was different, taking them more to heart. Ben had never realized before how deeply. All this time, he'd understood Mark's need to distance himself as a personal rejection. But it was bigger than that, and at the same time, more essential to Mark. He was struggling to find out who he was, beyond this town and his automatic identity in it.

"But what about your mother? The way you've acted toward her?" Ben asked. "I don't understand that."

Mark glanced up at him. "I know it wasn't Mom's fault. I know she couldn't help being sick—but she was, Dad. I'm not saying she didn't love me then or doesn't love me now. But there was something missing, something important. And you never wanted to face that." There was no accusation in Mark's voice now, only weariness. "I knew I'd never have a chance of getting past it if I couldn't admit it."

Ben accepted Mark's words without argument. He *was* protective of Carolyn, never wanting to see any flaw in her. But just because he understood and had adjusted his expectations to her ability to give, didn't mean Mark had been able to. Wasn't that what he was really saying?

"I'm sorry. I really am," Ben said quietly. "I didn't really get it before now. It's almost funny," he went on, "because I said almost the same thing to your mother about you. I said we can't heal this if we don't face it and talk about it. But she didn't want you to feel accused or attacked when you got home. She wanted you to come back, no questions asked. Unconditional forgiveness. Unconditional love," he added, feeling his throat tighten with emotion. "Despite what's gone on these last few days, I always promised myself that if you ever came back, the first thing I would tell you was how much I love you. How much both of your parents love you and that we only wanted to understand and resolve these differences that have kept us at odds all these years, Mark. That's all your mother wanted you to know," Ben quietly concluded.

Mark shut his eyes for a moment. "But it's too late for Mom," he said sadly.

"We don't know that," Ben reminded him, putting a hand on his shoulder. "I'm sorry it's taken this crisis to bring us together and talk this out. But that, too, is God's plan for our lives. Your struggles, your questions, every urge that led you away from this place was part of your journey back again, too."

"I know. It's been like a huge circle," Mark said. "A few days ago I would have been horrified to see that. But not now, for some reason. It seems right to me somehow," he admitted.

Ben waited a moment, then he said, "Let's go back upstairs and check on your mother. I'm sure Rachel needs to get back to the baby."

Chapter Twenty-One

Following his doctor's orders, Dan stayed at home and off his leg all day Tuesday. Once again, Lindsay went down to the newspaper office to turn out the next edition.

He called her at five and learned that she was going to work late with Sara. "A story just came in on the emergency services grant. I need to change the front page," she said hurriedly. "I think there's some spaghetti sauce in the freezer for dinner."

"I'll find something. Don't worry," he managed to say, just seconds before she hung up.

She was in the thick of it now, he thought, realizing what he had sounded like to other people for most of his life. He fixed himself some dinner and waited, reading a book. When Lindsay finally came home, he followed her into the kitchen, curious.

"So what's tomorrow's headline?"

" 'Mayor Wins Battle for Federal Funds.' "

He nodded. "Good one. I'm sure the mayor will like it."

"She gave us a good statement. You know Emily," Lindsay said, giving him an inquisitive look. He frowned and looked away, feeling uncomfortable. Maybe he'd call and congratulate Emily. They'd barely spoken since their argument on the beach. He kept picturing the way she looked on New Year's Eve, an evening that had felt partly like magic and partly like a bittersweet breakup scene in a movie with a realistic ending.

He missed her something awful. He could barely admit to himself how much. But he knew he shouldn't call. He didn't want to lead her on anymore, to get her hopes up again. He sighed and turned back to Lindsay, who was browsing in the refrigerator.

"I left some pasta for you. It's on the stove."

"That's okay. I'm not that hungry." She emerged from the fridge with a jar of peanut butter and a loaf of bread and began making herself a sandwich.

"Sara got the story," she told him. "It's her first headline. You should have seen her face when she saw the dummy. Want to read the story? I brought the copy home."

"Sure, I'll read it later," he said.

"She's been dogging Warren Oakes for weeks now," Lindsay continued, "but he wasn't giving much. But she worked the other angle and gained Callahan's confidence. She even got him to fax us a copy of the official letter Warren got today by messenger."

"Sidestepped Warren. Nice move," Dan said, with admiration.

"We knew the *Chronicle* didn't have it yet, so we wanted to get it in for tomorrow. Besides, it's important news for the village."

"And everybody loves to read about a battle between Village Hall and the county," he said. "That always plays well."

Dan watched her sit down with her sandwich and a glass of milk. She was all revved up after an exciting day at the paper, just like he used to be. He understood completely.

"How's your leg?" she asked, between bites.

"It's a lot better. Doesn't hurt now at all. But I have had it up a lot."

"Will you be going in tomorrow?"

"Oh, only for an hour or two, I think. I just need to wrap up some stuff."

"Oh . . . like what?" she asked, her interest piqued.

"I've called off the sale to Crown," he told her.

He sat back in his chair, watching her reaction. Lindsay looked as if a glob of peanut butter had stuck in her throat.

"I thought it was all set," she managed to say.

"It was. But I hadn't signed anything yet. You were right." *You and Emily,* he silently amended. "I couldn't do it. I don't know what came over me to think I could."

"Well, I'm happy you changed your mind." He watched a slow smile spread over her face, and he felt his heart warmed by it.

"Lindsay, I humbly offer you the job of owner, publisher, and editor-in-chief of the *Cape Light Messenger,* which as you know has been in our family for generations. The last two at least have never missed a scheduled issue. I know you will bring even more honor to this title and our great family tradition."

She looked up at him. He couldn't tell what her reaction was at first. Her eyes narrowed with disbelief—or was it just uncertainty?

"Are you sure you want me to?" she asked him.

She had reason to doubt him now, and he regretted that. It was time to set the record straight.

"That day we argued, after you got that message from Ted Kendall, I didn't know what I was talking about," he confessed. "I was so focused on Wyatt and set on the plan of him taking the paper, I had no idea what you'd really been doing there and what you were really capable of. But more than that," he hurried to add, "I had no idea of your feelings about the *Messenger.* You've not only got the head, but the heart for it. That's what it takes, honey. True love, utter devotion. If you still want it, it's all yours," he offered.

She pressed her lips together, looking as if she might cry. "Yeah, Dad. I do want it," she said.

"Good then . . . that's just great." Dan felt relief and happiness rising up inside him. He stood up awkwardly, wobbling on his new cast, then he reached across the table and hugged her.

"Congratulations, honey. I'm so proud of you and so happy. This ended up just right after all," he said, feeling amazed at the fortunate turn of events.

"Thanks, Dad. I'm happy, too." She sighed and wiped a few tears from her eyes.

Dan smiled at his daughter, knowing that somehow in his stumbling plow-horse way, he'd made the right choice after all.

SARA GOT INTO THE OFFICE EARLY ON WEDNESDAY, EAGER TO SEE THE day's edition and her first headline story. Lindsay was already there, working at Dan's desk. She cut the string on the bundle of fresh newspapers and handed Sara a copy. "Here you go, hot off the press."

Sara thought of her parents in Maryland and then about her mother's network of relatives and friends. "I better take a few," she said, making Lindsay smile.

"Sara," Lindsay said, "sit down a minute. I need to talk to you about something."

Lindsay looked serious, so Sara thought it must be about the sale of the paper. Sara hadn't heard much about the situation lately, but everyone had assumed it was still imminent. Ed Kazinsky was already trying to work out a deal with Crown News to keep his column.

"I have some news," Lindsay began. "My father isn't coming back to the office anymore."

"Because of the sale?"

"No, the sale is off. My dad told me last night. We talked, and I'm going to run the paper now. I'm the new publisher."

Sara felt breathless for a moment. "Wow! That's terrific! I'm so happy," she said honestly. She felt like jumping up and giving Lindsay a hug, but she knew it wouldn't seem professional. "I was hoping something like this would happen."

"So was I, but I'd basically given up," Lindsay confided.

"Why did Dan change his mind?" Sara asked.

"I'm not really sure. He finally took his blinders off, I guess," she said, somewhat cryptically. "But aside from all that, I thought we should have a frank talk about your work here. You're doing well, Sara. This issue proves it," she noted, glancing at the day's edition. "It took some real reporting to get that story. You've really learned a lot the last few weeks."

"Thanks, but everyone around here has helped me figure things out. Wyatt and Jane and you," Sara told her.

"Well, you have a real future here. If you want it, that is," Lindsay clarified. "I guess I want to know if you're really committed to staying here, in this town. Or do you think you'll go back to Maryland soon? Or just move on?" she asked directly.

Sara felt put on the spot. She hadn't thought much about this question, not since her parents had visited a few weeks ago. She knew she could put Lindsay off with some vague, I'll-get-back-to-you answer. Instead, she took a deep breath and followed her first instinct.

"I'm settled here. I'm going to stay—for a long time," she answered in a steady voice.

Once she'd said the words out loud, she felt certain that she truly meant them. She did feel settled here, as if she really belonged in Cape Light.

Since Luke had left for the city, she missed him terribly. But she wasn't going to run back home. She'd take that heartache with her anyway. This was her town now. She was going to stay.

"Good, I'm glad to hear it," Lindsay said, with a wide smile. "I'm counting on your help."

IT WAS THE FIRST DAY THAT RACHEL DIDN'T HAVE ANYONE TO LOOK after the baby while she visited the hospital. Since she and Jack had brought William home, a steady stream of volunteer baby-sitters and household help from the church had been at her door. Ben had also been deluged with offers to clean, wash clothes, and cook. The congregation seemed intent on caring for his family now, which Ben found very gratifying. Maybe he wasn't such a bad minister after all, he thought.

But today Rachel's help had canceled, and Mark, who sometimes watched the baby, had already left to be with Carolyn. Ben watched his daughter come into the room, carrying his new grandson in a strap-on pouch that made Rachel look like a mother kangaroo. She also toted a large blue bag that, he knew by now, was filled with diapers and other necessities.

Ben rushed to the door to help her. "Honey, you didn't have to come this morning. You could have stayed home with William. I would have called you if there was any change at all."

"Come here, pal." Mark stepped over and easily took his nephew in his arms so that Rachel could get her coat off.

He was very comfortable handling the infant, Ben realized. But of course, he'd been around the baby a lot lately, staying at Rachel's and watching William when no one from the church could come.

Ben had been so focused on Carolyn—and on Mark—he hadn't spent much time with the new baby. He looked at the child from across the room, a sweet, innocent bundle. Carolyn would have barely let that baby go long enough for Rachel to hold him, Ben thought.

They sat quietly together for a few minutes. Then Rachel said, "Let's say a prayer together."

It seemed to help her when they all prayed together for Carolyn at her bedside. Ben felt comforted by the effort, too. He drew closer to them and they joined hands.

"You start, Dad," Rachel said. Mark had handed the baby back to her, and she cradled him in one arm, holding Ben's hand with the other.

Ben bowed his head. "Dear heavenly Father, please look upon my family with mercy and compassion. Please spare my dear wife's life and help her thrive again—"

The baby suddenly started squalling, and Ben abruptly stopped his prayer. William's fierce, piercing cry shattered the stillness of the darkened room. It was hard to believe such a little thing could make such a big sound, Ben thought. He almost felt like putting his hands over his ears.

Rachel started to comfort her son, rocking him in her arms. "There now, William. What's the matter?" she said soothingly. "I don't think he's hungry. I just fed him before I left."

"Check the diaper area," Mark suggested.

Rachel did and shrugged. "Not that."

"Maybe it's gas," Ben said. He could barely remember a thing about baby care, but that was one thing he recalled.

Rachel walked and bounced the baby, patting his back and trying to bring up some air, but the infant cried even louder, rhythmically, gasping for air.

Rachel looked rattled. Ben and Mark watched, not knowing what to do.

"The baby . . . the baby's crying. . . ."

Ben heard Carolyn's voice and thought he had to be imagining it. He quickly ran over to the bed, and Mark followed, looking as if he'd heard it, too. Rachel stood back watching, not understanding what was going on.

"Carolyn . . ." Ben took her hand and put his face close to his wife's. "Can you hear me? Can you open your eyes?"

There was no response at first, then her eyelids shuddered and finally opened. She stared straight up at the ceiling for a moment, and Ben thought she'd lost her sight.

Then she blinked and turned her head toward him. "Ben . . . what's wrong? Why is the baby crying?" she asked, as if they had just been in the middle of a conversation.

He couldn't speak. His throat felt choked with joy and tears. He squeezed her hand and dropped his head to her chest. "Thank God," he cried. "Thank God. Thank God," he repeated over and over again, just about losing all self-control.

Mark hovered over his mother's bed. "Mom, you've been sick. You were in a coma, but you woke up."

"Oh, Mark. It's you! Oh, my heavens," Ben heard Carolyn say, her speech slightly slurred but full of such feeling it nearly broke Ben's heart.

Rachel stood at the other side of the bed. She was the one crying now instead of the baby, who had abruptly and mysteriously stopped.

"Oh, Mom. You woke up. Thank God," she said. "Look, here's your new grandson. He's a week old today." She held the baby near to Carolyn so she could see him. "We've named him William, after Jack's father."

Carolyn stared at the baby, her mouth forming a perfect circle. "Look at him. He's come to us at last," she said. "Like an angel down from heaven."

"And you've come back to us, my dearest love," Ben said. "Heaven is missing two now."

ON THURSDAY NIGHT SARA CALLED HER PARENTS TO TELL THEM ABOUT her front-page story.

"That's great, honey," her mother said at once. "We can't wait to see it."

"I put it in the mail today. You should get it soon," Sara promised.

"How is everything else going?" her mother asked.

"Um . . . fine." She didn't know whether or not to tell her parents about all the ups and downs at the paper. She decided it was best to just simplify the story and cut to the chase.

"Wyatt left the newspaper. His sister, Lindsay, is going to run it instead," she explained.

"How does that affect you, Sara?" her father asked.

"Well, Lindsay seems to like my work, so it's good, I guess. We talked, and she wanted to know if I was committed to staying on the paper."

They didn't respond to that at first. Then her mother said, "And what did you tell her?"

"I said I was committed. I feel like I belong here now, and I'm going to stay—indefinitely," she forced herself to say.

She knew this was difficult news to drop on her parents out of the blue. But maybe after their visit it wouldn't come as that great a shock.

"Well, that's your decision, Sara," her father said, surprising her with his reasonable, resigned tone. "You do seem happy up there."

"Yes, you do. You're doing so well at the paper, it would be a shame to give that up," her mother told her encouragingly. "Can you send us more copies of that edition with your headline? I want to send some to your aunt and my friends."

"Oh, Mom, don't be silly," Sara said, feeling embarrassed.

"No, honey. I want to," her mother said. "I bet Emily was happy to hear that you're staying," she added. But in a positive tone of voice, Sara thought.

"I haven't told her yet. Maybe I'll speak to her tonight."

They talked for a few more minutes. Then Sara hung up, wondering if she should call Emily. She really wanted to call Luke. She knew that despite everything, he would be happy to hear about her first headline. Should she even try to call him in Boston, she wondered, glancing at the phone. She had the number at his parents' house, where he must be staying.

No, that would be too much. Especially since they'd parted so angrily. She didn't know what to do.

She pulled out her journal and started to write:

I guess I feel sad for myself tonight. I have something to really celebrate and no one to celebrate with. But maybe that's what it means to be older. To really be on your own. It's great to be with someone in a relationship, but you have to figure out how to be happy with just yourself first, I guess. Luke said that because I'm young, it's hard to understand that sometimes things just don't work out. I think it's hard to understand at any age. Look at Emily. I know she feels bad about Dan, but at least she has her faith to help her.

Sara stopped writing, remembering Luke's suggestion to write God a letter.

She turned the page and started to write again.

Dear God, It's me, Sara Franklin. I don't think it's good not to pray at all or to not go to church and then ask for favors. But I'm trying to get in touch with you, I guess, and this is my way. I wish I could be more like Emily, more patient about life. More trusting that things will work out all right one way or another. I know I can't ask you to change Luke's feelings for me. But could you help me see things differently, so that no matter what happens, I can really understand and at least feel resolved about it?

Sara paused. That was all she really had to say.

Thank you, God, for your help and for listening to me. And thanks for the headline story today. That was good. Send more my way.

She laughed at herself. She closed her journal, feeling much better, as if she could already see things a little more clearly.

EMILY WAS WALKING THROUGH THE HOSPITAL LOBBY, HEADED FOR THE elevators when Dan spotted her. He felt his heart jump in his chest. She looked beautiful, in a slim black coat, blue shawl, and leather gloves. No hat, of course, her hair in windblown perfection. As usual she somehow appeared harried on the outside, yet serenely calm within. His felt his mouth go suddenly dry as he stepped into her path and caught her eye.

"Emily . . . hello."

She looked up at him, her blue eyes wide. "Hi. How are you?"

"Oh, getting along. You had a busy week," he pointed out. "I meant to call and congratulate you on your victory over Commissioner Callahan."

He saw her blink. *Then why didn't you?* he could nearly hear her say. *Because I'm a fool,* he answered for her. *A complete fool to give up a woman like you.*

"He caved pretty quickly once the federal agency got involved. I was surprised myself," she remarked. "I guess I won't get impeached at the next town council meeting, after all."

"I guess not," he agreed. He smiled at her, not knowing what to say next. He felt so . . . so emotional all of a sudden.

Her eyes are so blue, he thought. Nobody else has eyes that color. Or maybe it was the shawl that made them look so deep today.

"You're wearing the shawl," he said.

"Oh . . . sure. I wear it all the time." Her tone was offhand, as if it didn't matter much to her at all. Yet he could tell in the restless way she looked away that it did matter to her.

"I heard you called off the sale to Crown News," she said.

"I couldn't go through with it. You were right." He met her gaze again. "I gave Lindsay the paper. You were right about that, too." She finally smiled at him, and he felt himself smile back.

"I heard about that from Sara," she said. "Gee, what happened to your leg? Did you break it again?"

He looked down at his new cast and shook his head. "Not really, but I got up on it too soon. I have to wear this for about two more weeks."

"Oh, well, that's not so bad. It won't delay your trip much, I guess. Much more, I mean." She looked at him, her expression questioning, he thought. He felt suddenly uneasy.

"Uh, no, it's no big deal. I haven't thought that much about it lately—with everything else happening."

He heard the dour note in his voice but couldn't help it. His trip. It seemed like a burdensome task now, not the grand adventure he had once looked forward to with such great anticipation. Now it was more of something he had to get over with. Lately it all seemed so pointless. He only hoped that once his doctor said he was ready, his old enthusiasm would somehow rekindle.

Gazing at Emily right now, he couldn't imagine how it would.

"Going up to see Carolyn Lewis?" he asked.

"Yes. Are you?"

"I just saw her. You can hardly squeeze into the room," he warned. "But she seems happy to have all the company." He paused and looked down at her. What was she thinking right now? Did she care about him at all anymore? She was so adept at hiding her emotions, he couldn't really tell.

If he could only just . . . just talk to her. Really talk to her. Something real and essential that would cut to the bone, not all this chitchat.

He watched her take a breath and glance at her watch.

"I guess I'd better get up there," she said quietly.

"Of course. I won't keep you. See you around, I guess."

"Sure." She smiled gently, then touched his arm. "See you, Dan. Take care of yourself."

"You, too, Emily. You, too." He briefly touched her hand and felt it slip out from his grasp. Then she turned quickly, hugging her shawl around her shoulders, which made him remember how it felt to hug her close.

He turned, too, and headed through the lobby for the exit, his eyesight suddenly blurry.

IT WAS A QUIET DAY AT THE PAPER ON MONDAY, AND LINDSAY URGED Sara to go out on a real lunch break, since it was her turn to stay and help with the layout that night.

It was cold and windy outside, and the Beanery, just a block away, seemed the perfect choice. Sara took a table near the back and picked up the menu. When she looked up, Luke was walking into the café. He was alone and headed for the take-out counter. Her heart pounded in her chest as she sat wondering what to do. She waited a minute for him to look around and see her there. When he didn't, she called out to him.

"Luke . . . hello," she said. He turned and saw her. Then he smiled, and she felt better.

"Hi, Sara. Waiting for someone?" he asked.

What a question, she thought. "No, I just have a rare real lunch break today. Want to sit down?"

He hesitated a moment, then pulled out a chair next to her.

"So, what's been going on?" he said casually. "Anything new at the paper?"

"Yeah, a lot. Wyatt left, and Lindsay's taking over. Dan was going to sell out to Crown News, but he changed his mind at the last minute."

Luke sat back, looking interested in her news. "Wow, that is a lot. When did all this happen?"

"The last couple of weeks, while you were in Boston."

He seemed distracted for a minute, then said, "I just got back this afternoon."

"So, when do you start your new job?" she forced herself to ask him.

He looked down at the table and fooled around with the fork and spoon. "I decided not to work for them after all. Not up in Boston, anyway. I'm going to stay here," he said, lifting his gaze to look at her. "I'm going to work at the new center, like I'd planned to before."

"Oh, that's funny," she said, feeling quietly elated at his news. "I've decided to stay here, too. Permanently, I mean. I more or less promised Lindsay I wasn't going to take off on her, and I even told my parents the other night."

He stared at her across the table and sat back in his chair. "That is funny," he agreed, "because I finally figured out I didn't really want the job or want to go back to the city. The real reason I even considered it was because I thought you were leaving, too, eventually. I didn't want to be left alone here in town, thinking about you," he admitted.

Wow, Sara thought, but didn't say aloud. She didn't know what to say. Had he just admitted he still cared about her? She had to know for sure.

"So, how do you feel now?" she asked quietly.

A slow, warm smile spread over his face, and he reached out and took hold of her hands. "I feel great. I promised myself when I left Boston this morning, I was going to see you and at least try to set things straight between us—and here you are."

"Here I am," Sara agreed, feeling amazingly happy. "I felt awful after we argued," she admitted. "I shouldn't have run off like that—"

"That was my fault," he cut in. "I mean it. I should have told you that night that I loved you. That's why I really came looking for you. But I chickened out. I didn't think you were ready to hear it. Maybe you aren't ready now," he said, casting a questioning look at her. "But at least you know my real feelings."

"I love you, too," she said quietly. She moved closer and put her arms around him, pulling him close in a tight hug. He turned his head and smiled at her, then kissed her, taking her breath away.

Sara held him close. She had missed him so much. She missed talking to him, confiding in him, and just having fun with him. She'd missed turning to him for advice and encouragement. She hadn't realized how important he was to her until he was gone. That had been a painful lesson to learn, but at least, Luke had forgiven her.

Finally, she pulled away. Still holding him close, she said, "I think I took you for granted. That was wrong. I'm so sorry. I'll never do that again," she promised.

"I believe you," he said, smiling at her. He sat back and took a box from his jacket pocket. Then he handed it to her. "Here. This is for you. Your Christmas gift. A little delayed."

"I'll say it is," she teased him, excited to open her package. "So you did get me something after all. I thought you didn't bother."

"I bothered. I was just too mad to give it to you," he admitted. "I hope you like it."

She opened the box and pushed back some tissue paper. She found a beautiful handcrafted necklace with amber beads and a small silver medallion that had an Asian symbol engraved in it.

"Oh, it's beautiful." She lifted it to her neck to try it on. "What does the symbol mean?"

"Double happiness. It's also a symbol for love."

"Oh." Sara leaned over and happily kissed him again.

Her phone rang, and she pulled back to dig the phone out of her knapsack. "You have a cell phone now?" Luke asked her.

"Just for work. Lindsay gave it to me. It must be her," she said, flicking it open to answer it.

It was Lindsay, who called to send Sara to cover a story in Newburyport. Sara took down the information and hung up. She looked at Luke, wondering if he'd get annoyed and feel pushed aside by her job.

"That was Lindsay. I've got to run. The teachers in Newburyport are threatening to strike. Sorry," she added, with regret. She reached over and took his hand. "Can I see you later, after work? It might be late," she added, remembering that she had to stay late that night at work.

"Call me when you're done. It won't be too late," he promised.

He walked her out to the street, where she kissed him good-bye again and gave him another hug. Then she ran to her car, amazed at how some things really did have a way of working out.

CHAPTER TWENTY-TWO

SARA DROVE TO NEWBURYPORT, INTERVIEWED A SPOKESPERSON for the teacher's union, and came back to town before she realized that she'd never eaten lunch. *I must be head over heels for Luke,* she thought, laughing at herself. She'd been so wildly happy about their reconciliation that the teachers' meeting went by in a blur; she only hoped her notes were good. As she passed the Clam Box, she pulled over and parked, then ran in for a take-out order.

It was already three o'clock, and the lunch crowd was gone. She didn't see Charlie behind the counter. As she looked around for someone to help her, she felt a hand tap her lightly on the shoulder. She turned to see Lucy, wearing her waitress uniform.

"Hello, front-page-story reporter," Lucy greeted her. "Can you autograph my copy? I saved it under the counter."

"Lucy, come on." Sara felt herself blushing. "What are you doing here?" she asked curiously.

"Charlie and I decided to get back together," Lucy said, with a sigh. "I moved back home with the kids over the weekend." She looked a little embarrassed, Sara thought. As if she were almost ashamed to have reversed herself this way.

Sara reached out and touched her arm. "Are you feeling okay about it?"

"I thought it over a lot. I needed to do what was best for the children, you know? When there are kids involved, it's different. It gets more complicated," she said, shaking her head. "Charlie's agreed to go into counseling. He's even trying to control his temper. He read this book about it and does little things to keep his cool," she said, smiling a bit. "I guess we both want to bring our boys up in a happy home. I couldn't say no. I have to at least try."

"I hope it works out for you, Lucy," Sara said sincerely. "I hope you're happy."

"Thanks, Sara. It feels like the right thing to do. For now anyway," Lucy said. "Gee, that's a pretty necklace. A Christmas gift?"

"Yes, but a late one." Sara touched the medallion with her hand. "Luke just gave it to me," she said, with a little laugh.

"Luke, huh? I thought you two had a fight, and he took a job in Boston." Lucy smiled knowingly, as if she'd never believed Luke would leave town—and leave Sara.

"He didn't take the job. He just got back today, actually. And gave me this present."

"So it all worked out. You know, some things are worth waiting for," Lucy added, with a grin. She pulled out her order pad. "I've kept you waiting long enough, haven't I? What will you have today, honey?"

CAROLYN STAYED IN THE HOSPITAL A FULL WEEK AFTER WAKING FROM the coma before the doctors decided she could finally go home. Once the word got out, Ben was besieged with offers to get the house ready for Carolyn's return. He put Sophie Potter in charge and gave her the names of others who had offered to help, so that she wouldn't have to do everything alone.

All the paperwork at the hospital went slowly. It was well past noon before Ben was able to meet Carolyn in her room. She sat in a chair, dressed and ready to go. Fortunately the long-term effects of her stroke were few. She had lost some mobility in her left arm and had the slightest slur to her speech, but with therapy the doctors believed she would soon be back to her old self.

"Ready to go?" he asked eagerly.

"I can't wait," she said happily. She adjusted the turban-style hat Grace Hegman had given her and checked her image in the mirror in her makeup compact. "I'm not used to the way I look with short hair—well, no hair, really." She sighed and snapped the compact shut.

"You look beautiful to me," Ben said honestly. "Besides, a bad haircut is a small price to pay for what you just survived, wouldn't you say, dear?"

"True enough. God was good to spare me. I'm thankful every minute of the day," she said in a far more serious tone.

"Yes, we all are," he said softly. He rested his hand on her shoulder. "When I thought you might not make it, I felt so lost. I didn't know how I would ever carry on. I felt as if my faith had just about failed me," he confessed quietly. "I can see now I was thinking only of myself, imagining how empty my life would be without you and not thinking at all of your salvation or even God's greater wisdom and will. I feel ashamed," he added. "I've asked God to forgive me."

"Oh, Ben. I know you're a minister, but you're also human." She reached up and patted his hand. "Your feelings were only natural, it seems to me. I'm sure God has already forgiven you."

He leaned down and kissed her cheek. "Let's get you home now," he said, pushing on her wheelchair. "I think it's time."

They returned to the rectory midafternoon. As they pulled into the drive, Carolyn noticed familiar cars parked nearby.

"Oh, those are just friends from the church who offered to get the house in order. I didn't think they'd still be here, though," Ben said. "They must have waited to say hello." He turned to her with concern. "Are you up to it?"

"Oh, yes. I feel great. Besides, I'm so used to having visitors these past few days, it would seem a little quiet in the house without anyone," she admitted, with a laugh.

They had expected a few visitors, but when their front door opened,

Ben could see it was more than the handful of helpers he had assigned. It was a large party—a surprise party of sorts, he realized at they walked in.

"Welcome home, Carolyn." Sophie came up to Carolyn and gave her a hug. "I know this might seem a little overwhelming, but people were actually arguing over who should have the privilege of coming over here today to help. We even tried to pull straws. I knew I couldn't keep them away, so we put together a little party. We hope you don't mind," she added.

"Mind? I think it's wonderful of you all," Carolyn said, sounding close to tears. She hugged Sophie and then Grace, who was standing right next to her.

"We won't stay long, and we'll clean up every last crumb," Tucker Tulley promised. Dressed in his policeman's uniform, he looked very official, as he cast a warning look at the group.

"We just wanted to wish you well," Jessica said.

"And everyone wanted a closer look at William," Emily Warwick added.

Guided by Ben, Carolyn had walked into the living room and gazed around. "Where is that darling boy?" she asked.

Rachel brought the baby over to her mother. "Here's your grandson," she said, her eyes shining with happiness. "Welcome home, Mom," she murmured, kissing her mother's cheek.

Mark appeared at Ben's side and patted his father's back. He didn't say anything, just stood beside Ben and watched Carolyn, a small smile on his lips. Though the gesture had been unconscious and fleeting, it had touched Ben's heart.

The somber winter afternoon turned to a dark frigid night, but no one in the rectory seemed to notice. Small groups of visitors came and went, careful not to overwhelm or tire out the guest of honor.

The party was now winding down, Ben noticed. When he had entered the rectory this afternoon, he had honestly felt overwhelmed and even distressed by the unexpected gathering. But now, as he sat surrounded by friends and well-wishers and saw the radiant glow on his wife's face, he realized he'd been worried for no reason. Worried about the thorns instead of appreciating the roses. He would have to do better than that now, Ben promised himself. He would have to learn something from this ordeal.

The affection and fellowship of their dear friends was the best tonic for Carolyn—and for himself as well.

LATER THAT EVENING EMILY ARRANGED THE KINDLING AND LOGS IN HER fireplace. She still felt her spirits lifted by Carolyn's homecoming party, but she would be happy when January was over. She always found it a hard month, a letdown after the holidays, with spring nowhere in sight.

Then again, Dan would probably be gone by the end of the month or soon after, she thought, as she lit the fire. It was harder every day not to call or try to see him. She sometimes wished he would just go and get it over with. All these delays had been bothersome for him but sheer torture for her.

She curled up on the couch with a book Sara had loaned her and tried to concentrate. The fire made her sleepy and before long she felt herself dozing off on the couch.

She wasn't sure how long she'd been out when the sound of the doorbell roused her. She sat up and ran a hand through her hair, then stumbled to answer the door.

It was Dan. He stood on her doorstep with a box in his arms and an odd expression on his face, she thought. Or maybe she only thought that because he'd shaved off his beard.

"I just dropped by to bring you this," he said, holding out the box to her. She glanced at it. The five-in-one emergency lantern.

"Oh, what's the matter? Doesn't it work right?" she asked.

"It works just fine. It's just that I won't be needing it now. You ought to return it, get your money back. I've decided I'm not going on my trip. I even shaved off my beard. See?" He touched his chin. "Won't need it now."

"I noticed."

Emily could barely believe she'd heard him right. She didn't know what to say—and was afraid if she said anything, she would reveal how happy the news made her.

"Would you like to come in?"

"Yes, thank you. I would." He stepped inside and took off his down parka. Emily led the way to the living room.

"Oh, a fire. That's nice," he said, sitting down on the couch. "It's a cold night." He rubbed his hands together, looking uncomfortable.

She sat down on the other end of the couch. "So, why aren't you leaving? Is Lindsay having problems at the paper?"

"No, not at all. Took to it like a duck to water," he said. He sat leaning forward, his hands on his knees, as he stared at the fire. "Nothing's really happened. I've just been doing a lot of thinking. I know this might sound odd . . . but it feels like something is telling me not to go."

Emily smiled. It was true. It did seem like one unexpected thing after another had come along to keep him here. She sat back in the corner of the couch, with her legs curled under her. This is getting interesting, she thought.

"Do you mean just something? Or *Something* with a capital *S* . . . like God, for instance."

He looked even more uncomfortable now that she'd brought God into it. But she couldn't help asking. They'd only talked about spiritual matters in the most glancing way.

"I mean *Something* with a capital *S*, if you want to put it that way," he ventured. "You know I'm not much of a believer, but I can go that far. So many unexpected things have happened to me these last few months, Emily. It makes you think.

"Look at the way things worked out at the paper. Who would have guessed Lindsay, and not Wyatt, would be sitting in my chair right now? Or take my accident. If it wasn't for that, you and I would probably never have gotten to know each other."

"I've thought about that myself," she said carefully. She wondered where he was going with all this. She had her hopes, of course, but didn't dare voice them right now. Not after so many weepy nights and feeling as if she'd made such a fool of herself over him.

He sat there, staring at his hands for what seemed like a long time. At last he said, "I can't go on this trip. I can't leave you. I don't know how I ever thought I could," he stated finally, as if it was the most obvious truth in the world. "Why in the world would I take off on some stupid trip? I love you."

He finally turned to look at her. She could barely breathe.

"I love you, too. I have for a long time now," she admitted. "I never thought I'd get a chance to say it, though."

He moved toward her quickly and put his arms around her. "I just told you. I'm not going anywhere." He smiled tenderly, holding her face with the palm of his hand.

Emily felt stunned, as if she might be dreaming. Only the cherishing look in Dan's eyes assured her that this was real.

"But . . . what about everything we talked about on New Year's Eve?" she asked finally. He hadn't mentioned any of that. She was almost afraid to ask and ruin everything.

"You mean about wanting to get married again?"

She nodded.

"It was hard to hear that. I couldn't stop imagining coming back here someday and finding you married to someone else."

"Didn't like that idea, did you?" she teased him.

"No, ma'am, I did not," he said firmly.

"I didn't say it to make you jealous. I was just being honest." Secretly she was thrilled that he'd felt so possessive about her.

"That's what made it really stick," he admitted. "You acted as if you didn't care."

"Then I am a better actress than I thought," she said, with a laugh. Her expression became serious again as she forced herself to ask the hard question. "But what about having a baby? Did you imagine me pushing a stroller down Main Street, too?"

"That was harder, Emily," he warned her. "I have to admit, the prospect of changing diapers and walking the floor at four in the morning made the sailing trip seem more appealing again. I've done that already. I'm at a different stage in my life—or at least, I thought I was."

"Yes, I know you feel that way." She squeezed his hand.

"But I do love you. I want to make you happy, Emily. That's what it's all about." He sighed and smiled at her. "Let's just try and see where this takes us. One thing I've learned these last few weeks is you can plan too much. You can close yourself off to the possibilities. To the unexpected blessings that life . . . or *Something* . . . drops in your lap." His grin got wider. "You're the one for me."

"You are for me, too. No doubt about it," she said quietly. "But I don't want you to feel boxed into something."

"I think we both need time. Then we'll know what to do. The more I think about it, the more I feel I might like another crack at fatherhood. Especially with you," he added.

He really meant it. She could see it in his eyes. He wasn't just saying it to please her.

Emily melted into his embrace, reveling in the happiness of loving and being loved. Finally, she settled back in his arms, and they watched the fire, neither of them feeling the need to say anything anymore.

She sent up a silent prayer, thanking God for bringing Dan into her life. His love was an unforeseen gift from above. There would be issues and questions still to come, she knew. But she believed in her heart that she and Dan would work it all out somehow, in tune with God's plan. A favorite verse from the Bible came to mind. *"And we know that all things work together for good to them that love God. . . ."*

After a few minutes, Emily sat up with a start. "Oh, no! I just realized something."

"What's the matter?" Dan asked.

"Now you'll have to meet my mother."

Dan stared at her a moment, taking in her serious expression. He laughed out loud and hugged her tight.